FIDAN BA

The
SECRET
of
KARABAKH

A NOVEL

LUME BOOKS

LUME BOOKS

Published in 2022 by Lume Books

Copyright © Fidan Bagirova 2022

The right of Fidan Bagirova to be identified as the author of this work has been asserted by them in accordance with the Copyright, Design and Patents Act, 1988.

ISBN 978-1-83901-477-2

Typeset using Atomik ePublisher from Easypress Technologies.

Printed and bound in Great Britain by Clays Ltd, Elcograf S.p.A.

www.lumebooks.co.uk

In loving memory of my father the honorable Togrul Bagirov

Prologue

High on a green hillside, by a rock outcrop shaped like a cat curled in sleep, lay a young mother, her face turned to the earth. The cold wind snatched at the blood-soaked hem of her embroidered headscarf. Her arm was outstretched toward a child, dropped like a sack a yard away. The eyes of the dead child, a little girl, were closed. Her hair was the color of licorice, matted with dirt and blood. Wrapped around her neck was a pink woolen scarf decorated with chocolate-brown rabbits and butter-yellow ducklings; its fringe trailed in the congealing puddle of gore thrown from her body by a soldier's bullet. Between woman and child, like an umbilicus, was a twisted gray plaid blanket, twined round the woman's torso and the child's limbs.

They had been sheltering in the lee of the rock when the soldiers found them. The cracks of the two gunshots had echoed from the cat-rock and down the valley, stopping the screams and the pleas for mercy, halting the woman's exhortations to spare the child. No mercy came, only more gunshots farther down the valley.

Snow fell, dusting the grass with silver, blurring the outlines of the corpses scattered among the stones and bushes, a tide-wrack marking the limit of their exodus. Daylight faded quickly into a February dusk, shrouding the atrocity, leaving it to the eyes of the goats.

The soldiers were all indoors that night. If their souls were troubled, it showed little in their faces. They were at home here, in this place they had won for their people. Those enemies, those women and children, those workers and tradesmen and pensioners, from whom they had violently wrested it, had been usurpers, and had been put to the usurper's fate. Not murder, but execution.

So the murderers told themselves.

1

Cambridge/London

"Happiness and fulfillment," said Alana's mother, "is a line of open doors on Rodeo Drive and an Amex with no limit."

Of all things, this was the sentence that would stick in Alana's mind on this day – the day a new period in her life opened up like a sinkhole beneath her feet.

They were in the Promenade Room of the Dorchester Hotel. Catherine Fulton adored the place, though Alana found it rather soft and pretentious. Her mother had flown from Los Angeles, en route to Milan by way of Paris, and had broken her itinerary with a stopover in London to "enumerate the ways one might give balance to one's life, *amore*."

"I know, Mom," Alana interrupted as her mother repeated her mantra, pouring Earl Grey into her cup. "I've heard it before."

Catherine carried on, oblivious, underscoring her words with the ruby tip of a four-hundred-dollar fingernail.

Alana sighed; her mother was not kidding with that shopping-is-the-root-of-all-happiness stuff. It really was her soul-deep, God's honest truth. Catherine had just spent the morning filling the backs of cabs with shopping bags, and would do the same in Paris tomorrow, right after she'd finished refining Alana's sense of who she should be.

Sipping her aromatic tea, Alana watched a young couple sit down at a nearby table. He was handsome and dark; she was beautiful, perfect, dressed in exquisite beige cashmere with a blue shawl draped to expose a flawless shoulder, which he kissed in passing. Alana noticed the engagement ring: a pear-shaped blue diamond. Five carats, easily. Bliss oozed from them, a soothing balm that bit into Alana's nerves like vinegar.

"I said, are you listening to me, *amore*?"

"Yes, Mom. Look, I love that life is that way for you – the haute couture and the restaurants and all the people fawning around you. For me, not so much."

Catherine patted her hand. "I wish you would call me *maman*, like you did as a child." She raised a finger and looked grave. "*Amore*, you could have the world at your feet. The whole world. If you would only look up at the stars instead of always down at your … rocks and things." Catherine shuddered. "And dirt. I mean, look at your nails."

Alana looked. "It isn't 'rocks and things,' Mom. It's ancient culture and history. Anyway, I haven't gone digging in over five months. I spend nearly all my time in labs and libraries."

"Hmm." Her mother stared critically at Alana's hair. "*Amore*, tell me, what conditioner are you using? And when did you last get it styled? You had *such* beautiful hair when you lived at home, like a cascade of liquid ebony. This English weather isn't kind to hair, I can tell you." She patted her own, protectively.

Whenever Alana spent time with her mother, it was a reminder of how far she had diverged from the world she'd grown up in, a world of Malibu beach houses, upscale parties, high fashion, and the Hollywood scene. It was hard to believe that had once been her home.

4

Her mother's expression softened, and she touched Alana's hand again. "You know how much I love you, *amore*, and your father and I are *so* proud of all your accomplishments. And yet you look sad. Aren't you looking forward to coming home? Aren't you excited?"

Well, *there* was a question. Alana wondered if she should have it engraved above her bed so she could see it every morning when she opened her eyes. *Aren't you looking forward to going home?* Just to save her the slow, iceberg-crashing realization while the coffee brewed, and she remembered the future. Her doctoral thesis was nearly complete, and for the first time in ten years she had nothing set up to follow. Maybe she'd get a research post at Cambridge, or go excavate full-time in Turkey.

The past – the ancient history of humankind – was her life's work; she lived most of her conscious existence among the remnants of the ancient world, and her imaginative life was rooted there, among the long dead. Often, she yearned to walk among them, to be alive there, in a time long past.

"I know Howard is looking forward to you coming home," said her mother.

Howard. To almost every girl in the world, he was Howard Angelus, the super-hot second lead in *Phenomenal*, and if you were Catherine Fulton, he was the next best thing to royalty. She couldn't wait to welcome him into the family. Alana had been seeing him, on and off, for a few years; he was gorgeous, and she was fond of him, but did she really want to spend the rest of her life with him?

"You know how proud I am of your intellect," her mother said, her spoon hovering over a dish of cream. "But I still believe you'd be happier if you would only turn your hand to something productive." With a couturier's precision, Catherine sliced her scone while Alana glanced around at the peach and olive drapes and marble pillars. "You are so talented, darling. With a little work and some mentoring, you could achieve fame."

Catherine had never gotten over the fact that whereas she, Catherine Tessaro, second generation Italian immigrant from Baltimore, had worked her way up from the sewing room floor to become one of the biggest names in fashion retail, Alana, with all her advantages of birth and wealth, had gone off the rails, throwing over a fine art and fashion course in her sophomore year and switching to archaeology. After finishing her bachelor's degree at Stanford – with one of the highest grade-point averages in the history of the Archaeology Center – she'd taken a master's at Columbia before crossing the Atlantic to begin her PhD at Cambridge. In Catherine's eyes, these achievements were impressive in an incomprehensible way – and she bragged strenuously about them to her friends – but really, they were just a continuation of the train-wreck.

"*Maman*," Alana said firmly, "are we really going to do this now? I'm not eighteen."

She hated herself for getting angry. Catherine would bend over backward to help her only child – so long as it was on *her* terms. She would move heaven and earth to make Alana a princess, but only in a world where Catherine herself was the queen. She turned her warm, brown Italian eyes on her daughter and touched her cheek.

"Darling, you look beautiful … Underneath, I mean. Howard will have no regrets." Catherine tilted her head. "But your skin, *amore* … it's that hot Turkish sun and the dry climate, all that dust and dirt …"

"Mom, I haven't been in the Turkish sun since last fall."

"Oh, we'll get it fixed, darling, don't worry. Please don't stress your *maman*. Now, before I forget, we absolutely *must* finalize your gown for the Governor's Ball by the end of next week."

Outside, beyond this expensive room with its peach drapes and cream teas and autocratic mothers, was a world where Alana was in control. She yearned to get back to it. Alana pushed away her cup. "I hope you enjoy the ball," she said. "You and your imaginary mannequin daughter will be the stars of the evening." She stood up and kissed her mother's cheek. "Shop well, *Maman*. Be happy."

Catherine was so startled that Alana was almost out the door before her mother's cry of "AAALAH-NA!" reached her ears.

Out on the sidewalk, in the rush and roar of Park Lane, Alana leaned on a car to catch her breath. Her heart was pounding and her hands shaking. It had been a long time since she'd talked like that to her mother. She knew that, as soon as Catherine was on the subject of fancy gowns, wedding talk couldn't be far behind.

Alana set off briskly in the direction of Piccadilly, the adrenaline ebbing away. As she passed the Hilton, she started to feel an uncomfortable prickling sensation, as if she were being watched. She glanced around, but there was nobody there – just the regular bustle of people hurrying or strolling along, with not so much as a glance in her direction.

As she walked along Piccadilly, Alana began to feel the prickling sensation again. She tried to ignore it, but by the time she passed the Japanese Embassy, she couldn't bear it. She stopped and gazed back through the milling passers-by on both sides of the street. Nothing. Was she going crazy?

Alana turned to carry on walking … and then she saw him.

On the other side of the street, near the gate to Green Park, a man stood watching her intently. As her eyes met his, he looked away quickly, but not fast enough. He was middle-aged, with a stubble beard and graying slicked-back hair; he wore a slate-colored blazer and a black sweater over faded jeans. She remembered noticing him a few minutes earlier, walking by as she was coming out of the Dorchester. Alana's stomach turned. She was no stranger to unwanted looks and advances from men, but this one was especially disturbing. There was something about him that felt indefinably dangerous.

Alana picked up her pace, and after a few yards glanced back. The man had vanished.

At the entrance to Green Park station, she hesitated; the thought of walking in and descending into the underground with that man following her, unseen, made her flesh crawl. On an impulse she hailed a black cab and stepped in. As it pulled away, she looked through the rear window, but saw no sign of the man. She watched Piccadilly Circus swing by, and the manic bustle of Regent Street – chaotic, yet so calming when you looked at it from a moving car. Each time the cab jolted to a stop, she flinched a little less, and gradually relaxed.

Since living in England, riding in a taxi had become a novelty to Alana. She'd grown used to taking mass transit. After a lifetime of being sealed inside a cocoon of luxury, it was energizing to get down among the life and grit of a great city. She'd kept it secret from her parents that the Porsche 911 with a fixed glass roof they'd bought her had spent most of the past three years sitting in a garage in Cambridge, untouched except for the occasional weekend trek with fellow research students from the archaeology department to some remote ancient site or excavation.

She looked at her phone: 2:36 pm already. She was giving a tutorial in college at half past four. Damn. She'd forgotten how slow it was, getting across London by car. There were three text messages from her mother, evolving through indignation, anger, and resigned conciliation in under twenty minutes. Alana hesitated, then texted back an apology.

At King's Cross station, she dashed for the concourse, glancing at the departures board as she wove through the crowd. There was a train leaving in one minute. She accelerated to a flat-out run, skirting the snaking line of people at the Harry Potter photo stop, raced out along the platform, and swung onto the train just as the doors were closing.

As they hissed shut behind her and the train began to move, Alana saw a man running along the platform; he must have been only a few paces behind her, but he was too late. She only saw his face for an instant, but with a sickening shock she recognized the bearded man from Piccadilly. She pressed her face to the glass, craning her neck, but the accelerating train swept him rapidly out of her angle of vision. He became a blur, then disappeared.

As the train passed into the first tunnel, Alana was still frozen in place, looking at her horrified reflection in the glass. She tried to tell herself she'd imagined it, but it was him, she was absolutely certain, and if she'd been just a second slower, he would have caught up with her.

The train had trundled all the way out of London before Alana stopped shaking.

"Good afternoon, Miss Fulton."

"Hi, Keith." Alana gave a distracted half-wave to the college porter as she extracted the mail from her pigeonhole. She'd only been away for a few days, but it had built up: a package from Chicago (undoubtedly the book on Anatolian ceramics she'd ordered), various circulars, personal letters, and a thick envelope marked *Board of Graduate Studies*.

Her heart skipped, and she tore it open to find the formal instructions for submission of her dissertation. She skimmed the letter, the upsetting incidents in London forgotten.

She was so preoccupied, she scarcely noticed Keith trying to get her attention.

"Sorry, I was miles away."

"I said there was a young man asking after you."

"A young man?" Alana was nonplussed. "A student?"

"I imagine so. I didn't see him myself; he spoke to young Darren." Keith regarded her with the paternal look he reserved for young female members of the college. "I wouldn't have noticed, only it sounded important."

"Did he say who he was?"

"I don't know, miss. You'd have to speak to Darren. He's off just now. Back tomorrow."

"Oh. Okay."

"He was American, if that's any help."

"Okay. Thanks, Keith."

Alana racked her brain but couldn't think of any young American men who might be asking for her at the porter's lodge. There were two or three who were graduate students in the faculty, but none who'd be likely to come searching for her here.

She noticed the clock – nearly quarter past four! Her undergraduates would arrive for their tutorial soon, and she needed to find the right headspace. Walking out of the porter's lodge into Great Court, Alana shouldered her way through a knot of tourists and hurried along the path, shoving the big envelope into her bag.

Here in this ancient quadrangle, all honeyed stone, gentle rust-red brick, and trim grass, Alana felt her soul relaxing. Within this world of calm, ancient elegance, where little had altered through centuries of quiet scholarship, she felt insulated from the shocks and stress of the world outside. From the moment she first set foot in Trinity College, Alana had known she would be happy here. Whenever she ventured out into the cold, bright, hard world, she felt like an alien, especially in the alloy and plastic gleam of airports – either going home to LA to visit her parents, or the exhilarating pilgrimage to Turkey to visit the excavations at Çatalhöyük, the subject of her doctoral thesis.

Cambridge was the domesticated, safe, secure space in which she had made her life, while "out there" was a troubling, untamed wilderness in which she felt like a child.

Alana passed along the secluded private lane into New Court, a smaller Victorian version of the Tudor quadrangle she had just passed through, with a stately chestnut tree in the center. She clattered briskly up the wooden treads of staircase C to the top floor, anticipating a blessed few minutes' sit-down to the accompaniment of the kettle rumbling in the gyp room. She put the key to the lock, only to find that the door was already ajar.

Strange. Feeling a premonitory tremor of dismay, she pushed it open.

Her cozy, always-neat study bedroom had been turned upside down. Books and files pulled from the shelves and strewn about the floor; drawers and cupboards yanked open, her clothes spread all over the place. Even the bed had been overturned, the mattress stripped and slit open.

Alana couldn't breathe. Stepping through the wreckage, she stood in the middle of the room, her hand over her mouth, her brain reeling. The savage violence of it stunned her; it was as if the room had been not just burgled but *violated*.

She became dimly aware of female voices and feet clattering up the staircase. There was a rap on the door, then a breathless "Oh!"

Turning, Alana found her students standing in the doorway, mouths hanging open, her own horror reflected in their faces. One, a forthright Scottish girl, found her voice first. "What in the wide blue yonder's gone on here?"

"Are you *sure* you didn't leave it unlocked?"

The policeman's tone was beginning to try Alana's patience. "I'm absolutely sure," she said. "Whoever did this must have had a key."

11

The second police officer – a young woman – nodded at the door. "I wouldn't bet on it, not with an old lock like that. Wouldn't you say, Mr. Griggs?"

Keith the porter, an immaculate figure amid the wreckage in his dark charcoal suit and bowler hat, agreed that the doors and locks were very old and unsophisticated; indeed, the whole building was in urgent need of renovation.

At first, when she'd reported the break-in at the porter's lodge, Keith hadn't taken her crisis seriously: just a student prank, he was sure. But such complacent reassurances had died on his lips as soon as soon as he saw the state of the room. Alana didn't know anyone who'd prank her, let alone as brutally as this. This was vicious, hateful.

"Is anything missing?" asked the female officer. "Any valuables or cash not accounted for?"

Alana shook her head. This was what really bewildered her. Nothing seemed to have been taken. The most precious objects were her research notes and site records, which would be worthless to anyone else. As for saleable possessions, her laptop always traveled with her, and her Bowers & Wilkins Bluetooth speaker hadn't been touched. Even her extremely expensive Cartier wristwatch, a birthday gift from her parents, was intact. She rarely wore it, and it lived in her nightstand drawer; the drawer had been ransacked like all the rest, but the watch lay on the floor among the detritus.

The officer made a note. "Anybody you can think of who might want to intimidate or upset you? An ex-boyfriend, maybe?"

An image of the man who had followed her in London sprang into her mind. During the train journey, she'd gradually convinced herself that she had imagined it. She shivered and hugged herself. "I don't know. I mean, no, no ex-boyfriend."

"No one at all? No one you've fallen out with?"

"No, nobody. I mean …" Alana hesitated, and the policewoman looked expectantly at her. "It's just there was this creepy guy staring at me in London, and I got the feeling he followed me."

"When was this?"

"Just today. This afternoon."

"Did you know him?"

"I never saw him before in my life."

"Can you describe him?" Reluctantly, Alana did so. "We'll make a report," said the policewoman, closing her notebook. "You should hear something from CID within two or three working days."

Alana had expected detectives to show up and dust for fingerprints, and her heart deflated like a balloon. "Two or three *days*?"

"If you think of anything else or have any concerns, give us a ring. Ask for Detective Constable Philips at Parkside police station; he's the community minor crimes officer."

The porter coughed gently. "The young man," he said to Alana.

She looked blankly at him. "Young man?"

"A young man was asking after Miss Fulton at the lodge earlier today, while she was out," Keith explained to the officers. "An American."

Alana had forgotten all about this, and now a chill ran through her.

"Can you describe him?" asked the policewoman.

Keith shook his head. "I didn't see him. It was Darren Pellew, one of our gate porters, who spoke to him."

While this was being taken down, Alana gazed at the window. It was dark outside, and the reflection of the room in the wonky little glass panes made it look even more disheveled and ruined. All she wanted now was for these people to go and leave her alone. She yearned to restore order and begin to forget this had ever happened.

Eventually they departed, Keith giving a final touch of his hat brim and a fatherly smile. Alana closed and locked the door. For good measure she pushed her armchair against it. She felt as if she'd been personally assaulted, and couldn't get the image of the man in London out of her head.

With a supreme act of will, she suppressed her feelings and began picking up her scattered possessions.

It was nearly midnight by the time Alana finished cleaning up. When everything was returned to its proper place and the room looked exactly as it had when she'd last seen it four days ago, she sat on the bed, fighting down her emotions. Undoing the mess hadn't removed the sense of defilement, and she felt an indignant rage rising through the nausea. Why? Why her?

This room was small, confined – and yet it had been sufficient, a snug little nest. Her parents had wanted to buy her a luxury apartment in the town, but she'd refused. They'd provided her with a place in London, where she lived during her research visits to the British Museum. But in Cambridge, all she wanted was this little cocoon, from which she would emerge in due course with her doctorate. It had given her a sense of both security and destiny.

She glanced at the door – a frail-looking Victorian paneled thing held together by cracking glue and two centuries of paint. Even with her heavy old armchair pushed against it, it seemed a hopelessly inadequate barrier to keep out the unknown threat.

Alana's eyes stung, but she refused to let herself cry. *I am* not *going to let this drag me down*, she thought, and repeated the sentiment aloud: "This will *not* bring you down. You are stronger than this." As if to prove that she wasn't afraid, she removed the chair from the door. That was better. Now all she needed was a shower.

Having washed the grime of London from her skin, she sat at her desk with a small mirror propped up against some books and fired up her hairdryer. She reached for her hairbrush, but it wasn't in its usual place. She looked under the desk. No sign of it. Nor was it in her nightstand, her clothes drawers, or any other place she might absent-mindedly have put it when tidying. She guessed the cleaner must have tossed it into the trash by mistake. Alana dried her hair without a brush and forgot all about it.

It was getting really late. Yawning, she went back in the bathroom. Wiping the fog from the mirror, she studied her reflection. The heavy, raven-dark hair, the almond-shaped blue-green eyes, shadowed beneath from lack of sleep and overwork, the jawline unusually sharp with muscular tension. She relaxed, gently massaging her cheeks, and her face resumed its normal shape.

Plucking her toothbrush from its charging stand, she reached for the toothpaste ... and realized that the brush-head was missing. She stared dumbly at the naked metal spike.

A hairbrush and a toothbrush, both missing.

Had the burglar taken them? Alana wanted to laugh at the absurdity of the idea, but the laugh stuck in her throat. There was something deeply, weirdly perverted about the idea, something almost monstrous. Her hand trembled violently as she returned the headless toothbrush to its charger.

Dodging the streaming traffic, Alana crossed the street and went through the fortress-like gateway of the faculty, emerging from the arches into a quiet, tree-shaded quadrangle. At this time of day there were few undergraduates about. After a quick scan of her pigeonhole, Alana went briskly up the staircase to the Haddon Library, her shoes pattering softly on the smooth stone. That sound – and the place it led to – still felt reassuring. Alana had been drawn here by the need to get away from the confines of her room.

She'd slept badly, troubled by nightmares that still lingered oppressively at the edge of her thoughts. The most frightening had been the last, all the more troubling because she believed she'd dreamed something like it before.

She was standing alone on a green hillside strewn with corpses. Women, children, men, all dead and decomposing. Turning away in grief and revulsion, she saw a huge rock looming over her, shaped strangely like a coiled, sleeping cat. With a deep rumble, the rock suddenly moved and rolled toward her, crushing her, enveloping her in blackness, which became a dark, lonely room with a single rickety door. To her horror, the door handle began to turn. Sensing that whatever was outside was evil and malevolent, she hurriedly turned the key in the lock. The handle rattled and the door shook as the thing outside tried to force its way in. Alana pressed herself into the darkest, farthest corner and screamed until her throat was raw.

The screaming woke her, gasping, staring frantically at the door of her room. Everything was quiet. She lay there for a while, but even when she'd stopped hyperventilating, she couldn't get to sleep for fear of finding herself back in the nightmare. She padded through to the gyp room and made an industrial-strength pot of coffee, then sat until morning, poring over her dissertation without taking in a word of it. All the while, her room seemed to shrink in on her until she felt she could scarcely breathe. Her cocoon, her sanctuary, suddenly felt like a dungeon.

After some indecision she'd called the police to tell them about the hairbrush and toothbrush. She'd been put through to a Detective Constable Philips, who went to look for her case report – which apparently had to be fetched from the far side of the moon, judging by how long he was gone. In a tone of weary resignation, Philips made a note of the theft. He seemed neither surprised nor particularly interested.

Unable to be at peace, Alana had decided to seek refuge in the faculty library – one of her favorite sanctuaries.

Passing through the main reading room, she went upstairs to the long, dimly lit garret where the scholarly journals were kept. Mechanically fishing the latest issues of *Antiquity* and *Current Anthropology* off the shelves, she found an unoccupied desk in the far corner and settled down to read. She browsed articles about Nubian ceramics, Libyan rock art, German Iron Age grave goods, a French Neolithic tomb ... Normally Alana would have found at least a few things to take her eye or provide her with some new spark or fragment of knowledge that might feed into her own research. But today she struggled to concentrate.

She thought back over her time at Cambridge, the painstaking, obsessive process of building her thesis, and the years before at Stanford and Columbia. All of that had been channeled toward this moment – when the thesis was complete, and she faced the final test. Maybe the stress was getting to her more than she'd realized. Was she over-reacting? People got burgled all the time – why did this feel like such an earth-shattering event?

Alone in the silent reading room, she reviewed her life, her college years, the fun times with Howard, high school, birthdays, Christmases, evenings in Malibu when all that existed for her was the roll of the blue ocean and the warm, soothing Pacific breeze, weekends at her father's cabin in the cold, bright mountains ... It all came to her with unusual clarity and vividness. Seizing the thread, she followed it all the way back to her earliest childhood memories of kindergarten and ... and there it all halted, fading into the dark wall behind which lay the unrecoverable time of infancy. She couldn't recall any image before kindergarten, only fragments of an emotion that felt ... strangely like the sensation she had now – that same sense of bewilderment and simmering fear. The realization chilled her. Moving forward again through time, she realized that that a similar feeling had infected much of her early childhood, gradually diminishing, until by the time she reached adolescence it had disappeared.

It was like digging down through a trench, through layer upon layer of living occupation, and uncovering an unexpected black seam of burnt earth. Thinking about high school and college, Alana couldn't recall any other moments when she had felt that sensation. No wonder the emotion seemed so raw and unrefined, so primal – it was an emotion from earliest childhood. But why in the world would it surface *now*?

"Lanzy! Hi, how are you doing?"

The smooth sound of Howard's voice on the other end of the phone reassured her; it was the sound of home, which felt comforting in a way it never had before.

"Not so great," she said. "My room was broken into, yesterday." Howard was silent for so long, she wondered if the connection had been lost. She could hear a vehicle in the background. "Howard?"

"A break-in? Seriously?"

"I got back from London, and they'd trashed the place. Total mess."

"That's horrible, babe. I'm so sorry for you. Did they take anything?"

"Nothing valuable. Just my hairbrush and my toothbrush."

"Excuse me? Lanzy, did you say *hairbrush*?"

"I know, I feel like I'm losing my mind."

"Baby, I'm so sorry. Listen, it sounds like you need a little touch of H. O. W. A. R. D. to soothe your lonely heart."

Alana smiled. She and Howard weren't the best-matched couple in the world, but if there was one thing he was good for, it was cheering her spirits when she was down. "Where are you right now?" she asked. "Sounds like you're in a car."

"I literally just touched down at Heathrow. I'm on my way to the hotel."

"You're in London? I thought you weren't due till the weekend?"

"Oh, they changed the shooting schedule. I wrapped my scenes in Vancouver already, and I got hooked up for a meeting in London tomorrow. After that I fly out to start shooting *Well of Souls*."

"What's *Well of Souls*?"

"I told you about it, yeah? It's a comic-book spin-off for Netflix. *Heeeyy* – did I tell you I'm playing an archaeologist? I have to blow up the ancient ruins to save my girl and prevent the world ending."

"That doesn't sound like any archaeologist I know," said Alana. "They'd let the world end."

"Yeah, but this girl is *hot*."

"I'll bet."

"Maybe you can give me some tips before the shoot."

"On how to blow up ancient ruins? Howard, you didn't tell me *any* of this."

"Yeah, it's only a supporting role. But this meeting I have tomorrow, it's Christopher Nolan's next film. Can you believe it? Babe, I got a chance at the *lead*."

Howard's childlike zest was one of the things that drew Alana to him – that, and his soul-melting eyes and impudent pout. When his excitement bubbled up, it was so infectious that she almost forgot how little they had in common. She needed that right now.

"Howard," she said. "How would you like to meet up this evening?"

"You're in London?"

"I can be."

"You got a date, Lanz. Meet you at the usual?"

Howard had hinted more than once that she ought to let him have a key to her London apartment, but she'd always resisted. He could be erratic, and more than once he'd brought home strangers he'd met in bars. Besides that, Alana wouldn't feel comfortable allowing any man too intimately into her world. Throughout her adult life, all of her emotional energy had been devoted to study, while romantically she'd scarcely moved on since high school. She wondered often what Howard saw in her. A challenge, maybe.

After hanging up, Alana stared balefully at the Board of Graduate Studies envelope on her desk. Her thesis would keep for another day or so.

2

Vartan Sarkissian sat at his breakfast table, palms resting on the gold-and-rust-colored damask tablecloth, a plain porcelain teacup before him. He was lost in thought. His eyes, deep-set in the shade of his sharp, high-bridged nose, were glazed over, staring through the veranda windows.

The view was exquisite: the upper colonnade of the palace courtyard, draped with green flowering vines, and the white stone profile of the round tower. The pattering of the fountain in the courtyard below drifted in through the window. Vartan loved to gaze at this view as he breakfasted. The only part of it that offended his senses was the minaret of the palace mosque, partly concealed by a tall palm. Left to himself, Vartan would have dynamited the mosque long ago, but it was an ancient part of the palace complex, and the government in Yerevan, fearing an international outcry, had persuaded him to preserve it.

Vartan raised a hand and clicked his fingers. A servant came forward instantly and filled his cup with pale tea from an ornate silver samovar on a side table. Vartan raised the cup to his trimly-bearded lips and sipped. He looked at the samovar, studying the intricate engraved pattern of the Russian imperial eagle. If he closed his eyes, he could still hear the gunfire, the cries of despair, and see the blood trickling down that silver surface. He took another sip and set down his cup.

There was a murmur of voices at the door. His private secretary, Kamo, a slightly-built man with a thick goatee streaked with gray and a perfectly bald scalp, entered.

"We have it, sir," Kamo said, and held out a thin package. Vartan took it and slit it open without taking his eyes from the secretary's face. Kamo shrank a little under the glare. He knew the meaning of that look; there had been mistakes in the past, and Kamo's position would be perilous if there were any more.

Inside, Vartan found a Ziploc bag, which at first appeared to be empty. He held it up to the light from the window; inside were three long strands of dark hair.

"This is enough?"

"It is enough, I believe," Kamo said. "Only the merest sample is required."

Vartan held out the bag with the tips of his long fingers. "Have it tested."

Kamo took it, bowed, and retreated from the room. Vartan sipped his tea and resumed contemplating at the view.

A black SUV, coated with gray dust, ground its way up the steep, winding track, throwing up a cloud that enveloped the two identical vehicles following behind. The track cut back and forth across a slope of white stone scree peppered with pale shrubs and rough mountain grass.

The track leveled out onto the summit of a hump-backed plateau, green and tree-clad where it was watered by a stream descending from the higher mountains. A few tents clustered under some trees near an old stone goatherd's shack. The three SUVs steered toward this little settlement.

At the sound of engines, armed men emerged from cover, weapons at the ready. The three vehicles accelerated across the grass, fanning out, and ground to an abrupt halt. Their doors opened at once, and six men in military kit stepped out, submachine guns in their hands. The camp guards raised their AK-47s with a chorus of oily clicks as the weapons were cocked.

There was a silent, pregnant pause, then the passenger door of the middle vehicle opened, and Vartan emerged.

The men in the camp immediately lowered their weapons. One, a stocky figure in fatigues and an old army cap, hurried forward and bowed to Vartan. "We were not expecting you, lord, for several more weeks."

Vartan surveyed the camp, which was rather slovenly and unkempt. There was laundry hanging on the tent ropes, litter strewn around, and goats wandered among the detritus. "So I see, Vahe."

Vahe shrugged guiltily. "We've been extremely busy, sir. I'm sure you will be most satisfied." Vartan began walking, and Vahe fell into step beside him. "My apologies for the, er …" He indicated his guards, who were now standing down while Vartan's men formed a cordon facing the camp.

"Where is he?"

"He is exercising, sir."

Their walk had brought them to the outer edge of the plateau, where the hill fell away into a shallow valley, on the far side of which were serried green hillsides retreating into the distance along a winding valley into which the camp stream flowed.

"Here he comes now!" said Vahe, pointing a thick finger and offering Vartan a pair of binoculars.

Vartan trained the binoculars on the distant hillside. For a moment there was nothing, then he spotted the figure of a man running. His arms were oddly outstretched, as if he were balancing on a tightrope. As he came closer, Vartan realized that they were strapped to a thick pole, as if he'd been crucified. Despite this handicap, he ran hard and quickly over the uneven ground with scarcely a skid or stumble.

"Ando calls it the 'Goose Run,'" said Vahe with a chuckle, nodding toward a tall man nearby who held a stopwatch and watched the runner intently. "He has trained your boy well, lord."

Ahead of the runner, cutting across his path, was a long crevice in the rock.

"Three and a half yards wide," Vahe murmured. "And seven deep. A challenging leap even for an unencumbered man. Not a fatal height, unless one falls badly, but enough to break many bones."

The runner picked up his pace as he approached the crevice. Vartan held his breath. The runner hurled himself across, legs cycling in the air, back arched, arms rigid. His boots hit the other side, one foot sliding back toward the void, and Vartan's heart stopped; but with a twist of his bare torso the man recovered and ran on.

Vartan could make out his features now – scalp shaved, face thickly stubbled. Every muscle was stretched taut with exertion.

Suddenly, as the runner was passing a strew of large rocks, a man stood up as if materializing out of the ground. He was armed with a long wooden staff, which he swung with terrific force into the runner's midriff. The runner doubled over, dropped to his knees, and the attacker swept up his staff, ready to drive it, point first, into the back of his head. The runner twisted, swinging his tied arms, ramming one end of the yoke into the ground; he pivoted round it, catching his attacker with a powerful kick to the chest. Instantly, the runner was on his feet, swinging the yoke and catching the attacker in the head with it. The attacker fell back, and the runner, with teeth bared in an animal snarl, rammed the yoke, with his whole bodyweight

24

behind it, into the man's face, which collapsed like an egg, puffing out a scarlet mist.

"*Oof*," muttered Vahe softly. "Too slow, Sargis my friend, too slow; you've sipped your last wine."

The runner righted himself and carried on, sprinting now over the final leg of the race. As he ran past Ando, the trainer clicked his stopwatch with a flourish and a grunt of satisfaction. The runner skidded to a stop on the loose dirt, gasping for breath.

Vahe gave a sharp whistle. "Hayk! Over here."

The runner looked up and saw Vartan. His expression tightened warily, and he walked over, his arms still grotesquely outstretched. His skin was coated in dust with tracks of sweat flowing through it.

"I am told that your training progresses well, Hayk," said Vartan.

The young man bowed. He was young and handsome beneath the dust, with a short, sculpted nose and green eyes that sparkled in the sun. But the symmetry of his face was marred by a deformed left jawline; the stubble on that side was patchy over a puckered scar. His body was lean and muscular, marked here and there with long-healed wounds.

"Cut him loose."

The trainer produced a combat knife and deftly slit the ropes; the yoke fell to the ground with a thud, and Hayk eased his arms, suppressing the pain. He dropped to his knees before Vartan. "I am ready, my blood, my father."

"It does my soul good to see you again, my blood, my son. I believe you truly are ready. I have come for you. The day is at hand, Hayk." Vartan took the young, grazed, dust-coated hand in his and squeezed. "She has been found. We are very near."

The apartment door flew in, thumping against the wall, and Alana and Howard almost fell through it, laughing and holding on to each other.

"Let me get the light." Alana detached herself from Howard's grip long enough to reach the switch. Concealed lighting came on in the narrow hallway. She was a little unsteady, but hadn't drunk anywhere near as much as Howard, who was leaning back against the wall looking ready to slide to the floor.

"C'mon Mr. Leading Man." She gave him her shoulder and guided him to the living room.

They'd met up in a private club in Knightsbridge, a discreet, comfortable little place in a side street near Harrods, a warren of lounges stuffed with country house couches and open fires. Afterward they'd gone on to the American Bar at the Beaumont Hotel in Mayfair, where Alana drank a single margarita while Howard put away half a bottle of Scotch. He wasn't a good drinker at the best of times, and now he was like a marionette with its strings cut.

"I love you, Lanzy," he murmured as Alana settled him on a couch. The living room was comfortable but rather sterile: white brickwork, teak floors, furnished with gray leather couches. Big warehouse windows overlooked the river. Alana used the apartment as a pied-à-terre and had made little imprint on it.

"I know you do," she said.

"You know it's Valentine's today?" he said. "You forgot, didn't you? You didn't get me a card or nothin'."

"You didn't get me one either."

"I got you *me*, sweetheart," he said, spreading his arms wide. "Kiss me, baby."

Alana was powerfully attracted to Howard, almost in spite of herself. It was one of the tenuous strands that kept their relationship going. But not when he was in this state.

She took his hands and pressed them together between hers. "Let's sober you up and call you a cab."

He grinned. "I love it when you go all prom virgin on me. So damn sexy."

Alana placed his hands on his lap and went to the kitchenette. "You've got your big meeting tomorrow, remember," she called over her shoulder, filling the kettle.

He gave a long, grumbling growl. "Damn right. Hella meeting. Hey, Lanzy, you wanna come? I could introduce you to Chris Nolan?"

"He's 'Chris' all of a sudden? I thought you never met him before."

Howard waved away this objection. "He loves me. He saw *Phenomenal* and it blew him away."

"Uh-huh." Alana opened a fresh pack of coffee. The idea of Christopher Nolan loving that particular movie seemed implausible.

"S'why he asked to see me." Howard seemed to have forgotten the more credible version he'd told her earlier – that the meeting was the result of a long charm campaign by his agent, who was an old friend of Nolan's casting director. "Leading man, that's me," he said as Alana set a cup of coffee on the table in front of him. "Leading man in a Nolan flick. See you at next year's Academy Awards, baby; I'll be the good-lookin' dude pickin' up the best actor statue." He smiled blearily at her, then struggled to his feet. "I gotta use the bathroom."

When he'd gone, Alana went to the arched window and looked out at the night-time skyline of London. Below, the black surface of the Thames reflected the lights of Southwark and the towering spike of the Shard. To the right, London Bridge glimmered with traffic. This window had once looked out on a skyline of crooked roofs and spires, smoke, gaslight, and a fouled river covered in a forest of East India Company sailing ships. She loved to stand here and visualize how it must have looked to a dock-hand standing on the same spot two hundred years ago.

27

It soothed Alana's spirits to lose herself in the past. She'd left Cambridge in a rush, bringing out the little-used X1 from its garage and driving down. Her evening with Howard had been fun but had done little to calm her nerves.

She was jarred out of her thoughts by her phone ringing: a Cambridge number she didn't recognize. She swiped to accept the call.

"Am I speaking to Alana Fulton?" said a flat-sounding English voice.

"You are."

"This is DC Philips, Parkside police station. We spoke earlier today. There's been a development in your case."

Her stomach tightened. "Okay."

"Your description of the missing items – one hairbrush and one toothbrush – rang a bell, so I ran some cross-checks. I turned up a crime sheet on a similar incident a few months ago, just before Christmas. The room of a female student at Newnham College was broken into and ransacked, but nothing of value taken. However, the victim stated that the waste bin in her bathroom had been turned over, and – I'm sorry to be blunt – one or more used sanitary towels had been taken."

"Seriously? Sanitary pads?"

"Afraid so. Now, according to my notes, you're a student of archaeology."

"That's correct."

"Well, so was the victim at Newnham. Like you she's an American national. Additionally, she shares your surname."

Alana felt as if her stomach were falling out of her body. "You mean Elaine Fulton?"

"You know her?"

"Not really. She's an undergrad; I took a supervision with her a year or so back. We joked about having similar names."

"She's not related to you?"

"No, not at all." Alana's nerves got the better of her, and she began to babble. "Well, I imagine if you traced our ancestral lines back far enough, you'd find a common Fulton ancestor; she's from DC, I seem to remember, whereas my people go way back in New England, but …"

As she paused to draw breath, Philips interrupted. "I activated a wider search and turned up a third case in London. An assault. This was a fortnight before the Newnham break-in. The victim of the crime was, again, female and a student of archaeology at University College. Attacked late at night in the street between the students' union building and her hall of residence. She received a severe graze on her arm from the assailant's fingernails. The victim was unable to provide a description of said assailant other than that he was male, twenties, and white or possibly Middle Eastern."

Alana struggled to control the shake in her voice. "Was the victim American?"

"She wasn't, as it happens. She was Canadian. Her name was Alana Fisher."

Alana's breathing was racing out of control. "Okay. So this is some kind of serial killer thing?"

"Well, he hasn't killed anyone. Not yet anyway."

"Oh dear God."

"There's one other thing," said Philips. "I spoke to the gate porter at Trinity this afternoon, the one who reported a young man asking after you."

"Did he give you a description?"

"He did better than that – he gave me a photograph. He claimed to recognize the young man. He snapped a picture on his phone."

"He recognized the guy? He was a student?"

"Apparently not. Listen, if you give me your email address, I'll send you the photo. See what you think and phone me back, yes?"

After she'd hung up, Alana sat for a moment trying to stop her hands shaking and her gorge rising. She opened her laptop and set it on her desk. Her inbox was full of unread emails, the latest from rfphilips417@cambs.police.uk. She clicked on it.

"Your hand sanitizer's run dry," said Howard from the bathroom doorway.

Alana flinched and slammed the laptop shut.

Howard came up behind her and slipped his arms around her waist. "Who was on the phone?"

Her brain whirling, she gripped his hands and removed them, turning and ducking away from his embrace. "Cambridge cops," she said. "About the break-in."

"Poor baby," he murmured, and tried to nuzzle her neck. "Don't worry, Lanzy, your man's got you under his wing now." He wafted a fog of Scotch in her face. "Now, I think it's time you came to bed."

"Oh, I don't think so. I think it's time we got you a cab back to your hotel."

"Yeah, no, that place stinks. You lemme stay here? Ooh, PlayStation!" He pushed past her and stooped over the console under the TV. "Oh my God, you got Gran Turismo Sport!"

"Of course. You bought it for me." The game was still in its cellophane wrapping.

"Oh, babe, we are talkin' *all-night session*!" He winked at her.

"No, Howard, you have to go." Alana desperately needed to be alone.

"Baby, it's cold outside. Lemme stay?"

She hesitated. "Okay. But you sleep on the couch."

"You got it. Listen, okay if I take a shower first?"

"That's fine."

He smirked. "Wanna join me?"

"No, Howard, I do not."

The firmness in her voice penetrated the alcoholic haze. "You don't wanna?" She shook her head. Howard shrugged. "You are a mystery to me. I'm your leading man, baby, your leading man." He blew her a kiss and turned toward the bathroom. "Fire up GT Sport," he said over his shoulder. "I'll be back, and I am gonna *own* you so bad."

As soon as he was out of the room and she heard the shower start, Alana sat at her desk and opened the laptop.

DC Philips' message was terse. *Porter took photo because believed recognized person as celebrity liked by his wife. No positive identification. Do you recognize?*

The photo was grainy, shot through the inner window of the porter's lodge in poor light. Alana leaned close to the screen, zooming the image, and her stomach began to tighten nauseatingly. The man who had been seeking her, and who in all likelihood had ransacked her room and Elaine Fulton's and assaulted Alana Fisher, was caught in half-profile, and in spite of the poor quality, Alana would recognize the face anywhere. She had seen those sweeping eyebrows and wide-set eyes a million times; just a moment ago, those full lips had been inches from her own, and had blown her a kiss as he went off to shower.

3

Alana clawed her way up from sleep as if from drowning – clutching, gasping for breath. The first sense she regained was sight. Howard's face filled her vision. He was snarling, and Alana felt his fingers on her throat.

She fought back, struggling and screaming. He was mouthing words at her, but she couldn't make them out; terror took control of her. She punched him in the side, making him gasp; twisting her neck, she sunk her teeth into his wrist. He released his hold on her and leapt back. His voice suddenly snapped into clarity.

"Jesus, La! What the hell?" He stared at her in amazement, holding his injured wrist as Alana backed herself into a corner of the couch, bracing herself to fight.

Her confused senses began to untangle themselves. It was morning; she was on the couch in her apartment. She put her hands protectively to her throat, but although it felt raw inside from screaming, the sense impressions of Howard's fingers were not there but on her shoulders.

"What's going on?" she said warily.

"You were having a nightmare. I was trying to wake you."

"Oh my God! Oh Howard, you're bleeding!" The left wrist had a livid bracelet of teeth-marks. She jumped up and took his hands in hers. "I'm so sorry."

Rummaging through the kitchen drawers, Alana found her first-aid kit; emptying its contents on the table she extracted dressings.

"You wanna tell me what the bejeezus that was about?" said Howard, flinching as she disinfected and dressed the wound.

"I don't know. I'm sorry." Her mind was still livid with horror. The dream had been the same as the night before – the hillside and the bodies. Only this time, the image of Howard's face in the photograph had become entangled in it somehow, as if it were in some unimaginable way his fault. And then to wake and find him …

"That must've been one hell of a nightmare."

"What happened?" she said, winding the bandage.

"I don't know. I wake up and you're screaming. And I mean *screaming*, like, real blood-curdling horror-movie screams. I try to wake you up, but you won't. And then you *bite* me!"

The last Alana could remember was sitting on the couch with her laptop open, staring at Howard's face on the screen.

"I'm sorry," she said. Tying off the bandage, she picked up the computer, which had slid to the floor, and snapped it shut. "You're right. It was a hell of nightmare. I thought … I thought you were strangling me."

Howard looked querulously at her. It was the one expression that did nothing to enhance his looks; it made him resemble an indignant opossum. He stroked the bandage gingerly and flexed his fingers.

"Maybe you should get dressed," said Alana. He was wearing a bathrobe of hers.

As Howard stood up, the memory of Detective Philips's voice came into Alana's head – *The victim was unable to provide a description of the assailant other than that he was male, aged mid-twenties, and white …*

"Howard," she said suddenly. "Why were you in Cambridge Monday?"

The question burst out of her like a trapped air-bubble from a pipe. Howard stopped with his hand on the door handle. "Excuse me?"

"Why were you in Cambridge Monday?"

"Cambridge? Why would you think I was in Cambridge?" He was bewildered, but was there a trace of guilt? He laughed. "You're confused. I haven't been in Cambridge since, I don't know, last summer, I guess. We went on the river. You dropped your phone in the water, remember? I jumped in after it."

"I remember. So where *were* you on Monday?"

Howard opened his mouth, hesitated, and then seemed to decide to humor her. "What is it now – Wednesday already? Monday, I guess I was en route from Vancouver to New York. They wrapped my scenes Sunday. I spent Monday night in NYC and touched down here yesterday. Like I told you." His expression became quizzical. Alana studied him intensely. Was he acting? Was he capable of a performance this convincing? "You called me yesterday," he said. "Remember – I told you I literally just touched down."

"I …" She remembered the sound of a car in the background: the airport cab.

Howard came back to her and held her tenderly by the shoulders. "You've still got brain-freeze from that nightmare," he said.

He *must* be lying, surely? Alana, boiling with fear and frustration, wanted to knock his hands away. She should show him the photo, tell him the police were involved – that would jolt him out of this act. If it was an act. Howard was talented, but was he capable of a performance this convincing on the spur of the moment? Alana swallowed hard, pressing down her emotions.

"Just go get dressed," she said. She was too tired and confused to handle it right now.

"My stuff's in your beemer."

He hadn't bothered checking into his hotel, and his bags were all in the trunk of her car, which was in the parking garage underneath the building. She fished the car key out of her pocket. "Here."

After he'd gone out, Alana went through to the bedroom. She needed a shower; it would refresh her brain and help her think this through.

The bathroom floor was still damp and strewn with Howard's clothes and underwear. Alana gathered them up irritably and took them through to the bedroom, dumping them in a heap on a chair. His jacket slid to the floor, and something fell out of the pocket, skittering across the polished boards.

It was a small, padded envelope; she picked it up and was about to return it to the pocket when she noticed that it was addressed to Howard by way of a PO box in London. Why would he have a mailbox here? He had an agent in London who received official mail for him. Looking inside, she found a tiny Ziploc bag, which she extracted. It contained a diamond about the size of a small pea.

Alana shook the stone onto her palm and held it toward the light. She was no jeweler, but she'd seen enough precious stones in her life to be pretty certain this was the real thing – and high quality, too. Just under a carat, clear and beautiful, it could be worth as much as eight or nine thousand dollars.

She heard the front door open and a suitcase trundling along the hallway.

Howard appeared in the doorway just as Alana was scooping up his towel from the floor. "Yeah," he said, looking around the room. "I was a little messy. Sorry."

She tossed the towel on the bed. "Get dressed," she said. "I'll give you a ride to your meeting."

Alana swung off High Holborn into Shaftesbury Avenue, straight into a bumper-to-bumper logjam. Howard looked at his watch, wincing as he brushed the bandaged wound.

"Relax," she said. "There's plenty of time."

Several minutes ticked by in silence. Alana could sense Howard growing more tense and anxious. "Seriously," she said. "Your meeting's at, what, eleven-thirty? We still have fifteen minutes."

"I could walk from here," he said. "It's right across there."

At that moment, the jam began to clear. "See?" she said.

Howard's mood was strange; she'd never known him so anxious about an appointment before. If anything, he was usually infuriatingly casual about such things. But then, she supposed, this was his career; for Howard his career was everything – and it was Christopher Nolan, after all.

"Listen," he said suddenly. "Are you really sure you oughta go back to Cambridge?"

"I might as well. If you're heading straight to the airport after your meeting …"

"Really, La? After a break-in? I don't know about you, but that'd so freak me out. Tell me you'll stay in London."

Alana had thought the same herself. Returning to Trinity and that room made her skin crawl. But London hadn't been the escape she'd hoped for, and she wanted to speak to DC Philips in person.

"I haven't decided," she said.

She followed the spiral of one-way streets leading into the middle of Soho. Turning into Dean Street, she noticed Howard rummaging, increasingly frantically, in his jacket pockets.

"Lost something?" she asked.

"What? No ... I mean, no, it's just ... nothing." He gave up and stared out the window in undisguised consternation. As they circled Soho Square, he spoke again. "Babe, please tell me you're not going back to Cambridge." He turned to look at her. "I don't think you should. I don't think it's safe."

Alana glanced at him. "Not safe? It might be a little creepy, but why wouldn't it be safe? It was only a break-in." She hadn't told him anything about the other cases that connected to hers.

His thumbnail worked nervously at the leather door pull. "I worry about you. You're La Babe," he said with a smile. "I mean, a break-in ... that's serious shit."

Alana's bewilderment was mounting by the minute. If Howard had been lying through his teeth to her all this time, and was somehow implicated in the break-in and the other incidents, why would he suddenly be so concerned about her? She glanced sidelong at him. She'd always felt a little distant from Howard; she was fond of him, and often believed that she loved him, but had never really felt that he was her soul mate. Now he seemed like a stranger.

"It's right here," he said, pointing. They were in a narrow, shabby street. Alana pulled over outside a blank blue door between a restaurant and a vacant store. There was no sign or nameplate, just a number and a bell-push.

When they kissed goodbye, Alana could taste the anxiety in his mouth, and see it in his eyes. "Have a good meeting," she said. "Give my regards to Mr. Nolan. Tell him I liked *Inception*."

"Sure." Howard retrieved his suitcase from the trunk. Alana saw him in the mirror patting his jacket pockets again. He leaned in through the passenger window to say a last goodbye, his eyes flicking across the seat and floor, as if searching for something he'd dropped. His gaze met hers, and he smiled.

"See ya, La Babe," he said.

"Make it a good one."

"Love you."

"Me too."

She drove away. At the junction with Charing Cross Road, the traffic came to a halt again. Twisting in her seat, Alana dipped her fingers in her back pocket, extracting the crumpled padded envelope and the Ziploc with its pea-sized diamond. She stared at the stone, wondering. As the traffic moved, she tossed the Ziploc onto the passenger seat and hit the gas, turning left and heading north.

Alana's foot eased down, and the Porsche surged past a line of trucks. She'd been lost in thought for the past forty miles, one robotic part of her mind driving the car. As the third truck flicked by, there was a chime from the dashboard, and she realized she was doing over a hundred. Easing back, she pulled across to the slow lane and let her speed drop to seventy.

It was almost like waking from a fugue state. Since leaving Howard in Soho, everything had been a fog of fruitless wondering. Beside her on the passenger seat, the diamond glinted in a shaft of sunlight. She hadn't meant to steal it; hearing him enter the apartment, she'd slipped it into her pocket.

Her working theory was that Howard had got himself involved in drug trafficking; he traveled a lot, and she knew he indulged, using at least one dealer in LA and possibly others in New York and London. Was he in trouble with criminals? Were the break-in and the other crimes connected with that, somehow? Were gangland hitmen trying to terrorize her in order to put pressure on him? If not, why had he been so worried about her returning to Cambridge? It hadn't felt like the natural concern of a worried boyfriend.

She switched on the radio, hopping from station to station – a burst of Mariah Carey … a forecast of rain and high winds … pizzicato strings and a thunderous crash of brass and timpani … the prime minister was expected to make a statement to parliament on the terrorist attack at … a cheesy jingle … She switched it off again.

A few minutes later she was driving along the familiar, welcoming street leading into Cambridge. The road passed along the picturesque college backs – an idyllic avenue lined with tall trees and lawns bordering the willow-draped River Cam, with the stately rear elevations of the colleges on the far bank: King's, Clare, Trinity, St John's.

Alana slowed to a halt, preparing to turn in at the rear driveway of Trinity. Traffic cones had been placed across the entrance, and she had to brake hard. On the far side of the green, the iron gates leading into the college were closed and a police officer stood guard. Beyond, at the far end of the long driveway, she could make out movement under the great arch at the back of New Court. It was too far away to tell what was happening, but she could see the fluorescent green of police high-vis jackets. Probably a royal visit or something, she guessed.

A car horn blasted behind her, and she straightened up and drove on.

Twenty minutes later, having put the Porsche back in its garage, Alana walked along Trinity Street, wheeling her small suitcase behind her. A large crowd had gathered on the sidewalk opposite the college forecourt. Several TV crews had set up cameras, and there were more police. A sign was up – *COLLEGE CLOSED TO VISITORS*.

Alana walked past the police, through the arch and into the porter's lodge. Inside she bumped into a fellow PhD student. "Hi," she said. "What's going on?"

His pouchy eyes glittering with excitement. "It's the police," he said. "They've closed off New Court. They're saying it's terrorists!"

"*Terrorists?*"

"It's been on the news. Haven't you heard?"

"I just got in. Are you serious?"

Alana stepped out into Great Court, where another crowd – made up of students and college dons – stood rubbernecking and discussing this sensational event with varying degrees of earnestness and excitement. The far corner of the vast quadrangle, where the passage led through to the lane and New Court, had been taped off. There were more police, together with firefighters and some people wearing what looked from a distance like bulbous space suits.

"Here she is!" said a familiar voice.

She turned to see Keith, the senior porter, pointing at her and beckoning to someone behind him. A man appeared and, following Keith's direction, fixed his gaze on Alana. He was about forty, with intelligent gray eyes and deep lines either side of a small, tight mouth. He wore a suit in the careless manner of someone who hates suits but is habituated to them. He flashed a police ID.

"Miss Fulton? DC Rob Philips," he said. "We spoke yesterday. I've tried to phone you a couple of times since. I was hoping you might have some thoughts on the photo I emailed you."

"I'm sorry, I switched off my phone," said Alana.

"Would you come with me, please," he said. It wasn't a question.

"Come with you? Where?"

"Just across there." He pointed toward the range of grand buildings making up the far side of the quadrangle. "My colleagues would like a word with you in private."

4

Alana followed the detective, ducking under the cordon of police tape. The crowd bristled with envy, wondering why she was granted such privileged access to the scene of the crime.

"Has there really been a terrorist attack?" she asked.

Philips didn't seem to hear. He led her across Great Court and up the stone steps to the grand doorway of the college dining hall, where uniformed police were coming and going.

Passing through the lobby, Alana entered the familiar church-like space. Tall stained-glass windows cast colored pools across the white walls; high above was an intricate hammer-beamed roof of dark timbers decorated with carved finials and edged with gilt. The walls were paneled in honey-colored oak up to the base of the windows and hung with portraits of former masters in every costume from modern suits to Victorian frock coats and Tudor ruffs.

Alana felt, as always in these surroundings, a sense of security mingled with darkness. This place was timeless, comfortable, a sanctuary of scholarship and history; but it was also a relic of a strange and frightening former age. People had been burned at the stake during the lifetime of this college, just a short walk from this spot.

The town had its roots in medieval soil, and those roots still showed above the surface.

Four long, plain tables ran the length of the room; Philips led Alana past these toward the dais on which the high table of the Master and fellows stood under a full-length portrait of the college founder, King Henry VIII. Alana had dined at that table a few times – as a graduate student she was entitled to do so four times a year, and take wine afterwards with the fellows in their combination room – but had never felt comfortable. It felt more like a performance than a dinner.

Now it was swarming with police officers; computers, phones, and other equipment had colonized the tables, with a row of whiteboards alongside. Philips led Alana to where a middle-aged man and woman in civilian suits were studying a computer screen.

Philips cleared his throat. "Excuse me, ma'am, sir," he said, and they both looked up. "This is Alana Fulton."

Alana could tell, as soon as their eyes met, that the woman was in charge. She was in her mid-forties, with a round face and a tight mouth with slightly protuberant teeth. Her large hazel eyes were penetrating and hard. They scanned Alana's face.

"I'm pleased to meet you, Miss Fulton," she said. "I'm Detective Chief Superintendent Fiona Grayson, from the regional CTU."

This conveyed nothing to Alana. "CTU?"

"Counter Terrorism Unit," said Philips.

"I'd like a chat with you," said Grayson. "If that would be convenient?"

"Sure. Of course."

Alana was led back through the hall, through the lobby and into the kitchen wing. The offices had been commandeered by the police, and the far end of the building had been cordoned off. "The kitchens are within the potential area of effect," Philips whispered to her, but before she could ask what he meant, she was ushered into an office.

Grayson and Philips sat on one side of the large desk, and Alana was invited to take a chair opposite them. Grayson opened a thin folder.

"Miss Fulton," she said, "you are not under arrest, and you're free to go at any time. However, I'm obliged to caution you. You do not have to say anything, but it may harm your defense if you do not mention when questioned something which you later rely on in court. Anything you do say may be given in evidence. Do you understand?"

Alana's skin turned cold. "Court?" she said. "What is this? What's happening?"

"As I said, you are not under arrest and are free to go whenever you like. You are entitled to have a legal representative present if you wish – either your own lawyer or the duty solicitor. Do you wish to have a representative present?"

Alana was too bewildered to comprehend. She felt like a swimmer caught in a riptide, dragged under by forces she could feel but not understand. She shook her head vaguely.

"This interview will be recorded." Grayson nodded at Philips, who pressed a button on a bulky black box next to him. "Interview with Alana Fulton," Grayson said. "Present are DCS Grayson and DC Philips. Interviewee has declined legal representation." Grayson took a sheet of paper from her folder and laid it in front of Alana. "For the recorder," she said, "I'm showing the witness image CTC-4-024. Miss Fulton, do you recognize this person?"

It was the photo Philips had emailed her.

"Kind of," said Alana.

"Could you clarify?"

"It *appears* to be Howard Angelus," said Alana cautiously.

"Are you referring to Howard Angelus the film star?"

"Yes."

Grayson studied Alana's face, as if looking for a reaction. "You are in a relationship with him. Is that correct?"

"Yes."

"Can you confirm that that is him in the photo?" Grayson's voice had a naturally harsh edge to it, and she put her questions in a monotonously calm, dispassionate tone which was already beginning to grate on Alana.

"As I said, it *looks* like him." Alana replayed Howard's denial in her head; it still felt utterly genuine. "But I don't think it *is* him. People get mistaken for celebrities all the time."

Grayson consulted a handwritten paper. "The college employee who took the photograph says he recognized the person provisionally identified as Howard Angelus as a celebrity and took the photo to show his wife. He said that the visitor inquired about you by name, asking, 'Is Alana Fulton in her room?' to which Mr. Pellew replied, 'No, I believe she is away.' 'Is it okay if I call on her?' the visitor asked. Whereupon Mr. Pellew informed him that he must sign the visitors' book. Mr. Pellew says the visitor declined to do so and left." Grayson looked up from the paper. "Can you think of any reason why a random person who just happens to resemble your boyfriend would be asking for you at your college?"

"Well … no. I guess not."

"Were you aware of Mr. Angelus visiting Cambridge on Monday last?"

Alana hesitated. "No."

Grayson went on, consulting another handwritten sheet: "When the then-unidentified visitor was mentioned to you on Monday last by the senior porter, you claimed to have no knowledge of who it might be."

"That's correct. I had no idea who could be asking for me. I thought it might be some student."

"Have you seen or spoken to Howard Angelus since?"

"Yes. I met with him in London last night."

Grayson glanced at Philips, who said, "When I emailed you this photo yesterday evening, did you recognize it?"

"Yes. I mean, of course I recognized that it *looked like* him." There was no point in denying it. "It was a shock."

Grayson eyes brightened. "A shock?"

"Well, I didn't know he'd been in Cambridge."

"So you do acknowledge that it's him?"

Alana shrugged helplessly.

"For the recorder, the witness is shrugging," said Grayson. "What did you do when you recognized the photo?"

"I asked Howard this morning if he'd come to Cambridge on Monday. He denied it. I believed him."

"Can you think of any reason why Mr. Angelus would come looking for you in Cambridge and then keep it a secret?" Grayson asked.

"No." Alana's chest was tight, and she felt like she could cry at any moment. What did they want from her? What was going on? "Listen," she said. "Could you please just tell me what this is about—"

"You say you believed him," Grayson interrupted. "Past tense. Do you mean you no longer do?"

"I, I don't know what to believe." This wasn't a chat or an interview; it was an interrogation. "Listen, I want to know what's going on here. I mean – terrorism? What in the world could I have to do with that? And Howard? He's just an actor! It was just a minor break in – just nothing. I don't understand how it's got blown up into all this … this craziness."

"This isn't about the break-in," said Philips. "Although we're working on the possibility that the two incidents are connected."

"Which two incidents? What's happened here?"

Grayson went on: "At about eight o'clock this morning, a weapon was discharged within the bounds of this college."

"A weapon? You mean a gun?"

Philips answered, his voice grating over the words like a boat running onto rocks: "No. A chemical weapon. An extremely toxic military-grade nerve agent."

Alana sat with her mouth open. Her hands were shaking. She took a deep breath. "Okay. I think I want a lawyer now."

"I confess, I'm rather astonished you know nothing of this," said Professor George Coniston.

Alana's parents didn't retain a lawyer in England, and as Professor Coniston was vice-master of the college and happened to be on hand, he'd stepped in. Besides being Hazeley Professor of Law, he had authored two of the standard textbooks used in training criminal lawyers. He was a corpulent old-school English conservative in a tailored pinstripe suit and salmon-pink club tie, with thick, unnaturally black hair oiled down.

"I've had other things on my mind," said Alana. "It's been a weird couple of days."

"You're not aware, then, that the prime minister addressed the House of Commons on this precise subject less than an hour ago?"

Alana shook her head. "I'm just … spaced. I mean, a chemical weapon? Here?"

"I can only tell you what is public knowledge. A nerve agent, believed to be of military grade, was released in a room on staircase C, New Court this morning. More than a dozen people have been hospitalized. A cordon has been imposed in a wide radius around the point of release. They've sealed off Trinity Lane and Garret Hostel Lane, as well as parts of the neighboring colleges."

"Staircase C? That's my …" The coldness in Alana's stomach spread to her legs, and she thought she was about to fall down. "I live there," she whispered.

Coniston regarded her with concern. "You are naturally a person of interest, Miss Fulton, because it seems that the point of release was in your very rooms." He paused, watching her closely as his words sank in. "I understand that you are not a suspect *per se*, but regarded as a *potential* suspect."

Alana's head spun, and she pressed her fingers into her temples. "My rooms …" She couldn't even begin to process this. "Is anyone dead?"

"Not at this point, although that may change. The chemical is believed to be *Prevoskhodstvo* – or PVS – an extremely toxic nerve agent of Russian military origin. All the people who were in adjacent rooms have been affected to varying degrees. The other occupant on your landing is the most severely poisoned."

"Isobel?"

Coniston consulted his notebook. "Dr Isobel Bailey, aged thirty-eight," he read. "She is in the intensive care unit at Addenbrooke's." His face was grave. "I'm afraid there is little hope for her."

Alana stared in horror. "Oh, sweet Jesus."

"Three other people are also in intensive care. In addition to the hospitalized victims, more than two hundred people are being screened for possible contamination. If you had been in your room," Coniston added, "you would certainly have been killed immediately."

Alana leaned heavily against the old oak panels of the narrow lobby. She couldn't speak. She felt nauseous, dizzy.

"I say again, you are not currently a suspect. However, this is an extremely serious incident, with inevitable international ramifications. There is speculation in parliament and the media – and even a rather dour warning from the prime minister – that Russian intelligence is behind the attack."

To Coniston's surprise, Alana laughed out loud at this. Her nervous system, in a state close to emergency shutdown, was producing irrational reactions. In her disordered mind, the idea of her vacant room being targeted by Russian intelligence was not only palpably insane but hilarious. She startled herself with her laugh, and instantly shut it off.

"Of course, it may not be Russians," said Coniston. "A security specialist on the news seemed to think it could be ISIS. You may not be the primary target. It could be random." He glanced at DC Philips, who was standing by, and touched Alana's arm. "Come along, let's get you a cup of tea before we face the music."

A few minutes later, Alana found herself sitting at a table in the dining hall, a cup of strong, brown, gloopy English tea in front of her.

"When we go in there," Coniston was saying, "ensure that you keep your answers truthful, concise, and simple. Do *not* elaborate unless specifically asked to do so. The fewer words you use, the fewer bear-traps you will lay for yourself. And above all, do not become flustered." He peered at her and smiled. "I sense that you are not the sort of woman who is easily flustered."

She met his eye. "Only by patronizing patriarchal lawyers," she said.

Coniston grinned. "Good, that's the spirit." He beckoned to DC Philips. "I believe we are ready to proceed."

The recorder chimed. "Interview resumed at 14:37," said Grayson. "Persons present as before. Also present: Professor George Coniston. Miss Fulton, please be advised that you are still under caution."

48

Grayson went on, her voice as cold and unemotional as before: "Please describe your movements during the past few days – let's say since Sunday the twelfth of February."

Following Coniston's advice, Alana stuck to the bare bones – dates, times, places, no elaboration. On Sunday she had spent the day in her apartment, studying research data. The following day, Monday, she was scheduled to travel back to Cambridge to take a supervision. She met her mother at the Dorchester just after lunch, then took a taxi to King's Cross.

With a stab, she remembered the creepy man on Piccadilly who had tried to board the train after her. But she suppressed any mention of him. *No elaboration.*

On returning, she had found her room ransacked, and called the police. She spent the night there. After speaking to Howard, she had driven to London in the afternoon and met up with him. They spent that night together in her apartment, then she drove him to an appointment in Soho and returned to Cambridge. The rest they knew.

The only thing they were really interested in was Howard. "Did he seem at all agitated to you?" Grayson asked.

"I guess so," said Alana.

"Can you think of any reason for that?"

"Howard's dedicated to his career; always strung out about some part he might get. Right now his heart is set on a leading role in Christopher Nolan's next movie."

"The appointment you took him to – was that connected?"

"Yes, it was a meeting with the man himself."

"With Nolan?"

"Yes."

"Where exactly did it take place?"

49

Alana gave them the address. Philips wrote it down, and at a nod from Grayson, left the room.

"How would you describe your relationship with Howard?" Grayson asked.

"I'd describe it as weekend-serious, weekday-casual." Seeing the detective's blank look, she added: "When we see each other, it's pretty serious. He knows my parents, I know his, we vacation together. But we don't get together all that often."

"But what is the relationship *like*? Happy? Argumentative? Indifferent? Contented?" Grayson paused. "Violent?"

Alana thought hard. What *was* it like? It was a question she had asked herself increasingly of late. "Mostly happy, I guess. Howard's a lot of fun. Sometimes a little tense. Certainly never violent; Howard's not like that." She became aware that she was kneading her fingers together anxiously and made herself lay her hands flat on the desk.

"Was it tense yesterday?"

She took a deep breath. "A little."

"Your research is based in Turkey, I believe," Grayson said.

"That's right."

"Do you go there often?"

"Once a year for a month or so. I'm not a digger so much; my work is largely theoretical."

"You have friends in Turkey?"

"Yes, a few among the local archaeologists."

"Is this line of questioning relevant?" Professor Coniston interjected. "My client's research can have no—"

"Tell me their names, please," Grayson interrupted.

Grayson pursued this line doggedly for several minutes, asking for details, and whether these Turkish friends had ever visited her in England. None ever had. Had she ever been threatened or felt in danger while in Turkey? No, she had not. What about in the UK or at home in the States? No, not until two days ago.

"What happened two days ago?" Grayson asked.

"I was followed by this guy," she blurted out, startling herself. In that moment she realized that, subconsciously, it was that incident rather than the break-in that was at the root of her feeling of insecurity.

Grayson's eyes showed a glimmer of satisfaction at having provoked an admission. "Tell me about that," she said.

Alana described the man in as much detail as she could and recounted the incident at the train station.

As she was finishing the story, the door opened and closed. "For the recorder, DC Philips has re-entered the room," said Grayson. The detective constable sat down again, giving his superior a nod and passing her his notebook. Grayson looked at it, and Alana saw both their faces harden. Whatever was written there was bad.

"You claim that Howard arrived in the UK yesterday, Tuesday the fourteenth of February. Is that right?"

"I don't *claim* it. Howard claimed it."

Grayson gave Alana a cold look, then pushed a printed sheet across the table. "Airline records show that Howard Angelus arrived in the UK on Monday the thirteenth at nine am. That he was in Cambridge a few hours after that is confirmed by the photograph. Can you explain?"

"No, I can't," said Alana.

"You have no idea why your boyfriend would keep his presence secret from you – despite the fact that he was asking for you at your college?" For the first time, Grayson was beginning to lose her cool, a note of impatient irritation entering her voice.

"No idea at all."

"Where is he now?"

"If he's running to schedule, he should be boarding a flight to Amman."

Grayson's eyes widened. "Amman in Jordan? Now why would he be going there?"

"He's shooting a Netflix show."

"Amman is close to the border with Syria, isn't it?" Grayson said.

Alana opened her mouth, but Professor Coniston cut in. "My client's knowledge of Jordanian geography can have no relevance. Also, we are straying far into the realms of speculation."

"Is there anything else you would like to tell us about Mr. Angelus?" said Grayson.

Alana tried to shut out the image of the diamond sitting in the palm of her hand.

Grayson's tone turned hard as granite. "A dozen people are in the hospital right now, at least one of them is likely to die. Is there anything else you would like to tell us?"

"You think I don't know how awful this is?" said Alana, close to tears. "I'm damn lucky I'm not in the hospital too. Or worse. I didn't intend to go back to London yesterday – I was meant to be *here*. You get that? Just one flaky decision saved me from a slab in the morgue." She rose to her feet. "I can't stand this. I have to get out of here."

"Please sit down, Miss Fulton," said Grayson.

"You know what, I don't think I will," said Alana. Her eyes were filling up, and tears running down her cheeks. "This is bullshit! I could've died in that room, and it's only luck I'm still alive. You're responsible for counter-terrorism in this country? Those people in the hospital – that's on you. You screwed up. So you can save your insinuations and go find whoever did this."

"Well," said Coniston, lighting a cigarette. "That was not helpful."

Alana stormed down the steps. "They were practically accusing me of being a terrorist!" She pointed to her chest. "*I'm* the victim here! Somebody was trying to kill me!"

Coniston looked steadily at her. "You were the intended victim, one supposes. Fortunately not the *actual* victim."

Alana rubbed her hand across her face. "Oh God, poor Isobel. I'm sorry, I'm so sorry. I should go visit her."

"That is not possible, unfortunately. The special ICU is under containment; nobody can enter due to the risk of contamination."

Alana turned away, watching the activity by the passage to New Court. Some firefighters were helping a colleague into a bulbous yellow hazmat suit. "Professor, thank you so much for stepping in."

He smiled. "Wait till you see my invoice." He nudged her arm. "I'm joking. The police will almost certainly wish to question you again before very long. Should you still desire my help, ring me." Flipping open his wallet, he gave her a card.

"Thanks. Oh wait, there's one thing I didn't understand. Philips going out and coming back in, like he'd found something out. And the look they gave. What was that about?"

"Indeed, that was interesting." Coniston opened his notebook. "He left immediately after you mentioned Mr. Angelus's meeting venue. I'll look into it." He pursed his lips. "Now I must leave you; I promised the Master an update on developments." They shook hands, and he walked off towards the Master's lodge.

Alana returned to the crowd still hovering by the gatehouse. It had thinned somewhat, but there were still dozens of spectators who stared curiously at her. She'd have to check into a hotel now that her college rooms had become a chemical ground zero. She hadn't showered in nearly forty-eight hours and felt rank. Howard's presence in the apartment that morning had made her feel uneasy about getting in the shower. Her trust in him, which had never been rock-solid, was now utterly shaken.

She tried to recall exactly what Philips had told her about the other incidents. The Newnham break-in had been about two weeks before Christmas, he'd said, and the attack on the woman in London a couple of weeks before that. It wasn't much to go on. Opening her phone's calendar, she skipped back a few months. The Newnham incident must have been between December ninth and twelfth, which meant the London attack was maybe between November twenty-third and thirtieth.

The date gave her an idea, but it wasn't precise enough. She googled *London assault November* … She tried to recall the victim's name. It was like her own, but what exactly? She tried *London assault November student Alana* …

And there it was, buried deep among the results, an item in the *Evening Standard*: Alana Fisher, age twenty-one, Canadian, assaulted near her student hall of residence in Maple Street around 11:40 pm … assailant male, white or possibly Middle Eastern, mid-twenties. Scrolling to the top, she found the date the story was posted: Tuesday, November twenty-ninth. So the attack was Monday the twenty-eighth.

Her hunch was correct. Feeling an almost euphoric flush of relief, she double-checked her calendar. The Thursday before the attack had been Thanksgiving; she and Howard and her parents had spent the holiday weekend in a villa on Maui. Her parents had left on Sunday evening – the twenty-seventh – and Alana and Howard had flown back to LA together the next day. Therefore, at 11:40 pm UK time, when the assault happened, they had been landing at LAX.

The fear that had been poisoning her since seeing his profile on her laptop the previous night – that Howard was the burglar, that he had attacked that woman – melted away.

Standing among the onlookers, Alana became aware that people were glancing curiously at her and whispering among themselves. Time to leave, she felt. She was wondering whether to try the Hilton hotel in Downing Street or the one by the river, when she was jostled from behind by someone pushing their way hurriedly through the crowd. Simultaneously, she felt a piece of paper being pushed roughly into her hand.

Twisting round, she saw the person who'd jostled her – a figure in a pink hoodie and baseball cap – shouldering a path rapidly through the crowd away from her.

The thing in her hand was an envelope with her name on it. She tore it open. Inside was a small piece of expensive, textured paper the size of a compliment slip, but with no letterhead. On it was written, in purple ink in a neat italic hand:

You are not who you think you are.
Your future will not be what you expect.

Added below in black ink, in a different, bolder hand:

You are in danger.

5

The old man negotiated the steeply descending path, prodding ahead with his staff as if he were blind. Despite the gray in his mustache and the lines on his face, he was neither infirm nor frail, but carried himself with the dignity of an aristocrat, unaccustomed to picking his way along uneven mountainside paths. On his head he wore the traditional Azeri *papaq*, a black woolen hat like a Cossack's, and a long, old-fashioned greatcoat with silver buttons – not really suitable for hillwalking in winter.

On his right the landscape fell vertiginously into green foothills patched with bushy copses. The valley bottom was far away and hazy. The old man paused and glanced up at the sky. There would be snow before the year's end. If he was fortunate, it would hold off until he had completed this journey and returned home.

The way twisted, skirting the foot of a large rocky outcrop. Rounding the bend, the old man came up short at the sight of a figure sitting on a flat stone beside the path. He wore mottled green military camouflage, and was looking out over the valley, wreaths of cigarette smoke dribbling from his black-bearded lips, snatched away by the wind.

He sensed the old man's presence without turning. "Don't be afraid," he said. "Come, sit and rest. Or pass by, if that is your wish."

Warily, the old man stepped closer, eying the green-clad figure. "I took you for a soldier," he said.

The younger man chuckled. "Behold my regiment," he said, gesturing with his cigarette at the herd of goats scattered across the hillside below. He touched the sleeve of his combat jacket. "I took this from a dead Armenian soldier. You like it?"

"If a live Armenian catches you wearing it, you will be a dead Azeri, friend."

"Huh. I didn't kill him. Though it would have been justice enough if I had; four of my family they murdered when they took Xanyurdu." He spat on the ground. "Like enough one of his own killed him. Like mad dogs among the herd; as quick to draw one another's blood as to take down their prey."

The old man nodded reflectively. "I wish that were true, friend. We would be free of their occupation in no time."

"The faithless don't scare me. I know how to hide myself. These hills are mine, not theirs."

The old man smiled wryly, leaning forward on his staff. "Yours?" he asked. "Perchance the Khan of Karabakh has taken to goat herding? What is your name, fellow?"

"My mother named me Huseyn. Who wants to know?"

Receiving no answer, Huseyn glanced up at the old man, drawing deeply on his cigarette and surveying the fine, hawkish features, the well-made clothing. The old man's skin was paler than that of most Azeris – the color of creamy caramel – and his eyes were an icy blue-green.

Huseyn, flustered, started to scramble to his feet. "Lord, I—"

"Peace," said the old man. "Be seated. Perhaps I shall join you after all. It has been a weary walk and I have some miles to go yet. A rest would be welcome."

Huseyn brushed down the flat rock beside him and waited while the old gentleman seated himself before resuming his place. He took out half a loaf and some cheese. "You are hungry, lord? I have plenty and to spare. My wife—"

"Thank you, Huseyn, but no. One of your cigarettes would be most appreciated, however."

Huseyn fumbled open the pack. The old gentleman took one and examined its flattened shape. "Turkish," he said. "These also came from your dead Armenian?"

"They did."

The two smoked in silence for a minute, two plumes entwined and whipped away by the wind.

"You are going to Khojali?" Huseyn asked. The old gentleman nodded. "You will meet plenty of live Armenians going that way."

"I had hoped to pass them by."

The goatherd shook his head bitterly. "Not today. The town is surrounded now. Their soldiers are everywhere."

"You have seen this with your own eyes?"

"I have." Huseyn opened his mouth to elaborate, but his attention was caught by a sudden heaving movement beneath the old gentleman's coat.

The old man chuckled and reached inside; from between the folds of gray worsted popped the black and white head of a puppy. "He has slept soundly for the past mile at least. He is woken by our voices, or more likely the smell of cheese." The old man ruffled the puppy's ears. "A gift for my granddaughter."

"My little girl has a pup," said Huseyn, breaking off a morsel of cheese and offering it to the puppy, smiling as the sharp little teeth snatched. He glanced at the old man. "This dog will never reach your granddaughter if you keep to this path."

"You know a better way?"

Huseyn pointed. "Down there, where the ground makes those ripples, go straight ahead instead of following the path. It's steep, but you'll come to another track below. Follow that until you come to a thicket; go around, and you'll find a path where the soldiers don't go. You can get to the town safely that way, if you go warily. Stay on that path, lord!"

The old gentleman held out a hand, and the goatherd took it, bowing his head. "Go with God, Huseyn," he said. Tucking the puppy away in his coat, he rose to his feet.

Following the goatherd's instructions, he left the path and headed straight down the precipitous slope. A few yards down he looked back doubtfully. Huseyn raised his thumb and nodded encouragingly. The old gentleman was about to turn away when his eye was caught by the rocky outcrop he had passed. It was strangely shaped, like a cat curled in sleep, as lifelike as if it had been carved by an artist. How extraordinary that he had never noticed it before.

With a gesture of farewell to the goatherd, he carried on down the slope.

The little girl stood outside the open doorway, swinging from the handle and gazing at the people sitting inside. Elderly folk mostly, seated in hard chairs ranged around the walls. There was also a young woman with two children, and two men in the olive green of the local militia, one a youngster with a bandaged head, the other bearded, with a wounded leg and a crutch propped against the wall beside him.

The bearded militiaman noticed the tiny girl watching him and smiled at her. She saw a grizzled, weather-worn face. He saw a pure and perfect being, unscathed, new as a rosebud. Her eyes were wide and hazel-green, set off by a cream-colored headscarf, around which was wrapped a sugar-pink woolen muffler embroidered with chocolate-brown rabbits and butter-yellow ducklings.

"Ayna, where are you?" A woman's voice. "There you are! Close the door, child, you're letting the cold in." The little girl turned to see her mother coming along the garden path. With a last glance at the wounded militiaman, she swung the door shut. "We don't want the patients to get chilled, do we? Come here, my sweet."

Her mother squatted, taking care with her swollen belly, and adjusted Ayna's pink muffler, wrapping it more snugly around her neck and tying it gently at her throat. She smiled warmly, and Ayna smiled in response, like a flower in sunshine.

"Now come," her mother said, standing and taking Ayna's hand. "Your grandfather is here." She added softly, "Perhaps he has a gift for you."

They walked together back to the house, a large modern bungalow standing on a rise above the street. Entering through the garden door, they found Ayna's father sitting in his armchair, his medical bag open on the coffee table before him; he was sorting through the contents and talking to someone sitting with his back to the door.

"Here's my little girl," he said. "Come greet your grandfather."

Ayna came to her father and, turning, saw that the other person was an old man with a thick gray mustache and thin receding hair; his nose was large and high-bridged, and his wide-set eyes were blue and bright. He smiled, and Ayna pressed herself back against her father.

"She does not remember me, Tengiz," said the old man with a chuckle. "You do not know me, child?"

"You know your grandfather, don't you, sweet?" murmured her father in her ear.

Ayna looked at the old man intensely, thinking hard. "I know you," she said at last.

"I know you too, Ayna. Indeed, I have come all the way down from my home in the hills specially to see you. Do you know why?"

"It's my birthday," said Ayna, and in a sudden rush of confidence, added: "Do you like my new scarf?"

"I do," said her grandfather. He leaned forward and said in a conspiratorial whisper: "I have brought you a present also. Would you like to know what it is?" Ayna nodded again, more shyly. "Nurbanu," he said to Ayna's mother. "Go get it."

"Where are your brother and sister?" said the old man as they waited.

"Leyli's at school," she replied, "and Hakan is sick."

"He drank some bad water," said her father, checking boxes of antibiotics. "Since the siege began, the supply has been erratic." The old man nodded and sighed. "I'm amazed you managed to get through the lines, Papa."

"Ah, yes. Thank Huseyn the goatherd." He looked at Ayna. "I see from the shape of your mother you will soon have a new baby brother or sister." Ayna nodded. She had edged closer to her grandfather, and now rested her elbows on the arm of his chair. "You will no longer be the smallest in the family."

At that moment, her mother came back into the room with a little wriggling bundle of fur in her arms. She set the puppy down before Ayna, who covered her mouth with her hands, eyes wide in amazement. She dropped to her knees, squealing in delight as the puppy climbed all over her, licking her face.

"You like him, eh?" her grandfather chuckled. "One of the shepherds in the village bred a litter. This little fellow has been with me for a few weeks. He's almost housebroken already."

Nurbanu patted her husband on the shoulder. "The waiting room is full, Tengiz," she said. Tengiz clicked his bag shut. "Will you be back for dinner?"

He shrugged. "Who can tell? Once I've tended to the regulars, I have my rounds among the refugees." He looked at his father. "It's getting worse. We need more doctors here. More medications, more supplies, more of everything."

The old man thought he detected an accusatory tone in his son's voice. "Tengiz, we are doing all we can. But all of Karabakh is under pressure, even Shusha itself."

Ayna, fixated on the puppy, scarcely noticed her father leaving. "Mommy, may I show Hakan the dog?"

"All right. But don't disturb him if he's sleeping."

She ran out into the hallway and along the passage, the puppy racing at her heels, and burst into her brother's room. "Hakan! Look, I got a dog! I'm gonna call him Rolan – what d'you think?"

Hakan, who had fallen asleep with a comic-book open on his chest, was startled awake by the puppy bounding onto his bed. Hakan had recently turned five, a year older than Ayna, but she treated him as if he were the younger and she had a duty to watch out for him. Once last summer, when he'd blasted the garden hose through their parents' bedroom window, she had magnanimously taken the blame, sparing him a period of hungry exile in his room. Even their sister Leyli, who was nearly seven, tended to treat Ayna more like an equal than a baby sister.

"They're talking about the war again," said Ayna, picking up Hakan's comic-book and leafing through it. "This is baby stuff," she commented.

"We're going to win," said Hakan, lying back on his pillow and ruffling the puppy's ears. "Why 'Rolan'?"

Ayna shrugged. "I like it. It suits him." She regarded her brother; with his black hair and almond eyes, he was as pretty as either of his sisters. "Why do you think we will win? Papa says they're surrounding us and killing us everywhere."

"We're strong," he said. "This is our land, and that makes us stronger."

Ayna considered this for a moment in silence, then poked her brother's leg. "Hey, did you know Grandfather is here?"

"He is?"

"He brought me Rolan. I'm not supposed to wake you because you're sick."

"I'm not sick anymore."

"Then come and see him."

"I will. Come on, Rolan!" Hakan rolled out of bed and ran out, the puppy following, yapping excitedly.

Ayna sat on the bed for a moment, pondering. *This is our land, and that makes us stronger*. What a strange boy her brother was. How could the land make you stronger?

She gave up the conundrum and followed the sound of high-pitched barking and her grandfather's sudden booming laughter.

6

You are in danger.

You are not who you think you are.

Alana felt the blood draining from her face, her stomach knotting. The shock and bewilderment, coming on top of the interrogation and everything else she had been through, instantly resolved into anger. How dare the world do this to her?

Scanning the crowd, she caught sight of the man in the pink hoodie. He had reached the gatehouse, dodging through the crowd. He pushed past some people coming in through the small side gate and was gone.

Shoving the note into her pocket, Alana took off in pursuit, weaving through the crowd. The cobbled forecourt in front of the college was blocked by a truck unloading a portable police office. There was no sign of the hoodie. She ran around the truck into the street, which was still crowded with onlookers and TV crews.

And there he was. His way blocked by a BBC truck, he darted in through the gate of All Saints Garden, a small triangle enclosed by fences. It was a dead end. Alana sprinted in pursuit.

As Alana ran in through the gate, hoodie guy skidded to a stop in front of the spiked iron railings at the far end. Her heart leapt – she had him! Quick as a rat, he doubled back to where some dismantled market traders' stalls were kept stacked under a tarp against the fence. He leapt up on top and hurdled the fence. Alana followed him, dropping down into the narrow alley.

He reached the end well ahead of her and swerved right into Bridge Street. Alana followed, colliding with an elderly couple, nearly knocking them down, and ran on, throwing an apology back over her shoulder. Ahead she could see the pink hoodie weaving through the knots of shoppers and students, sprinting flat out. Alana ran as hard as she could, but years spent in libraries and study had softened her muscles and drained her stamina, while this guy ran like an athlete.

She saw him duck into another alley, and followed, but by the time she emerged at the other end he was nowhere to be seen.

Alana scanned the crowds. Nothing. Taking a gamble, she headed right, toward the market square. At the corner was a sidewalk café, and as Alana approached it, she heard a man's voice raised furiously: "Watch where you're going, you stupid sod!"

Hoodie guy was sprawled on the ground by an overturned table. The middle-aged couple who'd been sitting at it were picking themselves up from the wreckage. The young man was on his feet in an instant; leaping on top of the next table, he cleared the barrier and sprinted on past the market stalls, heading toward the passage between the Guildhall and the Grand Arcade mall. Skirting the barrier and overturned chairs, Alana set off in pursuit.

Her strength was flagging badly now, but she kept the pink hoodie in sight as he crossed the little piazza outside the mall and dashed into the side entrance. Entering a few seconds behind him, she heard the squeak of his sneakers bounding up the staircase to the parking garage. Taking the stairs two and three at a time, she followed, overcoming her fatigue and weakness. In her mind, this unknown man was the source of this whole nightmare – he was the terrorist, the burglar, the attacker, the key to the puzzle in which she was trapped. Adrenaline was taking Alana beyond tiredness, drawing on reserves of energy and strength she didn't know she possessed.

She had hurled herself up ten flights, lungs bursting, when she heard him slam through the swing doors into the parking levels one story above. Did he have a car? She didn't care; she'd jump on the son-of-a-bitch's hood and smash through his windshield if necessary.

Following through the door, she ran out into the path of a car; fortunately, it was slowing for the turn; she rolled across the hood and hit the ground running. Hoodie guy was racing across the level, heading for an open-air section. She saw him reach the exterior barrier and run along beside it, peering over frantically as if looking for a way to climb down.

Alana put on her last reserves and ran hard, aiming for him like a missile. Intending to grab his arms and pin him from behind, she stumbled in the last yard and collided violently with him. His feet were on the raised lip of the concrete, and she felt his center of gravity shift over the steel barrier; he toppled and begin to fall. The yellow brick wall of the Corn Exchange and the black asphalt of the street five stories below flashed across the edge of her vision as the man twisted out over the drop, falling away.

Instinctively, her fingers gripped, coiling into the soft pink fabric of the hoodie, gripping the flesh beneath. Alana felt his fingers gripping her forearm, then the top of the barrier pressing hard into her midriff as his weight tried to pull her down.

She opened her eyes to find herself gripping his left arm in both her hands. His right arm swung free; his legs kicked frantically in the void. He was mewling in terror. Her fingers were weakening, and his struggling was making it worse.

"Keep still!" she gasped. "I can't hold on."

He had been staring down, fixated on the distant ground, but at the sound of her voice he looked up, and for the first time Alana saw his face.

She almost dropped him. A part of her wanted to, but her instincts held firm. She didn't want to believe it, but it fitted. "You!" she said furiously. "How can it be *you*?"

He stared at her in horror – like an animal, uncomprehending but knowing that it is facing death. Feeling her grip start to give, she pulled, trying to haul him back over the barrier. "Stop struggling! Hold on and climb." He grabbed at her with his free hand, and she hauled with all her strength. At last he managed to get a hold of the rail, then a foothold. Grunting and gasping, he slithered over the barrier like a landed fish and collapsed onto the concrete.

Alana fought for breath, her eyes never leaving Howard's face. In a rage she launched herself at him, slapping him, back and forth, again and again, cursing incoherently.

"What are you doing to me?" she screamed. "What are you doing?"

Howard tried feebly to shield himself from the blows; at last he managed to seize hold of her wrists, and she collapsed, sobbing.

He took her hands in his. "I'm trying to save you," he said. "You're in danger. I'm trying to save you."

High on a parapet of pale, weathered stone, Vartan stood looking down into the courtyard below. This was a part of the palace complex he rarely came to; the stink of it was enough to drive away dogs, let alone a civilized man.

The palace of Shusha had for centuries been the fortress home of the khans of Karabakh; now it belonged to him. A great walled stronghold – palace, mosque, stables, castle keep, and garden. From where he stood, the curtain wall ran down the rocky hillside to a square tower, then along to a round tower and back up the slope, making an enclosure acres broad. The section into which Vartan was looking consisted of a large courtyard and, on the crest of the hill, two large buildings of white stucco with red pantiled roofs. They had once contained the apartments of the khans' wives and adult children. Now, they were a prison. At first it had served as a holding pen for captured Azerbaijani soldiers during the war, nearly three decades ago; since then, it had become the state prison for this district of Karabakh. The windows were barred, the stucco was discolored, cracked, and in places had fallen away from the brickwork. Here and there were scorch marks and scars from the battle in 1991, in which the palace had been captured from the last khan, Togrul.

Vartan turned and rested his hands on the stone embrasure, beside a tray bearing a porcelain teacup and a glass flask encased in wrought silver. He gazed out toward the mountains, beyond which lay what remained of Azerbaijan, a lurking threat. Togrul, the old khan, was still out there, still alive, lurking in his hiding place, watching for a chance to take back this place. Vartan's people's hold on Karabakh, so dearly bought in blood, was in danger, all thanks to one old man who was supposed to be long dead, combined with the incompetence those who called themselves Vartan's allies. His hand tapped rhythmically on the wall, his ringed index finger going *chak-chak-chak* on the stone.

"Sir?"

His secretary, Kamo, was hurrying along the wall-walk toward him.

"Is it true?" said Vartan quietly as Kamo came up beside him.

"Sir, I'm afraid it is. The Archimandrite is here to see you, as you requested …"

Vartan looked round to see a second figure coming along the

walkway at a statelier pace – a stout man in a long black clerical robe with a cowl. Kamo gave a bow as he approached. "Very Reverend Father," he said. Vartan looked the newcomer up and down coolly.

Archimandrite Gevorg Harutyunyan was an imposing figure – a broad physical bulk wrapped in ecclesiastical black, the *veghar* – the priestly pointed cowl – framing a face as brown as weathered teak and as flat as a spade, from which a thick steel-gray beard descended almost to his waist. Behind him followed two young male acolytes: his personal assistants. Harutyunyan smiled complacently at Vartan, unperturbed by the warlord's piercing stare.

"My lord Vartan," he murmured.

Vartan went on staring in silence, then gave a curt nod. "Father," he said quietly, and the priest raised a spidery eyebrow at the misnaming. "I do not give you your title," Vartan added, "because at this moment I do not revere you so much as desire to see you strung by your fat ankles from this battlement."

Harutyunyan's smile took on a hostile edge. "My lord Vartan, what can the matter be?"

Vartan glanced at his secretary. "Tell me, Kamo, can this be a man of God that stands before me?" His voice suddenly exploded into a furious roar: "Or is it the lying bastard offspring of an ape and a goatherd? Huh? Should we seek his blessing or split his liver with a tent spike?"

Kamo blanched, and he turned his eyes toward the archimandrite, who remained unfazed.

Vartan lowered his voice. "You did it, didn't you? What I've seen on the news reports – that was *your* doing."

"Based on the intelligence you supplied, we judged it necessary to move with all dispatch."

"Intelligence I supplied? I gave you a preliminary report. Preliminary! Nothing more."

69

"Nonetheless ..."

"Five months it has taken! Five months of careful work. All we needed was the final confirmation from the genetics lab. One last little piece of data. And you prelate monkeys have blasted it all to pieces with your impatience!" The priest opened his mouth, but Vartan cut him off. "Where do you think she will be now, huh? You think she will ever go back to that place again? You know what my agent had to go through to trace her there?"

"It was a risk we had to take."

"It was a completely unnecessary and reckless risk. It's bad enough that you failed and undoubtedly scared her away. But imagine if you had succeeded – we would be facing utter disaster!"

"How so?"

Vartan pinched the bridge of his nose. "Without her we have no leverage, and without leverage there can be no legitimacy." He gestured to the countryside and the mountains. "How long now since Armenia shed its blood to win Karabakh? My blood, the blood of my brothers. More than twenty-five years as a province answerable to Yerevan. And yet look at any map in the West, and what is Karabakh? Still part of Azerbaijan – or at best a disputed territory. This mission is our only chance for recognition of our claim."

"The Holy Apostolic Crusade for—"

"Holy nothing! This is blood and soil!" Vartan hissed. "Now, because of your clumsiness, it will take more time, more blood."

He unstopped the glass flask and poured an exceptionally pale-looking tea into the porcelain cup.

"Do not presume to judge my actions, my lord Vartan," said the priest. "I will brook no opposition in the council. What is more—"

He got no further. As quick as a snake, Vartan dashed the contents of the teacup into the face of one of Harutyunyan's acolytes. The young man let out a soul-freezing scream and fell to his knees, hands over his face, wailing and sobbing as the acid burned into the skin. The other acolyte shrank back in horror, while Harutyunyan stared down at them both with eyebrows raised.

"You were saying?" said Vartan.

Harutyunyan glared at him, then gestured angrily at the acolyte cowering by the wall. "Take him away! I cannot hear myself think!"

The young man dragged his shrieking companion to his feet and helped him hobble away.

Harutyunyan was silent, watching Vartan as he replaced the cup on its saucer and stoppered the flask. "So. Did you get your final confirmation?"

Vartan glanced at the priest. "We got it. She is the one."

Harutyunyan smiled complacently. Vartan turned and surveyed, from the golden, curlicued Armenian cross resting on the portly chest to the pointed *veghar*.

The archimandrite followed his gaze. "You know what they say about the *veghar*?" he said. "Why the cowl is pointed on top? To protect from the devil. So that a demon may not sit upon the holy man's head." He chuckled, reaching out and patting the warlord's shoulder. "Take care not to try and find repose upon my skull, my lord Vartan."

7

Alana gently sponged Howard's arm. There was a dirty graze where she had dragged him back over the concrete wall of the parking garage. Washing away the grit, she soaked a cotton pad with antiseptic and dabbed the wound. He flinched violently and mewled like a cat.

"Keep still," she said. "The more you struggle, the more it'll hurt."

In her mind she saw herself as a child, with skinned knees after falling off her tricycle, her mother cleaning her up just like this, brisk and precise but gentle – the hands of a dressmaker. Alana could swear that even as a six-year-old she'd made less fuss than Howard was making now.

An hour had passed since the incident in the parking garage, but he was still pale and shaking. They had scarcely spoken since; Alana had been too stunned and angry, while Howard was almost catatonic from shock. She had led him down in the garage elevator and around the corner to the Cambridge Hilton, which adjoined the Grand Arcade, where she booked two rooms. Once she'd settled him down, she'd walked back to Trinity to collect her suitcase, which she'd dropped in Great Court when the chase began. On the way back to the hotel, she bought a first-aid kit.

Once Howard's arm was cleaned and dressed, she ordered him to take off his hoodie and t-shirt. His midriff was one large bruise from ribcage to waist. "Well, there's nothing I can do about that," she said. "D'you think you've cracked any ribs?"

Howard shook his head vaguely. "I don't know," he muttered, and winced as she touched his side. "Yeah, I reckon."

She found some painkillers in the kit. "Here, take two of these."

With nothing practical left to do, Alana was overwhelmed by the cold, sick sensation left behind by the dissipating adrenaline. She fished the note out of her pocket.

You are not who you think you are. Your future will not be what you expect. You are in danger.

"Are you ready to explain what this means?" she said as calmly as she could.

Howard blanched at the sight of it. "I don't know what it means," he said.

"Did you write it?"

"No, I did not. I wish I'd never seen it."

"Who gave it to you?" He was silent. "Please look at me, Howard. Who gave it to you?"

He forced himself to look at her face but couldn't hold her gaze. "I ... I don't know."

"Was it the same person who sent you the diamond?" Now she saw his eyes again as he looked up at her, astonished. "I found it in your jacket this morning. Howard, why do you have a PO box in London?"

Part of her wanted to scream at him, physically drag the truth out of him, but the other part felt as bewildered and scared as a child.

Everything in her world had been secure and comfortable; now it was dissolving, and she felt like crying.

"Baby," said Howard. "You don't wanna know anything about this, I swear. I wish I could tell you, I wish I could, but I don't know anything."

"You must know where the note and the diamond came from?"

Howard rubbed his eyes. "It started a couple years ago. We were shooting *Phenomenal* in New Jersey or Boston or one of those hell-holes back east. I got this letter. I don't know who it was from. It mentioned you."

Alana's skin began to prickle. "Go on."

"Whoever sent it made out you were incredibly important and valuable. They wanted me to watch out for you, take care of you. I'd get paid. I didn't answer. Then they sent a guy to talk to me." Howard glanced up at Alana, who was staring at him with such intensity he didn't dare stop. "We met in a parking lot. He didn't tell me a name. He was south Asian or maybe Arab. Something like that. Maybe mid-thirties, clean-shaven, Paul Smith suit – nice cut, British accent. He told me all I had to do was look out for you, and report on how you were. Make sure you were safe. Didn't matter if we weren't together all the time, just so long as I checked in on you from time to time. I'd be paid in diamonds. He gave me the first one right there and then."

"Why?"

"They never told me, just that you were important, and they wanted to know you were safe and okay. I reported through the mail. Postcards." Anticipating her question, he shook his head. "I don't know who received them. They were all to 'John Smith', addressed to a PO box in Baku."

"Baku? In *Azerbaijan*?"

Howard nodded. "It'd be like, *John buddy – Having a wild time in Malibu. Everything great. Howard.* That kind of thing. I wasn't allowed to mention your name, just the place you were at – if you were okay, I had to write a positive message, if something had happened to you, it was negative. Like, if you were sick, it was 'bad weather', or if it was worse, I was supposed to say the house burned down. If it was, like, an emergency, I had a number to call. Every couple months there'd be a diamond delivered to my box in London."

Alana pressed her fingers into her temples. This was insane. Somebody in Azerbaijan, of all places, was paying her boyfriend to *spy* on her? *Azerbaijan*? She thought of Turkey as her professional home ground, so Azerbaijan was kind of her backyard. But she'd never actually been there and only had the most basic knowledge about it. Baku – why on God's green earth would anyone in Baku be interested in her? Not just interested, but obsessed.

It couldn't be to do with archaeology. Something connected with her parents, maybe? She had a vague idea that Catherine might have a retail outlet in Baku, but she wasn't sure, and her father's news channel had probably touched down there at some point. But nothing she could put her finger on. An elaborate abduction plot? With two very wealthy parents, she'd long got used to being a potential kidnap risk; her father, who had contacts in the overseas security industry, had made her take a brief course in avoiding capture when she was a teen.

"Last Sunday I got a call from that number I just told you about," said Howard. "They told me to come to England to check on you. I had to stick close to you without arousing your suspicions and wait for further instructions. I said I had to finish shooting, but they said … Never mind what they said, I don't like to think about it. So I walked off set and got on the next flight. That's why I came to your college Monday morning, looking for you."

"Kind of fell down on the whole *not arousing my suspicions* part."

"Oh God, babe, I can't believe what I've done. I just *walked off set*!

I'm gonna get sliced and diced and sued to hell. That producer is *such* an asshole; he never wanted me hired in the first place."

"How about your meeting with Christopher Nolan? Was that real?"

"Yeah, it was. I mean, no, not exactly. I mean … I didn't meet Nolan, just his casting director. Or rather, his casting director's assistant. And we didn't exactly hit it off."

He looked so desolate Alana felt sorry for him. She was about to speak but was interrupted by her phone ringing.

"Miss Fulton? It's George Coniston here." She was in such a bewildered state, she had to think for a moment before recognizing the name and the upbeat, plummy British accent of her legal adviser.

"Oh hi, Professor."

"I hope you're well. That was rather a stringent going-over they gave you. Now, I have news for you. Some of it good, some of it … interesting."

Casting a glance at Howard, Alana went out into the corridor, pulling the door shut behind her. "Go ahead," she said.

"The pleasant news is that I don't believe the police are interested in you as a suspect, despite Superintendent Grayson's confrontational tone. Not that they would have had much of a case. However, they will certainly want to speak to you again, so please don't go anywhere. You are under no obligation to hang around, but I would advise in the strongest terms that you stay put."

"Okay. And what's the other news?"

"About that Soho address which so exercised our police friends. I drew on a favor or two and managed to tap into the same information source as the estimable DC Philips. The address visited by Mr. Howard Angelus this morning contains the offices of two companies. One is a feature film production company. Perfectly legitimate business. The other is somewhat less so; the offices on the upper floor are owned by a firm which lets them out by the week. During the past few days they have been occupied by an overseas private equity company called Furness-Rayan Investments, based in Jordan. The company is suspected of money-laundering in connection with a second company, believed to have links to Al Qaeda going back to the late 1990s. That may explain why Superintendent Grayson was so intrigued when you mentioned Mr. Angelus going to Jordan."

Alana closed her eyes and leaned against the wall.

"Understandably," said Coniston, "the police are decidedly interested in speaking to him. You said he was flying to Amman this afternoon, if I remember correctly; therefore, one supposes that he has already gone?"

Alana opened her eyes, concentrating on keeping her breathing steady.

"Miss Fulton?"

"Yes," she said. "I … I guess that would be the case."

Later, she would search her soul to try and understand what made her tell this lie. A residual affection for Howard? A belief that he was an innocent dupe? Sheer naive foolishness?

"In that case, the police may have already detained him," said Coniston. "On the other hand, they may not have reasonable grounds to arrest a foreign national on the evidence they possess, even under terrorism laws. Especially a fairly rich and well-known American citizen."

"Arrest? You think they might arrest him?"

"It's possible. However, you appear to have been the intended target of this attack, and you testified that he was with you when the incident occurred. Moreover, the Soho address does match up with his stated appointment. The Jordanian connection is really rather tenuous. Still, if you happen to speak to him, please pass on my advice that he get himself promptly equipped with legal representation."

"I will."

"And as for you – you will be remaining in Cambridge?"

"I'm not sure. I'm in a hotel right now."

"I understand. Do be cautious. You are not a suspect, but your position is, shall I say, delicate. In a terrorism case, all possibilities are on the table."

"I'll take care, Professor. Thank you."

Alana hung up and stood trying to piece together her thoughts. She walked to the end of the corridor, where there was a window looking over Downing Street. It was dark now, and there were lights on in the archaeology department. The churchlike windows of the library glowed softly, and her supervisor's office was lit up.

You are not who you think you are.

What in the world was she supposed to do with that? As a piece of advice, it was about as much use as a fortune cookie. What was the point of sending someone a seemingly important message if you made it so vague and glib as to be incomprehensible?

And yet … it seemed to touch something inside her: something so deeply buried, she couldn't even guess what it was, like an unidentifiable but somehow unsettling noise somewhere in the house at night.

She gave up trying to fathom the feeling and went back to room 413. She'd left the door ajar; pushing it open, she was greeted by a sight that stopped her in her tracks.

Howard was sitting on the end of the bed, just as she had left him. Cradled in his hands was a small angular black object. Had she known more about such things, she might have identified it as a South African-made Vektor CP1; as it was, all she saw was a small, vicious-looking handgun.

He heard her sudden intake of breath and looked up, startled. Alana was almost beyond being surprised by anything. Taking a moment to steady her voice, she said, "I figure you didn't buy that in England." Howard shook his head. "And you didn't bring it on the plane."

"No," he said. The gun shifted in his hands, his fingers closing around the grip. He looked terrified.

Slowly, warily, Alana moved towards him. The muzzle of the gun was pointed in her direction, tilted down toward the floor. It looked almost like a toy, with curved and angled surfaces and sweeping lines molded into its frame. Trembling, never taking her eyes from Howard's, Alana reached out and laid her hand on his. Gently, trying to read the expression in his face – frightened, almost unrecognizable – she pushed the weapon aside. Taking hold of the barrel, she tried to prize it from his hand, but his grip on it tightened.

"Howard," she said softly. "Why have you got a gun?"

His fearful expression turned to puzzlement. "I ... I don't know."

"What?"

"I mean, they gave it to me for protection. To protect you. But I don't know who from."

"I think you should put it away now, don't you?"

Howard seemed to come out of his trance-like state. "Yeah. I mean ... yeah." He reached around and tucked the weapon into his waistband at the back.

Alana exhaled in relief. "Where did you get that thing?" she said.

"The same person who gave me the note."

"Was this in the office in Soho? Furness-Rayan Investments?" He looked at her in surprise. "I know about the other office in that building, Howard. That call just now was my lawyer. I know that company has links to terrorism."

"I don't know anything about that. They fixed it up to meet me there when they knew I had a meeting with the film company. They gave me the note and the gun and the keys to a car and told me to get the note to you that day. They said you were in danger, that I might need to protect you. But I should keep a distance."

"Why? Who are they?"

"I don't know. Some Middle Eastern guy. He talked about 'we', like he represented someone else, an organization or something. Oh God, I wish I'd never gotten into this."

Alana believed he was telling the truth at last. If he wasn't, he'd have to be the greatest actor in the world, and whatever else Howard Angelus might be, he wasn't that. She felt a pang of affectionate pity for him. She folded her hands around his and sat beside him on the bed. "Tell me what it means. *How* am I not who I think I am?"

He shook his head. "I told you, I don't know. Maybe you should ask your parents?"

Alana felt a thrill of adrenaline; it hadn't occurred to her that this was the obvious answer. Insane, half-formed theories had flitted across her mind – that she was some kind of agent who'd been hypnotized to impersonate Alana Fulton, or that there was no such person, that Alana Fulton was a fake identity created for some nefarious purpose, or that her brain had been swapped with somebody else. Everything that had happened to her in the past few days felt so utterly unreal that nothing, however crazy, seemed beyond the bounds of possibility.

The mention of her parents brought her back to earth. They were real, her childhood was real. If anyone would know who Alana truly was, it was them. She felt a profound, heart-wrenching longing to be with her father. He had always made her feel safe and secure and loved; the sound of his voice, the smell of him, the lines on his face crinkling as he gave one of his confident smiles – all these things had been a balm since she'd been a little girl, as far back as she could remember. Now she felt like a child again, lost and scared.

Her phone – which she'd set on the floor when she tried to pry the gun from Howard's fingers – started buzzing. The name *Daddy* and his familiar face filled the screen. It was as if he'd known and had reached out to save her.

Fumbling in her excitement, she tapped the button. "Daddy!" she said. "Oh, Daddy!"

"La-la, sweetheart. I just got out of a meeting, and I saw the news. Baby, are you all right?"

Alana let out a sob of relief at the sound of his voice, as sweet and dark as molasses, creaking deeply like seasoned timber. "Daddy, I'm fine. I wasn't there. I was in London with Howard."

"Your mother told me you were going back to Cambridge. I got a heck of a shock when I saw that report. Was that in your actual dorm?"

"Yes, Daddy, it was." She thought it best not to mention that it was in her actual room.

"Where are you right now, honey?"

"Cambridge. I came back this afternoon and it was all going crazy in Trinity. I'm in a hotel now."

"Is anyone with you?"

Alana hesitated. Coniston's words came back to her. What if the police were looking for him? What if they were listening in on her phone? "I ... No, I'm alone."

John Fulton's voice rumbled with displeasure. "You shouldn't be on your own, honey. Where's Howard?"

Alana closed her eyes. "He was scheduled to fly out today, for work. Listen, Daddy, I need to talk with you."

"That's what I'm here for, little boo."

"I mean in person. Can you come to London?"

Her father hesitated. "I have meetings tomorrow, but ... No, listen, the hell with that, I'll be on the next flight."

"You're still in Geneva?" Alana knew he'd been heading there on business, but had assumed he'd have returned to LA by now. Officially he'd retired and left his companies in the hands of their directors, but John Fulton had never liked relinquishing control.

"I am. But look, I'll kill some of the meetings and postpone the rest. My daughter comes first."

"No. No, Daddy, I think I'd rather come to you. I feel like getting away from here anyway."

"All right. Listen, from tomorrow evening I'll be at Gstaad. I promised I'd meet your mother; she's flying in from Milan or some place. You haven't heard from her yet? I guess that's just as well; she can't have heard about the attack. We'll be at the usual place. Come join us there." Alana couldn't speak; the swell of emotion was too strong. "Don't say anything to your mother, La-la. Let's hope she doesn't see the news in the meantime."

8

A February wind, harsh with cold and damp, rushed through the narrow confines of Downing Street, gusting between the university buildings.

Lying on a blanket on the steep tiled roof of the archaeology department, elbows hooked over the ridge, right shoulder pressed up against the brick chimney stack, was a young man. His face was lit dimly by streetlight reflected from the windows opposite: dark stubble, fine nose, and the misshapen line of his left jaw.

Without taking his eyes off the hotel on the opposite side of the street, Hayk reached into his black rucksack, which was wedged against the chimney. He drew out a telescopic rifle sight and trained it on the hotel's fourth floor, only a little below his level. Panning from window to window, he stopped at the one closest to the corner of the building, facing onto Downing Street.

There she was.

Hayk would recognize her face anywhere. He had looked at so many photos, studied her features so closely, burning every line and contour into his memory, that he believed he could have known her in the dark, by touch alone. She was on the phone. He kept the crosshairs trained steadily on her face. She was smiling, looking out the window, directly across at the library, right below where Hayk lay. He didn't flinch; he knew she wouldn't be able to see him in the dark, even if she looked right at him.

It gave him pleasure to watch her like this, in the flesh. He could stay here all night if he had to. Although he was only lightly dressed in a dark blouson and black jeans, the cold didn't bother him in the least. He was hardened to it. Aged sixteen, he'd spent the whole of the Christmas week alone in the mountains above Shusha, fending for himself the way Vartan had taught him, back in the days long ago, before he'd advanced so far that Ando had to take over his training.

He watched her hang up the phone and turn to speak to someone else in the room. Hayk could see a man's sneaker and part of his leg and a hand, but nothing more. Clearly young, white, dark hair on the bare arm. Hayk could guess who that was: the boyfriend, the snake. Hayk's orders were to eliminate him. He glanced at his rucksack, which contained his folded-down sniper rifle, and wondered whether to attempt the shot from here.

Hayk ran the calculations in his head. The windage would be considerable, but the range was short. On the other hand, the angle of the glass in relation to the trajectory would compromise accuracy.

No. Even if the boyfriend came right to the window, the risk would outweigh the objective. Whatever Hayk did, it must be at close quarters. He liked working up close; from a distance you didn't feel the heat of your enemy's breath and blood, didn't sense his terror and surprise. Hayk began to pack up his observation post. It was time to move in closer.

The hot water cascading over her skin and the slick caress of soap felt like every sensuous delight Alana had ever experienced all rolled into one. For two whole days she'd been without a shower. The last had been on that unimaginably remote night following the break-in. Only two days ago, but it felt like an eon. What a joy to get clean again.

She'd come to her own room for the purpose, leaving Howard in his. She felt she didn't know him at all anymore, and the thought of making herself vulnerable in the same room made her skin crawl. And yet, leaving him alone was a risk; she hated to think what he might get up to if she wasn't watching him.

Alana showered as rapidly as possible, toweling herself down and throwing on her clothes while her skin still glistened with droplets and her hair was dripping. Hurrying across the corridor, she opened the door to room 413.

He wasn't there.

Alana swore through clenched teeth. "Howard?" she called.

From the bathroom came the sound of a toilet flushing. The bathroom door opened, and Howard stood looking at her with his perfect eyebrows arched in surprise.

It seemed weird when she thought back on it later that the shock and relief somehow reignited her affection for him – *he's here after all, good old, dumb old Howard*. On an impulse she kissed him lightly on the cheek. "Stay right there," she said. "I'll be right back."

Alana hurried back to her room to retrieve her hairdryer. Gathering up her things, she wondered at what she had just done. Surely Howard couldn't win his way back that easily – by simply not running off and getting into God knew what shenanigans, and by appearing with that cute, perplexed look on his pretty face? Of course not, it was just relief. And yet … there was still a residual affection that couldn't be erased utterly in so short a time.

Carrying three take-out coffee cups and with a thick folder clamped under his chin, DC Rob Philips climbed the steps to the Trinity dining building. In the evening gloom the great hall was a blaze of illumination. More staff had shown up during the day, and the incident room was bustling.

Philips spotted Detective Chief Superintendent Grayson at the high table, where she was in conference with a couple of serious-looking civilians and two senior officers with so much silver braid on their uniforms they looked like a pair of Christmas trees. She caught Philips's eye, excused herself and joined him in front of a whiteboard covered with names, photos, and arrows in green and red.

"Flat white, ma'am," he said.

She took one of the coffees. "Good chap. Cheers." She peeled the lid off and gestured at the board with it. "I'm not seeing the pattern. Are you?"

Philips looked. "Don't ask me, ma'am. I'm just a foot soldier."

"You and I both know that's not true, Robert." Grayson sipped her coffee. "Your man here," she said, and gestured at the center of the chart, where two names were written in green – *Alana Fulton* and *Howard Angelus* – with arrows linking them. A web of lines connected them to Alana's parents, her father's corporate media interests, Howard's one-time association with an environmental direct-action group, his travels to the Middle East and Russia, and his suspected contact with Furness-Rayan Investments. "We can't fix on a link between Angelus, Furness-Rayan and any of its known terror-related connections," Grayson said. "Samples of the chemical used in the attack have been sent to Porton Down for analysis, and the preliminary result is that it's basically Russian. But Furness-Rayan has no connections with Russia whatsoever, either directly or through its subsidiaries or associates."

"Seems unlikely," said Philips.

"Exactly," said Grayson. "A Middle East-located financial enterprise having no business at all with Russia is … odd." She indicated a printed list that was pinned to the board. "These are all the countries where they *do* have connections."

Philips looked at the list. *Afghanistan … Albania … Armenia … Austria … Azerbaijan … Bahrain … Bhutan …*

"Speaking of the Middle East …" Philips tapped on Howard's name. "This lad never caught his flight to Jordan this afternoon. And he's not recorded on any other exit points from the UK."

"So he's still here?" said Grayson.

"Apparently. I think we'd better have a little chinwag with Mr. Angelus, don't you, ma'am?"

"I agree," said Grayson. "Find him and bring him in."

Philips took a slug of coffee. "I'm on it," he said, and turned away.

"You know where he might be?" said Grayson.

Philips shook his head. "No, but I know where Miss Fulton is."

"Good. I think we need another chat with that young lady, victim or no victim."

"*Amore*, are you all right? I just heard, please tell me you aren't hurt? I couldn't bear it. You are all right, aren't you, my sweetie? Please tell me you are."

"Yes, *Maman*, I'm fine."

The phone had rung while Alana was drying her hair and Howard was calling room service for dinner. Her whole life, Catherine Fulton had taken hardly any interest in the news except when it crossed over with showbiz and lifestyle; from time to time she'd watch *AM Joy* or (if her husband and daughter weren't around) *Fox & Friends*, all but oblivious to the political difference between them. She'd heard the news about Cambridge from a business associate. Fortunately, she seemed to have little idea just how close to Alana the poison attack had come – let alone any inkling that the whole thing might have been targeted at her.

It took over twenty minutes to placate her, by which time a waiter from room service was setting dinner on the table. Alana hung up with relief and a last *I love you Maman*, then sat down to eat.

She was surprised at her own appetite. She often got so wrapped up in work that she forgot to eat, but her hunger now was of a different order. Her insides felt knotted up with tension and anxiety, and she didn't think she'd be able to eat at all, but as soon as she took one forkful of poussin chicken with red wine and smoked bacon sauce her appetite surged, and she ate it all down while Howard was still sawing away at his 10-ounce rib-eye.

She rested her elbows on the table. "Will you come with me? To Gstaad, I mean."

"Of course. I have to protect you," he said, glancing at the pistol, which he'd laid on the table after the waiter had gone. "Don't laugh," he added with the flicker of a smile.

"What about your Netflix series?"

He looked down at his plate. "That doesn't start shooting till next month."

"Uh-huh." Another lie uncovered. "You can't take a gun on the plane."

He picked it up and tapped the frame, which made a dull sound, not at all metallic. "Polymer frame," he said. "Can't be detected."

Alana pursed her lips. "I kinda think they'll have thought of that, don't you? And it must have metal parts in it, surely?"

His cunning expression melted away. "I don't know."

"Anyway, that's not the only problem."

She explained what Professor Coniston had told her – the police assumed that Howard had left the country. But if they checked boarding records – which they surely would – they'd find out he was still here. They might have done so already, in which case they'd be looking out for him.

"But I haven't done anything," he said.

"Maybe not, but all the same … even without an illegal handgun, it could be a challenge getting you on a plane." Howard looked like he was about to start whining about the unfairness of it all, and Alana couldn't stomach that. "There might be a way around it," she said, and reached for her phone.

Hayk snapped shut the lens cover on the rifle sight and tucked it back in his rucksack. Kneeling on the ridge of the roof, he quickly rolled up the blanket he'd been lying on and packed that away too. Slinging the rucksack on his back, he picked his way down the steep slope and vaulted over into the valley made by the junction of the library roof and the neighboring building.

Stepping deftly downwards, he came to the lip of the vertiginous drop, four stories up, where there was a narrow ledge. With the agility of a lemur he ran along the ledge and dropped, catching it with his fingers then climbing down the succession of stone-mullioned windows, dropping the last two yards into the low shrubs skirting the building.

A group of people came out of a building opposite. Hayk shrank back into a dark section of the quadrangle. As soon as they had passed through the arch into Downing Street, he followed them. He crossed the street, walked on past the hotel's main entrance, and turned into the dimly lit alley beside it.

The alley was split in two, the roadway sloping down toward an underground loading area, and the sidewalk sloping upward to a series of service doors and an entrance to the hotel's parking garage. Hayk took a moment to assess the layout, then headed for the latter.

Inside the garage, he ran swiftly up the stairs to the top level, which gave a view over the whole illuminated center of Cambridge. He walked to the south corner and leaned over the wall. Just as he'd anticipated, he was looking down on the roof of the hotel. The building had two wings running back from the frontage on Downing Street, and between them was a well three stories deep, at the bottom of which were glazed skylights over the hotel's recreational areas.

There was a window in the west wing that was unlit and partly open. There was his way in. The room he'd seen his target in was on that floor. Swinging himself over the wall, Hayk lowered himself to the west wing roof a few yards below. He attached a rope to an air-conditioning unit and rappelled down the face of the building.

The window wouldn't open all the way, but there was enough of a gap for him to squeeze through. Hayk could tell from the faint odors of flesh and perfume that a person had been here within the past half-hour. He listened, but could hear no sounds from the bathroom, and all the lights were off.

He opened the door silently and peeked out into the corridor. There was nobody about. Closing the door quietly behind him, he followed the corridor. At the far end it turned, and the number on the nearest door was 413. This was the room he had been watching from the library roof. The two of them were in there right now.

Slowly, silently, he turned the handle. It was locked. Closing his palm around the grip of the silenced pistol under his blouson, he rapped on the door. There was no response, so he knocked louder. Still no answer.

Taking a small, flat crowbar from his rucksack, Hayk thrust its tip into the door jamb. He glanced up and down the corridor, then, with one swift movement and a loud splintering noise, the door flew violently inward.

9

An unmarked car pulled into the drop-off area in front of the Cambridge Hilton. DC Philips got out the passenger side and walked into the lobby.

The two clerks were both busy – one on the phone, the other checking in an American couple with a vast quantity of luggage. Philips leaned on the counter and looked around, taking stock of the people coming and going, noting anyone loitering. He felt an urge to smoke, and his hand wandered to his jacket pocket, even though there were never any cigarettes there anymore. At last the male clerk hung up the phone and directed a watery smile at Philips.

He flashed his ID. "DC Rob Philips, Parkside police. Do you have a Miss Alana Fulton staying with you?"

The receptionist's expression didn't flicker; his eyes traveled from the ID to Philips's face and then to his computer screen. He tapped the keyboard. "Rooms 412 and 413," he said.

Philips wrote the numbers in his notebook. "Two rooms?"

"It's not uncommon for such significant guests to book several rooms." The clerk's expression faltered. "Although they do usually choose the more luxurious suites."

"Was anyone with her?"

The clerk consulted his screen again. "Apparently not."

"Anyone who might not have registered?"

"I didn't check her in. Wait a moment." He nudged the female clerk dealing with the Americans. "This gentleman's a police officer. He'd like a word."

The clerk, an immaculate forty-year-old with trim bronze-colored hair, extricated herself from the American couple and came over, giving Philips a bland smile.

"I believe you checked in a Miss Alana Fulton earlier today?"

She looked blank, and her colleague prompted her: "Rooms 412 and 413."

"Oh yes. That's right," she said.

"Was there anyone with her who didn't check in?"

"Yes, there was a young man."

"Can you describe him?"

"Well … young, like I said. I didn't see his face. He was wearing jeans and a hoodie with the hood up." She lowered her voice theatrically. "I thought he looked a bit scruffy, to be honest. It did cross my mind he might've had an accident or something. I asked was he all right, and she said he was fine."

"I see. Thanks. Rooms 412 and 413, you say?"

The male clerk nodded. "The lifts are just round the corner there."

"Is that for us?" Alana asked, hearing the sound of knuckles rapping loudly on a door. It seemed kind of muffled, like it might be a neighboring room.

Howard shook his head. "Don't think so."

Alana had been packing her suitcase – having only just unpacked it an hour earlier – ready to set off for the airport. She walked toward

92

the door. As she reached it there came the sound of wood splintering and a door banging open.

She peered through the spyhole. She could just make out that the door to room 413 – Howard's, which was diagonally opposite – was wide open. As she watched, a figure dressed all in black, wearing a small rucksack and carrying a handgun, came out of the room, glanced up and down the corridor, then walked away to her right.

Alana shrank back from the door in alarm. The man had passed in a flash through the little sphere visible through the spyhole, but the face – distorted by the lens – registered in her horrified brain. Male, not tall, olive-skinned, with dark stubble and strong, angular features. She wasn't sure from that momentary sight whether the odd shape of his jaw was his own or a product of the fisheye lens. But she was absolutely certain of the cold, hard expression and the very deadly-looking gun in his hand.

She leaned against the wall with her heart thumping. She believed she knew now, without a shadow of doubt, who was responsible for the chemical attack. She had no idea who that man was, but she knew he was a killer. Alana and Howard had been in room 413 only five minutes ago; if she hadn't had to pack right away, they'd have been caught.

You are in danger. For the first time it hit Alana what that meant. Somehow, for reasons she couldn't begin to guess, somebody wanted her dead.

"What was it?" said Howard from behind her.

"We have to go," she said faintly, and turned to look at him. "We have to go right now. Get your things together."

Howard stood flat-footed, staring at her.

"Now!" she yelled. "We have to leave this minute!"

She crammed the last few items into her case and zipped it shut.

"Where's your car?" she said.

"It's in the big parking garage next door. The Grand Mall or whatever. Alana, what's going on? What happened just now?"

Alana looked him in the eye as steadily as she could. "That danger you warned me about? It's found us."

Checking the spyhole, she opened the door a crack and peeked along the corridor. Completely deserted. Beckoning Howard to follow, she went left, toward the elevators. As they reached the corner, she glanced back. The corridor was still empty.

It was only four floors, but the elevator seemed to take forever. When it stopped on the second floor, Alana's heart almost stopped. The door opened, but no one got in. She peeked out: nobody there. As the doors swished closed, she could feel her heart thudding and hear her own heavy breathing.

The lobby was quiet, with only a few people passing through. Alana looked through the glass into the street, where a young family were getting into a taxi in the pull-in directly outside the doors. She thought of the dark, lonesome walk along Corn Exchange Street to the entrance of the Grand Arcade and shuddered. On an impulse she went to the reception desk.

"Hi. Is there a direct way to the Grand Arcade car park from the hotel? It looks like rain outside."

The bronze-haired desk clerk looked at her in surprise. "Miss Fulton, isn't it? There was a policeman looking for you a minute ago."

Alana didn't know what to think. Would it be better to put themselves into the protection of the police and risk Howard getting charged with something he didn't do? She recalled the sickening sensation she'd experienced in that interview room – of feeling like the accused while knowing she was the intended victim. That was nothing compared with what Howard could expect.

"Oh … er, yeah, I just spoke with him," she said glibly. "So, the car park?"

The clerk's smile didn't flicker. "Of course. Just go through the lounge here and through the double doors at the end."

Alana was moving before the clerk had finished speaking. "Thanks," she called over her shoulder. With Howard following close behind, she half-ran through a large room that she perceived only as a blur of beige and tables. At the far end was a double door, which she slammed through, almost colliding with a group of men in suits. There was a wide corridor beyond, with event rooms leading off it.

Stopping in confusion and looking frantically around, Alana felt panic rising. "Where is it?" she said. "Did we get the wrong door?"

"There!" said Howard.

The corridor angled to the right, there was a lobby area with a small reception desk and a second double door with a discreet sign beside it: CAR PARK & GRAND ARCADE SHOPPING.

Alana took off, dragging her little suitcase behind her. Cautiously she pushed open the door and peeked out. There was an area with a stairwell and two elevators, and another door, signed GRAND ARCADE. Nobody was about. Howard headed for the elevators, but Alana stopped him.

"No, that must be the hotel parking. You're in the public, right? We'll have to go that way."

The door led to the mall's side foyer, all gray stone and fake beige marble. There were elevators along one wall, parking ticket machines, and a door leading to a stairwell. The foyer opened out into the ground floor level of the parking garage. The entrance into the mall itself was shuttered for the night. The only people in sight were an elderly couple using one of the ticket machines.

"Dammit," Alana muttered. "Do you still have your ticket?"

"What?"

95

"Your parking ticket. Do you still have it? We can't leave without it."

Howard patted his pockets while Alana twitched with impatience. He found his wallet and rifled through the cards, notes, bills …

"Hurry," Alana whispered, glancing back through the door.

"Got it!" Howard extracted the ticket from between his credit cards.

Alana stood guard while he inserted it in the machine. The elderly couple finished paying and left, leaving them alone in the foyer. Alana looked from side to side, wide-eyed with fear, listening for any sound of footsteps. She noticed the black grip of the pistol sticking out of Howard's waistband as he reached up to insert his card in the machine. She grabbed it, dropped out the magazine to check it was full, slotted it back, and gingerly drew back the slide to check there was a round in the chamber.

Howard stared at her in amazement. "Where did you learn to do that?"

"My Daddy made me take lessons."

The moment she'd turned eighteen, her father had taken her to a range and made her take a handgun course. John Fulton wasn't a gun guy himself, other than for hunting, but he wanted his daughter to be able to defend herself. First there'd been a kidnap avoidance course, then the gun lessons. Alana had disliked both intensely, but the shooting lessons she truly hated – the hideous, painfully loud noise and the powerful leap of the weapon when it was fired. She had never gone near a gun since. Until now. The Vektor's weight felt strange and unpleasant in her hand.

Silence. The ticket machine was making a long job of processing the card payment.

Alana could hear distant sounds of a car engine on some upper level and the faint rushing of tires on concrete. She thought she heard footsteps echoing in the stairwell, but when she glanced through the door there was nobody there. She kept the gun lowered, down by her thigh, ready to use it or conceal it.

At last, the machine whirred, released the card, and spat out the ticket. Alana snatched it and slipped it into her pants pocket. At that moment the elevator at the end of the line chimed and the door hissed open. Alana froze and pressed her back against the ticket machine, gripping the pistol tight but not raising it.

Nobody came out. Alana moved cautiously toward the open door, heel and toe, the gun held out in front of her, both hands on the grip. She inched up to the door, pulse racing, hugging the wall, then, gathering her courage, swung round to face it.

It was empty. Alana deflated like a balloon, breathing heavily, feeling like she might faint. She waited a moment, then stepped into the elevator and beckoned for Howard to follow.

"Which level?" she asked, her finger hovering over the buttons. Howard's mouth opened and closed dumbly. "Which level did you park on, Howard?"

"I … I can't remember."

Alana wanted to bang her head on the wall. "Think, Howard, please!"

"It was the one … the one I almost fell … I was trying to get to my car."

The picture came back to her mind of chasing the hooded figure between the parked cars, out into the open-air section … She couldn't recall the number of flights of stairs she'd run up, so she made a guess and hit the button for level 4.

As the elevator hummed, Alana studied Howard's face. She hadn't told him exactly what she'd seen through the spyhole. Instinct had warned her not to mention that the man had a gun. Howard's face was pale and scared, but he wasn't panicking; Alana wondered how he'd be if he knew there was an armed killer looking for them.

DC Philips stepped out of the elevator and walked briskly along the plush-carpeted corridor, noting the room numbers.

He sensed something was wrong as soon as he saw the door of room 413 standing ajar. Coming closer, he saw the splintered frame and the broken lock. Cautiously, he pushed back the door and stepped into the room. It was clear; the bed was ruffled as though someone had sat on it, and there were the remains of a meal on the table, but no other signs of occupation. In the bathroom a hand towel had been used, and one bar of soap unwrapped. In the wastebasket he found wrappers from first aid dressings and blood-stained tissues.

The door of room 412 was locked, and there was no answer to his knock. A housekeeper was pushing her cart along the corridor, and Philips asked her to open the door. The room was empty.

Nobody checked into a hotel and then left so abruptly unless they were absconding. Absconding from what, though? Maybe Mr. Angelus was guiltier than he'd suspected.

The detective took out his phone. "Rob Philips, requesting backup. I'm at the Cambridge Hilton in Downing Street. Floor four, rooms 412 and 413. Signs of a break-in, potentially dangerous suspect has absconded, possibly still on site."

He ran back along the corridor to the elevators.

In the lobby the female receptionist spotted him and said brightly, "I see you found her then?"

"Miss Fulton? No I didn't."

"Oh. She said you had …"

"Where did she go?"

98

"That way. She asked how to get to the Grand Arcade car park."

Philips wasn't a particularly fit man – too many desk hours and junk food lunches – but he managed to run pretty fast, slamming through doors and finally skidding to a halt in the mall foyer. He stared around frantically at the ticket machines, the elevators, and the entrance to the bottom level of the parking garage.

She could be anywhere. Where should he start? He tried to estimate how long it had been since she'd passed through here. Ten minutes? Fifteen? She might be long gone. But if she was still in the building it didn't matter which floor her car was on – there was only one way out.

Philips ran through the ground floor level, heading for the exit, pulling out his phone as he ran. "Backup to Grand Arcade car park exit, Corn Exchange Street. We're looking for Alana Fulton and Howard Angelus. Fulton's vehicle is a blue Porsche 911 with a fixed glass roof, registration number: Charlie uniform five seven bravo alpha Charlie. Angelus is potentially dangerous. Request armed response vehicle. Repeat: request ARV at scene."

The elevator stopped at level four and the doors opened. Alana looked out across rows of cars gleaming in the bright fluorescent light. Although the mall was shut, the level was pretty much full: people going to concerts or movies or out to dinner. Cambridge was as busy as London by night. Alana wished she'd taken the risk after all and gone to the main entrance at the far end of the building, where there would be plenty of people around.

Whatever, this didn't seem to be the level with the open area. She ducked back inside and pressed five. The elevator hummed and stopped, and the door opened. This level was a little less full. Still not the right one, though. She pressed for level six. Her nervousness was escalating with each rise of the elevator.

Level six was the right one. Beyond the last but one row of cars was the area open to the sky, where they'd been earlier that afternoon. Nodding to Howard, she stepped out and walked across the narrow concrete waiting area.

Suddenly, hands grabbed her from behind. She was pulled backward violently, losing her footing and falling, only held up by the strong hands gripping her arms. At the same moment, a car flashed past her field of vision, and the long, furious blast of a horn filled the level with echoes.

"Jesus, Lanzy, you nearly got hit," said Howard. "Watch where you're going, for Christ's sake!"

Alana extricated herself from his grip. "Thank you. Where's your car?"

Howard pointed. "At the far end, couple rows over. Red Toyota."

The level was only half-full, and there was no sign of life. Warily, Alana walked along the row, the gun held down at her side, watching, listening. Ahead, the concrete formed a bright road sloping gently down toward the exit ramps. Every parked car and every pillar she passed Alana half-expected a black-clad figure to leap out at her. Before they'd reached halfway, her heart was beating so hard she could barely stand it. It felt like this cold, echoing space and this long, sloping row of cars was her life now, an unending series of potential threats; she was doomed to walk along it forever in a perpetual state of nervous, creeping fear.

At last she saw a compact red Toyota Yaris, parked against the end rail between a blue sedan and a silver minivan; she glanced at Howard, who nodded. They were almost there. "Give me the key," she whispered. She'd have to drive; she knew how to get where they were going, and he didn't. He passed it to her, and she crossed the last few yards to the car, pressing the button and feeling elated as the car chimed and lit up.

Over the rail there was a fine view over the illuminated city; Alana gave it only a passing glance as she opened the rear door and threw her case onto the back seat. She slammed the door and was turning away when, in the corner of her eye, she caught a black shadow momentarily blanking out the city lights. There was a soft thump of feet landing lightly on the concrete, and then a hand was on her throat.

Alana opened her mouth to scream as the hand pushed her back with phenomenal strength against the blue sedan. The fluorescent light above her whirled, and the fingers pressed hard into her neck, pinning her to the car.

Her screams came out in a guttural rush, suddenly choked off by the assailant's grip. She saw his face. The deformed jaw in the pretty face, the olive skin, the dark stubble. His right hand pinioned her by the throat while in his left hand a semi-automatic pistol with a long, fat silencer pointed across the Toyota's roof directly at Howard's terrified face.

Alana sensed that the man wasn't holding Howard at gunpoint; he was taking a second to steady his aim before firing a kill-shot.

She acted instantly, without thought. The man's attention was focused on Howard, assuming Alana would be too terrified to move. She twisted in his grip and lashed out with her foot, catching him on the shin. The pistol coughed, whacking a hole through the minivan's window and setting its alarm howling.

The gunman steadied himself, and his grip on Alana weakened. She tore herself free and ran, heading toward the nearest bank of elevators, yelling over the wail of the alarm: "Help! Help us! Help!"

A group of men and women exiting the nearest elevator stopped in their tracks. Alana glanced back. Howard was still rooted to the spot. The man in black was nowhere to be seen.

"Are you all right, love?" said a female voice.

She felt a soft touch on her hand and turned to see a middle-aged woman looking at her with concern. Her friends, who looked like tourists, had gathered around.

Alana hesitated and looked back at Howard, who had come to life and was staring around him like someone waking from a dream. "I … Yes, I'm okay now. We were just … you know, horsing around."

The woman looked nonplussed. "Well, if you're sure?"

"I'm sure." Alana forced a smile. "I'm sorry to have startled you."

She returned to the Toyota. The man in black was nowhere to be seen. The minivan's alarm cut out, leaving behind an echoing silence.

Alana had dropped the Vektor when the gunman jumped her. It was lying on the concrete by the rear wheel. Checking that the tourists were out of sight, she picked it up and looked around the nearby cars in case the man was hiding. Then, cautiously, she approached the end rail. She was sure he'd come at her over the rail from outside the building.

She glanced over. Directly below was a drop of about ten feet into the open top of the garage's spiral entryway; looking up, there was the rail of the floor above. She couldn't begin to imagine how anyone could climb in or out that way. Alana's hand, resting on the icy steel rail, was shaking. She flexed her fingers.

"Did … did that really just happen?" said Howard.

He looked utterly terrified; his jaw was tight, the muscles working beneath the pale, waxy skin, his eyes haunted.

"Get in the car," she said. He didn't move. "Please, Howard, get in the car. We have to go."

Mechanically he opened the door and sat in the passenger seat. With one last glance around, Alana ducked into the driver's seat. She started the engine and pulled out, every nerve in her body alert for threats.

Driving up the row, she accelerated hard, tires squealing as she turned at the end. Straightening up for the first ramp, she saw a car pull behind her – a black Mercedes with dark windows. Glancing in the mirror, she couldn't make out the driver at all, just a smudge behind the windshield. Putting her foot down, she swung onto the down ramp, Howard gripping the dashboard as she turned violently at the bottom, tires squealing. Alana threw the car down another ramp and along the rows, down yet another ramp, going as fast as she could, on the very edge of losing control in the confined space. At last they reached the bottom level and she accelerated onto the spiral exit-way.

As the Toyota sped down the twisting concrete tunnel, she glanced at the mirror. If the Mercedes was still following, it wasn't close enough to be seen around the bend of the spiral.

Howard kept watch for the pursuing car, his emotions divided between terror of the gunman and fear of Alana smashing the car across the wall. The former was the greater, and he urged her to go faster.

The spiral ended, opening into the exit area. Alana slowed at the sight of the barriers.

"Ram it!" yelled Howard. "Don't stop! Just bust through it for Christ's sake!"

Alana just couldn't do it. Good behavior had been too thoroughly drummed into her. She steered into one of the exit channels and braked in front of the barrier, searching in her jeans pocket for the ticket. She found it and wound down the window.

"They're coming!" said Howard.

Alana heard the rush of tires on the concrete as the Mercedes shot out of the spiral. Fingers shaking, she tried to insert the ticket in the slot. The Mercedes pulled into the next channel. Alana's free hand reached for the gun, in a cup-holder behind the gearshift. The Mercedes driver's window wound down, revealing a young blonde woman who glanced curiously across at them as she inserted her ticket.

Alana let out a sound halfway between a sob and a laugh. Her ticket went in, the barrier rose, and she eased the Toyota out into Corn Exchange Street.

DC Philips, gasping for breath, felt like he was on the verge of a heart attack as he ran up the slope toward the exit. He arrived just in time to see two cars – a black Mercedes and a red Toyota – pull out through the barriers.

He reached the barriers just as the second one was going down, and leaned on the ticket box, fighting for breath. He looked up to see three patrol cars, blue lights flashing, come racing down Corn Exchange Street and slam to a halt outside the exit. Several officers spilled out of them and started blocking the road.

Philips beckoned to one of them. "We've missed them. Call it in. Tell them to put an all ports watch for Alana Fulton and Howard Angelus."

10

Alana made the turn into Downing Street slowly, forcing herself to drive calmly and not draw attention from the police cars racing past them.

"D'you think they were for us?" Howard asked anxiously. "Or for that guy?"

"I don't know. Either way, it's not good. Who was he?"

Howard shrugged helplessly. His brain was overloading. In two years of "protecting" Alana, it had never occurred to him that it might come to actual danger.

Waiting at a red light at the end of the street, Alana looked in her mirror, expecting at any moment to see the blue flashing lights come back out of Corn Exchange Street and head their way. They didn't. The traffic light turned green and she pulled away, turning right and taking the route to the airport.

"I guess London Stansted would be nearest?" said Howard. "Are there flights to Switzerland from there?"

"We're not going to Stansted," said Alana.

"Where then?"

"Cambridge."

"Cambridge has an *airport*?"

Alana glanced at the clock on the dashboard. As far as she'd been able to understand from her mother's confused instructions, there was only a minuscule time window available, and if they missed it … It was 7:38 now. The rendezvous had to be no later than 7:55.

She put her foot down and the Toyota sped through the streets, then out along the main route leading out of town. It was 7:45 when they passed the last intersection and came to a long strip lined on both sides by car dealerships – huge flag-decked lots filled with Range Rovers, Jaguars, and Fords. Alana carefully scrutinized each turning they passed, looking for the right entrance. She'd only been here once before, early in her first year, and couldn't remember what to look out for.

"That's it," she muttered. "I think."

She pulled into an entrance to what looked like a parking lot, which was hard to distinguish it from the auto dealerships.

"Why are we stopping here?" said Howard, looking around in panic. "Where's the airport?"

At that moment they heard the high-pitched whine of a low-flying plane. A sleek executive jet passed low overhead, descending, and disappeared beyond some nearby buildings.

Alana pointed to a small brick building about the size of a neighborhood convenience store. There was a sign on it: CAMBRIDGE CITY AIRPORT.

"We're here," she said, steering past the building and heading for the entry barrier.

As the Toyota stopped at the barrier, a second car turned into the outer parking lot from the street – a black Mercedes with darkened windows. It came to a halt. The driver's window rolled down, revealing a young woman with blonde hair.

She watched for a moment as a security guard at the barrier spoke to the driver of the Toyota. "What now?" she said over her shoulder. "You want me to wait?" Her accent was British, but with a trace of something foreign in the way she bit down on the consonants.

"Wait. But don't park. Keep motor running."

The rear door opened, and Hayk got out. Scanning the area, he moved swiftly toward the shadows at the foot of a two-story building beside the parking lot. Finding a drainpipe, he tested its firmness then began to climb.

From the car, the woman watched as the barrier rose and the Toyota was waved through. Seeing Hayk's shadowy form reach the roof of the building, she rolled up the window and drove along to the end of the row, where she waited with the motor idling.

Her little suitcase trundling behind her, Alana walked across the concrete apron toward a sleek white Gulfstream jet parked in a holding area, its lights glittering in the damp darkness and its engines emitting a low hum.

On one side of her walked an airport attendant, with Howard following behind reluctantly, as if he were trying to hide in their shadows. Alana was nervous too. Her parents had pulled a lot of strings to make this happen.

The Gulfstream belonged to VisWorld Corp, the parent company that now owned Excorpora Media, the news reportage cable TV operation founded by John Fulton in the early 1980s. He retained a major holding in the company and a seat on the board of VisWorld, which entitled him to certain privileges. This evening's request had tested those privileges pretty heavily.

Fortunately, the jet had been en route to Heathrow from New York when he made the call; applying some leverage, he'd managed to secure a stop-off at Cambridge. There was absolutely nothing John

107

Fulton wouldn't do to ensure the safety of his only daughter, a point he'd made emphatically to his contact at VisWorld – combined with a hint that Excorpora might get exclusive interview access to the central figure in the Cambridge terror attack.

The captain was waiting at the foot of the steps. "Miss Fulton," he said warmly. "And Mr. Angelus. May I say how pleased I am to welcome you aboard this flight. As time is pressing, I will have to ask you to carry your own baggage. May I see your passports, please?"

Alana could feel the lump of the pistol grip pressing into the small of her back and prayed there wouldn't be a security search involved. She'd traveled on private charters and company jets often enough to know there usually wasn't, but never in such weird circumstances.

The captain gave both passports a brief look-over before handing them back with a smile. "Welcome aboard," he said, and ushered them up the steps.

Lying flat on top of the airport building, Hayk trained his rifle scope on the Gulfstream, watching the two figures go up the steps.

His finger hovered on the trigger, holding the crosshairs on the woman's upper torso as she paused at the top of the steps. She wore a white jacket with a fur collar, which stood out vividly in the light spilling from the open door. His finger trembled. Thinking of who this woman was and what she represented, he longed to squeeze the trigger and put a bullet through her heart. Even at this range, he was confident of the shot. She turned her head to smile at the captain, and Hayk stroked his fingertip along the warm edge of the trigger, beginning to apply pressure … and stopped himself.

His rage had been cultivated and brought to bloom by Vartan, but Ando had trained him to focus the energy of his feelings like a beam of light, and to aim it consciously, controlling its intensity and its target. To kill this woman was not the mission. At least, not yet. The woman (he knew her name perfectly well, but hated to pronounce it, even in the privacy of his own mind) must be taken alive.

The boyfriend, though? He was an irritation, and entirely expendable. Hayk had judged him a coward, and his behavior in the parking garage had confirmed it. But Hayk's estimation of the woman had been disastrously inaccurate. Knowing what he did of her background, he'd expected her to be weak and easily cowed. When she fought back, it had taken him utterly by surprise. If he'd judged her more accurately, he'd have handled her differently, and by now the boyfriend would be dead and she would be in Hayk's hands.

His finger hovered on the trigger. The captain's body was obstructing the boyfriend. Through the scope, Hayk watched the woman duck in through the door; the boyfriend entered after her, followed by the captain.

A few minutes later, the Gulfstream's engines ramped up and the plane taxied out. By the time it took off, Hayk had disassembled and packed away the rifle. He would have to report immediately and account to Vartan for his failure.

11

A bright February sun cut across the rim of the mountains above Khojali. Lying on her back on the soft, frost-laden patch of grass beside the road, just outside the garden wall, Ayna squinted against the cold light, her eyes tracing the green furze of the mountain ridges.

Her parents had warned her against looking into the sun and lying on the ground in the winter damp. Ayna tried to obey, but she did these things anyway.

She was humming a tune and listening to the resonance of her own voice in her skull. She could hear the distant clatter and pop of gunfire, but it didn't disturb her; it had been a part of her environment for months now and was no more remarkable than the weather. Ayna knew that the noises terrified her mother and made her father anxious – especially the thump of artillery shells. She also understood that the ugly, bloody injuries her father often had to bandage were connected.

There was a lull, and against the calm murmur of the street Ayna heard a helicopter taking off from the airfield at the edge of the village. A moment later she saw its dark shape climbing into the blue sky; it was swallowed in the sun's halo, and then, circling north, disappeared behind the mountains.

Her grandfather lived sometimes beyond that ridge, near Aggadik, when he wasn't at his main home in Shusha. Ayna had asked her mother why he didn't live with them here, in Khojali. "He has responsibilities," her mother said, which Ayna didn't understand at all. "More than ever now. Besides, I think this house would be a little small for such a great man, don't you?" Ayna thought this was absurd; her grandfather was no taller than her father, who lived here quite happily. She was too little to remember her only visit to the palace at Shusha; and now, with the siege, it would be a long time before her parents would have a chance to take her there again.

Suddenly the dazzling light was blotted out by a huge snout. Hot snuffling breath blew on her face, with the brush of a wet nose. She giggled, riffling her fingers in the fur of Rolan's shaggy neck. He wagged his tail wildly and nuzzled her face all the more, making her curl up in a fit of breathless giggling. Only three months had passed since her birthday, but Rolan was already larger than her.

She fended him off and scrambled up. The moment she was on her feet, Ayna was conscious of the boy watching her from across the street.

He was about the same age as her brother, Hakan, although maybe a little bigger, and paler skinned with blue eyes and hair that was almost blond. His clothes were threadbare, and his skin streaked with dirt. She knew him by sight as one of the Azeri IDPs (internally displaced persons) from the city of Khankendi, which had fallen to the Armenian forces. The refugees lived in the hostel at the end of the road. Ayna was a little afraid of the place; a rambling mass of old buildings in which nearly a hundred families lived. They had crowded out the hostel and spilled out into tents and makeshift shelters scattered down the hillside. The chaos and distress of it scared her. Ayna frowned at the boy. He smiled, and she frowned harder.

"I like your dog," he said suddenly.

Ayna stepped protectively in front of Rolan, knotting her fingers into his fur. The boy crossed the street toward her, and she took a step back. As he came closer, she could see nothing but friendliness in his expression. His eyes were large, and his face open and warm.

"My name's Neymar," he said. "What's yours?"

"Ayna," she said warily. "This is Rolan," she added, noticing that the dog was looking at the boy with friendly interest. Ayna trusted Rolan's judgment of character; they always liked and disliked the same people. "You can pet him if you like."

Neymar stroked the smooth, mottled gray fur on the dog's head. "My papa knows your grandfather," he said. "We used to live in Shusha before we went to Khankendi. We had to run away from Khankendi when the Armenians came there."

"Why don't you go back to Shusha?"

"My mama says the Armenians will come there soon, and everyone will run away."

"My grandfather is brave. He would never run away."

"He will," said Neymar flatly. "Everyone has to. All the Azeris have to run, or the Armenians will kill us. My mama says they will kill us here. She wants to go to Baku where my cousins live."

"Have you been to Baku?" asked Ayna.

Neymar shook his head, teasing his fingers around the soft folds of the dog's ear; Rolan tilted his head; he could stand all day and have his ears fondled. "I don't want to. My papa says this is our country and we must stay here."

Ayna knew this to be a solemn truth, having heard the same from her father and grandfather.

Neymar took some crusts of stale bread from his pocket and began tossing them to Rolan, giggling as the dog jumped and snapped them up in his jaws. Ayna laughed, the last trace of her reserve melting away.

112

The game was interrupted by the loud, howling drone of a military helicopter taking off from the airfield. It turned tightly, like a lumbering goose, then roared low over their heads, climbing steeply and flying away east.

"My papa says that's why the Armenians want Khojali so bad," said Neymar. "They want our airfield."

"I know that," said Ayna. "My father says that too. And that's why we must fight to keep it."

"Neymar!" said a woman's voice. "What in the world are you doing?"

He gave a guilty start. "Playing," he said.

The woman came striding across the street toward them. She was young, but her face was prematurely lined, and the dark hair showing under her embroidered headscarf was streaked with gray. Ayna noticed how frayed her dress was, and how washed-out its pink and brown floral pattern. "You are wasting food," she said angrily. "You know how scarce it is. And to feed it to a dog!"

"I'm sorry, mother," said Neymar. "He's my friend's dog. He's nice."

The woman looked at Ayna. "I know you, child," she said in a calmer voice. "You're a Karabakhsky."

"She's Ayna," said Neymar.

"Well …" His mother seemed mollified. "You will give my best wishes to your parents," she said, almost meekly. Ayna nodded. "Now, Neymar, come home."

The boy obediently followed his mother. Halfway across the street he suddenly ran back and took Ayna's hand. "I'll see you again," he said, then hurried to catch up with his mother.

Ayna watched them walk away, feeling how strange it seemed that he didn't look back once.

12

Gstaad

Turning her head on the fat white pillow, Alana gazed, blinking, into a bright halo filtered by the lace edging of the drapes and the border of frost on the glass.

She slid out of bed and padded drowsily across the warm wooden floor to the window. Pushing back the drape, she was rewarded with a view of the sun rising in a clear sky over the peak of the Giferspitz, black and jagged as a broken knife-point above the slopes of the Wasserngrat. The snows were tinted lilac-gray in the shade of the mountain, and the pine forests were black. The pointed turrets of the Gstaad Palace Hotel, on its knoll above the town, caught the sun and glittered like fairyland.

It felt so good to be back here. To be in this place where comfort met unreality and – above all, right now – safety. Beneath, though, was an uncomfortable seam of memory lingering from her dreams. She couldn't recall what the dream had been about, but it was set in a landscape where there were mountains – not dark, rearing peaks like this, but green ridges. The dream had felt pleasant but harbored a sense of foreboding which still lingered like a faint echo.

The flight from England had been fraught. The Gulfstream already had four passengers on board – a couple of senior VisWorld execs and two men from some European-based subsidiary, all reclining with their ties loose in heavy leather seats around a polished walnut table upon which were drinks, a laptop, and piles of documents. They'd looked at Alana and Howard with astonishment – not least because of Howard's haggard appearance. They knew who Alana was and the pull her father had in their world, and they treated her with respect.

Avoiding their questions, Alana and Howard had retreated to the other end of the passenger cabin and sank gratefully into the deeply comfortable seats. The plane made the short hop to Heathrow, where the execs disembarked. There was a long, tense wait while the plane was refueled. Alana declined the offer of a car to the private executive lounge in the terminal, expecting at any minute to see blue lights through the window and hear the howl of sirens. Her chest ached with anxiety by the time the plane took off again. She hardly remembered the flight – it was just a blur in which she and Howard barely spoke.

When they touched down on the short runway at Gstaad, her parents' Range Rover was waiting on the concrete, the familiar sturdy figure of John Fulton standing beside it. Alana hurried down the icy steps and ran into his arms, crying with relief while he swung her off her feet, his deep bass voice booming with laughter. Then the comforting leathery interior of the car, the headlights picking out the snow-covered road and glimpses of the steep chalet roofs of the town. The familiar smell of the apartment. Her mother's near-hysterical greeting. And then sweet, sweet sleep …

The sun was above the mountains now, light spilling down into the valley, flowing through the winding streets of Gstaad, pouring over the gables. She loved this place. Her parents rented this small apartment every year for the skiing season and spent as much time here as their schedules allowed. The apartment occupied the attic story of an old building on the Promenade, opposite the Hotel Olden. It was centuries old, with carved gables and huge, jutting eaves like the half-furled wings of a duck; the apartment was redolent with the aromas of ancient timber and polish, and lingering in the grain of the wood was the ghost of generations of tobacco pipes.

Alana threw on some clothes and stepped out onto the balcony. There was an inch of snow on the wooden railing, despite the eaves projecting out several feet beyond it. To her surprise, Howard was already there.

"Hi," he said shyly.

They had taken separate rooms for the night. She had her regular room, and he took the spare.

"Hi yourself." She studied his face, shielding her eyes from the sun's glare. He wasn't smiling.

She brushed some snow from the rail and leaned on it. Without a word, Howard passed her his phone. It was open on the Twitter feed of the *Hollywood Reporter*. Alana's stomach dropped: *UK Police Seek Howard Angelus in Terror Hunt.*

Alana tapped on the link and read the story.

UK police are seeking Howard Angelus (Phenomenal, Hunger at Noon) in connection with the chemical attack on a Cambridge, UK college dorm building Wednesday in which dozens of students were hospitalized. Several victims are on life support and reported to be in a critical condition. UK police are treating the attack as terror-related, although the UK Foreign Secretary in an online article has accused the Russian government of being involved.

Alana Fulton, daughter of couturier and fashion retail giant

116

Catherine Tessaro and Excorpora Media founder John Fulton, who is a student at Cambridge and a resident of the dorm, narrowly escaped the attack. Fulton is in a long-term relationship with Howard Angelus, the two were seen together at the 2016 Governor's Ball and on the red carpet for the London premiere of Phenomenal, *the Kristen Stewart starrer in which Angelus turned in a critically acclaimed supporting role.*

That was the whole article. Alana went to the BBC News site, but their version of the story was just as oblique, giving nothing away about exactly why the police wanted Howard.

"Someone's gonna rat on me, aren't they?" he said. He took back his phone with shaking fingers.

"It doesn't say they want to *arrest* you. Just that they're looking for you." Even as she said it, she was conscious of how lame it sounded. Howard wasn't consoled.

"Good morning, both of you." John Fulton stood in the door to the living room, wearing a plaid robe and hugging himself against the cold. "By God, you're out and about early. Don't you kids even *get* tired? Come on in and get breakfast. I have some coffee brewing that'll blow your socks off."

His voice soothed Alana, and with a rush of delight she took her father's arm and stepped indoors with him. Daddy hadn't lost his ability to make her feel safe and loved and at peace with the world. Howard lingered on the balcony, then followed disconsolately.

Alana sat at the breakfast counter between the living room and the small galley kitchen, looking into the swirling, smoky surface of her coffee.

"I'll give you ten bucks and a fifteen percent raise for your thoughts," said her father, swirling the coffee pot before pouring a refill into his cup.

They were alone. Howard had gone to shower, and Catherine never got out of bed before nine. She'd been complaining of jet-lag, and it was doubtful she'd set foot on the floorboards all day.

Alana looked at her father's face. Many people thought John Fulton handsome, but it wasn't an accurate description; his face was long and chiseled, with a straight, blunt nose, but there was something hangdog in the set of his jowls and the mournful downward slant of his eyes. His looks belied his character, which was good-humored and upbeat, but also sharp as a shard of glass. A good deal of his success in business had come by way of his looks wrong-footing people about his personality. To Alana, those same features represented everything good and wise in human nature.

Feeling in her jeans pocket, she extracted the slip of gilt-edged card, rather bent and battered after its travels, and laid it on the counter, pushing it across to her father.

"What's this? A party invitation?" He smiled, put on his eye-glasses and peered at it.

You are not who you think you are.
Your future will not be what you expect.
You are in danger.

"It was given to me in Cambridge. I don't know who it's from, but I think it means something."

He studied her face. "Means something? Means what?"

"I don't know, but I can't stop thinking about it. *I'm not who I think I am.* Daddy, there's one person in the world who knows truly and absolutely who I am, and I'm sitting opposite him right now. What does it mean?"

His expression was unreadable. "Who gave it to you?"

"It was passed … anonymously."

Her father rested his elbow on the table and his chin on his hand, as he often did when thinking hard.

"Daddy?"

He sighed. "I really don't know how to answer you."

"Do you mean you don't know the answer, or you don't know how to tell me the answer?"

"If it means what I think it means …" He shrugged.

Alana's breath caught; she had hoped for reassurance, for this disturbing note to be authoritatively dismissed, for it to mean nothing.

Her father looked at her, chewing his lip. He drank his coffee in one fast slug, set down the cup and stood up. "Let's you and me go for a little walk. I have a notion to see what this fine morning looks like from the hills."

"Do you still believe in God, sweetheart?"

Alana, leaning on the cable car handrail, turned away from the view to look at her father. She wore the same quizzical half-smile John remembered from his daughter's childhood.

He gestured at the view from the car window – the mountains and forests, with the scatter of Gstaad spread out below and slowly receding. "When you look out at all of this, do you think God made it?"

Alana looked, turning her gaze from the base station far below, ahead to the Wispile, the great smooth ridge which lay like a vast hump-backed whale. For both father and daughter the Wispile was a favorite spot; John Fulton usually rented a little cabin up there and liked to retreat to it whenever the buzz of Gstaad got too much. He owned a similar place in Sequoia National Forest, and ever since Alana could remember he had spent whole weeks up there alone, occasionally allowing his precious little girl to accompany him.

"I don't know," said Alana, bracing her feet as the car lurched over a pylon. They were the only passengers at this early hour, ascending in beautiful isolation, suspended far above the earth. Her eyes roamed over the rolling, folded white ground and the scattered rugs of snow-dusted pines, the great jagged peaks of the Geltenhorn and Wildhorn rising into view beyond the Wispile. "I know I used to, when I was a kid. Do you still believe?"

His eyes sparkled under their drooping lids, and he gave the smile that had always reassured her and made her feel that all was right with the world. "Oh, absolutely," he said. "I just know that God is all around." Standing with his hands on the rail, looking out, he spoke softly, his voice almost guttural. "When I first met your mother, we weren't much more than kids. I was just starting out with Excorpora."

"In your garage?"

"In my garage. Just me and a couple of college buddies, some old electronic gear we picked up at a bankruptcy auction and an awful lot of duct tape. Cable TV was just getting off the ground then. It was all local content then, you know, neighborhood-based …" He glanced at Alana. "Yeah, I know, you've heard it a million times. Anyway, the point is I met Catherine Tessaro – or Caterina as she still called herself then – when she came to book ads on our NYC service. She was starting to do okay in design and was diving into retail. One store. One! Can you picture what that was like? Catherine Tessaro with one store and a truckload of verve and ambition."

Alana nodded. She'd heard this story before, but never tired of hearing it, wondering if she would ever meet anyone as perfectly matched to her as her parents had been to each other. Or rather, as the story made them sound.

"What I'm trying to get to, in my wandering way," her father went on, "is that for us, our businesses were … well, we were obsessed back then. Excorpora for me and Tessaro for her, they were kind of like our children. You understand?"

"I understand."

"For the longest time, we thought we'd never want to have children. When we finally got around to changing our minds, we were told we'd almost certainly never be *able* to have kids." The cable car reached another pylon, lurching and plunging. "So when you came along, it was like you were a gift from God." He turned to look at his daughter. "The answer to our prayers. That feeling has never changed."

Alana's eyes tingled. She hugged her father.

"That's why it's so very hard to say this." He gripped her by the shoulders and gently pushed her away so that he could looked in her eyes. "I'm not your father," he said.

Alana didn't know what to say. She could feel his pain, and in that moment, she believed she loved him more than she ever had in her life before. She squeezed his arm, and said the only thing she could say, which happened to be last thing he could possibly have expected.

"I know, Daddy," she said gently. "I already know. I've known that for years."

John stared at her in astonishment. "I ... How could you know?"

"Daddy, I know Mom fooled around before I was born. I know she cheated."

"Alana—"

"I overheard her and Vivian talking – oh, years back, when I was a senior in high school. They were talking about you and about me, and ... well, *stuff*, you know. They had no idea I was listening. Vivian thought Mom was jealous of me and you, the relationship we had, that we were so close." Alana turned to look at her father. He was watching her with something almost like fear. "At one point, Mom said, 'John loves that child as dearly as if she were his own.'"

John looked down at his hands gripping the rail; his knuckles must be white underneath the gloves.

"Later that night," said Alana, "I heard Mom crying in her room. It was the one time I saw her really broken up about something like that." Alana pried her father's hands from the rail and held them in hers. "So you see, I know. And it *doesn't matter*. I don't care about any of it. Whoever's genes I'm made from, *you're my father*. You. You're my Daddy, and I love you." She took off his right glove and kissed the back of his hand.

His eyes were shining. "Alana—"

"That's all that matters, Daddy. I'm your La-La, your precious jewel. Forever and always."

John's voice cracked as he spoke. "You don't know how beautiful it is to hear you say that." He touched Alana's cheek. "I used to watch you playing when you were little, and when you smiled at me it was like a stab in the heart. Grief and joy. I never knew how you'd take it if you knew, when you were old enough to understand."

"Well, now you do."

"It makes my heart happy. But Alana, that isn't what I wanted to tell you. I mean, not all of it. There's more."

"What do you mean?"

His tone of voice gave Alana a nervous stab. She wondered if he was going to tell her who her biological father was and felt sick. Alana's mind raced, trying to recall what she knew about the two or three men she believed her mother had had flings with.

John untwined his fingers from Alana's and told her the absolute last thing she expected to hear. "I'm not your father," he said flatly. "And Catherine is not your mother. Neither of us made you."

She stared at him. "No, that's wrong. I don't believe it." He opened his mouth, but just shook his head dumbly. "I'm *adopted*?

No, this isn't right. Daddy, I've seen my birth certificate." She could picture it vividly in her head. She'd first seen it when she applied for her own passport at sixteen and had kept hold of it. It showed that she was born December 7, 1987, at Cedars-Sinai Medical Center, Beverly Grove. *Name: Alana May Fulton; mother: Catherine Fulton née Tessaro; father: John Harold Anthony Fulton.* All there in black and white. After overhearing her mother's revelation, Alana had spent a lot of time staring at it, reading her father's name over and over, wondering if he knew he wasn't really the father, or if he found out later.

"Oh, La-La," said John, his voice cracking. Alana felt as if her feet were sinking into soft sand, the world starting to fade around her. She clutched at the image of that birth certificate – her right to exist, to be herself. It was real, concrete, undeniable. She could hear her father speaking. "… all we could, both of us, myself and Catherine. I wonder now if it was enough. Or maybe it was too much."

"What was too much?"

"After what you went through, I've sometimes wondered if we tried too hard to help you go on forgetting it all."

"Forgetting what?"

"You weren't our biological child, Alana sweetheart. You weren't born in Beverley Grove, or even in the United States. We took you in because your real family were gone."

"What do you mean, *gone*?"

"They died. All of them."

123

13

With her mother's soft, firm grip enclosing one of her hands, in the other Ayna held the stiff leather of Rolan's leash, which yanked and slackened as the young dog scurried ahead or stopped to investigate some scent on the brickwork of a roadside wall.

They were on their way to visit Nurbanu's elderly aunt, who lived on the north side of the village. It was quieter there, away from the airfield, and the Armenian lines were not quite so close. The air was harsh and cold, and Nurbanu had dressed Ayna in her warmest clothing, topped off with the candy-pink woolen scarf the little girl loved, with its chocolate-brown bunnies and egg-yolk-yellow ducklings. Rolan, who was usually allowed to roam free around the house and grounds, had been collared and put on his rarely used leash. Ayna didn't like to go anywhere without her pet; Nurbanu believed the girl loved that dog more than she did her siblings.

Walking down the street, Ayna laughed in delight at the way the dog lolloped from scent to scent. She was so distracted she scarcely noticed that her mother gripped her hand less gently than usual, or that a nervousness flowed from her mother's fingertips to her own small palm. Ayna glanced up at her mother but saw nothing in her face other than calm there.

There was a sudden backward jerk on the leash, almost yanking it out of Ayna's grip. "Rolan!" she squeaked. The dog was standing rooted to the spot, staring ahead, shoulders hunched, ears folded backward, growling uncertainly.

"What is it, boy?" said Ayna. "What's the matter?"

She went to pet him, but he backed away, staring past her down the street.

Nurbanu looked at the terrified dog. The anxiety she was trying to suppress was suddenly amplified, although she could see nothing to be scared of. The road ran downhill and joined with the main village street, a broad thoroughfare winding through from northwest to southeast. There were few buildings in sight, just hedgerow, scrub and trees. All was quiet. A lone Azeri woman carrying a bundle on her shoulder was walking along the main street toward the farm near the next bend in the road. Nurbanu recognized her as one of Tengiz's patients: Mrs. Radjabov. Her husband and two sons worked for the farmer, and Mrs. Radjabov herself did laundry. Nurbanu had often seen her taking food to Azeri refugees who'd had to flee Armenia in order to stay alive.

The dog's low growling grew into a full-throated, teeth-baring snarl. He backed up suddenly, then turned tail and ran, almost pulling Ayna off her feet; she stumbled a few paces before the leash was ripped from her grasp. "Rolan!" she shrieked. She tried to run after him, but her hand was locked in her mother's.

Nurbanu was staring down the street. From beyond the corner, she could hear men shouting and the sound of running feet. Suddenly, a young man in a white shirt came hurtling into view, running as if demons were at his heels. He was heading for a copse of trees on the far side of the main road. There was a clatter of gunfire; puffs of dust kicked up near the young man's feet, then red splashes blossomed on his white shirt. He fell sprawling in the dirt. Nurbanu, paralyzed with horror, recognized him as Mrs. Radjabov's eldest son, Vugar.

Mrs. Radjabov let out a blood-curdling wail; dropping her bundle, she ran to him, falling to her knees and trying to raise him, sobbing. He twisted violently in her arms, jerked and lay still. At that moment a group of soldiers carrying AK-47s came into view. Mrs. Radjabov, convulsed with grief and rage, shook her fists at them, screaming imprecations. One of the soldiers raised his weapon and shot her three times in the chest. She slumped sideways across the corpse of her son.

Ayna watched in stunned bewilderment. She looked up at her mother, who had one hand over her mouth as if she were going to be sick.

One of the soldiers noticed them standing there and began moving in their direction. Nurbanu snapped out of her daze, swept Ayna up into her arms, turned on her heels, and fled.

Gunfire was breaking out sporadically from all directions. Somewhere Ayna heard a man's voice yelling: "The Armenians are coming! They are coming! The siege is broken!"

14

A dull light was skulking in through the window when Alana woke with a start, sweating and shivering, the pillow damp beneath her face. Her eyes, blinking, saw the peak of the Giferspitz shining gold in the light of the sinking sun.

The dream that had startled her awake was still playing its last scene over and over in her mind, superimposed on the fading sunlit mountain, blurring with her tears.

On the far side of her bedroom door she could hear the muffled sound of her father talking, and the familiar tone of her mother's voice raised in high emotion, which her father was trying to quell. Alana couldn't make out their words, but she could guess the import.

Mother and father. She mentally corrected herself: *John and Catherine.* If what they were telling her was true, they were not her mother and father, and everything – all certainty, all foundations, all love – had broken and been cast to the winds. Everything was false, everything was deception and lies.

The dream – a scatter of disjointed fragments – wouldn't die down. It wasn't the first time she had dreamt such things, and she was afraid it wouldn't be the last. Reaching back beyond the dream memory, like a child floundering in water out of her depth, looking for a grown-up's hands to lift her, all she could catch hold of was the waking memory of that conversation on top of the mountain. In its way, that was worse.

The moment the cable car door opened at the top of the run, Alana walked out and strode through the little station building, leaving her father in the car.

Out on the hilltop, in front of the Berghaus Wispile, the mountaintop restaurant, a dozen or so early-morning skiers were heading for the slopes. Alana, scarcely aware of her surroundings, strode past them along the path that descended the side of the ridge. Her mind was a mess of confused images and words, her feelings scattered and jumbled. Unconsciously, she was heading in the direction of her father's cabin, which stood by a small copse of spruce and pines below the ridge-back on the western side of the mountain.

John Fulton's heart had shrunk and cracked in his chest when she stormed out of the cable car. He stood for a few moments, too afraid to face the devastation he'd just set loose. Finally, gathering up his courage, he went after her.

He guessed where she would go and found her standing in front of the little cabin, her back turned, staring stonily at the view while he delved in his pockets for the key. The door swung open with a woody moan, and he went in. It was as cold inside the cabin as it was outside, and John busied himself kindling a fire in the stove. He heard the door close behind him and the light scuff of a boot on the boards. That was reassuring; so far, Alana was acting exactly the way she always had when she was angry and upset with him. There was nothing new or frightening there. So far. Once he'd got a good blaze going, he turned to find her sitting on the high-backed wooden settle in the corner.

She still wouldn't look at him.

John closed the stove door and sat on a stool. He stared down at his hands as he talked, as if he were reading from a script. Thinking back on this later, Alana realized that that was exactly what he *was* doing – reciting words he'd long been preparing in private, maybe for years.

"I had a good friend," he said. "His name was James Aldridge. You maybe don't remember him, but you met him when you were a child …"

Alana sighed heavily, and John glanced at her.

"I promise this is going somewhere, honey. There's a lot to tell, and this where it starts. We were in college together – James was in pre-law while I was a freshman. He wasn't cut out to be an attorney; he crashed out of law school in his junior year and took off to become a reporter. While I was graduating from Yale like a good little robot, James trekked halfway across Soviet-occupied Afghanistan, nearly got killed twice by different sides, and sold his reports to the *New York Times*."

John looked at Alana, who was staring sightlessly at the floor, as if she wasn't even listening. But he knew she was digesting every word.

"After I'd got Excorpora off the ground, I was looking to set up a cable news service. CNN was in its early days then, and the market was wide open. They were the first twenty-four-hour news channel in America, and we were the second. Anyhow, I brought James on board as foreign news and intelligence editor. He'd built up connections in the CIA's Middle East service, as well as on the jihadi side, that gave us scoops like you wouldn't believe.

"In 1988 James went to Azerbaijan to cover the conflict with Armenia. They were both Soviet satellites in those days. The relaxation of rule from Moscow under Gorbachev had let loose all kinds of frictions in the provinces, and boy did the Azerbaijanis and Armenians have frictions. Centuries of strife and rivalry. The big bone of contention was a territory called Nagorno-Karabakh."

"I know," said Alana flatly, without taking her eyes off the floorboards. "They had a civil war over it."

"Okay. Well, James spent most of the next three and a half years covering that war. In late 1991 he got a major lead on a CIA monitoring operation in Karabakh, a combined set-up involving the CIA, the State Department, and a couple of European agencies. They were trying to jump ahead of the United Nations – you wouldn't believe how slowly they can act when there are lives being lost."

Alana stole a glance at her father. He caught her eye and smiled wanly; her expression hardened, and she looked away again.

"James loved the Middle East and Asia," John continued, "but Azerbaijan had a special place in his heart. He told me about how remote it felt from the West, but also how strangely civilized. A tiny country between Russia and Iran, on the coast of the Caspian Sea. Beautiful place." John nodded toward the window. "A lot of mountains. The war was essentially an ethnic clash. What else are wars ever about? *My group is more precious than your group and we want your stuff, which by the way happens to be our stuff that you stole.* Armenians and Azerbaijanis both claimed entitlement to the same tracts of country, and they were tearing bloody hunks off one another over it. The CIA team's task was to scout the situation, establish relations with local leaders, and feed intelligence back to our government."

"Why?" Alana was interested in spite of herself.

"Peacekeeping, ostensibly, but there were other reasons. Besides being beautiful, Azerbaijan possesses a whole heaven and earth of oil – enough to make Russia and the West take notice."

For reasons she couldn't even begin to guess at, Alana had started feeling uncomfortable, on top of her boiling anger. Something was nagging at the back of her mind. She stood up and went to the window; taking off her thick padded glove, she scraped a fingernail along the edge of the pane where there was a smear of old dried paint on the ice-cold glass. She dug hard at it with her nail, relishing the distracting pain it caused her.

"There was a place," her father went on, his voice dull and distant in her ears. "Right in the heart of Karabakh, among the mountains. A small town named Khojali. It was filled with refugees from the fighting. Both sides wanted that town, because small as it was, it had Karabakh's only airport, which made it a major strategic asset."

The numb sensation turned to a tingling. Alana thought she was getting sick – her father's voice was growing dimmer and duller in her ears, but his words clanged like bells. Trying to push it away, she conjured up her birth certificate in her mind, focusing on its comforting words – Alana May Fulton ... County of Los Angeles ... Beverly Grove ... mother ... father.

"As far as I can recall from what James told me," he was saying, "the field unit established contact with an Azeri man in the area, a potentially valuable asset, a kind of patriarch who had a lot of influence in Karabakh. He lived in the hills and had family in Khojali town. His son and daughter-in-law and their three children."

Alana thought she was going to faint. What she felt wasn't exactly dizziness – it was more like electrodes being attached to her head, but instead of being on the skin, they were plugging right into her brain. She was being hooked up to something. Images came trickling along the wires into her mind; images she'd seen in dreams. A house ... a woman's face ... children ... and blood.

And suddenly she knew.

131

"You've told me this before," she said.

Her father's voice stopped. There was a long, aching silence, then: "No, I never told you."

Her fingers gripped the window frame. "You did. You must have."

"I didn't, honey." She turned around. Her father's face had turned gray under its creased, leathery tan. "I couldn't tell you before … I wouldn't."

"You did, you told me. You told me the story!" she yelled at him. "I didn—"

She screamed: "*Then why do I already know it?*"

What enraged her so much wasn't that he was lying to her – pretending he'd never told her something he obviously had. It was something else, something much deeper and more painful. Alana couldn't remember all of the story, but she knew it was horrible – a story no father should tell his little girl, even when she had grown up. It was a story from a nightmare.

"You remember what happened?" her father asked.

"I … I don't know." There were tears and her voice was cracking. "I know they all … they all died."

"La-La, honey …"

She stared at the mountains and the sky, turning from mauve to sapphire at the horizon. "I see blood," she said in a hoarse whisper. "I see it in my dreams. White cloth dyed red in blood. Red everywhere, running red, ground stained red." She looked at him through a blur of tears. "Why?"

John couldn't meet her gaze, and looked down at his hands, digging his fingernails into a patch of callus at the base of his thumb.

"When James first met his contact – the old patriarch – Khojali was surrounded by Armenian forces. They went on holding the place under siege for months. Then, on February 25, 1992, they moved in and captured the town. The Azerbaijani inhabitants hid or tried to flee. The Armenians massacred them all."

Alana could see it in her head. The images from her dreams – the lines of people across a hillside, the angry faces, the fearful, hunched figures, the blood, and the corpses.

"The old man's son tried to get his family to safety, making for the hills. They never got there. I don't know exactly what happened, James never found out, but I guess they got caught." John took a deep breath, like a sob, and his voice cracked as he went on: "The only survivor was a little girl. She was only four years old. James was in Baku at the time, but a couple of weeks later he returned to Karabakh and visited the old man and met the little girl. The old man told James the story I've just told you."

John paused and glanced at his daughter, then went back to concentrating on the patch of callus, gouging it as if trying to erase it.

"The grandfather wasn't able to look after the little girl, couldn't give her the care she needed, and naturally he was scared in case the Armenian soldiers came there and killed both of them. He was planning to retreat eastward to Baku with a group of his followers. He begged James to take his little granddaughter with him to safety. 'Take her to America,' he said. 'Give her a chance of life.' James was such a good guy, you wouldn't believe it, there wasn't a thing he wouldn't do for people who needed him. He did as the old man asked. He took the child with him. He pulled every string and called in every favor he was owed to get that girl into the United States. He brought her to DC, where Catherine and I were living at the time. James wasn't married, and with his way of life he couldn't devote time to looking after a child. So he came to me."

John paused. "Catherine was reluctant. You know what she's like, but give her her due, she agreed to take care of that little girl. We grew to love her, and we made her ours. We gave her our last name, Fulton, and kept the name James had given her: Alana."

There was silence. At last Alana turned to look at him and saw that there were tears running down his face. "And we love her still," he said. "But she's a grown woman now – and such a fine woman! And the time is overdue for her to know the truth."

"Why didn't you ever tell me before?"

John shook his head. "We intended to. I promise you we did. But as you started to learn English, so we could talk with you, you seemed to have no knowledge of your former life. It was like you'd totally blanked it out. And you seemed so happy with us, we couldn't bear to stir up traumatic memories. You were like a fresh new bloom, so we just let you be. We thought maybe we'd be able to tell you once you were grown up, but … well, the moment never seemed right."

Alana gazed steadily at him. "What's my real name?"

"I … We never knew. James had taken to calling you Alana, and he told us that your grandfather – the patriarch – had said it was a suitable name for you."

John reached out and cupped his daughter's face in his hands. "I'm so sorry, my darling. I am so, so sorry."

Through her bedroom door, Alana could hear Catherine crying, and John's voice murmuring, trying to comfort her.

All the way from the cabin to the cable car station, Alana and her father had walked in silence; they rode the gondola down the mountain in silence, and walked home in silence through the busy fairytale streets.

Lying on her bed, Alana watched the sky darken and the jagged tree-line turn black, the lights coming on in the windows of the Palace Hotel. At last she understood the dreams, and why they disturbed her so much more than mere nightmares should; they were not dreams, but the remnants of memories.

Her thoughts kept returning to her birth certificate. How could anything be true if *that* was false? Her father had told her a wild story about how James Aldridge had approached a contact high up in the CIA asking for help, threatening to publicize everything the agency was up to in Azerbaijan. Strings were pulled, and John and Catherine were provided with all the official paperwork they needed to legitimize their little girl. There were even corresponding entries in the records of Los Angeles County and the Social Security Administration. As far as government was concerned, "Alana May Fulton" was as real and bona fide a person as anyone else in the United States.

And her father expected her to *believe* that? What he hadn't been able to explain was why somebody in Baku would be paying Howard to keep watch on her and why somebody seemed to be trying to kill her. Were they the same person? That man with the deformed jaw who had appeared in Cambridge was the proof that none of this was imaginary. She couldn't get his face out of her head; the pitiless brutality of it terrified her.

Now that she knew the truth about her dreams, they had become more frightening than ever. Alana was caught like a nut in a vice, between the yearning to fill in the voids between the fleeting images and a dread of confronting the terrible things her unconscious mind had suppressed.

It was a little after seven in the evening when Alana raised herself from her bed, standing with some difficulty on limbs that seemed to have turned to jelly.

She'd eaten nothing all day. Her parents had knocked softly on her door several times asking if she needed anything, but despite the desperate love in their voices, she had asked them to leave her be. Hunger was gnawing at her. She opened the door quietly.

All three of them – John, Catherine, and Howard – were sitting at the kitchen table in silence, and all three looked up as she came in. Howard was visibly nervous as she crossed the floor. Her father's gaze darted anxiously back and forth between Alana and Catherine, whose eyes were red from crying.

Alana stopped. "I just," she began. "I just wanted to say I understand. I mean, not *'understand'* – I don't understand anything right now – but the one thing I get is your part in this. You'll always be my mother and father, and—"

Catherine rose to her feet and tried to embrace her, but Alana stepped back. "Don't," she said. "Just don't. I love you, but I'm not sure I can ever forgive you."

"We're so sorry, *amore*," Catherine sobbed. "So, so sorry." She turned to John, who wrapped her in his arms and kissed her on the forehead.

Alana yearned to be hugged by her father's long, strong arms, but she couldn't let it happen, not yet. She kept her eyes on Howard, who remained seated, watching the scene with a distant, inscrutable expression.

15

In the snug, luxurious comfort of the Rialto Bar, Howard munched eagerly at a limp slice of sospiri pizza, admiring the large black and white photo of James Dean hanging on the wall behind Alana. She hated that photo – which was why she tended to sit right under it, because it was the only place in the Rialto from which it couldn't be seen. She often complained about Americanism obtruding into the Swiss setting. Howard loved the picture; James Dean was his idol, and his greatest aspiration was to be like him. Right now, he was wondering whether he ought to take up smoking again.

Alana was preoccupied with her phone. Her fork hovered over an exquisitely golden folded crêpe with its circles of raspberry coulis and rosettes of cream, occasionally moving in as if to cut into it, then veering away as she found something new to look at on the screen.

Howard sighed. "Are you gonna eat that crêpe or absorb it by osmosis?"

"Uh-huh," she murmured vaguely. Her fork cut off a golden triangle, swept it through the crimson coulis and raised it to her lips … where it hovered for a moment before descending again to the plate. Alana frowned at her screen, scrolling eagerly.

"Did you know," she said, "Azerbaijan was one of the first countries anywhere in the world to grant women's suffrage? *Two years* before the United States? After the fall of the Russian Empire in 1918 Azerbaijan became a democratic republic – the first one in the Muslim world – and gave *full voting rights* to women. America didn't give us that until 1920." Her voice was hoarse with excitement. "Britain granted partial suffrage in 1918, but it took another ten years to give us equal footing with men. *Azerbaijan was way ahead of the whole western world* – can you believe that?"

Howard nodded encouragingly, but she wasn't looking at him. He sighed again and shifted his gaze to a portrait of Sophia Loren.

Two days had passed since Alana had learned the truth. If it *was* the truth – she was still a long way from really believing it. She had recovered from the initial shock, and the grief over the identity that had been revealed as a sham had begun to transform into a yearning to discover her newly-revealed past. Another person might have taken much longer to begin their recovery, but the hunger for knowledge that had driven Alana through life was aiding her now. The urge to research whatever she didn't understand was so honed and trained that it had become an instinctive response to stress and the fear of uncertainty.

She had probed her father for information about Azerbaijan, but there was little there to be extracted. Her own dream memories were too fragmented to help her. They were like disjointed movie clips, without context, sometimes giving a bright and detailed pan across a scene, more often distorted and clouded or shorn of meaning. James Aldridge, the only person who had known all the facts, could tell her nothing; after two decades on the front lines, he had got in the way of a sniper's bullet in Afghanistan in 2004. With his death, any chance of ever learning the full truth about her past had gone. All she had left was this – to go in at the ground floor and research the country of her birth.

What she learned fascinated her. She knew little bits and pieces about the rich prehistory of Caucasia – the region including modern Georgia, Armenia, and Azerbaijan – through its connection with her own research on Neolithic Turkey. She knew about the waves of Scythians from central Eurasia that had swept over the Caucasian Mountains in the Iron Age, and the Medes from Persia, and Alexander the Great's conquering horde, and the Turkic influence from the west. And she was dimly aware of the Kingdom of Caucasian Albania, the prehistoric culture that had practiced the Zoroastrian religion and built the foundation of what would become Azerbaijan.

Alana's mind, being that of a trained researcher, absorbed the new knowledge quickly, but there was always more to know. She felt a grief distinct from the sense of losing her family and home, a deep sorrow that she had not chosen the archaeology of her homeland as her specialism. How could she not have known? Surely some kind of ancestral instinct should have pointed the way?

Meanwhile, the little household in the apartment above the Promenade adapted itself to new circumstances. Catherine Fulton, coming down from the emotional peak of the first day, had begun acting the part of the tragic heroine, as if this were all about her. Her nerves were shot to pieces, she said, and she simply must depart the hive of Gstaad for a secluded spa center on Lake Como in the Italian Tyrol.

John, dismayed at his own inability to do anything to help his daughter, had also retreated into himself, spending most of his time in his cabin, reading, listening to old Appalachian folk songs, and carving wood with a hunting knife.

Alana and Howard had the apartment to themselves most of the time, and on the second day he had persuaded her to venture out.

They'd strolled the full length of the snow-decked Promenade, bought chocolates and croissants at the Early Beck boulangerie, eaten lunch by a roaring fire in the rustic Alpine setting of the Hotel Olden, drunk Moscow mules in the lobby bar of the Palace Hotel.

But all the time, Alana's mind was elsewhere. Gstaad impinged on her only as a backdrop, whose childhood associations made her feel safe. The lethal danger that had come for her in England receded. She figured there was no way anyone could trace her or Howard to here. She was secure, undiscoverable. They'd probably assumed she'd hidden out in England or returned to America.

All the while, Alana hoped that her research might yield some kind of clue to why she was of so much interest to somebody in Baku that they were willing to pay diamonds for information about her and – assuming the same people were responsible – put a killer on her tail.

Alana and Howard walked side by side up the steps into the Gstaad Palace Hotel. Time was when they would have been hand in hand or arm in arm; Alana wondered if the distance between them now would ever be bridgeable. She had once believed that she loved Howard, but that feeling had been nourished by Hawaiian sun and her own contentment. He had breached her trust by spying on her – even if he believed it was for benign reasons – and his behavior in England had revealed aspects of his character that she had suspected before, but never seen out in the open.

"Lanzy," he said as they entered the lobby. "I have to dash to the bathroom. Wait for me?"

"Okay, but no Hollywood refreshments, right?"

He gave her his innocent little boy look. "I'm stone clean, baby. Order up a couple of mules, yeah? I'll be right back."

He was gone before she could object. They were supposed to be going skiing on the Eggli slopes, and there was only a couple of hours of good daylight left. Alana always skied from the Palace; they'd known her since she was a kid, and they gave her a special deal on ski rental. Muttering under her breath, she ordered two Moscow mules in the lobby bar and sat down to wait.

The drinks came, and there was no sign of Howard. Daintily lifting the slice of lime out of the little copper mug and laying it on a coaster, she sipped at the sharp vodka-ginger ale cocktail.

A man sitting alone a few tables away caught her eye. He smiled momentarily, then looked away. Alana felt a tiny rush of attraction, which made her take a second look. He was about her age; his hair was a fairish brown and combed back, his features were a little off from being perfectly handsome, but firm and pleasant, and he had the brightest blue eyes she had ever seen. They were gentle, and his brief smile was warm. He was dressed in a skiing jacket and jeans, as if he'd just that moment come from the slopes, and was sipping a beer and reading a magazine.

It took only a moment to register these details. Alana suppressed the feeling of attraction and looked away.

She took out her phone and opened an e-book she'd been reading, about Caucasian Albania under the Caliphate. Instinct told her that somewhere in all this history she would find a clue as to what was happening to her. Most of the academic historical literature was in Russian, and this was the only thing she'd been able to find in English. If nothing else, it was helping to orientate her on the big picture. In the early medieval period, there had essentially been two states: Armenia and Albania. The latter, which had no connection with European Albania, consisted of modern Azerbaijan with various other territories tacked on. The ancient Zoroastrian religion had been replaced by Christianity by the middle of the first millennium AD, but then the region came under the sway of the Islamic Caliphate in the early seventh century. The array of Arabic, Persian, and Turkic place names, layered with Armenian and Azerbaijani, was infuriatingly opaque, and Alana wondered whether she would ever master it.

She was so absorbed in reading, that it was only when she took the last sip of her mule and set down the empty cup that she realized Howard still hadn't returned from the bathroom. He'd been gone for over twenty minutes.

Irritated, Alana strode across the lobby, looking for the men's room. She rapped on the door. "Howard?" she called. "Howard, are you in there?" Nothing. Glancing around, she opened the door a little way; there was nobody inside, so she stepped in. The place was empty. All the stall doors were open and unoccupied.

She took out her phone and called him. "Sorry. The number you have reached is unavailable right now. Please try again later." She tried his other phone, the one he reserved exclusively for business calls, but that just rang and rang. With a rising feeling of alarm, she called both numbers several times, with the same response.

There was no sign of him in the ski rental place or any of the hotel's other bars and restaurants. It wasn't the first time this had happened; he'd probably hooked up with some Hollywood pal or a director he wanted to suck up to. Gstaad was full of them at this time of year. Probably forgotten all about her. "Well, the hell with him," she muttered.

Alana walked out of the front entrance and stood at the top of the steps, looking out for a cab. She was so preoccupied she didn't notice that the attractive man with the curly hair and bright blue eyes had followed her out of the bar and was watching her from just inside the entrance.

She went to the bottom of the steps. One of the regular black minivans that shuttled guests from the hotel to the train station and the ski slopes was just pulling in at the pickup point. The driver got out and held open the door for her.

"I guess that's fate," she said. "Can you drop me at the Promenade?" He gave a little bow of assent.

Alana stepped inside and sat. There was one other passenger in the rearmost seat, fast asleep and breathing noisily. Curious, she turned to look at him just as the door slammed. There was a movement in the corner of her eye, and in an instant something hard and cold was clamped over her mouth and nose; there was a hiss of gas, drowned out by the engine starting. She managed to struggle spasmodically and give out a muted scream before her muscles went limp and she lost consciousness.

In her last waking moment, it registered in Alana's mind that the man sleeping in the backseat had been Howard.

In a long, narrow stone corridor deep beneath the old palace of Shusha, a single electric lamp burned yellow, its pallor seeming to deepen the gloom as much as dispel it. Beneath the lamp was an iron-bound door, its timbers darkened and hardened by age to the color and texture of stone. Behind this door lay somebody's future.

Far above this dismal passage were the floors containing the apartments where the old khan's children had lived. Their drapery and carpets and fine furnishings were long gone, replaced by bars and steel beds and crude latrines. The family wing was now a prison, and its echoes carried throughout the building, even to this lonely subterranean passageway.

The stillness of the passage was broken by footsteps. Vartan came striding from the darkness and halted, gazing at the impenetrable ancient door for a moment, then drew a long key from his pocket

143

and inserted it in the lock. It turned with a squeal, and the door groaned like an animal as Vartan pushed it inward. He switched on a flashlight and stepped inside.

It had once been a storeroom or pantry; now it resembled a dungeon. The plaster was green with rot and crumbling away from the stone. The flagstone floor was damp and littered with the droppings of rats; as the flashlight swept round, two of them scurried away into the darkness.

This would do. She would not elude Hayk a second time, and what more appropriate place in which to end her days could be found for her than this? Was this not her rightful home, after all? Soon she would return to it, and to the company of her ancestors.

Alana surfaced from a dreamless sleep to find that she couldn't move, and seemed to have gone blind. Her senses were utterly disorientated. She was startled by a muffled thump and felt her body jolted forward by a sudden lurch of the ground beneath her. She could hear a car engine idling softly, and realized she was sitting upright. She was in a vehicle, slumped on the seat.

Suddenly there was a noise like a roll of thunder right beside her ear; she gasped and shied away from it, even as her brain told her it was just a vehicle door sliding open. A hand seized the back of her hair, yanking her head up, and a male voice with a strange accent snarled in her ear: "Make one foolish act and it goes bad for you."

She was pulled out of the vehicle, staggering, feeling snow beneath her feet; her vision began to return, giving her nothing but a dazzling blur of white.

"Now walk," said the voice, pushing her forward. Alana stumbled, the hand still gripping her hair. Something hard pressed into the small of her back. She didn't need to see it to know it was a gun.

Her vision was beginning to focus. She stumbled a few steps, and a dark blur appeared in front of her against the white background, resolving into the shape of a closed van parked by the roadside. The van and the hotel vehicle were pulled in at the side of a narrow country road. On one side was a wire fence and a rising snow-covered hillside dotted with trees, on the other a stony-bottomed stream with a thin trickle of water flowing through the ice. Alana looked back, and instantly wished she hadn't; the minivan driver was slumped in his seat, with what remained of his face pressed against the side window, which was covered in his blood. Now Alana understood the hard thump she'd heard as she woke up – the sound of a silenced pistol in the enclosed space.

Unlocking the rear door of the van, her abductor pushed her inside. As he did so, she saw his face at last, and her gorge rose. It was the very same youthful Middle Eastern face, its beauty marred by the brutally misshapen jaw.

He noticed her staring at his disfigurement and slapped her hard across the face. "You want same, like this? Not move or you get." He went back to the minivan and returned a moment later pushing Howard along. He was in a state of abject, weeping terror, stumbling through the snow and cowering as he was shoved violently into the back of the van beside Alana.

"Wait!" she said as the man went to close the door. "Who are you?"

He paused and gazed intently into her eyes. "You not know?" he said. She shook her head, and he leaned close. "I am death for you," he said softly.

The door slammed shut, leaving Alana in darkness, with only the sound of Howard's weeping for company. The engine started, the vehicle swayed and pulled away suddenly, throwing them both off balance. It drove along for a minute or so, accelerating, then braked hard and took a tight right turn. Alana, holding on to part of the vehicle's interior frame, sensed they were heading uphill, along one of the hundreds of steep, winding mountain roads. Were they still near Gstaad? She hadn't seen enough of the landscape to recognize it, and had no idea how long she'd been unconscious. It was still daylight, so not long, she guessed. She searched her pockets, but her phone had vanished, along with her purse and watch.

"Howard, do you know what time it is?" No response. "Howard!"

"Hngh?"

"Do you have your phone? Or your watch?"

He fumbled at his pockets. Alana could see him dimly in the light leaking in through a vent. She had never seen a person so scared; he was haggard, eyes wide, staring, tearful.

"No," he said. "It's gone."

Alana swore under her breath. She moved closer to him. "Howard, there has to be a way out of this, but you're gonna have to help me." There was no response. "Howard, I need your help. We don't have much time; we have to figure out a way out of this *right now*."

"I can't," Howard whined. "We're gonna die. I never signed up for this! I never wanted *this*!"

He started to cry, his sobs interspersed with bitter complaints and curses against life and the world, and against her for getting him into this. Watching him, the last trace of affection Alana felt for him withered and died. She'd always known, deep down, that this was the fundamental truth of Howard's character. She couldn't even feel pity; her heart shut against him.

Bracing herself against the swaying and jolting, Alana tried the rear door handle. Locked, of course, and the side door too. She searched the dark interior, hoping to find a wrench or a jack, but there was nothing but a coil of climbing rope, a pair of boots, a tarp, and a plastic snow shovel. If there was some way to engineer an escape with these objects, she couldn't imagine what it was.

Her senses told her that they had stopped ascending so steeply and were driving along a more or less level road with frequent bends. Evidently, they hadn't reached a highway yet, which meant they couldn't be very far out of Gstaad – unless their captor was taking them deeper into the Alps, in which case they might be in the middle of territory Alana knew nothing about.

She was on her feet, probing the vent in the roof, when the van suddenly braked hard, throwing her off balance and hurling her against the plywood bulkhead. The vehicle slewed, skidding, then righted itself and came to a halt.

Silence. Even Howard's sobbing stopped, and he looked up from behind his hands. The sound of the driver's door opening. Footsteps crunched on the snow, and the rear door was flung open, letting in a flood of dazzling light. The long, blunt finger of the pistol pointed at them, and the face with its deformed jaw peered in. "Give me that," he said, gesturing at the snow shovel. His face was taut, and his voice shook with anger. "Careful and slow."

Alana didn't take her eyes off the pistol's hollow black muzzle as she reached for the wooden handle of the shovel and pushed it slowly toward him. He took it and slammed the door violently.

As if in answer, there was a deep, grinding rumble, vibrating the whole vehicle: almost like thunder, but deeper, like the sound of the earth beneath tilting on its axis. There was a violent thump against the side of the van, and it lurched sideways. A deafening metallic drumming filled the vehicle as if the sides and roof were being battered with mallets and crushed. Alana crouched on the floor with her hands over her head.

Eventually it stopped. In the hush that followed, Alana was surprised to find herself still alive and unharmed. The van was filled with light, and after a moment's dull puzzlement she realized that the rear door had sprung open. She crept warily to it and peeked out.

Immediately she recoiled in terror. The rear of the vehicle was poised at the edge of a precipice. Catching her breath and looking again, Alana saw that the van had slewed across the road and come to rest with its back end against the crash barrier. There was a sheer drop of maybe ten feet or so, then a snowy slope

Climbing gingerly onto the barrier, Alana looked around the van. There had been an avalanche. Not a major one, but enough to bury the road for fifty yards ahead. The van was half-buried. A few trees had come down with the slide, including a hefty spruce which had partially crushed the vehicle's roof. Alana could see no sign of the armed man. Figuring it out, she guessed there must have been a small slide blocking the road; he'd taken the shovel to try and clear it, not realizing it was a precursor to an avalanche. A fatal misjudgment.

She ducked back inside. "Come on!" she said to Howard. "Let's make a run for it!" She grabbed the coil of rope and slung it over her shoulder. "Come on!"

Howard didn't move; he just stared in bewilderment. "I can't," he said.

"Come on, we have to go." He just shook his head. Alana sighed. "Okay. I'll get help. Stay warm."

She climbed back out onto the barrier, inched along it, and scrambled up onto the bank of snow that had half-buried the vehicle. Still no sign of the gunman. Alana was about to head back down the road when she had an idea.

Clambering over the snow, she peered in through the driver's window. Inside, on the passenger seat, was a duffel. It must contain the man's supplies, and maybe more weapons. Out in the wilderness, with no knowing where she was, she needed all the help she could get.

The door was blocked by snow, so she found a rock and smashed the window, then crawled inside. She had her hand on the bag when she saw the gunman, and gasped.

He was lying on his back, a few yards ahead of the vehicle, a black smudge on the snow. The avalanche had buried him up to his chest, and he was bleeding from a gash in the side of his head. He had the shovel in one hand, and had been trying to dig himself out. His pistol lay on the snow nearby. He stopped digging and stared at Alana.

Without pausing, she backed hurriedly out through the shattered window, leaving the bag behind. The man scrabbled frantically for the pistol, but it was just beyond his reach. In a fit of panic, instead of heading for the clear road, Alana ran up the nearby slope toward a dense stand of pines.

As she reached the first tree, she glanced back. The man, stretching desperately, got hold of the pistol grip and aimed. Alana pressed on up the hill. A shot slapped a chunk of bark from a pine a yard from her hand; another kicked up a puff of snow; then she felt a sharp blow to her right hip. Ignoring it, she kept running, running, running, into the trees.

16

Ayna pressed herself back against the truck wheel, drawing her knees up to her chest, covering her ears with her hands. The gunfire was still going on outside, echoing in the streets. The refugee boy, Neymar, crouched in the dim light, watching her anxiously.

She didn't know where she was, just that it was a tiny, dank garage under somebody's house. It smelled of oil and gasoline and mold, and was deep in gloom, with only a wintry moonlight coming through its grimy windows.

There was a distant scream, then a gunshot cracked right outside the door. Ayna flinched and squeezed her eyes tight shut. She knew the soldiers must find their way in soon.

Everything was a confused jumble in her memory – how she had ended up here, alone with the refugee boy; how she had got so much blood on her blouse and sweater; what had happened to her family.

It was all just fragments.

Mrs. Radjabov crumpling over her son's bleeding body in the road; her mother's hand gripping hers, sweeping her up into her arms; being pressed against her mother's swollen belly, her chest heaving as she ran. Others were running too, yelling, screaming.

When they turned the corner, Armenian soldiers were already in the street outside her father's medical office. Ayna heard her mother gasp. In the gathering dusk, Nurbanu carried her daughter around the back of the building, along the edge of the garden and up to the house. Ayna's father was there, and her brother Hakan and sister Leyli, hiding behind the couch in the lounge, terrified.

Tengiz told his wife to take the children and flee the village. "They're saying the road to Aghdam is open for evacuation," he said. "Our militia will guard everyone. Go! Take the children. I have my patients."

"Your patients will be killed! *You* will be murdered! I won't go without you. If you don't come with us now, you are killing us all."

Ayna closed her eyes tightly and clung to her brother and sister.

There was a blank, and then …

Her ankles freezing in the snow when her mother set her down on the far bank of the winding Gargar river … Finding her brother Hakan's hand in hers as they trudged through the frozen marsh and the woods with hundreds of other villagers, friends and neighbors among them, but all of them strangers in the darkness … the sound of gunfire in the distance …

Resting by the forked bole of a tree. Ayna felt Hakan shivering beside her; he and Leyli had been indoors when the attack began, and weren't dressed for the cold. Hakan's face was pinched and his teeth chattering. "Here," she said, and took off her precious pink woolen scarf, offering it to him.

Hakan shook his head. "No. Leyli needs it more."

Leyli was hugged close to their father; her lips and eyes were growing dark and bluish. Ayna draped the scarf around her sister's neck, knotting it snugly under her chin, and kissed her icy cheek.

Another blank, and then the worst part. Ayna tried to shut

151

it out of her mind, but it wouldn't go away. It felt like a dream, because it made no sense.

Her mother's face contorted with anguish in the bright glare of flashlights. "Run, Ayna, run!" Somehow, they were back in their own house again, in the lounge; her mother was being held by men whose faces Ayna couldn't see. Her back was against the sideboard, where the silver samovar stood. Ayna stood rooted to the spot. "Run, baby, run," her mother pleaded. "*Please*, baby, run my sweet—"

And then there was blood; her mother's belly, full of new life, was split open. A man's hand forced her head back over the samovar. The knife sliced through fabric, through flesh, and the blood was everywhere. Ayna felt a warm splash of it across her face.

Then she ran.

Neymar had found her in the street, crouched against the garden wall where they had first met, paralyzed with shock.

He didn't know where his own parents were; they had either fled without him or were already dead. He'd been to the hostel, but it was in chaos, with Armenian and Russian soldiers everywhere. There were Soviet armored vehicles in the streets now. Neymar had crept from street to street, looking for a way out, hoping to find his parents, and instead had found Ayna all alone.

Taking her hand, Neymar pulled her to her feet and together they flitted through the darkness.

A street near the school, suddenly soldiers all over the place; a tank had closed off the end of the street, and soldiers were going from house to house.

"In here," said Neymar, and then Ayna was on her knees, crawling through a gap in a rotting wooden door. The space inside was confined and reeked of car smells and decay. Ayna stood up and banged her head on something; in the faint moonlight coming in through the cracked panes she saw the outline of an old pickup truck.

"Nobody lives here," said Neymar. "Maybe the bad men won't look."

How long they sat in the dank garage under the abandoned house Ayna didn't know. Left to herself, she might have remained there, incapacitated by terror, until cold or hunger killed her. But Neymar wanted to find his family, and he wasn't about to leave her behind. Once more he coaxed her to her feet.

It was darker than ever, and the village was growing quiet when they crept outside.

17

Alana leaned against a tree and looked cautiously back the way she had come. The road and the van were hidden from view by pines, and the snow-covered slope between was clear. There was no sign of her abductor.

There was a searing pain in her right hip. She recalled feeling a sharp knock, and assumed she'd collided with a branch. The denim was torn as if by a saw blade, and blood was seeping. She'd been shot. Probing the wound gingerly, she found it was little more than a graze, but it was bleeding and painful as hell, and she had nothing to bind it with.

She took another glance back. He must be trapped under the avalanche still. Limping and holding on to her hip, Alana set off again through a copse of spruces and pines.

The ground leveled off and the trees gave way. A rail fence crossed her path, and Alana clambered over it, wincing. She found herself on a narrow lane. From here she had a partial view across the valley through the trees. There was a big ridge on the far side, maybe a mile away, with a cable car run, but Alana couldn't see enough to recognize it.

Weighing up her options, she headed right – uphill – fearing that going downhill might take her back to the scene of her escape.

She hadn't walked far when a narrow track cut away from the road and angled down a shallow slope to a cluster of farm buildings and a house nestled in a broad dell surrounded by trees. Pushing open the gate, she headed down the track. There was no sign of movement at the farm or the surrounding fields. Approaching the entrance to the farmyard, Alana's conscience nudged her. Did she have the right to bring danger to an innocent family? Instead of opening the gate, she climbed the fence into the field and skirted the barn.

The air was getting colder and the light beginning to fade. The clouds were darkening, and even as Alana looked up, the first big flakes of snow began to fall. She felt herself beginning to panic, and made a conscious effort to control her breathing and heart rate.

And then she saw him.

Just an impression of movement in the distance, by the pines on the far side of the dell, resolving into the shape of a dark-clad man, moving lithely, vaulting easily over a fence. Her heart pounded and her lungs convulsed, beginning to hyperventilate. A flurry of snow blurred her vision and he disappeared. But Alana knew he was there and coming for her. He'd not only tracked her; he had anticipated where she would go and headed her off.

Crouching with her back against the barn wall, she caught another glimpse of him – about two hundred yards away, heading right toward her. His head tilted slowly from side to side, scanning the snowfield. He hadn't seen her.

Keeping low, Alana moved quickly back the way she'd come, easing quietly over the fence, then went through the gate into the farmyard. Finding the barn door half open, she crept inside.

It had that barn quiet – spacious, muted, calm, thick with the odor of livestock. The concrete floor was dry and dusty, strewn with straw. A steel fence divided off the near end, where a dozen cattle stood chewing hay and watching her benignly.

Alana took two steps and froze. Standing by a steel trough in the center of the barn was a little girl, about five or six years old, dressed in a thick padded anorak and a rainbow-colored knitted hat. She stared curiously at Alana.

Holding her finger to her lips, Alana moved quickly, silently across the floor, took the girl by the hand, and led her to the other end of the barn, where there were several large stacks of hay bales.

"Who are you?" asked the girl in Swiss German.

"I'm a friend," said Alana. "We have to hide."

"Is it a game? Are you the lady from the school?"

"What?" Alana was struggling with a bale of hay, pulling it across some others to form a hiding place.

"Mommy said the lady would come get me to school if I missed another day."

"I'm not the lady from the school. Now be quiet and get in here. Shimmy down right there." She spoke a garbled mix of English and German, but the little girl seemed to understand, squatting down between the two bales, which were screened from the rest of the barn by a tall stack and roofed over by the one Alana had dragged into place.

"This is fun," said the girl softly. "I'm Ingrid. What's your name?"

Alana looked at the child in the near-darkness and squeezed her hand. "You can call me Ayna," she whispered.

What had made her think of that name? Nobody had ever called her that. An image came into her mind of a little girl crouched in terror in a garage, with her mother's blood on her skin, the soldiers shouting outside, and a little boy telling her it would be time to go soon because he needed to find his parents …

Emerging from the dizzying flash of memory, Alana gasped like a swimmer ducked beneath the water without a chance to take a breath, bursting back through the surface.

Ayna. She had been Ayna.

In the hush, with only the soft murmur of the cattle, she heard the faint scrape of a boot. Alana held her breath, listening, and shielded Ingrid with her body. Did she hear breathing? Another soft footstep, and a dark shape detached from the shadows beyond the edge of the stack of bales. It was him, creeping along cautiously, heel and toe, the long, fat silencer leading the way. He began a smooth, quick turn to cover the area behind the bales, and in the fraction of a second before his eye fell on the hiding place, Alana launched herself at him.

They landed sprawling in the dust, the pistol skittering away and clattering off the cinderblock wall. Alana was on her feet an instant ahead of the gunman, sprinting for the door.

"Halt!"

His voice sounded thin and harsh in the echoing barn. The pistol gave two rapid coughs, dirt kicking up in front of Alana's feet. She was almost at the door, bracing herself to feel the next bullet hit her square in the back. In a flash she was outside, vaulting over the gate in spite of the burning pain in her hip, over the fence, and high-tailing it across the dell.

Battling through the swirling snow, she reached the rail fence and glanced back just for a split second. He was twenty, maybe thirty yards behind her and closing. Lungs aching, Alana heaved herself over the fence, lost her footing, and went tumbling, cartwheeling down a steep wooded slope. Pine branches whipped and thrashed her all over as she slid down toward a sheer drop. The coil of rope around her body caught on a branch, and she hung over the drop for a moment before the branch cracked and she fell, coming to rest in a drift.

Alana scrambled to her feet, head spinning. The man was picking his way carefully down the slope above. Without pausing to get her bearings, Alana ran on.

She was completely disorientated. She caught a glimpse of a building in the distance and made toward it. Risking another glance back, she saw the gunman gaining on her again – closing the gap from fifty to forty yards – and summoning up her remaining energy, she slogged on through the deepening snow.

Just a few dozen yards farther on the field ended; Alana slithered down a bank and found herself on a narrow road. She began running along it, heading downhill.

Rounding a bend, she skidded to a halt. The road was blocked by an avalanche. Another one! Clambering over banks and chunks of snow discolored with soil and grass, she was nearing the far end of the fall when a vehicle came swimming into view. It had slewed across the road, presumably caught in the avalanche. Coming close, she recognized it; it was the van she had escaped from. She'd come full circle.

Alana edged past it, noticing the hole where the gunman had dug himself out, and the broken-off scoop of the shovel discarded next to it. Sliding down the last bank of packed snow onto the road surface, she rounded the back of the van, wondering if she had the strength to keep going or should just lie down and die, and whether Howard was still cowering inside the van.

He wasn't. Alana found him hunched against a telegraph pole beside the road. His face was a waxy pale gray and utterly lifeless, and a pool of blood had spread across the banked-up snow beneath. The snapped-off wooden shaft of the snow shovel had been rammed through his body.

Alana covered her mouth with her fists, gasping for air and screaming voicelessly into the padding of her gloves.

"Put your hands behind your head."

The gunman's voice was right behind her. She had no more strength or will left to run. Slowly, shakily, she raised her hands and clasped the back of her head. Instantly the coil of rope was taken from her, her wrists were seized in a strong grip, and her arms twisted and fastened together with a zip tie behind her back. The gunman swung her around, and for the second time Alana found herself looking full into his face at close range.

His features were pretty beneath the furze of stubble, marred only by the white scar and the deformed jaw. But his defining feature was the inhuman coldness in his eyes, which turned to smoldering hatred when he spoke. Hate, it seemed, was his only human quality.

He spun her round. "Walk."

Gripping her bound wrists and pressing the muzzle of the pistol into her back, he forced her to walk down the road. Alana didn't even think of resisting. She was done.

They rounded a bend and had walked about a hundred yards when a bright blue Audi came up the road toward them. Alana felt hope flutter in her chest. The gunman forced her into the middle of the road, pressing the pistol against her temple. The Audi slowed to a halt. The gunman gestured, and the terrified driver, a man in his sixties, opened the door and got out. Another gesture, and he raised his hands and walked to the side of the road. His eyes, wide as saucers behind his thick eyeglasses, stared at Alana in bewildered horror.

"In," said the gunman, pushing Alana toward the open door. "You drive."

She climbed awkwardly into the driver's seat, her hands still tied behind her back. He got in the backseat behind her and passed two loops of the rope around her neck, tying them off behind the head restraint. Alana couldn't move, let alone escape. She felt a knife prick her skin as he cut the zip tie, freeing her hands.

"Now drive."

Alana executed a shaky turn in the narrow road, and the Audi headed back down the mountain, leaving its owner stranded by the roadside, hands still raised.

At the first junction, Alana recognized the parking lot and base station of the Wasserngrat cable car. At last she knew now exactly where they were. Gstaad was near, and they were heading back toward it.

As she drove, Alana couldn't shake off the sickening image of Howard's corpse; she felt nauseous and shaken, her hands trembling on the steering wheel and fumbling the stick shift as she negotiated the steep, tight turns of the mountain road.

"Who are you?" she demanded. He said nothing. "*Who are you?*" she repeated.

The pistol jabbed her neck. "Drive. Don't talk."

In the rear-view mirror she saw him take out a phone and make a call. He spoke a language she recognized, but although it stirred memories, she couldn't understand it. All she made out was one word, which he said several times – *rendezvous*.

He hung up, and she felt another prod in the neck. "Left here."

It was the turn for Lauenen. Alana's heart sank as the faint hope that she might get another chance if they drove through Gstaad dissolved. They were now heading away from the town again, south along the valley between the Wispile and Wasserngrat – roughly the same direction they'd been going before, but on a busier road, which was less likely to be blocked. But it made no sense; none of these roads went anywhere; they were all dead ends. This one led a couple miles or so to the village of Lauenen, then split off into a maze of mountain tracks, which dissipated among the massive hills at the base of the high Alpine massif flanking the Rhône valley. You couldn't get anywhere by going this way.

Possibilities flooded into Alana's mind, none of them encouraging. Was he taking her to some remote mountain hideout? Or to a lonely spot, away from the resort area, where she could be executed?

"Who *are* you?" she demanded again. "Where are you taking me?"

"You come meet someone," he said. Alana thought she sensed something like pleasure in his voice.

"Meet someone? Who?"

"Someone who has waited long for you. Owe you great debt."

Alana's hopes revived a little at this. "What debt? Who are you talking about?"

"Big great debt," he said, and added with relish: "Only repaid in blood."

"Jesus. Who are you talking about? There is no debt."

The pistol nudged the back of her neck, and she shuddered, the car wavering on the road. "Just drive."

"If you're going to kill me, why not just do it and get it the hell over?"

"That happens, no doubt. First your help needed."

There was a rush of sound, and a helicopter swept overhead at low altitude, following the same road. As it raced ahead, the gunman said, "That is for us. Drive faster." Alana hesitated, and the pistol slammed against the side of her head. "I said faster! Go, go!"

Alana pressed her foot down hard, and the Audi shot along the winding road, careering around bends; the surface was patched with snow and ice, and the rear wheels kicked out at each turn. With no safety belt and her neck roped to the head restraint, a head-on crash would be like a hangman's drop. Alana focused every ounce of her concentration on not losing control. Finessing the car through a long S, she brushed a hedgerow, scraped a fence post, and flew onward, the entrances to farm tracks flashing by. The road took a long bend to the right, running parallel to a rushing mountain stream. On the other side, beyond a line of bare birch trees, another road converged with this one; ahead she could see the point where they met, on a steep leftward bend.

"Faster!" barked the gunman.

With a prayer, Alana put her foot to the floor, heading into the bend. With every fiber of her being focused on the car, she saw only a flicker, a sliver of gray on the other road as a speeding Peugeot shot out of the turn and T-boned the Audi.

With a superhuman strength born of animal instinct, Alana gripped the steering wheel and braced herself in the seat as the airbag exploded in her face. Her head whiplashed sideways, hitting the side window. The Audi pirouetted on the slushy ice, swept away the flimsy wire fence, and ploughed sideways several yards up the hillside before coming to rest.

Alana opened her eyes, surprised to find herself still alive. She didn't dare move. It was impossible to tell which hurt more – her neck or the side of her head. Her hands were still gripping the steering wheel, her arms embracing the airbag. With an effort, she flexed her fingers and released her grip.

There was no sound from the back seat. Glancing down, she saw the pistol lying in the front passenger footwell. She longed to reach out for it but couldn't; the rope still held her fast. "Shit," she muttered, and tried to untie it. Her fingers were shaking too much, and she couldn't even find the knots, let alone untie them.

"Relax," said a voice behind her, and she froze. "Let me." The accent was like the gunman's, but the voice was different – softer, warmer. Fingers probed at her neck, there was a slicing sound, and the ropes fell free.

The door beside her opened, and Alana looked up to see a man in a gray snow jacket. He held a pistol, trained on her abductor, who was slumped unconscious on the back seat. The man squatted down and studied her closely. He looked a lot more anxious than the last time she had seen him, in the lobby bar of the Palace Hotel, but he had the same brown hair and the brightest blue eyes.

18

As the whirling rotors slowed, Irina Ledovskaya stepped out of the helicopter into a cloud of powdery snow whipped up by its landing. Her phone earpiece rang. She clicked it.

Vartan's voice – usually coldly detached – rushed eagerly into her ear: "Does he have her?"

"He has reported success." She heard Vartan sigh with pleasure. "I am at the rendezvous. He is on his way." Irina looked back along the valley. "He reported fifteen minutes ago, and I flew past him about six miles back."

"Call me immediately when he arrives." Vartan hung up.

Taking a pair of binoculars from the helicopter, Irina surveyed the valley. The road ended at a farm on the slope below. In the other direction, the Alps rose in a sheer, impassable wall. The valley was a dead end. And yet she could see no sign of the blue Audi. Given its speed when they overflew it, it should at least be in sight by now.

Five more minutes passed. Irina paced back and forth, looking for a clearer vantage point, but aside from a few random cars and trucks, the road was empty all the way back to Lauenen.

This woman had slipped out of Hayk's grasp once before; Irina had been there, and scarcely able to believe it. The way Vartan had described Hayk's talents, it should have been impossible. Irina believed in Vartan absolutely; if he said it was so, then it was so. There must be something about this girl, or perhaps something in the way Hayk acted around her. Irina didn't know him well, but she suspected he was letting personal feelings obstruct his objectivity.

Still no sign. Something had gone wrong. Irina climbed back into the helicopter and gestured to the pilot. "Take off. Scout the road."

The rotor blades whirled, sending up a storm of snow. Taking out a handgun, Irina checked the chamber and held it on her lap.

"I'm sure there's no fracture," said the man with bright blue eyes, gently probing Alana's neck and the base of her skull. "There's some nasty bruising, but you'll live." His accent was odd, somewhere between Russian and Middle Eastern, with a touch of American, and his voice pleasantly deep.

Alana tried to turn her head to look at the man who'd abducted her, still slumped unconscious in the back seat. "Ow!"

"Careful! It will be tender for days."

"I think it's broken. Are you a doctor?"

"Look at me now. Let me see your eyes."

Alana gazed at his blue eyes while he peered into hers. "I don't think you have a concussion," he said. "We should have you checked out properly, but we're a little pressed here. That guy will wake soon, and we cannot be here when that happens."

"Who are you?"

"A friend." He carefully pushed back her hair, studying her scalp. "Slight bruising. No lacerations," he murmured. "Some grazing on your neck from that rope. Lucky it wasn't tighter. Come on, let's get you on your feet."

He helped her out of the driver's seat, and she stood unsteadily on the steep slope where the car had come to rest amid a tangle of broken fencing.

"Can you walk?" Alana took an experimental step and nearly fell over on the slippery, uneven slope. Holding the man's hand, she stepped down on to the road. She found she could stand and walk without trouble, despite shaking in every limb.

"I'm fine."

"You are sure? Good. Wait a moment …" He went back to the Audi and scooped up the pistol from the footwell. "Better to be safe." He dropped out the magazine and worked the slide, ejecting the round from the chamber. He did it with skill, clearly well accustomed to firearms. Unscrewing the silencer, he threw it, the pistol, and the magazine into the river.

"That could've been useful," said Alana.

"I hate guns."

She studied him. "Who *are* you?" she said.

He glanced at her and gave a gentle, almost embarrassed smile. "My name is Noah," he said.

"Noah," she repeated blankly.

He nodded. "And yes, I am a doctor."

"That doesn't answer my question. *Who are you*? Why are you here? I don't want to sound ungrateful or anything, but …"

"I told you. I am a friend." He nodded back toward the Audi. "But *he*," he said, "is not. I better check he has no other weapons."

He stopped suddenly and muttered in his own language. Alana turned to look. The back seat of the Audi was empty; the gunman was gone.

They both looked around, but there was no sign of him. There was a small stand of trees nearby and a stack of cut logs, and

166

farther up the slope an abandoned cabin. He could be anywhere.

"We have to leave, right now," said the young man.

The Peugeot's front end was badly crumpled, but not completely staved in. The impact must have been less violent than it felt. Alana ran to the passenger door while her rescuer jumped into the driver's seat. He turned the key, and the starter moaned fitfully.

"Come *on*," said Alana, anxiously scanning the hillside above. The starter whined again and again. "Try the other car?" said Alana.

"You're right. Come on."

The Audi's right side was so badly damaged they both had to get in the driver side, Alana wriggling across to the passenger seat. It started first time, and the blue-eyed man backed it rapidly onto the road, dragging bits of the wire fence with it and leaving behind broken pieces of trim and glass. It came free with a metallic shriek and jolted on to the asphalt. All the time, Alana's eyes scanned the trees, the logs, the cabin.

As the car reversed, performing a violent U-turn to face back the way it had come, Alana glimpsed the helicopter above the trees, about a quarter of a mile away.

"That helicopter," she said. "It's with him. He's got help!"

The car revved and lurched away, its rear end fishtailing on the ice. Alana tried to twist around to see the helicopter, but her neck hurt too badly. The passenger side door mirror was hanging off its mount. Tilting it up, she could see the helicopter descending, circling over the crash site, then she lost sight of it behind the trees and the bends in the road.

For half a minute, Alana thought they might be clear away, but then the helicopter reappeared in the mirror, climbing above the treetops about half a mile back. It swung around, tilted forward and came speeding after them.

167

"They're coming! Go faster!"

Noah put his foot down, but the half-wrecked car was struggling. A hose must have broken somewhere, and billows of steam were leaking from a gap between the bent fender and the hood. Alana, whose seat was tilted sideways by the crushed-in door, hung on to the dashboard and gritted her teeth.

The helicopter flew overhead in a rush of wind and thunder, a glittering black bat shadow, its skids barely clearing the car roof. Racing on, it banked and swerved. They were coming to a long straight, with a few scattered houses on the left and a gentle rising slope on the right. The aircraft swung side-on and began to descend. It was going to land right in the road, blocking their path.

Alana stared at it in gaping terror as they sped toward it, every detail registering on her senses: the sleek, polished black lines, the profile of the pilot through the windshield, the side door opening, and a blonde woman framed in it – even in that minuscule, split fraction of a moment, Alana recognized her as the woman she had seen in the parking garage in Cambridge. The woman's arm pointed, straight and steady, at the car. Alana saw her hand blink brightly, and believed she felt her heartbeat once between the blink and the violent cracking sound as a hole appeared in the top left of the Audi's windshield.

Then Alana was hurled sideways as Noah swung the wheel right, slamming his foot to the floor. For a moment she thought he'd been shot, but he hadn't. The ruined, speeding Audi veered over the narrow verge, smashing through the flimsy wire fence, careering through snow, Noah fighting the wheel, swerving back toward the road. Alana saw it all as a perfectly detailed, slow animation. She felt herself rising, jolted by the violent motion, and heard the metallic rending as the g-forces dragged open the jammed passenger door; as Noah turned the wheel and the helicopter's tail flashed by overhead, the door swung wildly. Alana's grip on the dashboard failed, and she was flung toward the gaping opening.

Screaming, she flailed wildly, blindly, for a hold. Something hard brushed her wrist, and her hand instinctively closed on it and gripped.

That was when her mind clicked out of its strange, sensitive state and everything returned to frenetic, blurring speed. She was halfway out of the car, with snow and broken fencing flashing past her face as it jolted back onto the road. One hand was gripping the door pillar, the other swimming in empty space, searching for a hold.

Noah shouted something in his own language, and reached across, grabbing her sleeve and hauling her back inside. Steering with one hand, he swerved to straighten up, the switch in g-force slamming the broken door back against the car; it was too damaged to shut and banged and bounced against the frame. Noah drove on as fast as the car would go.

The helicopter rose again, turned, and came after them. Alana could no longer see it – the door mirror had broken right off during their swerve through the fence – but she heard it pass overhead. The road ahead was too narrow for it to touch down again. Instead it shadowed them, racing along a few yards above and to the left, receding and approaching with the bends in the road. Noah could see the blonde woman in the open doorway.

"Stay down!" he yelled.

The rear side window shattered. Alana ducked, and Noah crouched forward over the wheel. "They will not kill you," said Noah. "But you might get hurt in the crossfire while they're killing me!"

"What?"

A bullet banged into the driver's door, and Noah flinched. The engine was steaming so badly it was obscuring the view ahead, and Alana could feel it losing power.

"Just a few seconds more," said Noah softly.

As if to punctuate his words, the driver's window shattered, and a bullet smacked into the dashboard right by Alana's hand; she yelped and shifted her grip. Instantly, the bullets started coming faster, clanging into the bodywork, thudding inside the car. Noah gasped, a red splash blooming on the sleeve of his gray jacket. The car wavered, then straightened. Alana saw the blonde woman taking careful aim at Noah. The next shot would be lethal …

Suddenly, the helicopter slowed, falling back. Alana's view was blocked by a house, then another, then a whole unbroken row. Looking up, she saw they were coming into the outskirts of Gstaad, a straggle of houses and small industrial lots. As they passed a large lumber yard, the engine seized at last, and they rolled to a stop on the forecourt.

Noah sank back in his seat. "I guess we walk from here."

"It's not far into town," said Alana. "We can be at my parents' apartment in five minutes."

She pushed at her door, which had now perversely jammed shut. Noah put his hand on her arm. "We can't go there," he said. "It's too dangerous. They will certainly look for you there."

Alana stared at him. "Who exactly *are* these people? And who are you?"

Noah glanced behind. The light was failing fast, the road receding into gloom. "We need to go. They may be coming after us already." Seeing her reluctance to move, he added: "I'll tell you as we walk."

He helped her open the jammed door. As she stepped out, she staggered and nearly fell down. In the adrenaline rush she had all but forgotten the bullet graze on her right hip; now as she moved it burned with breathtaking ferocity.

"Well I'll be damned," she muttered. "I got shot. My first time."

Noah examined it briefly. "You can walk?"

She put her weight on the leg. "Yeah, I'm fine. How about your arm?"

The left sleeve of his jacket was wet with blood. "It needs tending to." He muttered something that sounded like a curse in his own language. "I left my pack in the rental car, with my medical kit."

"That settles it. We're going to the apartment."

Alana set off walking, and Noah hurried after her. "We cannot."

"Then where?"

"You need to come with me," he said.

"Where to?"

"Baku."

Alana stopped walking so suddenly she almost skidded on the ice. "*Where?*"

"Baku," he said. "Your homeland."

"*Azerbaijan?* You *so* have to be kidding me."

"You're in danger. Deadly danger. You've seen what they can do. Alana, if you don't want to die you have to come with me."

She stared at him incredulously. His expression was difficult to read in the gathering dusk. "Yeah, that works for Schwarzenegger. You, not so much, my friend."

"I'm serious, Alana. *They* are serious."

"You don't think *I'm* serious? I don't even know who you are. Why would I go anywhere with you?"

"Very well. But come, let's walk, I'll tell you as we go. Okay, my name is Noah Abdullayev. I have been sent to ensure your safety, on behalf of people who value you highly." Noah hesitated. "I know your story, Alana."

Alana stopped walking again and stared at him.

"Khojali," he said. "I know you lost everyone." He paused. "I know how it felt. How it feels still. I lost my family in that war too. My mother … and then my father."

171

The short-lived mountain twilight was fading fast, but his eyes shone clear and bright. "That conflict has never fully stopped, Alana. Even for you, living so far from it, it goes on. Indeed, for you more than anyone the war is still real. The Armenians want you, Alana. These people who are tailing you are from there."

"Why? What do they want from me?"

Noah shook his head. "I don't fully know. In Baku, if you will come, I will take you to someone who knows it all and who will do anything in his power to save and help you."

"Who?"

"Come. We must keep moving."

He urged her along, and she walked reluctantly.

"Who, Noah?"

"I prefer not to say right now. I will tell you all I know, I promise. But we have to get to Geneva. There's a flight this evening; I have tickets. We'll get a taxi in the town. But we have to hurry."

They walked in silence until they reached the corner of the Promenade. By the Graff jewelry store, Alana paused. "I'm going to the apartment," she said. "I've got to." She set off.

"Alana! *Alana*!"

Muttering to himself in Azerbaijani, Noah followed her.

The helicopter sat silently in a gloom eerily lit by its own lights. Hayk was in the rear seat, his head wound being tended to by the pilot.

"That makes three times," said Irina.

Hayk glared at her. "Two."

"Cambridge; here in the van; again in the car. Three times she's eluded you." Irina counted them off on her gloved fingers. "Vartan believes you are the best. I think he may be mistaken."

Hayk grunted. "How many rounds did you fire into that car

without stopping it? I tell you, this girl is not ordinary. And who was that man?"

The pilot soaked a pad with antiseptic. "This is going to sting like wasps," he warned, applying it to the bleeding graze on Hayk's forehead. Hayk gazed steadily into Irina's eyes, and didn't blink or flinch.

"I don't know," she admitted. "One of Karabakhsky's people, maybe."

"It's your job to know. What if he's CIA or DGSE? With the connections she has, he could be anyone. Mossad, even." He took his phone out. "Here, I got a photo."

Irina looked at the picture; it had been taken from near the crash site; the young man and the target were running to the Audi. She zoomed in, but the man's face was too grainy to make out. "Instead of shooting this, you could have shot him."

"They took my gun."

Irina sneered and handed the phone back. "Send it to HACA; they may be able to identify him. Did you place the tracker on her?"

Hayk nodded and switched apps. "It's working. There she is."

There was a green dot at the corner of Lauenenstrasse and the Promenade. "She is going to her family's apartment," said Irina. "You have one more chance."

Hayk brushed aside the dressing the pilot was trying to apply to his head. "I need your weapon, Irina." As she gave him her handgun, he stared coldly at her. "I shall inform Vartan that you think he is a deluded fool."

She smiled tightly. "Go. Do your job."

Irina Ledovskaya knew Vartan better than Hayk guessed, and she was aware that he had devices in his armory more effective than this blunt instrument. Why such a devious and ruthless man would feel such devotion to this boy was a mystery to her.

* * *

173

The apartment was dark and silent when Alana let herself in. Noah put his finger to his lips, and she closed the door silently behind her.

Together they stole across the little hallway to the kitchen. Noah cautiously checked each of the rooms in turn. "Clear," he said.

Alana had been holding her breath; she'd had a premonition that her father would be here, dead, but he'd evidently stuck to his plan to spend the night in his cabin. He'd be safe there; aside from Alana herself, nobody knew the cabin's exact location.

She switched on the light. "Okay, your arm first. My mother has a first aid kit that would keep an emergency room stocked for a week." She opened kitchen cupboards at random. "I could swear … aha, got it!" She brought out a green pack the size of a briefcase and unzipped it. "What do you need?"

Noah had taken off his jacket and rolled up his sweater and shirt sleeves to expose the gunshot wound. The bullet had cut a furrow across the flesh of his left forearm. It was oozing blood. "It should be stitched," he said, and rummaged through the contents of the kit, taking out a pack of butterfly sutures. "These will have to do." He washed the wound with antiseptic. "Now, please, Alana, pinch the wound like so."

She did as he showed her, squeezing the edges together while he gritted his teeth against the pain and deftly applied the adhesive sutures.

"Now let me see your hip," he said, patting down a dressing over the sutures. Alana turned it toward him. "I can't examine that. You'll have to remove your pants." She hesitated. "I'm a doctor and we don't have much time."

With a sense of embarrassment she wouldn't have felt with her own doctor, Alana shucked off her ruined jeans and tossed them aside. Noah examined her wound, which was similar to his, but shallower. He bathed, sutured and dressed it. His touch was gentle and surprisingly soothing. She remembered a similar moment just a few days ago, when she'd inexpertly tended to Howard's injuries. This young man appeared to be the very opposite of everything that Howard had been.

The image of the impaled corpse by the roadside and the blood-soaked snow fell into Alana's head with force of a blow. Her mind had been too overwhelmed to deal with it, but now she saw it with horrifying clarity. She gagged and let out a high-pitched whimper, her legs almost buckling under her. She had to grab the counter.

"Did I hurt you?" said Noah.

"No. No, I just … felt kind of weird. I'm okay."

Noah glanced around. "Your parents live here with you?"

"Dad's staying the night somewhere else. My mother's away."

"Good." He finished applying the dressing. "The people after you will not hesitate to harm them to get at you."

"Noah, who are these people?"

"I'll tell you on the way to the airport." He saw the look on Alana's face. "I swear to you, if you do not come, I cannot protect you. It's only by a miracle that you have eluded them so far. They will catch you soon, and you will have an eternity in which to regret it."

Alana scrutinized his face. She felt somehow that she could trust him. But could she trust her own feelings? It was an excruciating choice to make: to put her faith in this attractive, blue-eyed stranger who had dropped into her life out of nowhere, or take her chances with the kind of people who would kill anyone who got in their way.

"All right," she said. "But at least let me put on some pants first."

Slipping into the shadows, away from the cheerful lights of the Promenade, Hayk silently mounted the stairs to the apartment. He checked the tracker. The green dot was right in front of him. She was still inside. He drew his pistol and screwed on a silencer, then tried the handle. The door was unlocked.

175

It opened quietly on well-oiled hinges, and Hayk slipped through. The lights were on in the kitchen area; with the pistol steadily in front of him, he advanced. He could smell antiseptic and the aroma of the hair products she used; he'd inhaled it deeply as he was tying her to the head restraint, along with the natural smell beneath, recording both in his memory like fingerprints.

There was nobody in the kitchen. The dot on the screen showed he was almost on top of her. He moved to the nearest bedroom door and eased it open with the gun muzzle. Nobody. The other two bedrooms were also empty, and the bathroom too.

Where was she? He followed the tracker's directional indicator toward a corner of the room that was deep in shadow. Hayk moved toward it. Crumpled on the floor he found a pair of jeans, and holding them up to the light he saw a tear, and bloodstains. He fished in the back pocket and drew out the tiny tracking device he'd placed there two hours earlier.

He didn't waste time cursing. He called a number.

"Here," said Irina's voice.

"She's gone. Tracker is dead."

"Any signs of where she's gone to?"

"Nothing."

"We can trace her cellphone. I'll contact the Office. They can locate it. It could take a while; it'll have to be cleared through 104."

Hayk's gaze, scanning the kitchen from top to bottom, landed on a flat object lying on the counter. He picked it up.

"Don't bother," he said flatly. "I've traced it."

19

High on a bitter hillside, beneath a smoothed outcrop shaped like a sleeping cat, Ayna sat on the freezing ground in the dark, her knees drawn up under her chin, arms wrapped around them. There was snow beneath her, and a savagely cold wind cut at her face, but she wasn't conscious of either. Her mind was a constantly shifting kaleidoscope of unspeakable horror.

Ayna was scarcely aware of the presence beside her, watching her. It might have been her brother, Hakan, or her sister, Leyli. She wanted it to be one of them – and both of them – but it was not.

The two children sat under a sky that stooped low, threateningly, over the mountain tops, heavy clouds tearing here, letting through the stars and a waning moon that cast a deathly light over the nightmare.

Neymar watched Ayna closely. Her state of mind worried him, and he didn't know what to do. All she did was sit and stare and shiver like someone with a fever. He could hear her teeth chattering – like his own – but she wouldn't move. He had tried cajoling her, tried putting his arms around her to stave off the cold, but she just sat as unresponsive as the cat rock itself.

He began to wish they had remained in the garage. Then they would never have seen this horror.

The street had been quiet when Neymar put his head through the gap in the garage door. He could hear the pops of distant gunfire, and guessed it came from the far side of the village, near the airfield. It sounded as harmless as firecrackers.

"Come now," he whispered to Ayna. "It's safe. The soldiers are gone."

Ayna sat with her back to the pickup truck's wheel and looked at him. Her expression made Neymar shiver. He was too young to comprehend the desolation and terror in her eyes and the slack set of her jaw, but he understood that bad things had happened, and she had seen them. Quite what they were, he didn't know; she had scarcely spoken two words since they took refuge in here.

"Come on," he pleaded, holding out his hand. "The bad men will come back. Our mommies and daddies have gone. We have to find them." Still she just stared. "Come," he said, and began squeezing through the gap.

"Wait!" As if jolted by an electric shock, Ayna sprang to her feet and took his hand. Together they crawled out into the fresh air.

They stood in the shadows, surveying the empty street. "Where will we go?" said Ayna.

Neymar chewed his lip. "I heard grown-ups say Aghdam. Do you know how to get there? My mother has a cousin there."

Ayna felt sick; she heard her father's voice: *They're saying the road to Aghdam is open for evacuation. Our militia will guard everyone …* But then other people said it wasn't, that the enemy soldiers were killing people on the road.

"It's that way," she said, pointing.

It wasn't difficult to leave the village. Although there were Armenian

178

soldiers still patrolling, Khojali had no streetlights, and the children were small and cautious. Every now and then they passed bodies lying in the gutters or crumpled against walls. To Ayna's eyes, most looked too stiff and unreal to have ever been living. At one point a burst of gunfire close by made them jump out of their skins, but they passed on without being noticed and reached the main road leading north. A Russian armored vehicle stood at the intersection, and soldiers stood about chatting.

Ayna had been past this spot only hours before, and she remembered now why the people had crossed the river, heading for the hills. Ayna's family and their friends, along with hundreds of other villagers, had heard gunfire and realized that the road to Aghdam was anything but safe; to reach the city, they would have to leave the road and cut across the mountains.

It was still a mystery to Ayna how she and her mother had ended up back in Khojali, in their own home. She pushed the puzzle away from her, repelled by the memory of her mother's last cries and the blood.

"That way," she whispered to Neymar, pointing across the road.

The tracks of the exodus were easy to follow – a trampled path in the snow, as broad as a road, leading to the Gargar river, through the woods and beyond. As she walked, Ayna's mind grew blurred and fogged, and she could no longer tell whether it was now or then, and whether she was walking with the little refugee boy or with her family. Neymar began to worry about her when she started talking animatedly with someone who wasn't there. More than one person, it seemed: from her words, there seemed to be other children – a brother and sister, he guessed – and her mother, too. It was so vivid, Neymar almost believed they were really walking invisibly alongside, and it terrified him.

The trail grew fainter as it climbed the steep, windswept hillsides where the snow was thinner, but it was still easy enough to follow in the intermittent moonlight.

And at last they came to it: the place where the trail stopped. The place where Hell had visited itself upon the earth.

At least forty corpses were strewn across the hillside. A light fall of snow had softened their outlines, and in the darkness, they looked at first like hummocks in the turf. Men, women, children.

Ayna and Neymar halted, too terrified to advance through this charnel field. Neymar squeezed Ayna's hand, and they began skirting uphill, to go around. Ayna couldn't tear her eyes away from the shapes they passed: a mother carrying a baby, cut down and her infant slaughtered in her arms; two men who had fallen while running; a dozen men heaped together in a gully; a child of about three lying alone, wax-faced, eyes staring at the stars, a blanket that had been wrapped around him stretched out and tangled in his legs, as if he had been dragged away from his parents, who lay dead nearby.

Suddenly, Ayna stopped. Neymar felt her squeeze his hand so hard it hurt, and from her throat came a shriek so desolate it made his neck prickle with terror. She was staring down at the body of a child; a dark-haired girl aged about six or seven. She wore a woolen scarf, pale and colorless in the moonlight, decorated with the shapes of ducks and rabbits. Its fringed end lay in a black, frozen puddle of blood. Ayna screamed with an animal force, and although Neymar tried to pull her away, she stood rooted to the spot, staring wildly at her murdered sister.

Then Neymar's hands fell to his sides. A gray plaid blanket which was partially entwining Leyli's limbs stretched out across the snowy grass, its other end wrapped around the body of a woman, whose arm reached out, frozen in a last mortal effort to grasp the child. The woman wore an embroidered headscarf whose shape Neymar recognized, and although her face was turned to the earth, he knew that this was his mother.

The children's high-pitched voices, sobbing, were the only sound on that desolate hillside other than the hiss of the winter wind. Gradually their crying faded, and all that remained was the wind.

Neymar had searched the whole field of death, but had not been able to find any trace of his father. Ayna was too stunned to try to find her brother Hakan. His corpse could be anywhere out there in the darkness; just one among the many smaller hummocks in the snowy grass.

"Perhaps my papa saved Hakan," Neymar suggested tentatively as they sat huddled together, sheltered from the wind in the lee of the cat rock. Ayna didn't react. "I'll bet that's what happened." Still no reaction. "We should go look for them."

"They're dead," said Ayna. These were her first words since they had found the bodies, and she spoke them with a flat finality that made Neymar's heart die in his chest.

She wouldn't move, no matter what he said. They were both succumbing to the cold; Neymar knew they would die from it soon. Ayna's face was deathly and her lips turning dark.

Searching as close as he dared to the field of death, he managed to find an abandoned blanket and a bag in which a thick woolen sweater was packed among some household goods. The sweater was an adult's, and a large one at that. Neymar pulled it on, thrusting his small arms through the voluminous sleeves; then he sat close beside Ayna and drew it down over her so that her head came out the top alongside his. Finally, struggling with the bulky sleeves, he pulled the blanket around them both.

It kept the icy wind off their bodies, but as the night lengthened and snow began to fall again, the temperature dropped still lower,

181

and even inside their cocoon Neymar could feel it sucking the life out of them both. If they remained here much longer, they would die. But where could they go? Their people were gone, and the world was filled with enemies. It never crossed Neymar's mind to strike out on his own in search of help; nothing would have induced him to abandon a friend in this terrible place.

The eastern sky began to lighten, and gradually a weak sunrise seeped down the hillside and into the vale of Khojali, sickly and pallid.

Neymar woke from a doze to find Ayna leaning on him, eyes closed. The blanket had slipped from her shoulders and flakes of snow were on her hair. He shook her, but there was no response. He shook her again, and her eyelids fluttered but did not open. He pulled the blanket back into place, brushing off the snow and covering her head. It was difficult to move; his limbs were numb with cold and weak from convulsive shuddering.

Sensing a movement behind them, Neymar kept still; he heard heavy boots treading softly and turned his head slowly.

Towering above them was a large man – he seemed like a giant to Neymar – with a thick black beard and a large hook nose. He wore traditional loose hillman's clothing and over it a camouflage jacket, like the ones worn by the Armenian soldiers. Neymar's heart skipped in fear. The strange man stopped a few yards away and surveyed the dreadful scene before him.

"May Allah protect us," he murmured in a deep, grinding voice. He gazed for a while, then turned away, his face disfigured by despair. His eyes fell on the small bundle huddled on the ground at the foot of the great rock.

Neymar tried to speak, but all that came out was an incoherent whimper.

The man started as if he'd been struck. "Allah be praised, I thought you were dead!" He knelt down beside them. His delight turned to anxiety when he saw Ayna's unconscious face. "Don't sleep, child!" He gently slapped and pinched her cheeks with his weathered fingers until her eyes opened. "Good, good! If you sleep now, you will never wake. The cold will take you while your guard is down." She stared at him listlessly, uncomprehending.

"Who are you?" Neymar managed to say.

"Who am I?" His beard split in a smile full of crooked teeth. "You may call me Huseyn, child. Now come. It is not safe here from weather or wickedness."

Neymar's vision blurred and faded. The man spoke more, but his words were indistinct. Neymar's last sensation was of rising off the ground and floating, and he wondered if he was going to Paradise now.

Ayna awoke surrounded by white, and thought she was still on the snowy hillside. Her vision focused, and she saw that she was in a room all painted in white. Hung on every wall were embroidered horse cloths: ancient panels decorated with elaborate patterns of leaves, flowers, birds, and serpents in threads of bright red, gold, emerald, and ivory. Above her bed was a small window of stained glass, which cast a color-dappled light across her gray coverlet.

An elderly woman was tending the hearth, where a fire of split logs was crackling; as soon as she saw that Ayna's eyes were open, she hurried out, calling to someone. Ayna drifted on the edge of consciousness. There was a bustle at the door, and the elderly woman returned, followed by the familiar figure of Ayna's grandfather.

He was dressed as she had never seen him before; in place of the well-cut tweeds and blazers he wore in Shusha or when visiting, he wore what he thought of as his "country" outfit: a traditional light gray

Cossack-style tunic buttoned up to the collar, bound by a narrow belt of leather decorated with silver, with a gown-like overcoat of dark red.

Togrul's eyes brightened as he looked at his granddaughter. Even she could see the terrible grief in his face, but she had no idea of the strength of will it took for him not to bow down under the weight of it. He drew up a stool and sat beside the bed.

"Welcome to my little home in the hills," he said. "I should say welcome *back*, for you have been here before." He smiled. "I see you do not recall it. That is to be expected; you were a very tiny child when you were brought to stay while your father was away in Baku. There was still a kind of peace in Karabakh in those days. So recent, yet so long ago!" He folded his arms, looked sharply at her and smiled again. "But before that, and more importantly, you were born here."

Little of what her grandfather said conveyed much to Ayna, but this penetrated the fog.

"Oh yes," he said. "Right here between these very walls. It was a terrible winter. Your mother and father, peace be on them, were visiting and it was impossible for them to return to Khojali. If my old memory is not misleading me, it was in the chamber next to this one that you entered the world. 'You have given my house a precious jewel,' I said to your dear mother. 'This place will always be blessed when she is here.' They named you Ayna after your grandmother, whose portrait hangs in that room."

Ayna turned away. She wanted her grandfather to stop talking, to stop invoking her mother and father; the mere mention of them brought them so vividly to her mind that it was a bewildering, agonizing pain to her. Had it been a nightmare? That had often been the way: *Don't be frightened, my baby*, her mother would say in the exquisitely soothing way she had. *It was just a bad dream*. But it hadn't, and the more her grandfather talked, the more Ayna's mind hardened and thickened the defensive wall it was already unconsciously building between herself and everything she knew.

"Forgive me, child," he said softly. "To talk of the past is to keep alive those who have departed, but I see you are not ready." He sighed. "Truth be told, neither am I."

He rose and went out, leaving her gazing at the wall, her eyes tracing round and round the outline of a lily worked in green and ivory against a scarlet background, focusing her whole mind on its intricate threads.

Neymar sat at the big table in the warm, spacious kitchen, his back to the old iron range under the tiled chimney arch. In front of him was a dish of stewed lamb and a platter of fruit. He hadn't seen food in this quantity or quality for as long he could remember, but he ate little. He felt ill at ease in this house; his father – who came originally from Shusha – had spoken of Ayna's grandfather as a tremendous and powerful man, and Neymar went in terrified awe of him.

Beside him at the table, Huseyn the goatherd felt no such qualms, and ate his fill with relish, as did his wife and children. Ayna's grandfather, overcome with gratitude, had invited Huseyn to stay and bring his family for protection. There were several small cottages and outbuildings nearby with more than enough room for them and for other survivors of the massacre.

Half a week had passed, and each day a handful of stragglers found their way to the khan's old hunting lodge in the mountains and were fed and accommodated. They brought with them appalling tales of slaughter. It transpired that the killings in the streets of Khojali and on the hillside were less than a tenth of the full count of the dead. Togrul spoke at length with every survivor, but none could give him any news of Neymar's father or Ayna's brother.

Nonetheless, Neymar firmly believed that his father had survived and had rescued Hakan. They would be here soon.

Neymar toyed with his spoon, stirring his stew. Hearing voices raised outside, he rushed to the window, as he always did. A battered old pickup truck had pulled up in the yard and a small group of men and women climbed out. They were all ragged, dirty, exhausted. Neymar peered at their faces, one by one … and shrieked with delight.

He ran across the hallway and burst into Ayna's chamber. "He is here! My father is here! Come quickly!" And he ran out again.

Ayna had been sitting on her bed, chin on her knees, staring. It was all she did these days; she hardly spoke, barely ate. But as Neymar rushed out, his voice still clattering around in her head, Ayna's eyes came to life. She knew of his belief, and she had faith in his faith. If his father was here, Hakan would be too. She jumped off the bed and ran out of the room after him.

In the hallway she met her grandfather coming out of his study. His face lit up as she raced past him and out the front door. He followed her.

Neymar was ahead of her, running across the yard, crying out, "Papa! Papa!"

His father, a young man with a blunt nose and a week's growth of beard, as ragged and begrimed as the other survivors, ran to meet his little boy, sweeping him up into his arms, sobbing with joy, and staggering to his knees. Ayna watched in amazement at such unrestrained emotion from a grown-up. A hand settled on her shoulder, and she glanced up to see her grandfather.

Neymar's father put his boy down and came forward. "Allah be praised," he said. "Sir, I can never thank you enough. All blessings be upon you and your house."

"It is I who should thank your son, who brought my granddaughter to me, out of harm's way."

Neymar tugged at his father's coat. "But Papa! What about Hakan? Where is he?"

The young man stared at his son, and at Ayna, who took a step toward him. "I … I …" He stared imploringly at Ayna's grandfather, and she saw the look that passed between them. "I am sorry, I … he …" His mouth working helplessly, incapable of expressing what he had witnessed in words fit for children, he shook his head.

Hakan was dead. There was nobody left. Blackness closed in on Ayna. She felt herself falling. Voices swirled around her, incomprehensible, distant. And then there was nothing.

20

Baku

Three black SUVs in convoy climbed the steep, winding road into the city of Stepanakert. Sprawling across the crinkled folds of the mountains south of Khojali – this was its new name, Stepanakert, having been re-named when Armenia brutally invaded and appropriated the ancient city of Khakendi, and populated it with ethnic Armenians to make sure there would be no trace of Azeri cultural heritage left. Ancient Albanian churches had been renamed as Armenian, and Stepanakert was now the capital of occupied Nagorno-Karabakh. Its suburbs clung like lichen to the edges of the mountains, streets snaking around vein-like forested ravines.

The SUVs drew to a halt at the edge of a large patch of weed-grown waste ground. This unprepossessing place, surrounded on one side by apartment blocks and on the other by an industrial lot, was the site chosen for the city's new Christian cathedral. It stood unfinished, a red stone edifice clothed entirely in scaffolding.

Armed men emerged from each the SUVs, and from one stepped Vartan, wearing a dark blue suit and a black shirt open at the neck.

Lowering his sunglasses, he gazed up at the half-finished building with a mixture of wonder and dismay.

The Cathedral Church of the Holy Protection of the Mother of God was a massive rotunda, rising in three tiers and surmounted by a great cupola pierced by arches. It was Biblical not only in scale but in construction; the web of scaffolding covering it from the ground to the domed summit was built entirely from wood, jointed and doweled in the ancient manner. The windows had traditional carvings on their arched lintels, but no glazing yet, and the red stone walls were smeared with lime. It was a Sunday in Great Lent, and there were no workmen on site.

With two of his bodyguards following at a distance, Vartan walked up the slope to the entrance and stepped inside.

The main body of the church was a cloister-like space: a gloomy polygonal enclosure bounded by a dozen great semicircular arches. It should have felt cavernous and magnificent, but its flat latticed ceiling loomed, making it almost claustrophobic. The only light came from slit-like windows in the outer wall, and the unfinished floor was just dirt and rubble. Vartan walked warily into the center of the room.

"Welcome," said a harsh voice from the shadows, and Vartan froze. In the echoing space it was impossible to tell where the voice came from. Then a familiar heavy-set figure in ecclesiastical black emerged from the darkness beneath the arches. "You are late, my lord."

"Reverend Father," said Vartan softly and coldly.

Archimandrite Gevorg Harutyunyan stepped forward. As always, his bulky figure was clothed in a black cassock and his long gray beard was framed by the silver chain of his ornate cross. His formal cowl was pushed back, revealing a bald head as brown as his weathered face.

"Twice welcome," he said and spread his arms. "The Holy Mother of God Cathedral will be the wonder of the Republic and the heart of Stepanakert." He inhaled appreciatively. "It is not yet consecrated, but already I feel Christ's majesty in this place. Do you sense it too?"

"All I'm sensing is damp and delay," said Vartan. "If Noah had taken this long to build the Ark, he'd have washed away with the Flood."

The cleric smiled. "This house of God will be in the style of the ancient Cathedral of Zvartnots, and we honor this by using traditional methods. Come, walk with me. I will show you."

Vartan fell in step with Harutyunyan as they walked slowly around the arched cloister, the priest pointing out details of architecture and carving with the enthusiasm of an antiquarian.

"Speaking of traditional methods," said Harutyunyan, "I trust you are about to report the securing of the young woman. Unlike cathedral architecture, the Holy Apostolic Crusade will brook no delays." He glanced sidelong, but Vartan's face, obscure in the half-light, gave nothing away. "You have captured her?"

"It is imminent."

"Imminent? You mean to say you have not?"

Vartan said nothing, and the priest smiled thinly.

"My lord Vartan, you made a vow that your methods would bring a resolution to this matter. Indeed, your anger on the point cost me a particularly beautiful and devoted acolyte." Harutyunyan's voice was pleasant, almost ebullient, and Vartan knew why. "The Conclave will be severely displeased by your failure," he murmured.

Vartan stopped and turned to face the priest. "The Conclave gave me the authority to govern this task," he hissed in a voice like the sound of grit underfoot. "Not you, Father. *Me*. You think you can undermine me with this setback? You can think again."

"Now that she has outwitted you – how many times? Two? Three? – the Conclave will see that capturing her is beyond your capabilities, and that the only remaining course is to follow *my* recommendation."

Vartan stared hard at Harutyunyan. "Why not say it, Reverend Father? You wish to kill her. Fortunately, the Conclave is made up of wiser men than the one standing before me." In fact, Vartan wasn't at all sure of this; HACA's governing council had too many clerical members for Vartan's liking, and the Archimandrite's grip on it was growing. "Without the woman, the claim will not be achievable. She is essential to secure access and make the transfer legitimate."

Harutyunyan studied Vartan's hawkish face in the light from a window slit. "Are you sure that is your reason? Vartan, I know of your feelings about this woman and your intentions toward her. Vengeance is what you have in mind."

"It is not vengeance."

"A reckoning, then. Your little birds are not as discreet as you think. I know about the plan you have in mind for her, once she has served her ostensible purpose. My lord Vartan, I know well enough that you are capable of unconscionable cruelty, but what you are planning is beyond everything."

Vartan took a step toward him, and Harutyunyan shrank back. "Do not cower," said Vartan, and in an instant there was a knife in his hand; its blade touched Harutyunyan's beard. "*Priest*," Vartan added with contempt. "At least face your death in the expectation of entering God's kingdom."

Harutyunyan tried to back away and collided with a pillar. The knife pushed slowly through the gray beard. The priest felt it coming closer to his throat.

"Pardon me, lord," said one of Vartan's bodyguards softly. "A call for you."

Without moving the knife or taking his eyes off the priest's face, Vartan took the phone and listened.

"You are absolutely sure of this?" he said. "When?" He handed back the phone and began to smile. Leaning close to Harutyunyan's face, he said softly, "Bleat your little tale to the Conclave, you holy hypocrite, and see what good it does you. Soon I will have her, and will not even have to extend my grasp. She is being brought right to me. Of her own free will!"

He withdrew the knife, and with a mocking bow to the Archimandrite he left the chamber.

"We'll be landing soon. Yes, she is with me." Noah glanced up as one of the flight attendants came along the aisle to tick him off for using his phone during the flight. "No," he said, "she came willingly. Yes, I am absolutely sure. Listen, I have to go now." He gave the attendant his most disarming smile and switched off his phone. "I apologize; an urgent call on a family matter." She smiled back graciously and walked away.

Alana was fast asleep in the window seat. It had been an exhausting journey from Gstaad; all the way to Geneva she had demanded to know what was going on, who the people were that were hunting her, what they wanted from her. Above all, she wanted to know why she was being taken to Azerbaijan. He had fended off her questions as best he could, at the same time taking care not to lose her trust by being too secretive.

It was virtually impossible to do both, and he'd had to give way, insisting that they talk in Turkish so that the Swiss taxi driver couldn't overhear. Although Noah spoke the language passably well, Alana spoke it only haltingly, and this alone had saved him having to reveal too much. For security's sake, he was under orders to keep her in the dark at least until they were on the final leg into Baku, and she wouldn't be able to back out. To Noah's relief, after a layover in Istanbul Alana had slept almost the whole way.

He touched her hand. "Alana," he said softly. "Alana!" She jerked awake with a gasp. "I'm sorry, I didn't mean to startle you. I thought you might like to savor your first sight of the land of your birth."

Alana looked out the window. The plane was banking to begin its approach to Baku. The sky was cloudless, over a landscape illuminated by the rising sun. Shading her eyes, she saw a peninsula reaching out into the blue-green Caspian Sea, like a closed hand with a long finger crooked at the end. It reminded her a little of flying in over the Bay of San Francisco or the South of France, but here the land was flat as a table and patterned with a checkerboard of muted browns, grays and moss greens between the speckled sprawl of Baku's suburbs and coastal towns.

"How does it feel to return to your homeland?" said Noah.

"I don't know. It doesn't feel like home."

"Did you ever come to Baku as a child?"

"I don't know. I guess not. My family lived a long way from here." She gazed down at the landscape rotating, tilting, coming steadily closer. "I have no memories of Azerbaijan," she said. "Only nightmares."

Right now, she wasn't sure how she felt about any of this. There were only two reasons she'd come with Noah. For one, she trusted him and felt safe with him. But far more importantly, she felt an overriding need to understand what this was all about. Whatever the risks, she had to know the truth. Not only the truth about the people who had exploded into her life, but the truth about her past; and the truth about herself. If that truth was anywhere, it was in Azerbaijan, the country that had given birth to her.

If Alana was being honest with herself, trusting Noah came down in large part to the fact that he had beautiful eyes and a reassuring smile. Leaving Gstaad had been the great test of that trust. Noah had made her leave her phone behind. They would track it, he said. He'd disposed of his own phone for the same reason. He wouldn't even let her leave a note for her father. "You can contact him from Baku," he'd said. "We'll get you a phone – what do you call it, a baker?"

That had made her laugh for the first time in days. "A burner," she said. "It's called a burner."

Noah – or whomever he was acting for – had influence. There was a visa for Azerbaijan already prepared for her, and they were booked on an evening flight for Baku. The documents and tickets were waiting in an envelope at the information desk. Noah signed for it, Alana noticing the strength of his pen-strokes; there was something familiar about his handwriting, but she couldn't place it. She bought a prepaid phone in the airport and called her old college friend Katy in New York, who agreed to relay a message to her father: *I'm going away with a friend. Don't worry about me. I'll be back soon.* Noah had warned that her father's phone might be monitored. Her enemies had a lot of resources at their disposal.

Who those enemies were, he had revealed in the taxi on the way to Geneva, slipping briefly from Turkish into English. "They are known as HACA."

"Hacker?"

"H–A–C–A. It means Holy Apostolic Crusade for Artsakh. They are a kind of Orthodox Christian version of ISIS, a terrorist organization with only one goal: to confirm Karabakh in Armenian possession and in time to invade the whole of Azerbaijan and its oil fields in the Caspian Sea. You can find it on the European Union and Interpol index of state-sponsored terrorist networks."

"What's Artsakh?"

"It is the name the Armenians use for the Azerbaijani region of Karabakh. Artsakh is actually the former name of Karabakh, used when it was part of ancient Albania. Armenians stole that identity and claimed ancient Albanian history as their own. They destroyed most proof of this ancient heritage by appropriating it and re-writing history to their advantage. As you know, the Armenians believe it belongs to them by right, and that Azeris have no place there."

Karabakh. Each time she heard that name it was like bell tolling somewhere inside her – deep, resonant, hinting at something ominous but compelling. The landscape now rising to meet her was not Karabakh, but it was part of the same nation: her birth-land.

"To be not who you thought you were," said Noah softly beside her as the airport came into view and the seatbelt light came on. "To know that your future is not what you thought it would be."

It took Alana a moment to remember where she had heard those words before, and she turned to look at him in horror. Now she knew where she'd seen that bold, careful handwriting before. "*You are in danger*," she whispered.

Noah smiled, apologetically. "I added those words, I admit. But it wasn't my idea to send you the note. Indeed, I argued against it."

Feeling panic beginning to rise, Alana tried to remember how that note had come to her. It had come from Howard … who had been given it in London … by a company the police said had links to terrorism … and they had also given him a gun. She struggled to recall whether Howard had said anything that would tell her just how frightened she ought to be right now.

"I'm sorry," said Noah. "I shouldn't have mentioned it. I didn't mean to frighten you. That is why I advised against sending it. Please forgive me. It was sent with the best of intentions, I promise you."

"Who sent it?"

"It was sent on the order of the man I am taking you to see."

The back of her neck prickled. "Are you going to tell me who that is?"

"Some people call him Khan Karabakhsky; others know him by his given name: Togrul." Noah watched her closely as he pronounced this name, but she just looked blankly back at him. "He is your grandfather, Alana. I am taking you to see your grandfather."

All Alana's bewildered brain could conjure up was an image of her Grandpa Fulton, a rather cold and distant man who lived in retirement in Vermont, and of beloved Poppa Tessaro, whom she remembered as a limitless source of jollity and gelato; he had died in Baltimore when Alana was a teenager.

"My grandfather?"

"The father of your father. You do not remember him?"

"I …" She wasn't sure. There was a vague figure in some of her confused memory-nightmares who she thought might be him. "But he's dead. My family were killed in the war. All of them."

The plane had made its final descent, and the unusually violent jolt as the tires hit concrete felt exactly like what was going on in Alana's brain right now. The brakes came on hard, pushing their bodies forward.

"No," said Noah. "Not quite all."

21

"Togrul Karabakhsky," Alana repeated carefully as the taxi pulled away from the airport terminal, rolling the syllables off her tongue.

"I owe your grandfather a great deal," said Noah. "My life, indeed. He saved me during the war, when I lost my parents."

"You must've been just a little kid then."

"I was, like you. Togrul saved the lives of many people. After Shusha fell to Armenian forces, millions of Azeri survivors followed him here to Baku; they are the ones who still call him khan, out of gratitude and respect. He looked after us, arranging foster parents to raise the kids who were orphaned. Later, he helped support me through medical school."

Alana fell silent, only half-listening as Noah talked. If her grandfather was in a position to do all that for an orphaned boy – and Noah wasn't the only one, it seemed – why had he discarded his *own granddaughter* into the care of some visiting American he only half knew? And why was he only taking an interest in her now? If she was so important to her grandfather *now*, why hadn't he kept her with him all along, like Noah and those other children? Why send her away to live a false life? Whoever this Togrul Karabakhsky was – and she wasn't willing to accept that he could really be her grandfather – he'd better have some pretty comprehensive answers.

Two weeks ago she'd been looking ahead to turning thirty in December, with her future life happily settled, her origins buried and utterly forgotten; like the lowest stratum in an archaeological site, the truth had the potential to be excavated and revealed and understood, but only when the time was right, and in a systematic, careful fashion. What she was experiencing now was the equivalent of dynamiting the lid off an ancient tomb and digging to the foundations with a bulldozer.

Her thoughts were brought back to the present by a remark from Noah. "… so I ended up living in Manhattan."

"You lived in New York?" she said.

He nodded. "I got my MD at NYU."

"Really? I did my master's at Columbia. What was your class year?"

"I was Class of 2010. But I stayed on for three years as a resident at Harlem Hospital Center." For some reason he seemed faintly embarrassed by this admission.

"So we were practically neighbors? I can't believe it. I was at Columbia from 2012 to 2013. My friend Katy was my roommate. She got a job at Columbia after graduation."

"I know," said Noah, and blushed.

"What do you mean, you know?"

"Not about your friend's job, obviously. I mean I know you studied for your master's at Columbia, and I know that you shared an apartment on West 119th Street with two other students, both female. I know that most mornings you walked to your classes through Morningside Park, but always took a cab back if it was after dark. I also know your favorite restaurant was the Red Rooster and you always ordered the spicy charred glazed cauliflower and chicken and waffles." Avoiding Alana's incredulous stare, he looked out the window at the traffic streaming toward the airport.

"You *spied* on me?"

"No! Not spying." He shifted in his seat. "All through your life, your grandfather always made sure he knew where you were and that you were safe. When he learned that you were going to live in New York, he asked me to keep an eye on you. Until then I was at a hospital in Brooklyn; I transferred to Harlem to be close to Columbia."

"I was only there one year."

"Yes. When you went to Cambridge, Togrul asked me to go too."

"You *followed* me?"

"I'm afraid so." Noah squirmed with embarrassment.

"Just like that?"

"I completed my residency at Addenbrooke's Hospital in Cambridge. You will be relieved, perhaps, to hear that I know less about your life there. You divided your time between Cambridge and London, and the life of a hospital doctor is a very busy one. It was difficult enough in Harlem, but in England I never had time to look out for you properly. After two years I was fully qualified as a practitioner, so I returned to Azerbaijan."

"And who spied on me after that?"

"Togrul made other arrangements. Better ones. But I know nothing about that." Noah smiled. "I'm just a doctor. What do I know about spying? For anything else, you will have to ask Togrul yourself."

The highway from the airport had left behind the low-lying suburbs of red-roofed modern houses, passed through a big interchange near a massive white stadium, and became a broad boulevard lined with small modern office blocks and beautiful old apartment buildings in Imperial European style.

"So, if you can't tell me what's going on," she said, her innate curiosity starting to overcome her unease, "at least tell me about this place."

"Baku? Well, what can I tell you? It is the capital of Azerbaijan. It is very ancient, very beautiful, and very, very windy. Indeed, the winds are the reason for the name. *Baku* is from a Persian phrase meaning *city pounded by wind*. There are some who say this is wrong, that it means *gift of God*. Me, I think both are true. All year round the wind called the Khazri blows from the north across the Caspian, bringing snows from Russia in winter. But in the summer the warm Gilavar blows from the south. In Azeri mythology, the rivalry between icy Khazri and gentle Gilavar represents the struggle between evil and good."

"And who wins?"

"Nobody. Certainly not the people of Baku."

"And what are the people of Baku like?"

"What are they like? They are Azerbaijani – we usually shorten that to Azeri – for the most part. Which is to say, they love life and laughter and art and music, they adore good food, they work hard and prosper, and they serve Allah, Jesus and Hashem as time allows. It is a very unique, religiously tolerant and multicultural country. All religions have healthy representations, and followers live in harmony without conflict. Quite impressive, actually."

"Serving Allah isn't a priority, then?"

"Azerbaijan is a nation of Muslims – mostly Shi'ite – but it is officially a secular state. As for most Azerbaijani people, religion isn't a major factor in our lives. This is no more a religious country than France or Great Britain. For sure it's more secular than the United States." Noah smiled.

"It looks prosperous."

"The wealth comes from oil. You saw the refineries from the airport road. There are major oilfields under the Caspian Sea, and Baku had its first modern well over a hundred and sixty years ago. I'm told, however, that oil had been extracted in Baku long before that – before even the Arab Caliphate, when this was a great center of the Zoroastrian religion, more than a thousand years ago. Azerbaijan was ahead of the whole world with its oil; we were among the first petroleum-producing nations, about the same time as the United States. In fact the Rockerfeller, Rothschild and Nobel families have made their fortunes thanks to Baku oil. I hope now we will have time to show you the famous Villa Petrolea; it is now a private museum, the Nobel family's only former home outside Sweden to become a museum. It is quite a magical place."

As the boulevard approached another big interchange, a green space opened up on the right, in which sat a vast building shaped like a rising, curling wave, covered entirely in dazzling white tiles, scalloped in overlapping layers that reminded Alana of the plates of a Roman legionary's body armor.

"The Heydar Aliyev Cultural Center," said Noah. "It was designed by a British architect whose name I cannot recall."

"Zaha Hadid," said Alana. "Iraqi born. She died recently. I've seen pictures of this place; I'd love to see inside it."

The taxi was swept with the tide into the interchange and the great white wave was lost to sight. They came out onto a long avenue running along the seafront, where the city met the Bay of Baku, and where the main mercantile and government districts were. Monumental Turkic architecture, full of spires and arches, alternated with Italian Renaissance and modern. Alana felt that if Florence and Istanbul had married one another, the offspring might look something like Baku. They passed a fondant-yellow and white confection resembling a Tsar's palace in miniature, which Noah said was the Philharmonic Hall, then Alana had her first view of the Old City – the ancient medieval heart of Baku.

Like strongholds throughout history, from the early Neolithic settlements Alana studied through to the medieval period, Baku's medieval citadel was built on a fortified hill. The ancient walls still stood – not in a ruinous state like those of Roman London or the *bastides* of France, but immaculate, standing to their full imposing height, with round and square towers at intervals, all topped with battlements with rounded merlons in the Islamic style.

"Togrul lives in the Old City," said Noah as the taxi turned toward a massive double-arched gateway.

Alana's pulse quickened. She wasn't sure whether it was the draw of ancient stones or the prospect of a momentous encounter. The taxi pulled up at a barrier manned by security guards; it was raised, and they drove through.

"In Azerbaijani the Old City is called *Icheri Sheher*," said Noah. "The Inner City."

They drove along a cobbled street, the pedestrians parting to let the taxi pass. It was lined with stone buildings which were a mix of Italian and ancient Turkic styles. There were mansions and palaces cheek-by-jowl with religious structures which Alana guessed must date back to the city's earliest period; there were caravanserais, and ancient buildings Noah pointed out as *hamams* – traditional bath houses. Between them the houses, small and large, were tightly packed in narrow cobbled lanes. There were brightly colored awnings, massive oaken doors, intricate wrought iron gratings, and peculiar wooden structures like wardrobes projecting out from the upper stories of houses – some so large they reached the far side of the alley. These makeshift extensions were beautifully built, carved and polished, with elaborate windows.

Noah spoke to the taxi driver in Azerbaijani, and he pulled over at the entrance to a winding lane. "We get out here," Noah said to

Alana. "Togrul's house is some distance away, but it may be watched. We must make our approach discreetly."

Alana stood waiting while he paid the driver and had a brief conversation with him. Although the sun was bright, the air was chill, and Alana shivered. She'd bought extra clothes at Geneva airport, and was beginning to wish she'd made slightly warmer choices. Noah was right about the Baku wind, which came rushing down the lane, bringing a taste of the Volga winter, and the cashmere sweater and light jacket she had on weren't really robust enough to resist it.

As the taxi pulled away, Alana realized that she was empty-handed. "Hey, wait!" she said. "My bag is still in the trunk!"

"It's okay. He's taking it to your hotel. He'll book you a room and take your bag up for you."

"You trust him?"

"Of course. Tofiq is one of Togrul's people, a man of Shusha. I would not have spoken so freely in front of him otherwise." Noah chuckled. "You would not get such an extensive service, with rooms booked, from a regular Baku taxi driver."

"Uh-huh. So, which way is it?"

"First," said Noah. "Regard your feet."

"What's wrong with my feet?" She looked down at the rope-soled sandals she'd ill-advisedly put on in Geneva.

"They are standing for the first time on the ground of our capital city, in its ancient heart. In treading upon it, you become a part of its history, now and always." Noah smiled. "I am quoting. This was what Togrul said to me when he first brought me to Baku. It is doubly true for you, because you are of his blood. Now, let us walk."

With Noah leading the way, they passed down a narrow, steeply sloping alley bustling with locals and a smattering of out-of-season tourists and backpackers. They came to a busy street which Noah said was the Kichik Qala. There were pavement cafés and stores selling traditional clothes and crafts. The front of a carpet shop on the corner was entirely decked in fabulous Turkish and Azeri rugs in scarlet and gold; the seller had laid out more on the cobbles in front of his emporium. As she looked at the vividly colored patterns of flowers and serpents, Alana's memories stirred, but she couldn't place them.

"We are nearly there," said Noah softly. "Arrangements have been made." He lowered his voice to a whisper. "Togrul believes there may be a traitor close to him. A spy working for the Armenians. He does not know yet whether this person is in his household or his following or just somewhere in the neighborhood. Therefore extra care is required."

Before Alana could react to this alarming news, they both had to press themselves back against the wall of a house as a van came along the street, the driver blasting his horn irritably at the milling crowd. The van was loaded inside and out with builders' gear, and a protruding ladder almost caught Alana's shoulder. Noah shielded her and whispered urgently in her ear: "This is our Trojan Horse. Come – follow on. Keep between the van and the wall."

The vehicle carved its way slowly through the crowd, Alana and Noah staying with it. A short way along, there was a little flight of stone steps leading up to an extremely old and weathered building with barred arched windows and an aged, heavy wooden door.

"Here," said Noah, and with the van still shielding them from view they hurried up the steps. The door swung inwards as soon as they reached it, and in an instant they were inside, the door closing softly behind them, muting the noise of the van and the street.

Alana found herself in a vestibule, with walls painted a pale ochre and age-worn timber beams from which hung a single chased silver lantern. To one side was a heavy, high-backed wooden chair in which

204

generations of door wards must have sat. Beyond an inner arch was a small open courtyard.

The man who had opened the door was middle-aged and bald, with a gray mustache so profuse it obscured his mouth entirely. Above it, his gray eyes twinkled.

"This is Rashad," said Noah. "He is the elder brother of Tofiq the taxi driver. The fellow driving the van is their young cousin."

Rashad bowed, regarding Alana with a diffident, almost reverent, gravity. He and Noah conferred quietly in Azerbaijani, with frequent nods and glances at Alana. Although she couldn't understand the language at all, it had a familiar feel, as if the meanings in the words were only just beyond her grasp. It was bizarre to think that she must once have understood and spoken it fluently.

"The khan is waiting for us in the library," said Noah.

Rashad led them across the small octagonal courtyard; in four of its eight faces were arched windows, and in a fifth, directly opposite the passage, was a door as aged and cracked as the beams. Rashad ushered them through into a corridor lit by the courtyard windows, off which there were several doors and an archway. Alana glimpsed a staircase climbing up at one end. Everywhere were signs of antiquity – in the old hangings and paintings decorating the walls, the lamps on wall-sconces, the dark bookcases which lined almost every wall, even in the corridor. Everything was neat and clean but a little shabby and care-worn, the woodwork scuffed, the paintwork peeling, the gorgeous Azeri carpets going thin and threadbare in places where the traffic was heaviest. Alana had the impression of an ancient household maintained in high style on a limited budget. There was an aroma of old paper and leather book-bindings mingled with spices and perfumed tobacco smoke.

Through the archway was a sitting room with low chairs and a day-bed, and a large window with stained-glass panels. A fire burned in a tiled hearth, and the room was pleasantly warm after the outdoor chill. Two further archways, right and left, opened into a dining room and a large, asymmetrical chamber which Alana guessed must be the library; in addition to the ubiquitous bookcases, there was a large table with reading lamps and stacks of books, manuscripts, and even scrolls.

Her heart beating faster, her breathing quick and shallow, Alana followed Noah and Rashad into this room.

At one end, beneath a large stained-glass window, was a raised desk with a sloped top, of the kind a medieval scribe might use. Seated at it on a high stool, with his back to the room, was an elderly man, poring over a manuscript and apparently deep in concentration. His white hair was cropped short, and he wore a pale blue silk waistcoat over a white shirt. Rashad opened his mouth to speak, but without looking round, the old gentleman held up a hand: *Wait.*

They waited. When she got to know him, Alana would realize that this was all theatrics, and that Khan Togrul Karabakhsky was more excited about this encounter than she could imagine. Infinitely more, because while she had been anticipating it for about forty minutes, Togrul had been looking forward to and hoping for this moment every day for more than a quarter of a century. But he had a role to maintain, and that role called for gravitas.

"My most profuse apologies," he said at last, taking off his eyeglasses and laying them down, still with his back to the room. The sound of his voice shivered through Alana's body like a gunpowder fuse, lighting up flickers and flashes of long-forgotten memory. "I have been reading the most remarkable manuscript: a sixteenth century eyewitness account of the siege of Baku by Ismail the First, the Shah of the Safavid empire in Iran. Some regard Ismail as a baneful figure, bringing about the downfall of the incumbent dynasty, persecuting the Sunni majority and imposing Safavid rule. But in reality, he was the pioneer of the golden age for Iran. A prominent poet who went by the name Khatai, he influenced and contributed to great progress in Azeri literature, arts and architecture. He made the Azeri Turkish language the official language of Iran. But my goodness, what great achievements! Azerbaijan would not be what it is without him."

As he spoke – in heavily accented but otherwise perfect English – he turned to face Alana. She scarcely registered a word he said. Having anticipated a total stranger, to her dumbfounded amazement she recognized him instantly.

Togrul Karabakhsky had aged a great deal. Alana guessed he must be well over eighty. But he was still hale, getting down from the high stool without difficulty. His broad face with its magnificent curving nose was deeply lined, sunken and darkened by age, and the trim mustache was entirely white, but his blue-green eyes seemed as bright as ever.

They peered now at Alana, blinking. He reached for a second pair of eyeglasses, which hung on a braided gold cord around his neck and settled them on his large nose. "Azerbaijan," he repeated softly, studying her face, "would not be what it is today. We are all of us the products of our history, and few would wish themselves any other way, however harsh that history. Is that not so?"

He took one of her hands in both of his, which were smooth and dry as bare bones and trembled with emotion. "Oh my," he said in a whisper that cracked with emotion. There were tears in his eyes. "Oh, my little Ayna, how you have grown." He smiled. "You figure your dear mother so beautifully; I could almost believe it was she standing before me."

Alana's eyes were stinging; she opened her mouth, but she couldn't speak. Instead she gave a choked-off sob, which set loose the tears, and in an instant she was crying, struggling to speak. "I …" she tried to say, "I ... didn't know ... I can't remember ... Everything's gone." Her mind was in freefall, plummeting in a rock-slide of broken, ungraspable memories.

Her grandfather, with tears running down his face, pressed her hands together gently. "Hush. Let it all go. I understand. Come, be seated."

He led her through to the next room and sat her on the daybed. Then he turned to his other guest. "Noah Abdullayev," he said, his voice hoarse with emotion. He gripped Noah's hands in his. "What can I say? You have repaid my trust and love a hundredfold."

"It was a pleasure and an honor to do it," said Noah.

Togrul took Noah aside, out of Alana's earshot, and said quietly, "How close did they come?"

"Extremely. Their agent took her, and I believe she would have been lost if I had not intervened."

The old man's face paled. "Noah, my debt to you can never be repaid."

"Sir, you have paid it already, many years ago."

While they were talking, Alana pulled herself together, drying her tears. She felt as fragile as an eggshell; anything could set her off again. She pinched the bridge of her nose, focusing her mind, trying to infuse herself with calm. When her grandfather took a step toward her, she held up her hand. "Please don't," she said. "I can hold it in, but it's taking everything."

Togrul nodded sadly and turned back to Noah. "My boy, you will take tea with us before you go?"

Alana looked up in alarm. "You're not leaving?" She hadn't realized how attached to Noah she had become; he was her only friend in this strange country.

"I have to," he said apologetically. "I have my work to go back to." To Togrul he said, "I will take tea, thank you, but then I must go. If I leave within the hour, I should be able to reach Elamxanli by nightfall."

208

Togrul could see how distressed Alana was by this. She needed an anchor, and right now, Noah was it. "You are far too fatigued to set out today," he said to Noah. "I implore you, rest here for a day or two. I know full well how important your work is, but you will do it all the better after a proper rest."

Noah took a deep breath, and his eye caught Alana's. He let the breath go. "Very well," he said with a laugh. "I forgot how persuasive the Karabakhsky family can be. One day, and then tomorrow I must go."

22

The tea was strong and clear, served in bell-shaped glasses called *armudi*; it was similar to the Turkish style Alana was familiar with, but lighter in color. Now that the initial shock was past, tiredness was overtaking her; the tea woke up her senses a little, but she still had to fight to keep her eyes open. Togrul provided a breakfast of pastries, bread, and delicious fruit preserves, which he proudly declared were from his own kitchen.

Afterwards, Noah went out on some business of his own, and Alana was given a tour of the ground floor of the house, her grandfather pointing out little medieval architectural details, which he was sure would interest her.

"I have followed your career with great pride," he said. "Stanford, Columbia, Cambridge. You have earned distinction, and you will accomplish much, I am sure of it. I have acquaintances in Turkey who know of this great site you have researched and know something of the work you have published."

Alana was struggling to keep her mind focused. Her joints ached, and there was a pulsing in her brain; sounds were distorted, and her grandfather's voice came and went. One moment crystal clarity, the next he seemed to be speaking from the far end of a cave. There was a stone bench against the wall, and she sank on to it.

"My child, please forgive me. You are exhausted from your journey. What am I thinking of? Wearying you with talk when you need rest."

"Don't apologize. I'll be okay in a minute."

He called out: "Rashad!" The mustached manservant appeared in the doorway, and Togrul spoke briefly to him. "My housekeeper will attend to you," he said to Alana.

Rashad left, and a few moments later a middle-aged woman materialized as if by magic in the doorway. All Togrul's servants went about their work with silent stealth, so as to avoid disturbing his studies. The housekeeper was stout, with steel-gray hair pulled tightly back, and a round, amiable face with an upturned nose and jet-black eyebrows.

"Mary will show you where you can rest," said Togrul, and spread his arms apologetically. "I would have accommodated you as a guest in my house, but my advisers believe that you will be more comfortable in the Four Seasons."

"A nap would be great," said Alana. "But what about Noah? He must be at least as tired."

Her grandfather shook his head. "Noah is a doctor, and accustomed to long and arduous hours in the camp."

"Camp?"

"He is one of the medical staff at a large refugee settlement near Aghjabedi, close to the border of the Armenian-occupied zone. He could have pursued a lucrative career in America or Europe, or here in Baku, but his dedication to his calling is great."

The housekeeper inclined her head with a formal smile, and Togrul remembered his manners. "Go now, and sleep," he said.

Turning toward the staircase, Alana came face to face with a large man blocking her way; she gasped and took a step back. He was tall and heavily built, and positively the ugliest man Alana had ever seen; his jaw was large and protruding, his lower teeth overlapping the upper; his forehead sloped like the front of a tank, and either side of his thick, straight nose were tiny eyes which seemed to sparkle with pure malevolence. He loomed in front of Alana like a djinn risen out of the ground.

Mary sidestepped the monster and walked to the foot of the stairs, where she waited for Alana to catch her up.

"Ah, I apologize," said Togrul, pausing at the door of the sitting room. "I should have introduced Salim. He is one of my bodyguards, provided generously by the DMX, the Special State Protection Service." He whispered in Alana's ear: "I also find him somewhat discomforting; his colleague is a little more congenial."

Salim's small, cold eyes followed Alana silently as she walked to the stairs. All the way up, she could feel his gaze on her back, like spiders crawling on her skin, until she reached a turn and passed out of sight.

The guest bedroom was large, furnished in the same antique Turkish-Azerbaijani style as the rest of the house. The walls were painted white and hung with pictures and tapestries, but even here there were bookshelves crammed with volumes.

Mary bowed, said something polite in Azerbaijani, and left, closing the door behind her.

Despite her exhaustion, Alana felt too jittery to sleep. She had an urge to lock the door, but there was no key. It was absurd – this was the house of her grandfather, a man who had dedicated himself to her safety. And yet she'd had so many shocks and terrifying scares recently, she didn't know who to trust, and her thoughts were disordered and irrational. Opposite the door was a French window opening on to a wooden balcony. She tried the door, but it was locked, and the key gone. Togrul had advised her to stay away from windows while in his house, for fear of spies. She stepped back and drew the curtain.

Sitting on the edge of the bed, Alana felt a surge of physical relief; she lay back on the pillows, her brain buzzing, certain she wouldn't be able to sleep. She closed her eyes. Bliss. The pillows were heavenly soft.

Within five seconds she was unconscious.

After Alana had gone upstairs, Togrul heard the front doorbell pealing. He went out to the courtyard to see Noah being let in by Rashad.

"Come," said Togrul. "Both of you. Let us talk." The three men went to his inner sanctum, a comfortable study with a cozy atmosphere enhanced by warm light from a window overlooking the courtyard. "Well," said Togrul as soon as they were seated. "What do our two bodyguards think?"

"Salim still believes that the young *xanim** would be safer at the hotel," said Rashad. "Uzeyir disagrees; he advises that she remain here."

"I see. Very well. Let us speak with both of them. Call them in."

"Uzeyir is out of doors, making some kind of patrol. I'll fetch Salim." Rashad got up and went out.

"What do you think, Noah?"

Noah spread his hands. "I have no opinion. I know nothing of security."

"Do you have any thoughts on the identity of our traitor?"

"Sir, you know I doubt that anyone is betraying you."

"*Somebody* leaked the information that my granddaughter was in Switzerland." Noah said nothing, and Togrul went on gravely, "I have suspicions about Salim Zardabi."

"The bodyguard? Are you serious?"

"When have you ever known me joke about my family's safety,

*   Lady (Azerbaijani).

213

Noah? Salim is Iranian by birth. His parents were from Azerbaijan, but how can he be a true Azeri?" Togrul shook his head. "His loyalty is uncertain; I suspect he might be bought."

At that moment the door opened, and Rashad came in, followed by the flinty, unsettling countenance of Salim Zardabi himself. His sharp reptilian eyes glanced rapidly around the room.

"I am told, Salim, you are determined that the *xanim* should stay at the hotel rather than here?"

The big man nodded. When he spoke, his voice was as gruff and jarring as his face. "This house has too many exits in too many locations. The windows open on to the street, the main entrance is on the Kichik Qala, and the kitchen has a door and window on the side alley between the two. All the streets are narrow; it would be difficult to evacuate the client in an emergency."

"The client?" Togrul seemed to flinch slightly at his granddaughter being referred to in such a clinical way. "Whereas at the hotel …?"

"Only one entrance to each room, inaccessible from the outside, and video surveillance throughout the building."

Rashad exchanged a look with his master. "We have heard reports of the enemy's capabilities," he said. "They already tried to take her from a hotel in England, and only failed because of the *xanim*'s good fortune."

Salim stared at Rashad, eyes glittering, then shrugged. "There was no professional close protection in that situation."

"Thank you, Salim," said Togrul. "Your advice is noted.". Once the door had closed behind the grim giant, Togrul looked at Noah. "What do you think?"

Noah had been watching the DMX agent with interest throughout the interview. "I don't know. His looks certainly do him no favors, but a *traitor*? Really?"

Togrul shook his head. "Perhaps you are right. The devil of it is that

I cannot afford to lose a guard unless I am absolutely certain. I have only two, and that only by a favor from an old friend who vouches for both of them." He sighed. "Noah, my boy, you are tired beyond all reason. Go and sleep; there is a fold-down cot in my room. Ask Mary to prepare it for you." He squeezed Noah's hand. "Go with my good wishes and Allah's blessing."

When they were alone, Togrul said to Rashad, "My old friend, I trust your word more than that of any man living. Who do you think is betraying us?"

Rashad tugged at the gray curtain of his mustache. "I cannot tell, lord. My heart too misgives me when I consider Salim. But must we think ill of him just because he was born on the wrong side of a border?"

Togrul grunted. "Perhaps it is so. Whatever the case, I must press my government friend to provide us at least one more agent. Loyal or not, two will not be enough."

"Will your friend agree to so many for a private matter?"

"I believe so. He knows this 'private matter' has implications for the security of all of Azerbaijan. In the meantime, Rashad, keep those sharp ears of yours open."

Alana was woken by her phone ringing in her pants pocket. The cheap burner she'd bought at Geneva airport had a much more violent vibration than her iPhone, and it startled the life out of her. She jolted upright with a small scream, her nightmares still chasing one another through her brain.

The number was unfamiliar. "Hello?"

"Lana honey? Is that you?"

"Daddy! You got my message!"

"Yeah, I did. I'm calling from the restaurant. D'you want to explain what's going on?"

During the layover in Istanbul, Alana had called the Berghaus Wispile, the mountaintop restaurant near the cable car station, and asked the night manager to deliver a message – by hand, not phone – to Mr. Fulton in his cabin, promising him a very large tip. The message consisted of only her phone number, the instruction not to use his cell, and the phrase "Bun-bun," his pet name for her when she was little.

"I'm safe, Daddy. Don't worry about me. I've … I've come home."

"Malibu?"

"No, I mean my original home."

There was silence, and then: "*What?*"

Alana didn't dare to give specifics over the phone, just in case. "I'm with my grandfather – the one who gave me away."

John Fulton was utterly confounded for a moment, then the penny dropped. "Oh. Well, how in the world did you find *him*?"

"They killed Howard, Daddy." Alana's voice cracked as she said it, and she began to cry. Everything had happened so fast, she'd hardly had a chance to take it in, but she could still see the blood on the snow, and that hideous stick impaling his body, his eyes – which had been so beautiful – lifeless and staring, and his face streaked with red. "Daddy, you have to go somewhere safe. Don't go back to the apartment. Go straight to where Mommy is and take her to a safe place. Do you have somewhere?"

"Sweetheart, you have to tell me where you are. What in the world is—"

"And hire security. I mean full-on, badass secret service-type bodyguards."

"Dear God, Alana, what have you gotten mixed up in?"

"Get yourself a prepaid phone and text me the number. Don't ever call me on any phone that's registered to you. Listen, I have to go."

"Wait, aren't you gonna—"

216

"I love you, Daddy." She hung up, and sat with her head in her hands, trying to get her feelings under control.

Her watch was still set to Gstaad time, where it was a little after nine in the morning. She didn't know what the time difference for Azerbaijan was, but guessed it must be around noon. She'd slept for only three hours, and it had left her feeling thick-headed and queasy. She went in search of a bathroom.

As on the ground floor, there was a stone corridor with arched windows overlooking the octagonal courtyard. She found the bathroom next to the stairs. It was beautiful, with exquisitely intricate tilework in a pattern of radiating suns in colors of amber, aquamarine and turquoise, bordered by images of foliage and birds in emerald green and salmon pink. The fittings were antique, and she surveyed the gleaming copper pipes and complicated faucets above the huge, enameled bath in dismay. Fresh towels had been laid out, and Alana contented herself with rinsing her face in cold water.

The whole house was eerily silent. Faint sounds of the street could be heard, but from indoors there was not so much as a footstep or a creaking hinge. Alana had never felt so much like a stranger. She went downstairs with some trepidation, fearful of meeting the djinn-like bodyguard, Salim. To her relief, she found Noah in the library, reading. He looked up and smiled as she came in: that same comforting smile she'd begun to grow used to and (though she wasn't yet conscious of it) dependent on.

"Did you sleep well?" he asked.

"Oh, a little, I guess."

"Then you did better than me."

"Where is everybody?"

"Your grandfather is in his study." He whispered: "Hence the silence throughout the house."

Alana sat at the library table. "Does all of this feel as strange to you as it does to me?"

"I assure you it does. I am not used to intrigue, only broken bones and bad stomachs."

"My grandfather told me you work in a refugee camp."

"It's near the town of Aghjabedi in the west of Azerbaijan, in the region that borders Karabakh. It isn't really a camp; the last tent camps for refugees were closed several years ago. Elamxanli is a settlement for displaced families. There are many such settlements in Azerbaijan."

"Where do the refugees come from?"

"Nearly all are Azeris. Most fled the slaughter in Karabakh when you and I were children, when the Armenians occupied it. Others are ethnic Azeris driven out of Armenia itself. They lost their lands, their property, and their livelihoods."

"That's awful. Those poor people."

"Under Azerbaijan law, the IDPs – that's internally displaced persons – are treated well. Azeris coming from Armenia get citizenship, and all IDPs have special rights to housing, employment, free healthcare, and so on. I am the senior pediatric physician at my settlement's infirmary."

"Have you worked there long?"

"About a year and a half, ever since I came back from Cambridge."

Alana flinched slightly at this reminder of his role in spying on her, and Noah blushed and looked down at his book.

A woman's voice spoke suddenly from just behind Alana, and she almost jumped out of her seat. Mary had materialized again. Noah translated: "Mary says lunch will be in twenty minutes." The housekeeper smiled serenely and left as silently as she had come.

"Damn, I wish she wouldn't do that. That woman's like a Ninja."

Noah regarded Alana sympathetically. "You are jumpy. It's understandable."

Alana reflected that if Mary had worked for her, she'd have made her wear a bell, but kept the thought to herself.

Togrul emerged from his study just as a gong sounded from the next room. Alana was to learn that the old gentleman was never late to a meal; it was the one thing that never failed to prize him away from his books and papers. Inquiring solicitously about her nap and her comfort, he took Alana's arm in his and led her to the dining room.

Rashad was there already, and somewhat to Alana's surprise he sat down with them. She'd taken him for a servant, but as her grandfather explained as they ate, Rashad was a kind of steward; as a young man he had managed Togrul's affairs in Shusha whenever he was away in Baku or at his hilltop estate above Khojali. Now he was a combination of personal assistant and overseer of the household.

The table was laden with food in the Azerbaijani fashion: plates of fruit and sliced vegetables, and a large bowl filled with dolmas, which were quite unlike the cold vegetable dolmas she'd had in Turkey. These were wrapped layers of meat, vine leaves and rice, lightly spiced and topped with garlic yoghurt. There were three varieties of Azerbaijani-style pilaf – called *plov* – made with chicken, dried fruits and nuts, and fish. At first, Alana didn't think she'd be able to eat a thing; anxiety had left her nauseous. But as soon as she took the first mouthful, she became ravenous and ate steadily, refilling her plate twice.

Her grandfather watched her with affectionate satisfaction and made conversation with Noah and Rashad. The steward spoke no English, so his words had to be translated for Alana's benefit. It touched her that they went to such lengths to make her feel at home.

"This will not suffice forever, you know," her grandfather said, taking a ripe plum and slicing it. "You must learn Azerbaijani. You spoke it once, remember."

"I guess I must have," she said. "I don't remember at all." In the fragments of memory she had, it seemed as if people spoke in English if they spoke at all – her own brain translating the emotions into words. She set down her fork. "I want to learn all about that time: my mother and father, all my family. Most of all I want to learn what's going on – who HACA is and why they want to kill me."

Togrul and Noah exchanged a look. "They do not want to kill you," said her grandfather. "Precisely the opposite; they wish to take you alive. They wish this to such a degree that they will kill or destroy anyone and anything that blocks their path."

"But why?"

Togrul sighed heavily. "I knew it would come to this. To explain even a part of this, I shall have to teach you a lot of ancient history."

Alana smiled. "Well, isn't that lucky? It just so happens that ancient history is pretty much my favorite thing."

23

Togrul stooped before a chest with a dozen long, shallow drawers. "In here I keep my most precious documents," he said, opening a drawer and taking out a large, illuminated parchment. Setting some books carefully to one side, he cleared the sloped surface of his scribe's desk and laid the parchment on it. Alana could now see that it was an elaborate painting in a medieval Islamic style. At first, she thought it was a horseback hunting scene, but then realized it depicted a battle, rendered in green, scarlet, cobalt blue, and silver, with details picked out in gold leaf.

"This was made around 1520," said Togrul, and glanced over his spectacles at Alana. "It is only a copy, you understand, but a very exact one. It shows a battle before the city walls when Azerbaijan was invaded by Shah Ismail the First in 1501."

Under a sky of gold leaf and swirling clouds, knights in plumed turbans and gorgeously decorated blue and green tunics rode plump horses against one another, wielding huge scimitars and bows. On the city walls, soldiers in pointed helmets banged drums and blew trumpets at the combatants.

"The battle was a terrible, bloody defeat," said Togrul. "Baku fell, and the Shirvanshah dynasty, Sunni Muslims who had ruled eastern Azerbaijan for over seven hundred years, eventually gave way to the Shia Safavids from the Safavid empire that ruled Persia. Safavids, by the way, were of Turkic origin, they were Iranian Azeri Shia Muslim, not Sunni, and this difference created a lot of conflict between the Sunni Ottomans and the Shia Safavids, even though they both spoke the same language – ancient Turkish. Despite living on both sides, the Azeri form a single group. However, northerners and southerners differ, due to nearly two centuries of separate social evolution in Russian Soviet-influenced Azerbaijan and Iranian Azerbaijan, which today is part of Iran.

"All of these languages can be traced to the Turkish Oghuz, who moved into the Caucasus from central Asia in the eleventh century. Following the Russian–Persian wars of the eighteenth and nineteenth centuries, Persian territories in the Caucasus, some under merely nominal control, were ceded to the Russian empire. This included parts of the current Republic of Azerbaijan. The treaties of Golestan in 1813 and Tukmanchai in 1828 finalized the border between Russian and Persia, now Iran."

Togrul laid his bony hand on the image. "I show you this because it is emblematic of Azerbaijan's history. Like European nations, the lands between the Black Sea and the Caspian, between Asia Minor and Persia, have been shaped by war and migration. Peoples have moved and spread, religions and civilizations have come and gone, nations have been created, and the boundaries between them have been conjured out of soil and culture and language; the borders have expanded, shrunk, and blown away on the wind.

"The one thing that has remained constant is the land. And that is bound up with the human need to possess it. To live on the land, to work it, to spill blood for it, is to be at one with it."

He clenched and unclenched his gnarled old fist. "Now, examine that map."

There was a large modern map of the Caucasus on the wall between two bookcases. Alana went and looked at it. The land between the two seas was like a broad bridge linking Russia to the Middle East, walled on the north by the Caucasus Mountains. It contained three small nations: Georgia, Armenia, and Azerbaijan.

"See how they fold into one another," said Togrul. "Georgia protrudes into Azerbaijan, and Azerbaijan protrudes into Georgia. Armenia is squeezed between the two of them, with Azerbaijan's Nakhchivan enclave cut off by a branch of Armenia. You see, my child, unlike modern Armenia, where as a result of ethnic cleansing hundreds of thousands of Azeris who had lived there for centuries were expelled, Azerbaijan has always been a host of nations, welcoming for centuries people from all over the regions, and that is precisely how Armenians, or to use the correct term, *Hays*, infiltrated our region. The Hays came from modern Turkey, they never inhabited the Caucasus region. Today's territory of Armenia was ruled by ancient Albanians, but modern Armenians claimed that it was 'ancient Armenian'. The name of the land was indeed ancient Armenia, however the inhabitants of ancient Armenia were a Turkic tribe that lived here long before the Hays invaded. Not many dare to say so, but it is very clear from even a linguistic point of view that Ar and Men means 'I am a man' in Turkish; in Armenian it has no meaning. The Hays simply appropriated a Turkic heritage."

"Why do you call them *Hays*?" asked Alana

"I don't; that's what Armenians call themselves in their own language. And their country, Armenia, they call *Hayastan*. The Hays were a tribe that moved into our lands and after centuries of chauvinism and ethnic and cultural cleansing fabricated a history. Stealing our ancestors' tombs, changing and manipulating the engravings to their advantage. They have even claimed Albanian churches as Armenian churches. Some of them have claimed that Albanian prince Tigran was an Armenian warrior prince, shamelessly taking credit for his valor. Nevertheless my child, lies always find their way to the surface. There are historical records that prove all that I am telling you. Although they have managed to fool most of Europe and parts of the West, the truth will always remain the truth. Always remember, God sees everything."

He sighed, and then continued. "Our people have made mistakes, too. For instance, in 1918 first prime minister of what was then the Democratic Republic of Azerbaijan gifted the city of Yerevan to what became Soviet Russia, who made it the capital of Soviet Armenia. In the early nineteenth century, the Russian empire took over the Erevan khanate (Yerevan) and started populating it with Armenians from Turkey and Iran and gradually settled in, expelling Azeris and demolishing much beautiful architecture to erase its Azeri origins. When the Russian empire collapsed and the Soviet Union was established, it in turn established the Nagorno-Karabakh Autonomous Region which had by then a majority Armenian migrant population. It was in the interests of the Soviet Union to settle migrants in Azerbaijan, to limit calls for independence. The Russian empire and then the Soviet Union were highly dependent on Azeri oil, with more than seventy-five percent of that oil coming from Baku oil fields. The borders are the scars of long-ago battles. Or perhaps it is truer to say they are like the weed and foam left behind by a retreating tide, marking the farthest limit of its effort to invade the land."

Alana could imagine the pressures that had drawn these lines. "Historically, then," she said, "who are the Azerbaijanis? What is really Azerbaijan?"

Her grandfather smiled and sat down at the table. "You are a student of ancient history. You know better than to ask such questions. One might as well ask, who precisely are the Americans? What is America? You may talk of these things as if you know what they are, but try to answer the question and you discover that there is no definition. Like Americans, like the British or the French, like the lines on that map, Azeris today are the offspring of multiple tribes, a multicultural heritage, unceasing conflict, and unique circumstances. But we still have our shared sense of identity, our connection to the language, music, folk tales and – above all – the land for which all of us have bled."

Alana sat opposite her grandfather. She was beginning to understand where this was going, and what it might have to do with her. "This is about Karabakh, isn't it? Land and possession."

The old man sighed deeply and poured out two glasses of aromatic black tea from a pot, which had appeared silently on the table while they were looking at the painting. He took a sip. "The ancient core of the Azeri people comes from multiple Turkic tribes, but let's focus on the Caucasian Albanians, who settled this region millennia ago. But they are our forebears only in the sense that the English are Saxons, or the Americans are Europeans; it is a seminal element, you understand, not the whole.

"The name 'Albanian' had no connection whatsoever with European Albania. The name came from the Turkic nomadic tribe called the Alans, who lived in the region and were said by some to be descended from Noah." Togrul smiled at his granddaughter. "They later became mingled with –part of – the Albanian people. When James Aldridge told me that he had taken to calling you Alana instead of Ayna, it pleased me, for it is an echo of your long descent from that tribe."

"My father mentioned that. I mean my adoptive father, John."

Togrul frowned at his glass. "I shall carry to my grave the heartache

225

I felt when I watched James take you away from my house and from Karabakh."

Alana turned her tea glass round and round on the table, trying to control her feelings. She looked her grandfather in the eyes. "Why did you let me go? You kept others with you. You talk about heartache, but can you imagine how this feels for me?"

There were tears in her eyes. Togrul reached across the table and took her hand. "Oh my child, my child. I can never atone for the pain you suffer. When I look at you now, a part of me wishes that I had buried the secret deeper, cut you off entirely from all knowledge of where you came from, so that you would never suffer this, so that you would never be discovered and endangered." His eyes searched her face. "Why did I send you away? Because your life was at risk long before the first Armenian soldier set foot in Khojali. After that, your destiny and mine hung in the balance. The Armenians hate and fear both of us. But you in particular the want to destroy – for you are the future – but they also need you."

"What for? Why would they fear me?"

Togrul wiped away the tears that had come to his eyes and took a deep breath. He refilled his glass and sipped. "Let us return to ancient history," he said. "Where was I?"

Alana took a deep breath and sat back in her chair. "The Caucasian Albanians." Whatever answers were coming, they were taking the long way round. Alana couldn't help being fascinated by the journey; she knew bits and pieces from courses she'd taken in her sophomore year at Stanford, but little of it had stuck, and her professors hadn't brought to it the sense of personal investment that Togrul Karabakhsky brought.

"The kingdom of Caucasian Albania began in the third century BCE – which of course was the ninth to eighth century before the Hijra in the Islamic calendar. The kingdom coalesced out of no fewer than twenty-six tribal chiefdoms under the overall rule of King Aran. Some of Albania's borders were similar to those of modern Azerbaijan, straddling the Caucasus Mountains in the north and bounded on the south by the river Aras, which to this day forms part of the border with Iran. Other borders shifted, as borders will, through war and treaty, but they always included the land of mountains and rolling plains we know as Karabakh.

"The Albanians spoke a Turkic language. The Greek geographer Strabo describes them as tall, blond-haired and with gray eyes, as many are to this day; you yourself have blue-green eyes, and your grandmother was as blonde as oaken heartwood. Strabo calls the Albanians brave and warlike; they worshipped the moon, the sun, the stars and planets. Their ancient capital was the great walled city of Gabala, where they had a temple dedicated to the moon. They were pagans, naturally, and the Zoroastrian religion – with its belief in the power of fire and water – became dominant. There were wars and invasions. Empires rose and expanded in Persia and the Levant and the vast modern Russian lands. Peoples migrated, cultures spread, and the states of the Caucasus were part of that."

Togrul's brow furrowed, as if recalling a painful memory.

"In 313 CE, influenced by Rome, Albania was among the first states in the world to convert to Christianity. When the Roman Empire grew weak, the Persians took the opportunity to invade Albania. Thus began centuries of rule by invading empires and kingdoms, and incursions by warrior tribes – exactly as was occurring at the same time in Europe. Albania became a battleground between the Persian and Byzantine empires and the Khazar nomads, who came from what is now Russia."

Alana realized that her glass of tea had gone cold in her hand. She was beginning to wonder whether she ought to be taking notes. As her grandfather spoke, his deep voice rising and falling with an almost hypnotic musicality, her gaze shifted between his face and the wall map, tracing in her imagination the migrations and invasions across mountain, plain, river, and sea.

"All these changes were mere undulations and digressions in the track of Albania's history," he continued. "In the seventh century came a transformation that altered everything. Islam came. The word of the Prophet rolled in a titanic wave out of Arabia, bringing the whole of Persia into the light of the one true religion. All of Persia's vassals were affected. From then on, Caucasian Albania began to fade from existence, split into Islamic principalities ruled by princes called *khans*. There were more wars, more invasions, more blending and mingling of peoples with the Albanians – Turks, Persians, Arabs, Mongols. Slowly, the state of Azerbaijan grew out of the melting pot. Fundamentally it retained a memory of its past, but it was no longer Albanian. It was Azeri.

"Among the Persian vassal states was the Khanate of Karabakh." The old man's voice grew wistful, like a man speaking the name of a lost love. "The name Karabakh is traditionally said to mean Black Garden in Turkic and old Persian. Some modern scholars dispute that, as scholars will." He began to rummage among books and papers piled on the table, and finally found an academic journal printed in what looked to Alana like Azerbaijani. "Here we have it," he said, leafing through. "Two linguists – one Iranian, the other Azerbaijani – suggest that *kara* does not mean black at all but derives from an old Azeri word meaning large or great. An Armenian scholar," he added disdainfully, "has tried to claim it comes from an Armenian place name; they never cease with their irrational claims to Karabakh." He gave Alana a sour glance. "I believe we can dismiss that. So it is Great Garden or Black Garden – take your choice. I prefer the romance of the old meaning, though Karabakh is a green country; it has its share of brown and gray, but very little black."

"Black Garden," Alana repeated. "I think I prefer that, too."

"In the old times it was far larger than the region now generally recognized as Karabakh. The part of it within Azerbaijan you have heard called Nagorno-Karabakh, which is the eastern, mountainous half of the ancient khanate. From the beginning, the Khanate of Karabakh was Azeri, although many Armenians lived peacefully within it. It became semi-independent from Iran in 1750, with its capital in the city of Shusha.

"Karabakh was a much-desired land, and many attempts to seize it were made by Iranian khans; it was invaded, and Shusha besieged several times, and even sacked. But Karabakh retained its independence."

Togrul, whose lined face had become animated and passionate, lowered his eyes, and his voice grew mournful. "That did not last. While Iran and the Caucasian states fought their petty conflicts, in the north the Russian Empire had been growing. In 1813, having beaten Iran in a war, the Russians seized control of Karabakh. The khanate was abolished in 1822, and the last khan, Mehdigulu Khan Javanshir, lived as an influential and powerful figure, but with no official authority to rule. And so it remained ever after, under Russian imperial and Soviet rule, until the line of the khans descended from my father to me."

It took a few moments for her grandfather's closing words to click in Alana's brain. "Are you saying you're a descendant of the khans of Karabakh?"

"Father to son," Togrul said solemnly. "For over three hundred years. My forefathers lost the title, but the Azeris of Karabakh continued to regard us unofficially as their lords. You may call us khan, but you

229

must whisper it. Azeri names were Russified, and the name we acquired was Karabakhsky – a Russian form meaning from or belonging to Karabakh." He held Alana's gaze. "I am Togrul Karabakhsky. My son, your father, was Tengiz Karabakhsky, and you were born Ayna Chichak Karabakhsky."

Alana repeated the name: "Karabakhsky."

"Your pronunciation is impeccable. You see, you belong to that name, as you belong to Karabakh. And that is why you are such a threat to the Armenian extremists."

"What does the middle name mean?"

Mary appeared at that moment with a fresh pot of tea and glasses, delicious white figs from the garden, little crunchy red apples, organically-grown grapes and lots of fresh, aromatic cherries, along with preserves and cakes. Togrul poured out the tea and pushed the cakes toward Alana.

"Ah," he said. "Now that goes back to my late beloved wife, Seljan, your grandmother – she of the gray eyes and blonde hair. She was a great admirer of the *Book of Dede Korkut*, an ancient collection of twelve epic tales of Caucasian Albania set down in the seventh century. One tells of the wooing of a princess named Banuchichak, who was a highly accomplished warrior, archer, and hunter, and skilled in hand-to-hand combat."

"A warrior princess?"

"Oh, indeed. You have heard of Amazons, no doubt? Well, one of the places claimed as the location of the fabled female warriors is Azerbaijan. They are mentioned frequently in the *Dede Korkut*, and before that, Strabo wrote that the Amazons lived in Caucasian Albania." The old man got up and went to bookcase, from which he withdrew an old leather-bound volume. "It was reported that they were the cavalry in the battles against the invading Romans. Here, peruse this."

Togrul laid the book open on the table before Alana. On a page filled with Arabic writing was a picture of a woman sitting on a floor of gold leaf; she was clad in a blue tunic with crimson sleeves and a silver breastplate. At her hip was a scimitar, and on her head a hat with a long black plume. From the sculpting of the breastplate, she was clearly female.

"Strabo writes," said Togrul, putting on his spectacles and consulting another book: "*The Amazons spend their time isolated from men, occupying themselves with plowing and sowing, planting, taking their herds to pasture, and in breeding horses. The more courageous among them engage in hunting on horseback and exercise martial arts.* He writes further that in their youth, the warrior women had their right breast removed to help with use of the bow and the spear. They trained also with axes and shields."

Togrul laid down his spectacles. "There were women besides Amazons who were warriors and hunters, and they are prominent in Azeri folklore. Your grandmother loved such tales since her childhood, but most of all she loved the story of Banuchichak." He tapped the picture. "When you were born, she claimed she saw such strength in you. In her honor you were given the middle name Chichak."

"I wish I'd known her. Did she die in the war?"

"No. Seljan was taken by leukemia, when you were only an infant. I wish also that you had known her. She was not a soldier, but she was clever, and she possessed courage and an iron will. Now that I see you grown, I perceive much of her in you. I still feel the heartbreak of her passing, though at the same time I give thanks that she did not live to see the land she loved taken away." Togrul's eyes grew hard and cold. "I still belong to Karabakh, even though the Armenians finally succeeded in driving Azeris out, and Karabakh belongs by right to us."

231

"Sir, why haven't the international organizations and other countries done anything about this?" demanded Alana.

"Call me grandfather, Ayna" he said gently. "The truth is that since 1991, when the Armenian military occupied the internationally-recognized territory of Azerbaijan, there have been four UN Security Council and two UN General Assembly resolutions demanding that Armenia withdraw its their occupying forces. Armenia ignores them to this day. Also, the OSCE Minsk Group, co-chaired by France, Russia, and the US, was formed in 1992 to find a peaceful solution to the conflict, but to no avail. A ceasefire was agreed in 1994 but the Armenian side occasionally fires at us still. As you can see on the map, the Armenian armed forces occupied twenty percent of the Republic of Azerbaijan's territory – the Nagorno-Karabakh region and seven adjacent districts, including the town of Khankandi and the districts of Khojali, Shusha, Lachin, Khojavand, Kalbajar, Aghdam, Fuzuli, Jabrayil, Gubadli and Zangilan, as well as thirteen villages in Tartar district, seven villages in Gazakh district and one village in Sadarak district in Nakhchivan."

Togrul Karabakhsky's hand trembled with emotion as he handed Alana the map, which was a modern depiction of Azerbaijan.

"Grandfather, why are these cities marked in red? That's not Karabakh."

"Indeed my child these are the seven occupied districts that are part of Azerbaijan republic and had a majority Azeri population. When they attacked Karabakh they took a little extra land as their buffer zone." He looked down on the map with deep pain in his eyes.

"But these lands together are much larger than the territory of Karabakh! I've never seen anything like this before." She took a deep breath and continued. "So Armenia has not only occupied a sovereign country, Azerbaijan, but then annexed a greater portion of land by calling it "a buffer zone". They must think the entire world very gullible if they think they can portray themselves as the victims in this case."

"Very well said, my child. Very well said indeed. Armenia initially took control of these seven territories as a temporary measure, to prevent Azerbaijani attacks on Nagorno-Karabakh; they were eventually to be returned to Azerbaijan as part of a peace deal to resolve the conflict. But as time passed, that notion faded, replaced by a conviction that these are integral parts of the Armenian homeland, never to be surrendered."

They sat for a while in silence, Togrul's head bent over his glass.

Alana began: "Grandfather, I don't mean any offense ... Forgive me, but for a prince you seem to live pretty modestly. Why is that? I mean, Noah told me what an important man you are, and I've seen some of the power and influence you have. You paid for Noah's medical education, and he implied he wasn't the only one." She glanced around the room, at the scuffed furniture and worn carpets. "This house is beautiful, but it's not a princely palace."

Togrul laughed. "It is not, you are right. And yet this has been the Baku residence of the khans of Karabakh since my great grandfather's day. It was once considerably larger, but my father was obliged to sell portions of it to neighboring householders. The reasons were complicated and dreary, and are among the many things I have forgotten in my old age. Indeed, it is not a palace. The fortress palace of the khans is in Shusha. You should see it, child! White walls and domes inlaid with silver and gold; the imperial wings containing the royal apartments; tower upon battlement; gardens and courtyards planted with jasmine, rose, vines, orange and lime trees ..." He sighed. "I lost it when it was captured by the invading Armenian forces. I shall carry that shame and grief to my grave." He looked into Alana's eyes. "Ayna, my child, how could I live like a prince when I no longer have possession of my lands? When my people are scattered to camps and settlements far from their homes?" Togrul tapped a thick, yellowed fingernail on the table. "When Karabakh is returned, then I will truly be khan once more. And you, my child, will be khanim after me."

Alana contemplated this astounding suggestion in silence.

"Unhappy fate has laid this burden at your feet," said her grandfather. "My own father was a far-seeing man, and given to making prophecies. He foresaw that the Armenians would reach out at last to seize Karabakh during my lifetime. But he said of my son Tengiz, when Tengiz was only five years old, *This child's issue will bring back the fortunes of the khans. His blood will mark the loss of all, and yet his child's hand will restore all.*

"I never understood what my father meant, but when Tengiz grew to manhood he named his only son Hakan, and the forgotten prophecy came back to my mind."

At the sound of the name, an image flashed in Alana's mind – a little boy, laughing, a puppy licking his face … she could hear the high-pitched sound of his laughter. The image was so violently sudden, for a moment she thought she was going to be sick.

Her grandfather didn't notice. "The name *Hakan*, you see, is a joining of two Turkic words: *han* and *kagan*, both equivalent to *khan*. Prince of princes. Foolishly, I took this for a sign that the prophecy was true, and when the invasion and the battles began in Karabakh, I believed that Hakan was destined to win back, one day, all that was lost. When I learned that he had been murdered at Khojali, all my hopes failed. What little strength I could muster, I devoted to keeping you safe. But now I see you, and I know that Seljan was right. You are truly another Banuchichak. My hopes have begun to revive, and I believe now that my father's prophecy referred not to Hakan, but to you."

234

"Me? That's just … just …"

"This is why the Armenian militants fear you, Alana, and why they prize your life so highly. They too can see what I see. To me, it is a foundation of hope. To them, it is a bell tolling to portend their doom."

24

The courtyard was quiet, and although it was overlooked by windows, it felt like solitude. All Alana could hear was the muted sounds of the street waking up and coming to life. The early morning sky overhead was heavy with cloud, and the cold wind spiraled down into the courtyard, stirring fallen leaves and dust.

Alana hadn't slept well during the night. Her mind was preoccupied with all that her grandfather had told her the previous afternoon, and with his final revelation. It astounded and worried her that a man so learned – and so practical – could really believe in prophecies and destinies. Alana had no belief in such things. She believed in evidence and theory and reason, the knowability of the past and the predictive modeling of future events. Not fantasies conjured out of myths and family tales.

Gazing up at the courtyard walls, she noticed for the first time that the upper story only had windows on five sides; the other three had been bricked up. In the front vestibule she found doorways that had also been blocked. It felt like a metaphor for her existence: whole rooms and lives full of the past, closed off, shut away, inaccessible.

She turned back to the courtyard and saw a man watching her

silently by the inner door. It was Uzeyir, the second DMX close protection agent. She'd been introduced to him the previous evening. He was a far more comforting presence than his monstrous colleague Salim. Uzeyir Khalilzade was Karabakh-born – and thus absolutely trustworthy in her grandfather's eyes – and whereas Salim was an ugly, looming presence, everything about Uzeyir was compact and neat. His body was compact, and he had compact features in a compact head, decorated with a neat little black goatee. His mouth, though, was wide and generous and lapsed readily into a genial grin.

It had been Uzeyir who persuaded Togrul that Alana would be safer staying here than at the hotel. Two agents would not be sufficient to scout and protect her movements back and forth, he argued, and Salim had been forced to agree. Togrul had requested a third bodyguard from his friend General Azim Hajiyev, who was head of the DMX. General Hajiyev was not quite a true Karabakh man (in Togrul's terms), but came from the Aghdam district, and was sympathetic. The promised a third agent was expected to arrive later that morning.

"Nothing bad, miss?" said Uzeyir, whose English wasn't great.

"No, nothing bad." If there was one thing about Uzeyir that unsettled her, it was the look in his eyes when he smiled; it seemed like he was amused by something that only he could see. It made her feel he was about to jeer at something.

"Good," he said. "All good, nothing bad."

She found breakfast laid out in the dining room: a spread of tea, coffee, fruits, and bread. Noah had beaten her to it and was sitting at the table digging in with relish. He half rose from his chair as she came in.

"You slept well?" he asked.

"Yeah, pretty good," she said, untruthfully, and sat down.

The previous evening Noah and Togrul had enacted a benign

conspiracy to keep Alana's mind off the hostile world outside. They had talked of Azeri traditions and attempted to reintroduce her to the Azerbaijani language. It had felt bizarre, like listening to a hauntingly familiar-sounding song, only to find that it isn't at all how you think you remember it. Some words came back to her, but most did not, and the grammar was virtually all gone. All that remained was the rhythm and cadences.

She poured herself strong black coffee. "I still have no idea what I'm doing here," she said. "But thanks for bringing me, all the same."

"It has been a delight and a privilege."

"Togrul told me a lot of stuff yesterday. I asked him what the Armenians want from me, but he just talked about history. Noah, I *saw* what these people can do, the reach they have. There's no way they're taking this much trouble just to head off some fantastical prophecy about me being the next Princess of Karabakh."

"Now I have also seen what they can do, I agree with you."

"You do? So what do *you* think they want?"

Noah shrugged. "I can only speculate. I told you about HACA – the Holy Apostolic Crusade for Artsakh. These people are motivated by religious ideology. Like ISIS – fanatical and ruthless. Also like ISIS, HACA has practical requirements. Their ideology is focused on consolidating Nagorno-Karabakh as the Republic of Artsakh – a process already well under way. But their scope may be wider than that. And they must have finance. Azerbaijan is a resource-rich country. Armenia, not so much; it is not impossible that they have their hearts set on the wealth of all Azerbaijan. Karabakh may be their way in."

"Like the Romans," said Alana.

"Nothing ever changes."

"Least of all Azerbaijan's oil," said Alana's grandfather, appearing in the doorway. He came and sat at the table. Noah poured him some tea, and he took a sweet pastry from a dish and began to cut it up. "I hope you slept comfortably?" he said, looking solicitously at Alana.

"I was really comfortable, thanks." That at least was true.

"I was just telling Alana about the mineral wealth of Azerbaijan."

"Indeed, so I heard. Gold, titanium, copper, silver … all the precious minerals Allah sowed upon the earth are here. But chiefly oil. The fifth century Roman diplomat Priscus wrote that at Baku, *ex petra maritima flamma ardet* – from the rock of the sea a flame springs. In the thirteenth century Marco Polo came here: "*There is a spring from which gushes a stream of oil,* he wrote, *in such abundance that a hundred ships may load there at once. This oil is not good to eat; but it is good for burning. Men come from a long distance to fetch this oil, and in all the region no other oil is burnt but this.*"

"Oil is the mainstay of Azerbaijan's economy," said Noah. "There are pipelines taking it from Baku through Georgia and Turkey to the Mediterranean, bypassing Armenia. I dare say Armenia would give a great deal to have some of that wealth."

Noah and Alana exchanged a look.

"What are you thinking?" said Togrul.

"Noah thinks Armenia might see Karabakh as a steppingstone to taking all of Azerbaijan and its oil."

Togrul studied Noah. "You think this is why they want Ayna and me?"

"You do not think so?"

"I do not." The old man sipped his tea and broke off a piece of bread. "For HACA at least, Karabakh is the prize. Their colonization proceeds apace, but they have no legal recognition around the world. Their so-called republic there is as weak as a fledgling; legally, most of Nagorno-Karabakh still belongs to expelled Azeris and the descendants of those who were murdered. By far the largest and richest single portion belongs to the Karabakhsky estate, to which I retain title."

He gave a little bow toward Alana. "Which will pass to my heirs. If anyone is capable of beginning proceedings for restitution in the international courts, it would be my lineage. And that could cost Armenia and the so-called 'Republic of Artsakh' very dearly indeed. They might even lose possession of Karabakh entirely. To prevent that, there is nothing they will not do."

The third bodyguard arrived as scheduled, just before noon. He was a colleague of Uzeyir and Salim, but as different from them both as they were from each other. Rustam Mammadov was from an Aghdam family who had been driven out when the Armenians took the city in 1993, a year after the darkest day in the Karabakh war, when Armenian soldiers attacked the village of Khojali and killed all its residents in a single night. The Khojali massacre took place during the night between February 25 and 26, when more than 600 peaceful civilians were slaughtered. Almost 200 others, mostly women and children, were captured and remain missing to this day. Despite all evidence, the Armenian authorities have yet to acknowledge their responsibility. Rustam was the embodiment of the Caucasian Albanian archetype described by Togrul: blond, gray-eyed, and handsome. And whereas Salim projected an aura of cold, watchful cunning and Uzeyir's grin hinted at a secretive humor, Rustam's face was open, intelligent, and friendly.

Alana took a liking to Rustam as soon as she was introduced. He was immediately her favorite bodyguard; Uzeyir was second, and Salim she tried to avoid entirely. However, she was fated to have little contact with the new man. His specialty was the most important element of close protection: scouting. He would be spending most of his time out and about.

He had already conducted an initial patrol of the area around the

Kichik Qala and reported it clear. If HACA were watching Togrul's house at all, it must be by intermittent intelligence-gathering sweeps, not a continuous stakeout. Rustam knew the Old City and the government district inside out. "If anything smell bad or out of place," he told Togrul, speaking in a slightly fractured English for Alana's benefit, "I know it right away. Outsiders have been in Kichik Qala in this month, but not since a few days."

Togrul was visibly heartened by this news; his stooped shoulders and bent back straightened a little, and his habitually somber expression lightened. At the same time, Alana felt a weight lift from her. As welcoming and lovely as this house was, she had already begun to feel imprisoned.

Over lunch, she suggested that perhaps she might be allowed out to take a look at the city. "I mean, I saw so little on the way in from the airport, but enough to whet my appetite. There's so much I want to see." Togrul's somber expression immediately returned. But before he could raise objections, Alana went on: "I'm sure Noah would accompany me. Wouldn't you?"

"Sure," said Noah, with a wary glance at Togrul. "I have to leave tomorrow, but ..."

Alana beamed; she could see her grandfather's resistance weakening. "With the guards and Noah and everything, nothing can go wrong."

"I was correct," said Togrul. "You have your grandmother's spirit. Banuchichak indeed." He held up his hands in surrender. "Very well. But Noah – mark me – my granddaughter's life is in your hands. You, of all people, know what that means."

Alana and Noah walked along the Kichik Qala, Alana admiring the old mosques, ranging from a tiny medieval building tucked into a street corner to the Mosque Cuma, an edifice of honey-colored stone with carved arches and minaret. Uzeyir walked alongside, close to Alana, his dark, watchful eyes constantly on the move. Salim walked a few paces behind. Rustam was somewhere up ahead.

"What did my grandfather mean, that you *of all people* know what my life means?"

"I guess I know how important you are to him," said Noah. "Since I was a boy, he has talked of it."

Alana had so many unanswered questions. Some she was too afraid to ask – such as why the firm her grandfather had used to communicate with Howard was said to have terrorist connections. Others the wily old man found ways of deflecting – such as the details of what had really happened on the night of the massacre. Her memories of it were fragmented and contradictory. But when she asked, he began talking about her parents, Tengiz and Nurbanu; Alana was hungry to know more, and she only realized later that he hadn't answered her questions. She guessed he found it too painful.

"This is our destination," said Noah.

They were in a narrow side-street, beside a medieval stone wall of square-cut blocks, two stories high and almost featureless except for a few tiny slits high up. On the sidewalk, a train of miniature bronze camels led to a massive porch under a pointed arch, in which was a great double door of carved russet-colored wood.

"Originally it was a thirteenth-century *caravanserai*," he said. "What you would call in England a travelers' inn – but eastern-style."

He pushed open the door, and they stepped into an interior that was like the entrance to Togrul's house but on a far larger, grander scale. An airy stone passage led to a wide octagonal courtyard laid out as a restaurant, enclosed by two stories of arched alcoves. Eastern music filled Alana's ears, and there was the familiar aroma of spices and tea and ancient stone. Traditional carpets were spread on the flagstones, and tapestries hung on the walls between silver lamps. It had originally been open to the sky, but now a glazed roof kept out the wintry chill.

They sat at a table not far from where a three-piece ensemble was playing. "That is *mugham*," Noah explained. "Traditional Azerbaijani folk music. We are lucky we have a live band today."

The music was lively, feverish, and exotic; it sounded to Alana as if Turkish folk had been melded with Indian sounds, producing something both exciting and plaintive. While one musician beat a complex rhythm with his fingers on a large, flat drum – which Noah called a *daf* – the others played stringed instruments: a *kamancheh*, like an elongated lute, played with a bow like a cello; the other, similarly long and thin, was plucked like a guitar and sounded like a cross between a balalaika and a sitar. Its wavering bent notes were part of what lent the music an Indian flavor.

"We are doubly blessed," said Noah. "There are varieties of *mugham*, but this is *shikastasi* mugham, which comes from Karabakh. There used to be a famous *mugham* festival every year in Shusha before the Armenians came."

Alana watched Uzeyir discreetly patrolling the courtyard; he spoke to a couple of uniformed security guards, then moved on. The agents' presence unsettled Alana. The caution and watchfulness in their every move gnawed at her nerves, an ever-present reminder of the danger she was in. Was this her life now? She had friends in LA who had permanent security, and her mother had used part-time protection since a kidnap threat about ten years ago. You just got used to it, she supposed. But then, the threat those people lived with was hypothetical, a mere possibility; for Alana it was constant and never far away.

Noah ordered Turkish coffee for both of them. Few Azeri people drank coffee, and it seemed almost sacrilegious to order it in this place, but he'd acquired a great taste for it in America and guessed Alana would be missing it. He talked about his work at the settlement, but Alana was hardly listening. Her gaze wandered around the courtyard. The number of shady alcoves, especially in the gallery above, made her feel exposed. She watched people come in, move between the tables … and then she saw him: a slim figure, young, with black hair and stubble beard, standing in the shadows of the entrance passageway.

Alana gripped Noah's wrist so hard he winced. "It's him!" she whispered. "It's him!"

"Who?"

"*Him*! The one who killed Howard! Oh Jesus." Alana wanted to get up and run, but she was rooted to the spot. Noah stared at the man, trying to recognize him; to his eyes he looked like a more or less generic young guy, maybe familiar, maybe not.

Uzeyir, who'd been keeping half his attention on Alana, saw her react; following her line of sight, he spotted the young man. Uzeyir was on the move before Alana had even spoken to Noah. He crossed the space between tables rapidly and smoothly, alerting one of the club security guards with a nod. The two closed in on the young man. He noticed their approach and backed away into the passage.

Alana clenched her fists on the table. Her initial fear had transformed into rising anger. She started to get up. Noah put a hand on her arm. "Where are you going?"

"I want to see this son of a bitch face to face." She strode toward the archway with Noah following at her heels.

Uzeyir and the security guard had backed the young man up against the wall; he looked frightened and gabbled at them in Azerbaijani. The guard was examining the man's driver's license; he seemed satisfied and handed it to Uzeyir with a nod. Uzeyir glanced at it and looked around as Alana came marching up.

"This man you know?" he said.

Alana looked at the young man's face. His features were fine and dark, but his mouth was different, and his jawline was unmarked.

"No," she stammered, instantly consumed with shame and embarrassment. "No, I don't. It's not who I thought … I'm so, so sorry," she said to the young man.

He took back his license with a glare at the security guard, straightened his jacket, and, giving Alana a sour glance, stepped past them into the courtyard. Alana watched him join a table of other young people.

"I'm sorry," she said to Uzeyir.

"Not sorry," he said. "Always if there is a threat, say. Better to be safe."

"Thank you. You make me feel safe. Thanks."

Uzeyir grinned and nodded. He turned away and began talking into his earpiece mic.

"Shall we go on someplace else?" she said to Noah. "I've kind of made a spectacle of myself here."

"Sure. Let's go look at the Maiden Tower."

"Can't we just take a walk?"

Noah grimaced. "I kind of think your bodyguards need to know where you are going before you go there."

"No aimless strolling?"

"Forbidden, I'm afraid." He smiled. "You are a khanim, after all. This is how royalty lives, I guess."

There was a delay while Uzeyir and Rustam established that the route was clear, and they were kept waiting in the restaurant. Alana was growing ever more nervous. She met Uzeyir's eye; he was doing that thing again: looking as if he was finding some secret amusement in all this.

"You think I'm overreacting, don't you?" she said.

"Excuse me?"

"With that guy just now. You think I'm a nervous client, worrying about nothing."

The bodyguard shook his head emphatically. "No, ma'am. Danger is real. One agent of Ikskayicks already died guarding you."

"What?"

"He means XKX," said Noah, who sounded as surprised as Alana. "That's the Azerbaijan Foreign Intelligence Service, our version of the CIA." He spoke to Uzeyir in Azerbaijani and listened to his reply. "Uzeyir says there's a rumor in his department that an XKX agent got killed guarding you in England."

Uzeyir nodded.

Alana's mind raced back over everything that had happened to her in the past weeks; there was so much, she had to go through it piece by piece before she felt sure there wasn't a death she'd somehow forgotten about. "I had no idea there *was* an agent," she said. "My boyfriend was my grandfather's watchdog. When did this happen?"

"Few weeks," said Uzeyir.

He was distracted by a message in his earpiece and turned away. Alana looked at Noah, who shrugged. Uzeyir turned back and spoke to Noah rapidly in Azerbaijani.

"There's some kind of hold-up," Noah explained. "A suspicious vehicle came in the Old City gate. We have to wait while it's checked out."

Alana wandered along the passage. Noah hung back, sensing she wanted to be alone for a moment. Uzeyir quietly followed her. She turned round as he approached.

"Togrul tells me you're from Karabakh," she said, and he nodded. She reckoned he was around her age, maybe a few years older. "Do you remember the war with the Armenians?"

He shook his head grimly. "My family is from Khankendi, what is now called Stepanakert. Many Armenians there. Fighting started, my family moved all to Baku."

Alana had heard Khankendi mentioned as the initial flashpoint of the Nagorno-Karabakh war: located in the mountain valleys midway between Shusha and Khojali, it was Karabakh's largest city and had had a majority Armenian population due to the expulsion of the Azeris. It was now the Armenians' regional capital.

"Have you ever thought about going back to Karabakh?"

"Is not possible for Azeris now."

"But have you ever thought about it? Don't you want to find out where you came from?"

That odd jeering smile again. "Uh-uh. Know where I came from and know where I go." His eyes took on the glazed look that indicated he was listening to his earpiece. "Safe now," he said, and beckoned to Noah. "Can go now."

He swung open the door. As Alana passed by him, Uzeyir said softly, "Is possible."

"What is?"

"Go to Karabakh. But not safe."

Before she could press him to explain, they were out in the street and he was back in close protection mode, oblivious to anything but monitoring the street.

The Qiz Qalasi – the Maiden Tower – was visible as soon as they turned the corner from the caravanserai. A round tower of stone, eight stories high and fifty feet broad, marked all round with grooves, as if it had been turned in clay and had a comb run around it while still soft. A single enormous buttress rose almost to the full height of the tower, jutting out toward the sea which in medieval times had reached right up to the city walls. The whole building was framed by a lowering, darkening sky that threatened rain.

It was a tough climb up a lot of stairs, but worth it to come out on the open summit. Alana's first sight of the view was marred by coming face to face with the grim jaw and basilisk eyes of Salim, standing there in his stolid bulk like an extension of the tower itself. He nodded curtly at Alana and Noah as they emerged and took up position at the staircase doorway.

Determined to shut her mind to the bodyguards, Alana walked toward the parapet. She was slightly disappointed to find it unapproachable; a glass safety screen ran the whole circumference of the circular roof, reaching well over head height. Nevertheless, the view over the city was spectacular. South, the tower overlooked the blue Caspian, the marina, and the seafront parks. North gave a vista over the whole city, rising gently on its hills. Immediately below was the warren of the Old City. Noah pointed out the streets, indicating where there had once been certain quarters for different classes and professions: a quarter for clerics, a quarter for nobles, one for armorers and blacksmiths, another for Jews, and yet others for oil workers and sailors.

To the west of the Old City, three massive gleaming spikes rose above the apartment blocks, curved, their silvery surfaces catching the lowering sun through a gap in the roiling, darkening clouds. The three spires were like the petals of a colossal orchid, or the claws of some Kraken-like titan buried beneath the hill, thrust up through the soil.

"The Flame Towers," said Noah, following her gaze. "One of Baku's more striking buildings."

"They're beautiful."

"You think so? I find them a little in-your-face."

"That's what's so wonderful – so out of place but at the same time so harmonious. I love them. So tell me about this place. Why's it called the Maiden Tower?"

"Nobody knows for sure," said Noah. "But there are legends. Some are more savory than others."

"I'm intrigued."

"Well, they mostly go back to the Zoroastrian times. The most popular legend is that a king who ruled Baku had a virgin daughter who was so beautiful he fell in love with her and wished to marry her."

"That's pretty unsavory."

"The princess thought so, too. He made advances to her, but she resisted. In the end she was forced to make a bargain with him. Her father must build a great tower; when it was completed, if he still wished to marry her, she would be his wife. She hoped that by the time it was finished, he would realize the evil folly of his desires. So the king set his masons to work. They built and they built, and after several years the tower was completed. To the princess's dismay, he still desired her and once more pressed her to marry him. In despair, she fled to the top of the tower and threw herself to her death."

Alana touched the glass screen with her fingertips; she had an urge to lean over the parapet and look down, as she had often done on castle towers in Britain, enjoying the rush of giddiness, the gritty stone against her body, and the weight and mass of the fortification beneath. It frustrated her that she couldn't do that here.

"There's a much better legend," Noah said. "It also goes back to the days of Zoroastrianism, a religion in which fire was revered."

"I know. Fire and water – the purifying forces."

"Then you will know that the Zoroastrians constructed fire temples. The Maiden Tower – before it was remodeled as a defensive structure – is said to have been one of these temples, and a ring of perpetual flame crowned its top. I believe it's built on an oil well, so I guess that would be the source of the fire."

"Togrul said something about that – *from the rock of the sea a flame springs*."

"Well there you are. The story I heard when I came here as a kid is that there was a war and Baku came under siege. The invaders surrounded the city, cut off the food and water supplies, and sat back to wait for the citizens to surrender or die.

"Inside the city, the priests and their most faithful followers congregated at the fire tower and begged for aid from Ahura Mazda, the supreme deity of their religion. In answer, a ball of holy fire fell from the top of the tower, and from it emerged a beautiful young woman with hair the color of flame. The citizens fell down and worshipped her, and she comforted them. 'Do not be afraid,' she said. 'I will protect you from your enemy.' She asked for armor and a sword, and told them to send word to the enemy commander, challenging him to single combat with the city's *pahlevan* – its champion.

"The challenge was accepted. If the *pahlevan* won, the siege would be lifted and the army would depart; but if the enemy won, the city would surrender and suffer brutal sacking.

"The young woman put on the armor, concealing her face and her long red hair under the helmet, so that no one would know she was female. The city gate was opened, and she rode out in the guise of the *pahlevan* of Baku. The enemy commander was a big man and a fierce warrior, and he rode to meet the small, weak-looking champion. They fought hard for a long time, and the commander was awed by the skill and strength of the *pahlevan*. At last, with a great blow, the *pahlevan* knocked the commander from his horse. Leaping down, he put a knife to the enemy's throat, and was about to kill him when the enemy cried out, 'Halt! You win, I give up. But I must see the face of the man who has beaten me. Please, take off your helmet, *pahlevan*.'

"The *pahlevan* did so, and the enemy commander was amazed. He cried out, 'You are a girl! If even the maidens of Baku are such courageous warriors, I will never capture the city! I will march away immediately and never trouble you again.' Yet he was so captivated by the woman's beauty and bravery, he instantly fell in love with her and asked her to marry him."

"And did she?" said Alana.

"Of course. She admired his noble words, and he was a great warrior, so she fell in love with him, and they were married. The tower from which the flame-haired maiden had come was afterward always known by that name."

"Azerbaijan likes its tales of female warriors, doesn't it?"

"We do. I guess we lead the world in oil extraction and feminism."

Alana smiled. "Maybe."

Noah had been gazing thoughtfully out across the Old City as he talked. He glanced at Alana. "I believe Togrul regards you as highly as the people of Baku regarded the fire maiden."

"He doesn't even know me."

"Oh, but he does. He knows all about your achievements. And he knows how you evaded HACA's agents."

"That was thanks to you."

Noah smiled. "Of course, the true reason for the Maiden Tower's name is probably a simple metaphor; it has never been captured or breached by an enemy. It remains a virgin, so to speak."

Alana laughed. "Noah, you're blushing. A doctor shouldn't blush."

He looked up at the darkening sky. "I felt rain. Did you feel it?"

"No, I …" She was interrupted by a flicker of lightning from the north. Thunder rolled across the city.

"Come," said Noah. "The tower will be closing soon, and your grandfather is expecting our return." He walked to the staircase.

Alana stayed a moment, looking west, to where the sun was sinking through a gap in the bank of tumultuous clouds, its light turning the Flame Towers gold, so they truly seemed to be ablaze. Somewhere in that direction, hundreds of miles to the west, was the place where she had been born, and where the life she remembered only in fragments had been lived. She put her fingertips to the glass again, as if to reach out and grasp her past. This place, Baku, was not her home and was not her life. If answers were to be found, it was there, far beyond the horizon, in Nagorno-Karabakh, in whatever remained of Khojali, that she might find them.

Turning away, she walked past Salim, who stood sentinel by the stairs, watching her inscrutably with his tiny, dark eyes.

25

Alana was deep in thought as they walked home. As soon as Rashad let them in, she went straight to her grandfather. She found him in his library, his nose in a book. He looked up and smiled warmly.

"Did you see the Maiden Tower?" he asked. "And was it as magnificent as I promised?"

"I did, and it was. Thank you." She smiled. "Noah told me some pretty remarkable tales about it."

"I do not doubt it." The old man chuckled and got down from his stool. "There is an excellent volume on Shirvanshah fortifications," he said, running his forefinger along the spines of a shelf of books. "It has a very good chapter on archaeological research on the Maiden Tower." He found the book and pulled it out, looking at it doubtfully. "Unfortunately, it is in Russian. Do you read Russian?"

"I'm afraid not."

"Hmm. Well, you must learn it if you are to understand Azerbaijani archaeology and history. So much of the scholarly literature was written under Russian rule." Togrul considered the book, weighing it in his hands. "Look at it anyway. It has many plans and drawings.

With your expertise you may be able to understand the tower even without the text." He held it out and she took it.

"Thank you." She hesitated. "Grandfather," she began. It still felt very odd to address him in that way, but he smiled with pleasure every time she did so. "I was told today that an agent was killed protecting me in England. Is that true?"

Togrul's shoulders sagged. "Who told you this? Rashad?"

"Is it true?"

"They should not have said anything. I did not wish to alarm you. Yes, it is true. But believe me, you do not want to hear about it."

"But I do. Please. There can't be any more secrets."

Reluctantly, the old man opened a cabinet in the corner of the room. Inside was a safe; he dialed in the combination and took out a thin brown folder from which he extracted a document. He handed it to Alana.

It was a personnel file, all in Azerbaijani, with a man's photograph attached. The man was aged about forty, with sharp features, heavy bags under the eyes and steel-gray hair. He looked familiar, but Alana couldn't put her finger on it. Her eye ran over the incomprehensible words, and two jumped out at her: *Cambridge* and *Trinity*.

"Oh Jesus," she whispered. "Oh sweet Jesus Christ. This guy was a fellow of Trinity College."

"You knew him?"

"Not by name, but I saw him around the college a lot. He was on some kind of research fellowship. Ancient languages or something. *He* was a bodyguard?"

"No. He was a – what do they call it, an asset? – for XKX, our foreign intelligence service. He was not there specifically for you, but he was briefed to monitor your safety and report."

"Azerbaijan has spies in England?"

"It is necessary to safeguard our country's interests against Armenian influence abroad. I persuaded a friend in the government that keeping watch on you was a part of that mission. On your honor, Ayna, all this is of the utmost secrecy; it must never be divulged."

"I thought you had Howard watching over me?"

"The XKX man was limited by his principal mission. I needed someone close to you who could watch over you when you were in America and other places." Togrul's face was haggard. "The agent vanished from his post at the end of January. A body has never been found, to my knowledge, but it is assumed he was murdered by Armenian agents, perhaps HACA. I believe it was my fault."

"How could it be your fault?"

"I used leverage to obtain his file. I had an idea of somehow conveying his identity to you, so that you would know who to turn to if things went wrong. I never acted on the idea, but it was foolish even to possess such a document. I … I believe it was found and a copy passed to our enemies."

The old man sat down at the table. Alana sat close by him.

"Two months ago, there was a gathering here, a feast to celebrate the *Hamrayliyi Günü*, Azerbaijan's International Solidarity Day. It is the same day as *Yeni il bayrami*, what you call New Year's Eve. Many of the younger people like to celebrate the Western holiday, and this house was filled with guests that night. Many of my acquaintances of the Baku government and old friends from Shusha. Noah visited for a few days and brought some of his colleagues to my party." Togrul knitted his gnarled fingers together. "It was then, I think, that this file was found and passed to the Armenians." He looked at Alana with haunted eyes. "It is my shame, child, that there has been a traitor in my household. What is worse, it could be almost anyone, and I do not know if he is still here. I have my suspicions, but no proof."

"Does Noah know about this?"

"He and Rashad alone know of my suspicions. They are the men I trust more than any in this world. I would place my life and the lives of my family in their hands. If I could, I would put trust only in men of Karabakh, but compromises have to be made."

Alana digested this. How many more layers of falsity and deception did she have to dig through before she knew the whole truth? "Grandfather," she said, the memory of another face surfacing in her memory. "Was anyone else watching me in England?"

He nodded slowly. "There was another man. An XKX agent based at the embassy in London. He was briefed to watch your movements after the Cambridge asset disappeared."

Alana recalled the sallow-faced man staring at her in Piccadilly, the one she suspected had then tried to follow her onto the train at Kings Cross. She described him to her grandfather, but he shook his head. He knew nothing of the agent's identity. What would have happened if that man had succeeded in boarding the train? She might have been spared a world of terror and danger, and Howard might still be alive; or she might have been snatched there and then, and now be dead herself or imprisoned in some HACA stronghold in Armenia.

Never knowing for sure: that had driven her throughout her whole life, it was at the root of her obsession with the deep past. It wasn't a mere fascination, the way it was for her colleagues – it was a powerful, almost visceral need to find and possess the past, to know it and envelop herself in it. She had once tried to explain it to some friends. They were in a pub deep in the green heartland of Wales, during one of their weekend expeditions. A local scholar who happened to be present told her there was a word in the Welsh language – *hiraeth* – which meant something similar to nostalgia, an aching longing for the past, but with the difference that the past possessed a kind of immanence in the souls of certain people. For them, he said, the past had a magic potency. To Alana it seemed to describe exactly how she felt. But only now was she beginning to understand why.

She looked at her grandfather, who was gazing down at his hands, also deep in thought. "You've told me that your heart is in Karabakh," she said. "That it's our homeland."

"That is correct."

"I want to go there."

Togrul chewed his lip. "I have been expecting this. You are truly a Karabakhsky for boldness, that you express the wish so soon."

"I want to see the place where I was born, where I was a child."

"It tears my heart to say it, but you cannot. It is in Armenian hands. No Azerbaijani can go there."

"But I'm *not* Azerbaijani," said Alana. "I'm American, with an American passport. Surely I wouldn't be barred?"

Togrul shook his head. "That is true. You could go there if you wish. But once you have an Armenian stamp in your American passport, you will not be permitted back into Azerbaijan."

"You could arrange it, couldn't you? You're powerful. You arranged a back-room visa for me; you have secret service agents working for you."

"I had to draw on favors to get that visa, and the agents are a special arrangement with an old friend who sympathizes with our cause. I have no influence with the Ministry of Internal Affairs." He spread his arms helplessly. "I'm sorry, my child; it would be impossible." He studied her face gravely. "What do you hope to find in Karabakh?"

"Answers. Knowledge about myself."

"We all wish for that." Togrul gestured around at his library. "All of this is a search for answers. What, specifically, do you want to know?"

"I want to know what really happened in Khojali. To my family."

A heavy gloom came into her grandfather's face. "You do not want to talk about that, child."

"I do. I really do. I don't just *want* to talk – I *need* to. What I remember is so ... disjointed, so fragmentary. None of it makes any sense."

Her grandfather sighed heavily and clenched his fists, his gnarled old knuckles whitening. "What is it you wish to know?"

"I want to know what happened that night, when the Armenian soldiers came to the village. My little bits and pieces of memory contradict each other."

"Very well. I shall try to answer your questions. Come, let us sit."

Togrul called for Mary and instructed her to bring tea to the sitting room. He ushered Alana to a comfortable armchair beside the fire and sat opposite her. Mary set down a carved wooden tray bearing two *armudi* glasses and two chased silver pots; she poured a measure of aromatic black tea into each glass and topped it up with hot water from the second pot. It looked and smelled quite different from the tea she'd had before.

"*Keklik otu*," Togrul explained; "Tea flavored with thyme. Now," he said, settling back in his chair. "You may ask me your questions." His face was grave, almost forbidding, and she hesitated. "Perhaps it would be best, Ayna, if you were to tell me what you *do* remember."

"I remember a cold wind, and snow on the ground ..." The smell of the strong spiced tea somehow worked itself into her brain like an oil, in the way that only odors can, easing open locks and letting loose images. She knew this smell from somewhere in her childhood. An image came into her mind of a great silver samovar ... and blood ... a voice screaming: *Run, baby, run ... please run ...* She gasped and almost dropped her glass.

"Tell me, Ayna," said Togrul gently.

She began hesitantly, describing the fleeting, faint images of her parents: a good-looking man with a close-cropped brown beard and a kind expression, a beautiful woman, about the age she was now, with jet-black hair. And the even fainter images of her brother and sister. She saw a house and a garden, with a wall dividing it from the street, where she would sit in the shade on the edge of the road, playing with …

"A dog! I had a dog." She shook her head, as if trying to dislodge something. "I can picture him, but …" Somehow this memory felt especially important, with profound but elusive emotions attached to it. A feeling of longing.

"Yes, there was a dog," said her grandfather. He stood up and went to a bureau, opening one drawer after another, rummaging through. "Ah!" He came back with a couple of photographs and handed one of them to her.

Alana looked at it and almost choked. "Oh my God. Oh sweet Jesus." The photograph showed a little girl in a striped sweater and tasseled shawl sitting cross-legged on a patch of grass with a stone wall behind her; she was grinning at the camera, and her arms were wrapped around a dog with shaggy black and white and brown fur. "That's him," she whispered, and the name came to her. "Rolan … And that's me?"

"Your father took that picture. The dog was my gift to you. I had to walk through the siege lines to bring it to you."

Alana looked at her grandfather. "This must be not long before the massacre. I have no memory of what happened to him."

Togrul smiled and passed her the second photo. It showed the same dog, older, with grizzled gray around his black snout, sitting on a wooden bench. Alana put her hand over her mouth, tears welling in her eyes.

"He found me," said her grandfather. "After everything was over and you were gone, he arrived at the door of my house near Khojali, as thin as grass-stems and his fur full of thistles. He remembered where he had been born, you see. I brought him to Baku, and he lived with me in this house for, oh, many years. He was an excellent dog. Mary wept for a day and a night when he died."

Tears were streaming down Alana's face; she wiped them away, struggling to regain her composure.

When she had settled, Togrul urged her to continue. She told him all she remembered of the massacre: the soldiers, the shooting, fleeing through the snow and across the river; the hills, the dead bodies … But the part she kept coming back to was the part that made no sense.

"In my memories, I think I left the village twice. I remember being with my parents and brother and sister in a crowd of people, all trekking through woods, with the sound of shooting behind. But then I remember leaving *again*, but this time there's just me and another kid – a boy. I don't know if he was my brother or some stranger."

Alana reasoned that she must be remembering different parts of the same exodus. That was the only logical explanation. But she felt instinctively that it was wrong. And between the two departures was the unspeakable horror of her mother being murdered, apparently in the living room of their own house. "Somehow, my mother and I ended up back in Khojali after leaving, and I don't understand why. Am I misremembering it?"

Togrul had been watching her closely as she talked, leaning forward in his chair. He was silent for a few moments, then shook his head. "I don't believe so. I cannot explain it, but I think you are remembering it correctly." He took a deep breath and gazed into the fire. His voice was dull and hoarse, like wind through a rusty pipe. "Afterwards, I tracked down every survivor of Khojali, and spoke to eyewitnesses from Aghdam and the surrounding area. I needed to learn what had happened to my son and his family. You were in shock; you could not speak at all at first, and when you did at last, you seemed to remember nothing. And then you were gone.

"I spoke to the man who found Nurbanu's body dumped at the edge of town, in a ditch, among dozens of others." Tears glittered in his eyes. "The body of your sister Leyli was discovered on the hillside, together with many women, men, and children who had been shot there. I could never learn what had happened to the remains of Tengiz, my son, your father. But I spoke with two people who saw him shot in the street near his home. Your brother, Hakan was separated from the rest of the family during the exodus. For a few days we hoped he had survived. But a friend of mine, a man of Shusha named Amil – the father of the boy who helped you escape – saw Hakan shot on the hillside. Amil only survived because he was dragged away by his cousin."

As he talked, tears ran down cracks and folds in the old man's weathered face.

"In all my inquiries, I never could answer the question which now troubles you." Togrul clasped his hands together. "Your parents were not among the first to flee Khojali. If I know anything of my son, I imagine that he was reluctant to leave his patients. Tengiz and Nurbanu, taking you and your brother and sister, accompanied by some three dozen other people, left the village as evening was falling. They crossed the Gargar river and the woods, making for the hills. Word had spread that they must head for Aghdam, and that the Azeri militia would be there to protect them. Your mother carried you some of the way, your father carried Leyli, and Hakan was looked after by my friend, Amil, who had been separated from his own wife and little boy. Amil had no idea where they were – among the exodus or left behind in the village, or most likely already dead.

"Somehow, in the confusion, Amil was separated from you and the rest of your family. One moment he was walking in the darkness with Hakan in his arms, trudging through the snow, surrounded by desperate people, children crying, some people helping the sick and wounded to struggle on – and the next moment he was alone on the hillside. He searched and called out, and found his cousin and a few friends. But his cries had also attracted the Armenian soldiers. They came out of the darkness and began shooting. Amil and his cousin were the only survivors. Of the other – several dozen – men, women, and children, none survived."

Alana's gaze never left her grandfather's face as he talked; now he looked up, into her eyes. "That group was only one among many that fled Khojali that night," he said. "Almost all of those poor people were murdered: more than six hundred innocents hunted and butchered."

"How did I end up back in the village?"

"That has troubled me for more than twenty years. I talked with a teenaged boy who said he saw your father shot down in the street near his doctor's office, and you and your mother dragged away. After that I know nothing, until the goatherd found you and Amil's little boy on the hillside." Togrul wiped his hand across his face and pinched the bridge of his nose. "I could make no sense of it then and can make no sense of it now. My first thought was that Tengiz went back for some vital medical supplies; it would be like him to take such a risk, but he would not have taken his wife and child."

Alana closed her eyes. She could see an indistinct image of her mother's face, slipping in and out of focus, the features shifting and changing as Alana's brain tried to reassemble the right person. It kept trying to give her Catherine's image, and she pushed it away. When she finally succeeded in seeing a face that she believed was Nurbanu, it was instantly drowned in a horror of blood and screaming. When

262

Alana opened her eyes, Togrul was watching her with a look of desolation on his face.

"I guess we were both hoping to have our questions answered," said Alana.

"Give it time. Your memories will return," said her grandfather gently.

"I remember the little boy."

"Yes. His name was Neymar. His father was Amil, the friend I told you about who witnessed Hakan's death. Neymar's mother was killed in the exodus. I hold Neymar blessed above all others, for he saved you."

"What happened to him?"

"He and his father stayed a while with me. After that, Neymar was sent to live with his mother's relations in Baku."

"I think I remember your house in the hills. Everything was white and there were hangings, like the ones here."

Her grandfather nodded. "You stayed with me in that house for some weeks. You spoke not one word to me or anyone else. You were traumatized. At last it became too dangerous to be there, and I led all my people and a handful of survivors to my stronghold at Shusha. We were there only a short time before the city fell to the Armenians. We barely escaped with our lives. Many died fighting to cover our retreat." He sighed. "And so I came to Baku. An exile in my own country, with only my grief to keep me company, and my memories and books to feed my yearning for Karabakh."

Alana could see the pain in his eyes; yet as he gazed at her they twinkled, and he smiled. "But at least I knew that you were alive, and safe beyond the reach of anyone who would do you harm. One day, I knew, you would be the key to the future of that homeland. The key to Karabakh."

26

Elamxanli

The leave-taking went on for some time. Noah listened patiently as Togrul reiterated his concerns and cautions for Alana's safety: her importance, her vulnerability, and how it would break not only his heart but the very heart of Azerbaijan if this young woman, this Banuchichak, should be lost or come to harm. Noah reassured the old gentleman over and over again.

Alana had accepted that she couldn't go to Karabakh. Instead she had chosen the next best thing: traveling with Noah to his settlement near Aghjabedi, which was only a few miles from the occupied zone. The hills of Karabakh could be seen from there, he said. Alana felt that if she could at least be near the land of her birth, it would help her remember. It had taken all her powers of persuasion to bend her grandfather to her will, and Noah had lingered an extra day in Baku, waiting for her to overcome his resistance.

"Have I not already taken pains for her?" Noah said when Togrul took him into his study for one last talk. "I would risk all to save her and do nothing to put her at risk."

Togrul smiled. "I know, my precious boy. I know."

When it came time to say goodbye to Alana, Togrul kept her lingering in the courtyard of his house while the bodyguards stood by masking their impatience. The vehicles were parked in the back street behind the house, where the guards figured they would attract less notice.

"*Sagol guzel prensesim*," said Togrul, embracing his granddaughter a final time. "*Inshallah kisa zamana gorusuruz janim*. You have learned enough Azerbaijani yet to understand?"

"I caught *goodbye* and *God willing*," Alana admitted.

"It means *Farewell beautiful princess. God willing we shall see each other soon*." There were tears in his eyes. "Please come back safely to me."

Uzeyir had acquired an armored Range Rover from the DMX pool. He would drive Alana while Rustam Mammadov rode with Noah in his SUV.

When the farewells were over, the two vehicles pulled away, Alana waving to her grandfather. She had grown fond of him very quickly and would miss him. He held one hand in the air, stoically keeping his feelings in check as his most precious jewel vanished from his sight.

As the vehicles turned the corner, they passed the looming figure of Salim. Togrul would have preferred to send three guards with Alana, but his misgivings about the Iranian had got the better of him. The hard, bright eyes impassively watched the Range Rover drive by, exchanging only the slightest nod with Uzeyir.

Under a steady, cold drizzle, an Aeroflot 737 taxied to a halt in front of the terminal of Zvartnots International Airport.

Hayk gazed out the window at the gray expanse of Yerevan's main airport. The damp weather was a fitting backdrop to his return home. He retrieved his small backpack from the overhead locker. He had no other baggage; his weapons had had to be offloaded in Switzerland and would be in the back-channels of the international arms trade by now.

A car was waiting for him. While the other passengers filed toward the building, Hayk approached the slate-gray Ford pickup, where two familiar figures stood waiting, oblivious to the rain beading on their faces: the stocky frame of Vahe, his captain, in military fatigues and cap; and the tall, lean figure of his trainer, Ando. Their faces were stony. He was returning in failure.

Vahe put out his hand, and Hayk took it. "Welcome back," said the captain in a flat tone that was far from welcoming. Ando merely nodded. "Get in," said Vahe.

As the pickup moved away, Hayk repressed the urge to explain and excuse himself. There was no explanation and no excuse sufficient to account for his failure. He was the best they had – he knew it, they knew it – and yet he had not been good enough to complete this task. Vartan had selected and groomed and trained him specifically for this task, believing he was the only man to do it. The prospect of facing Vartan now was enough to shrivel up Hayk's soul. It was not so much what Vartan would do – Hayk could withstand any physical suffering that could be inflicted on him – but what Vartan would feel. Disappointment and shame were the terrors in this nightmare; torture and death were merely the means of expression.

A helicopter was waiting at the far end of the airport. They flew southeast. Throughout the flight, Hayk was debriefed by Vahe on every step of the mission, every tactical encounter picked apart, while Ando listened in silence.

The overcast began to break up, and as they crossed the border of Nagorno-Karabakh the green folds of the hills climbed up under open skies. By the time Shusha came into view and the helicopter set down on the open space outside the fortress walls, Hayk had grown even more acutely conscious of the enormity of his failure. It could not be forgiven.

The skin peeled away from the orange, the razor-sharp edge of the serrated knife easing into the pith, lifting it away in a continuous ribbon with a soft tearing sound. Vartan raised the knife up a moment, close to his eye, letting the late afternoon sun, which came slanting in through the open veranda doors, glint this way and that on the wet blade. He touched it to his tongue, savoring the bitter scent of the zest in his nostrils and the sharpness of the juice on his lip. It was a good knife, this – ivory handle, curved steel, beautiful, simple, and purposeful. He resumed peeling the orange, relishing the sensation of blade in flesh.

He heard a soft footfall behind him, and a quiet murmur at the inner doorway. "Let him come forward," he said.

The last inch of skin came away from the orange, falling onto the tabletop, and Vartan laid the fruit on a porcelain dish, a white pithy sphere with bright patches where the cut flesh had been exposed, oozing juice. He wiped the blade on a linen napkin but didn't lay down the knife.

"My son," he whispered to himself. "My blood."

Vartan turned. His secretary, Kamo, was at the doorway with Vahe and Ando. Standing with head bowed near the end of the table, beside the ornate silver samovar, was Hayk. Vartan rose from his chair and walked slowly around the table, never taking his dark, deep-set eyes from the young man's face. He came to a halt within arm's reach.

"*Thou art my son; and I am thy father,*" he said softly. "Do you know me?"

Hayk kept his eyes lowered. "*I am thy son in thought and deed,*" he recited; "*in truth and blood. My life is thine, my father, to spend as thou wilt.*"

"Will you not look into my eyes?" said Vartan. The tension in Hayk's body was visible; he trembled, but kept his gaze lowered. Vartan swept the samovar from the table; it flew, spinning, crashing, jangling, across the marble floor. "*Will you not look into my eyes?*" he roared.

Hayk was the only man in the room who did not flinch. He raised his head and met Vartan's gaze. Hayk's eyes were sparkling with tears. Vartan brought up the knife, the haft between his fingers like a cigarette, the blade glinting an inch from Hayk's throat. Hayk stared into his master's eyes and waited for the bite of steel in his skin. He almost wished for it, as a kind of consummation. Vartan's gaze seemed to be searching Hayk's soul, reaching inside him, seeing what he had seen. He stroked the point of the blade around the rim of Hayk's eye.

"Leave us," Vartan whispered.

Kamo ushered Vahe and Ando out of the room, followed them, and closed the door softly behind him.

Vartan's face softened and the knife clattered to the floor.

"My son, my blood," he said, and threw his arms around Hayk, burying his face in the young man's neck. "Forgive me."

Hayk was dumbfounded. "For … forgive … ?"

Vartan held him tight. "It was beyond you, I know. I should have foreseen it."

"Father, I am so sorry. I failed you, I—"

"Hush. Tell me later. All that matters to me now is that you are well."

He gripped Hayk by the shoulders, pushing him back, and smiled. Hayk had no idea what to make of this treatment. But he knew Vartan well enough not to talk, to let the mood play out, wait to see where it went.

"I should not have sent you. You were not ready, and I underesti-mated her ability. I of all people should have guessed, knowing the sires from which this bitch was bred. *You* know that. My sweet Hayk, why did you not *tell* me how unwise I was to send you?"

Hayk knew better than to try to answer that. He kept silent and allowed himself to be embraced once more.

"Come, sit and take tea with me." Vartan beckoned Hayk to a seat with the solicitude of a waiter. He frowned at the samovar as if wondering how it came to be lying upended under a bureau, then rang a bell. Kamo returned with servants, who rapidly cleared up the mess, righted the silver vessel, and set the table for tea. All the while, Vartan sat and gazed across the table at Hayk, smiling softly as if waiting to impart some joyful secret. Kamo, watching surreptitiously, sensed that there was still murder in his master's heart, despite the smile, an unslaked rage that showed in the tremor in his fingers and the tautness at the corners of the smile.

When the tea was set and they were alone again, Vartan leaned toward Hayk. "I have excellent news. God favors us. Your failure – which is *my* failure, I humbly acknowledge – has brought about a development I had not foreseen. I have a source within Karabakhsky's so-called organization, and I can now reveal to you this. His spawn, the she-beast, will soon be with us."

Hayk's heart quickened. "How so?"

"She is being brought to my very doorstep, in the care of someone she believes she can trust. Your failure has precipitated an outcome far better than if you had succeeded. Now fill your cup and I will tell you how we shall proceed."

Barely an hour out of Baku, Noah was already tired of the journey. Rustam Mammadov was a nice enough guy, but not the most congenial traveling companion. Their shared interest in soccer – which in Noah's case was neither deep nor extensive – had kept them occupied for barely twenty minutes. Since then, Rustam had quizzed Noah relentlessly about New York. Rustam had cousins living there – one had shares in a couple of nightclubs in the East Village, and the other was a rookie in the NYPD. They'd told him there was plentiful well-paid work for a bodyguard in NYC, and Rustam was full of dreams of living there.

For Noah, talking about New York was an unwelcome distraction from the challenges ahead of him. In truth, he missed that exhausting, dirty, wonderful city, even though all the time he'd lived there he'd done little but yearn for Azerbaijan.

Noah always found the first leg of the journey back to Elamxanli from Baku rather trying. Mile after mile of oil refineries along the coast eventually gave way to the seemingly endless, bleak strip of highway skirting the edge of Gobustan National Park, a vast moonscape of yellow rock hills and mud volcanoes.

He glanced in the mirror. The black Range Rover was close behind. Noah could make out the dark smudge of Uzeyir at the wheel and the paler one of Alana in the passenger seat. He sighed.

Regretfully, Alana watched the creased yellow-gray ridges of the Gobustan hills go by. Beyond those bleak rocks lay one of the world's great archaeological landscapes. The prehistoric rock engravings of Gobustan were contemporary with the cave art of western Europe, extending over tens of miles of otherworldly rock formations. Among them were the famed Gaval Dash, the so-called "musical stones" – giant slabs of natural limestone composite that resonated like a drum or a woodblock when struck. The stones were associated with rock art in places, and Alana was thrilled by the possibilities of a meaningful ritual connection. Her PhD research was on the art from a Neolithic culture that was, in effect, an inheritor of the Gobustan tradition. She longed to walk those hills and see it all for herself.

But that desire was insignificant compared with the one driving her on. Since leaving Baku, she'd been itching to ask Uzeyir what he'd meant about there being a way into Karabakh. But she hesitated to do so; he'd hardly uttered a word since the start of the journey, and as the first hour ticked to an end it grew harder to break the silence. She was reluctant to reveal just how interested she was in knowing the answer in case it revealed her intentions.

They'd been traveling for nearly two hours when the scenery changed abruptly. They passed a city named Shirvan, where the highway crossed a broad river. Immediately the relentlessly brown and gray country gave way to a flat green landscape of orderly agricultural fields under a vast sky, through which the highway cut in a dead straight line, passing by isolated modern settlements and farmsteads reminiscent of the rural Midwest.

"How far now?" she asked.

Uzeyir glanced at her. "Two hours. Maybe little more."

Alana groaned inwardly. She took out the chunky satellite phone she'd been given by Togrul. Cell reception was patchy west of Baku, and her grandfather couldn't bear the thought of her being cut off. She considered calling him, but decided against it. She thought about calling her father, but decided against that too. It didn't feel private enough here in the car. Alana hadn't felt this inhibited by another person's presence since she was a teenager. She put the phone away and watched Azerbaijan's equivalent of Nebraska rolling by.

Togrul and Rashad sat at the table in Togrul's study, a stack of papers and a huge ledger between them, both hard at work. They were engaged in their bi-annual review of the household accounts. For the first time ever, Togrul was struggling to keep his attention on the task at hand. His eyes repeated strayed to the cellphone lying on the table beside the receipt book. Togrul Karabakhsky had never owned such a device before, and found its presence unsettling, like a speck of grit in the clockwork of his mind. It had taken a matter of titanic importance to make him embrace such technology, and now that he had it, he couldn't leave it alone.

He laid down his pen and activated the screen, checking to see that there was a signal and that he hadn't missed any calls from his granddaughter. Glancing up, he saw Rashad's eyes on him.

"I know, I know," he said. "It will ring with *Sari Gelin* if Ayna calls, and with some kind of ugly American tune if it is anyone else." This had been the one thing that delighted him about the phone. *Sari Gelin* was an old folk lament that had been his late wife's favorite, and at his request Noah had set the phone to play it whenever a call came from Alana's sat phone.

Rashad smiled behind his mustache. "It will ring when it rings. Looking at it will not summon her. The reception is good, the phone has power."

Togrul nodded and picked up his pen, only to put it down again immediately. "It is a dreadful risk to let her go, Rashad," he said. "I cannot think how I was persuaded."

Rashad didn't look up from his ledger. "The *hanim* has your family's will, sir." He wrote a figure at the foot of a column. "What could you expect?"

"Caution. I expect caution, Rashad: courage leavened by prudence ... Still, at least her companions are all loyal men." He picked up his pen and scowled at Rashad. "Now, what were we dealing with before you began distracting me?"

"The builder's contract, sir."

"Hmm. Pass me that box of invoices."

* * *

Gripping the rusted bars of the gate and breathing heavily, Vartan studied the prisoners milling about the exercise yard. This enclosed courtyard had once been the khan's wife's garden, but was now a bleak quadrangle of weeds and cracked walls.

He pointed. "That one."

A burly guard marched into the center of the yard, seized hold of a prisoner, and pushed him by the neck toward the gate. Vartan looked at his face; he was little more than a teenager. Dirty, disheveled, trying to hide how scared he was.

"What was his crime?" Vartan asked, then shook his head. "It doesn't matter."

The guard unlocked the gate, pushed the boy through, and slammed it shut again. Without a word, Vartan turned and walked away into the darkness of the disused cloister along the foot of the curtain wall. Bewildered, the young prisoner followed him into the shadows.

Vartan was waiting for him. He held out a hand to the youth, touched his shoulder and his hair, embraced him. He could smell the fear, over the stink of the unwashed body, and it excited him, set his stomach trembling.

From his jacket pocket he drew the razor-sharp fruit knife; it glittered once in the half light as he drove it with the strength of rage into the crook of the boy's neck. The boy gasped and struggled, but Vartan's hand moved with the speed of a machine, striking again and again, setting loose rivulets of thick blood. He snarled like an animal as it soaked his skin and the boy weakened until he was a dead weight in Vartan's arms, sliding slowly to the floor. Vartan sank with him.

"My son, my blood," he sobbed into the neck of the dying youth. "Thy life is mine to spend as I will. Forgive me. Forgive me."

27

Alana scraped the blade of a trowel gently along a thin red vein of soil in the face of a trench. The dust fell away, revealing tight-packed layers of light browns and grays, with that reddish band dipping and rising as it followed the contours of what had been the ground surface thousands of years ago.

"You've found this layer across the whole site?" she said, looking up over the edge of the trench, which ran across the pitted, undulating surface of the excavation.

The student digger squatting on the baulk above her was a young man from Omaha called Bruce with a beard like a thorn bush. He nodded. "Uh-huh. Pretty much."

"A flooding horizon, maybe?"

"That's Bob's working hypothesis."

Alana stood up and looked around the site. For the first time since arriving in Azerbaijan, she felt like she was on familiar ground. For her, hearth and home were – often literally – to be found in a hole in the earth. And this particular hole was home in a deeper sense; this gritty gray-brown mass was the soil of Karabakh, part of the region known as the Karabakh Steppe, the outlying flatlands whose eastern fringe was still in Azerbaijani hands.

She had learned about this excavation entirely by chance – a happy coincidence that had brought Alana home in a way she could never have anticipated.

For nearly a week now she had been staying at Elamxanli, Noah's refugee settlement west of Aghjabedi. Having half-expected a kind of tent city or shanty town, impoverished and squalid, Alana had been surprised to find a large community of orderly streets lined with new-built houses, each within its own plot of ground. The houses were small and uniform, built of brick and adobe and painted alternately cream and marshmallow pink, standing out like blossoms against the emerald green of the fields and yards.

Elamxanli had a population of around four thousand, mostly young families who had known nothing before this, other than persecution. They were employed in the nearby vineyards and sunflower fields or in the connected winery and processing plants, all constructed under a government aid program. The settlement had elementary and high schools, and a thriving community life.

Noah's medical office – which he shared with three other doctors – was in the center next to the elementary school and was a hub of town life. He lived among the refugees (mainly ethnic Azeris living in Armenia) and internally displaced persons in one of the little houses, and arranged accommodation for Alana with his neighbors, an old couple named Yusif and Emine, whose children had grown up and moved to Aghjabedi. Their spare bedroom was small but neat and comfortable, with a window looking out over a vegetable garden and the corduroy slopes of the vineyard. Uzeyir and Rustam shared a room in Noah's house; they slept in shifts, so that at least one of them was constantly on duty, either scouting or standing guard at the door of Yusif and Emine's house.

The old couple were ethnic Azeris from the region of Armenia west of Nagorno-Karabakh. Their whole family had been driven out in a pogrom. Alana wanted to ask them about their experiences – imagining that it might somehow cast light on her own past – but they spoke no English, and Alana's Azerbaijani, though improving, still consisted of little more than social pleasantries. Noah had explained that Alana was a survivor of Khojali, and they had taken her to their bosom as if she were their own child. But they could scarcely communicate.

Seeing Noah in his everyday setting was a revelation for Alana. He had come into her life like a lightning bolt, and she had only half-believed that he had a regular life. Seeing him at work among the refugee families of Elamxanli, it was as if the Noah of Gstaad and Baku had dissolved and was replaced by a different person – grounded, content, and ceaselessly busy. He was a man who had found his calling and seemed absolutely settled in it.

They talked for hours during his off-duty periods, Alana improving her acquaintance with the language and the country. In the evenings, when she called her grandfather to report that all was well, Togrul noted her progress with delight. During Noah's lunch breaks, he and Alana would sometimes walk up the hill to picnic in the vineyard. It was during one of these strolls that she heard of the archaeological excavations near the town of Qaradagli. Among Noah's patients that morning had been a local truck driver who'd remarked that his uncle had suspended his barley crop for the season because Americans were digging up his fields. The name of Qaradagli rang a faint bell somewhere in Alana's memory. It was only about fifteen miles away, so she decided to drive over and check it out.

The decision was easier to make than to carry out. Alana was getting used to the discreet ways in which Uzeyir and Rustam haunted her life. They rarely talked or intruded, but every so often she would do some trivial thing – such as deviating from her usual route while walking from one part of the settlement to another – and one of them would appear at her side and ask if she was certain she wanted to go that way because they'd have to check it first. An excursion by car was a major tactical operation. Rustam drove ahead to check the route and scout the destination, while Uzeyir drove the armored Range Rover with Alana.

Qaradagli was close to the border of the occupied zone, and everyone working at the excavations was accustomed to official visits and the Azerbaijan government's sensitivity about security. Therefore, nobody was particularly perturbed by the sight of a burly DMX agent checking them over. However, they were rather surprised when the VIP visitor turned out to be a young American woman.

Getting out of the car, Alana looked up at a large sign on the fence. In English, Azerbaijani, and – incongruously – Japanese, it announced that the excavation was part of the Southern Caucasus Early Farming Project. The site director was absent, so Alana was greeted by the senior digger, bearded Bruce from Omaha, who gave her a tour. The project was a three-way collaboration between the University of New Mexico, Albuquerque, Tokyo University, and Azerbaijan's Institute of Archaeology and Ethnography, backed by UNESCO. There were other excavations farther north, near Barda and Ganja. The site director – whom Bruce referred to as "Professor Bob" – had been visiting Barda and was expected back today. Guessing that he was referring to Professor Bob Rheingold, the head of department at Albuquerque, Alana was glad to have missed him; Rheingold was notoriously harsh-tempered and unfriendly. Being publicly chewed to pieces for disturbing his excavations on a frivolous sightseeing visit would not have brightened her day.

About half the work force were students from Albuquerque, most of the rest were Azerbaijanis. It felt good to Alana that both sides of her –re the American and the Azeri – were represented here, in a place dedicated to uncovering the deepest roots of Azerbaijan's civilization. The sensation she'd felt since childhood when visiting ancient places – a contrary mix of soothing calmness and almost painful exhilaration, as if she were being possessed by the spirit of *hiraeth* – took her over as she walked among the remains of her prehistoric forebears.

Neolithic Qaradagli was a large settlement dated to around 5500 BCE. Like Çatalhöyük in Turkey, the focus of her own research, it was an early farming settlement built on a mound, but much, much smaller, and its buildings were entirely different. In place of the close-packed little mud-brick houses, Qaradagli had large circular buildings. Curious about their interiors, within ten minutes of arriving Alana was down on the surface of the excavation, where a dozen diggers were on their knees with trowels and buckets. Another five minutes and she was scraping away at a cross-trench with Bruce's trowel, examining the russet-colored band of soil.

The trowel's blade was worn to the size of a dessert spoon, but it felt big and cumbersome in Alana's hands. In her past two seasons at Çatalhöyük she'd worked exclusively on the wall paintings – red ochre geometric patterns and images of vultures, foxes, humans, and hunting scenes – and her main tool had been a scalpel, with which the layers of paint and plaster were meticulously unpeeled. Her doctoral thesis was on the performative nature of the art. The paintings in the houses had been plastered over and repainted dozens and dozens of times, apparently as often as once a month, suggesting that the power of the paintings lay in the execution as much as in the forms. The people of Çatalhöyük had buried their dead within the settlement, under the floors of their houses, and the bodies of children were given special treatment, decorated with beads and ochre; the wall paintings were often associated with their presence, and Alana suspect that acts of communion with the supernatural realm of the ancestors was bound up in the paintings.

"Do you happen to have a scalpel?" she asked. "This is kind of a blunt instrument. I'd like to take a look at the mud-brick strata."

"I, er ... no, I don't." Bruce called to one of the assistants making minutely detailed plans of the exposed layers. "Elisa, do you have a scalpel?"

"Yeah, sure." The young woman rummaged in a small toolbox. "Just a blade, okay?"

"That'd be great," said Alana.

A little foil sachet flew across site. Bruce caught it and passed it down to Alana.

"Thanks," she smiled. She liked Bruce, a gentle giant who seemed a little in awe of her. She opened the sachet and took out the tiny glittering blade. It was hardly ideal, but it was more her style than the trowel. Stepping down inside one of the buildings, where two diggers were slowly scraping back a layer of dirt, Alana knelt and began picking delicately at the gray edges between the mud-bricks.

"What're you looking for?" asked Bruce.

"Traces of pigment or plaster."

"You mean wall art? We don't have any here," said Bruce.

Alana worked the blade delicately, taking off minute slivers and grains of the crumbling material. "I have a hypothesis that domestic ritual art was a lot more common than we think. We just aren't identifying the traces."

"We do have a few pretty nice examples of painted pottery imported from Mesopotamia. But the people here were at a pretty early stage of settlement complexity."

"You think the flooding ended the occupation?" Alana asked, not taking her eyes off her work.

279

"Do *I* think? You're talking to the wrong dude," said Bruce. He glanced up at the sound of a car pulling up. "Aaand, speaking of the great Jehoshaphat, here's Professor Bob right now."

Oh shit. Alana's heart sank. Time to get chewed to pieces. A silver SUV, thick with brown dust, had pulled up near the site HQ, which consisted of a pair of large trailers, a small hut, and a pair of chemical toilets. But instead of the balding, furious figure of Bob Rheingold, the person who got out was a young woman with close-cropped red hair.

Alana could hardly believe her eyes. She clambered out of the trench and walked toward the car. "Bobbie?" she said. The red-headed woman paused in the act of hauling a large rucksack out of the trunk and regarded her curiously. "You don't remember me," said Alana. "I'm Alana Fulton. From Stanford?"

The woman's face brightened. "Alana. Sure, I remember you. You were in our Neolithic working group for a while. Didn't you go on to Columbia?"

Alana felt almost as intimidated as if it had actually been Rheingold. Roberta Fitch was a legend; a brilliant field researcher and theorist, she'd been in her senior year at Stanford while Alana was a sophomore. She'd gone on to direct major excavations in northern Iraq while still a grad student., and after getting her doctorate, she'd walked right into a tenure-track assistant professorship at UNM after only a year in a research post. In their world, those were superhero-level accomplishments.

"Yeah, I'm at Cambridge now," said Alana, almost apologetically. Her achievements, of which she'd been extremely proud, suddenly felt rather meager. "Just finishing my doctorate."

"What are you doing here? If you're looking for work, I could always use more diggers." Bobbie nudged her arm. "I'm kidding. Çatalhöyük, right? I caught your paper at Boulder last year. Submitted your dissertation already?"

"All printed and ready to go."

"That's fast work. I'm impressed."

Alana tried not to glow. "Well, I have to pass yet."

"I saw your paper. And I remember the piece you did for the Stanford group. Grooved ware distribution patterns in the British Isles, right? You'll pass. What are your plans?" Bobbie held up a hand. "Hold on. Let me drop my stuff and check these guys haven't broken my site while my back's been turned, then we'll get coffee."

Bobbie turned toward the HQ, and stopped short at the sight of Rustam, tall, blond, and handsome, standing guard near her car. Uzeyir, who'd been patrolling the fenced perimeter, came walking up at that moment.

"Uh-oh," said Bobbie to Alana. "Government spooks. We get them from time to time. This place is right on the edge of a militarized zone. I'll see what they want."

"Actually," said Alana, "they're with me."

"They're what now?"

Alana beckoned them over. "Professor Fitch, may I introduce Uzeyir Khalilzade and Rustam Mammadov from the State Protection Service."

Rustam shook hands warily, Uzeyir with the habitual mocking smile twisting his black goatee.

"Well, Alana Fulton from Cambridge," said Bobbie. "It looks to me like you have a story to tell."

Bobbie unrolled a map, weighing down the corners with random objects from her desk – a trowel, a rock, a full coffee cup, and a large sherd of prehistoric pottery. "The whole region is problematic," she said. "And not just politically. We're right on the boundary between the uplands of Nagorno-Karabakh and the steppe land. We have a modern political borderline smack dab on a Neolithic migration watershed; Qaradagli marks the first spread of early agriculture – the local version of the Shulaveri-Shomu culture – out of the highlands onto the steppe. And the zinger is, we can't get to the other side of the line."

"Because Armenia is occupying it," said Alana.

"Right." Bobbie pointed to a dotted line in blue Sharpie cutting across the map. "That's the border of the militarized zone. Behind it is a so-called security belt a mile to two miles deep, held by Armenian forces. We're here." She tapped a point right beside the blue line.

"That close?" said Alana. "I knew the border was near, but not that near."

"Any day of the week you could toss an obsidian blade from the top of the spoil heap and hit an Armenian soldier." Bobbie sipped her coffee. "UNESCO tried to broker a deal to allow our American and Japanese staff to run geophysical surveys on both sides of the border, but neither government would stand for it." She spread her hands helplessly. "I even put together a joint proposal for a totally independent project, with no Azerbaijani involvement at all, to run in Armenian-occupied territory, but the Armenian government kicked that into the long grass too. Foreigners are not wanted in Karabakh. At least, not if they have the slightest connection with Azerbaijan. That's how deep the hate is."

Alana's heart was sinking, but not for the same reasons. Her notion of somehow finding a way into Karabakh was looking more remote and foolish by the minute.

Bobbie was regarding her speculatively. "I know this is absolutely a left-field blindside," she said. "But would there be any chance of your grandfather helping somehow?"

Alana almost spat out her coffee. "My grandfather? Are you serious?"

Bobbie had shown little interest in the details of Alana's story (a heavily edited version), but had perked up visibly when Alana explained how she came to have two DMX agents escorting her.

"I mean, he's obviously a man of influence. Maybe he could arrange to have Baku ease up on their side of the restriction. If you were to explain how important this is ...?"

"I ... I don't know what to say."

"You've seen the material culture here," said Bobbie. "The structures, the Venus figurines, the ceramic decoration. You can see the parallels with Çatalhöyük ..."

"This site is a thousand years later than the population peak of Çatalhöyük," Alana said. "The Anatolian tell sites were pretty nearly depopulated before the bell curve even starts here."

"They overlap, nose to tail. Don't you see? We're looking at a pan-Caucasian-Levantine-Anatolian-Mesopotamian cultural package. *Not* the discrete pockets we're used to thinking of. Modern political boundaries are obscuring that, more even than they do in Europe."

Alana rested her elbows on the table. Her gaze wandered over the map and settled on the sherd of pottery. It was a common, reddish-colored ware, but its inside surface was painted with chevrons in a muddy green. After years of studying Neolithic art, her brain was attuned to respond like a compass needle to such patterns. She picked it up and turned it over. "Is this part of your assemblage? It looks different."

"That? No, that's late Bronze Age. We have some reoccupation at the northern end of the site. My hypothesis is that the settlement was abandoned due to flooding, then recolonized by a migratory wave around 1200 BCE. That's a piece of Khojali-Gadabay ware. I keep it around to illustrate that ancient culture doesn't respect modern political boundaries."

"Did you say Khojali?"

"It's a small town inside Karabakh, about fifteen miles from here. The type sites are there. Notorious for the Khojali genocide, an unprecedented massacre of the Azerbaijani population."

"I know. I …" Alana swallowed hard. Her hands were trembling, and she laid the pottery sherd down carefully. "I've heard of it."

"We're in the same river valley here; the Gargar flows through Khojali and down to the steppe and right by the site here."

Alana's head was beginning to buzz. A memory of freezing cold water numbing her ankles, of trudging through snow with wet feet, someone's hand in hers. Her breathing almost stopped, and she felt as if she were going to faint.

"Are you okay?"

She gripped the edge of the table. Her vision came back into focus, and she found Bobbie regarding her curiously. Every tiny detail of the woman's face was suddenly as vivid in Alana's eyes as a photograph: the flame-red hair cropped on all sides and piled in tight curls on top, the small, bright hazel eyes with the membrane-thin white skin already crinkling to crow's feet, the scree of freckles cascading either side of the thin nose, and every crease in the protruding, blood-red upper lip. Such a fragile envelope in which to enclose such a powerful spirit; so easily crushed and killed.

"I … I went a little dizzy. I could use a little fresh air."

Alana was shaken by the violence of her own thoughts; she'd had a fleeting urge to make the thoughts real: to feel and see the pale skin broken, delicate bones shattered, and blood set loose. The sensation passed in an instant, leaving her sick with horror and disgust. It was as if some malignant spirit had taken possession of her, and she had no idea where it came from.

She almost crashed through the trailer door and staggered out into

284

the open air, gulping for breath. She was dimly conscious of Bobbie's hand on her shoulder.

"Are you all right?"

"Yes. Sorry. I'm fine, just … I don't know, I got a little panic attack or something." She forced a smile. "Give me a second, I'll be okay."

Bruce was hovering nearby, trying to get Bobbie's attention. "Look, I need to make my inspection," she said to Alana. "Tag along. You'll see what I mean about the culture."

Alana accompanied Bobbie as she took a tour of the site. Recovering from her strange episode, Alana noted the woman's quiet authority with the diggers and her ability to master and analyze the hundreds of complex, overlapping layers and structures representing centuries of human life – pits dug, walls built and altered, removed, replaced, fires lit and abandoned, refuse disposed of – and conjure from it a narrative that fitted into the larger story of this region of the world, a story populated by nameless, faceless, but nonetheless physical people of flesh and spirit.

This was what Alana had got into archaeology for; it had always lived for her as it did for Bobbie, but now, for the first time Alana felt as if she were truly a part of the story being told. The people who had lived in these mud-brick houses were *her* people, somehow, and she felt the connection.

And yet at the same time she was a scientist; she knew perfectly well, from the irresistible mathematics of population genetics, that *everyone now living in the world* was descended from the people who had lived here eight thousand years ago. And by the same mathematics, Alana herself was just as much a descendant of European and Asian Neolithic populations as she was of the folk of prehistoric Qaradagli – or Karabakh, for that matter. Yet this was the place where she felt the connection – where the connection *meant* something. The river that had nourished these people, and whose wild waters had eventually driven them out, was the same river that her own feet had crossed and re-crossed, and in which the blood of her relations and neighbors had flowed.

Moreover, the monsters who had spilled her people's blood still occupied the land they had stolen. The land which, for the first time, she truly felt she belonged to. Her grandfather's stories of the deep past now began to take on a new and palpable importance to her.

While Bobbie was discussing the contents of a finds tray, Alana wandered to the perimeter fence and looked out across the landscape. The site was on the brow of a slight rise in the vast, flat steppe, and she could see clearly across the open space the mountains of Nagorno-Karabakh, rising green and sheer beyond the veil of haze. The Gargar river meandered toward them, vanishing in the distance. There was a deep crease in the mountain wall, which she guessed must be where the river valley cut into the heartland. Somewhere beyond that gap lay Khojali.

"It looks like a beautiful country," said Bobbie. "I'd give anything to be able to extend our survey there."

"What are those features?" Alana asked. "There, across the dip." She pointed at the slightly rising ground about a quarter of a mile away. "They look like earthworks."

"Earthworks is right, but not the kind we like. That's the Armenian front line."

Alana gripped the chain-link fence and stared. The defenses were more extensive than she'd first thought; the banks and entrenchments zigzagged across the landscape, stretching away for miles north and south. Among them were embanked spots which she guessed were gun positions, and she could make out concrete bunkers. The trenches were discontinuous, with long stretches looking abandoned, but elsewhere she could make out gun barrels and tiny vehicles crawling along.

"Do you have binoculars?" she asked.

"I do, but I've banned the use of them at the request of the government. You can wager your butt the Armenian army is watching us this minute. If anyone here looks like they're studying their defenses, it could cause an incident. I tell my American students that this spot is like the Berlin Wall or the DMZ in North Korea. We're here by the grace of the Azerbaijan government, and we can't afford to cause any upset."

Alana studied the defenses and the green mountains beyond. She hadn't realized just how thoroughly cut off she was from the place she hoped to reach. "It's like World War One," she muttered. "The trenches. And the land looks so dead."

"None of the security belt has been farmed or irrigated for two decades. Yeah, it's dead. Although …" Bobbie peered into the distance. "The lines don't look as busy as they used to. Taking a wild guess, I wonder if the Armenians are cutting back on some of their defenses. You see that road heading out west from just beyond Mammadbagirli?"

Alana looked. "You mean the village right there?"

"Yep, that's Azerbaijan's last outpost. My American diggers call it Mamma's Bad Girl. They have their hostel there. Well, that road used to be the main highway to Shusha, via Khojali and Aghdam. Aghdam was like the state capital of this district. The Armenians drove the Azeris out in 1993 and put the city to the torch. Now, that highway is just a ghost road. It's asphalt as far as Mamma's Bad Girl and then just holes and dirt. Nobody's traveled that road in twenty years. Nobody but ghosts."

28

The drive back to Elamxanli was tense. Alana drummed her fingers on the armrest, glancing from time to time at Rustam's profile. He drove with the same insouciant air he brought to everything, his elbow cocked on the window ledge, a faraway smile in his gray eyes, and a lock of his blond hair drooping over his brow. Neither her grandfather nor Noah had been able to tell her much about him; he was new to the team, an unknown quantity. Nevertheless, Alana felt instinctively that she could trust him. She couldn't deny that this was partly because she was attracted to him.

"My grandfather says you come from Karabakh," she said. It was about the only fact she knew about him.

Rustam glanced across at her in surprise. "From Aghdam, my family."

"I heard what happened there. I'm sorry."

He shook his head. "Very bad," he said. "We lose our home, lose everything, my mother and father, brothers. All gone."

"You remember it all?"

"Sure. I was kid, ten years old, when they come. We had to get out, the Armenians they burn and explosion everything. Houses, mosque, hospital, schools, all *kaboom*."

Alana thought of the ghost road to Aghdam and tried to imagine the flood of refugees coming along it, fleeing for their lives. That had occurred the year after Khojali, sometime after Alana had left this land for America.

"Do you ever feel the urge to go back?" she asked.

"Not understand."

"To return, go home to Karabakh. Do you want to?"

"Sure, I want Karabakh. But go to Aghdam?" He shook his head firmly. "No."

"You don't want to see the place where you were born?"

"Is dead place now. Only bones and ghosts."

Alana was silent for a while, then: "You know I'm from Khojali?"

Rustam turned to look at her, his eyes soft and sad. He nodded. "I hear this. Very sad place, like Aghdam." Then he smiled. "You don't talk like Khojali person."

"I grew up in America."

"New York?"

"Sure. I lived in New York for a while. But I grew up in California."

Rustam shook his head in wonder. "I go one day. I got cousins in New York."

"Really? What part?"

"East Village and Queens. Nice places?"

"Ah, well yeah. Interesting places, certainly. The East Village is pretty cool. You want to live there?"

"Is my dream. Good work there for bodyguard. Rich guys and lot of danger. Means lot of dollars for me, yes?" He glanced at her. "You like Azerbaijan? You come live here?"

Alana hesitated. What *did* she feel about it? Fascination, attraction, but did she actually *like* it? It felt alien to her, but there was something more. If she'd come as a tourist, she'd have fallen in love with it – with Baku and its architecture, with the beautiful language and the music and the wild, unsettling scenery, and above all the sense of deep ancientness. But she had brought terrible memories with her, and bad feelings, and an irrevocable sense of loss. Rustam was looking at her expectantly.

"I love it here," she said, and smiled.

She wasn't lying; she did love it, but in the way a child loves a parent who has caused her harm and abandoned her. It was an attachment, a longing, not really a feeling of affection. Perhaps the affection would grow in time. But Alana felt certain that that could only happen if she confronted her past, faced up to the harm, and in order to do that, she had to recover the whole truth about what had happened to her at Khojali.

"Do you think it would be possible to go back?" she said. "To Aghdam, I mean. To Karabakh, across the Armenian lines."

Rustam didn't understand what she meant, and she had to explain it a couple of times. "No way," he said when he finally grasped her meaning. "They shoot you or make you prisoner. Not possible to go through security zone."

"That place where we were today. My friend the professor said the defenses are really thin right now. Maybe a person might get through, if they had help." She directed a meaningful look at him. "Help from someone who knows what they're doing. You were in the military, right?" Alana had seen him exercising with his shirt off a few times, and noticed some military-looking tattoos.

"Yeah," he said. "Azerbaijan army, ten years."

"So …?"

Rustam shook his head firmly. "You cannot go to Khojali. Is impossible. Like Aghdam for me. Only ghosts."

Alana sighed. "Only ghosts," she murmured.

* * *

Togrul Karabakhsky lay awake, listening to the night noises from the street below his window. Sleep did not come easily to Togrul. As a young man he'd been able to switch sleep on and off almost at will, taking his rest to fit his needs. That ability was long lost, and in his old age, sleep chose for itself when to visit him. He often lay waiting in vain for it to come. Tonight, however, was different; sleep wanted him, but something in his mind was resisting it.

He rose from his bed and switched on the light. On the cabinet by the door lay the phone Noah had set up for him. He activated the screen. There had been no calls from Ayna for over twenty-four hours. Some intuition, whispering insidiously in the back of his mind, told him she was in danger. His finger hovered over the button that would call her.

No, he couldn't bother her in the middle of the night. He switched it off again, slipped it into his pocket and went out to the landing. Absolute silence. Looking down into the courtyard, he could see the open vestibule leading to the front door. He thought he could see someone moving down there. As he watched, there was a flicker of yellow light, which was suddenly extinguished.

Pulling his robe close about him, Togrul went downstairs. As quietly as he could, he opened the courtyard door – it creaked, as it always did, making his blood freeze. With as much stealth as an octogenarian could muster, he crossed the courtyard toward the arch. He could smell tobacco smoke. There was someone in the passage. He was about to call out a challenge when suddenly a bright light came on, dazzling him.

"Lord?" said a voice.

Togrul clutched at the wall for support. "Rashad! You fool! By all that is holy, what are you doing out here at this time of night?"

The flashlight dipped, illuminating the passageway. Togrul's steward sat in the door ward's chair, his bald head gleaming in the dim light. "Why, smoking." He stood up. "Sir, a thousand apologies. I didn't mean to alarm you. I sometimes come down here when I cannot sleep. I find it peaceful. Do you need assistance?"

"No, I do not need assistance. Take your hands off me!" Togrul was embarrassed at having taken fright so easily. It was unlike him. He looked around. "Where is Salim?"

Now Togrul realized why he had felt so unsettled; all the myriad tiny signs of the presence of bodyguards – the periodic checks, the soft tread around the house, the unobtrusive figure standing in the hallway or slipping in and out of the exits – to which he had become so accustomed that he rarely noticed them, were absent.

"I don't know," said Rashad. "Checking the street, perhaps?"

Togrul shook his head. "I haven't seen him since before supper. Have you?"

Rashad hadn't. Togrul immediately turned on his heel and headed back across the courtyard. "Where are you going?" said Rashad.

"To telephone Hajiyev."

"But it's the middle of the night! Surely General Hajiyev will be asleep."

"Are *you* asleep? Am I? Besides, I do not care. Our only remaining bodyguard has disappeared. He is up to no good, Rashad, mark my words. I never liked the look of that freakish Iranian."

"But sir …"

"My granddaughter is out there, Rashad. Ayna is out there!"

Alana lay with her eyes open, listening to the silence of the house. She couldn't have slept tonight even if she'd wanted to. Her brain was too active. It wasn't the stimulating intensity of thought she was used to in her work; instead it was an adrenaline-fueled spike bordering on panic.

After getting back from Qaradagli that afternoon, Rustam had immediately reported to Uzeyir what Alana had said about crossing the security belt into the occupied zone. The dark, compact bodyguard had given her a very hard stare and repeated his colleague's warning: Karabakh was a no-go. She received the same warning – expressed in friendlier words – from Noah.

What these three men did not know about Alana, but which her parents (both sets) had learned the hard way, was that to deny Ayna Chichak Karabakhsky something she had set her heart on was to make her want it more than ever. And the firmer the denial, the fiercer the longing. She wouldn't sulk or throw a tantrum; she simply watched and waited and calculated, and set about acquiring it.

She looked at her watch. It was after midnight. The old couple, Yusif and Emine, had gone to bed two hours ago, and she could hear Yusif's deep snoring through the thin wall. Alana got up, padded across the living room and kitchen, and silently opened the front door.

Rustam would be on sentry duty outside. Alana knew his routine: a patrol along the street, interspersed with circuits around the house and yard, never in the same order. It was Uzeyir's turn on downtime tonight, and he would be fast asleep in Noah's house.

Alana crept out on to the veranda. There was no sign of Rustam. A bright moon cast a bluish light and sharp black shadows on the street. Alana stole down the steps, every muscle tensed, expecting a creak to give her away. She peeked around the corner of the house, but still couldn't see Rustam. He wasn't in the street, either.

That was strange. Alana didn't have time to stand around analyzing the routines of nocturnal close protection. In her mind she heard her friend Katy's voice: *That draft you can feel, that's the window of opportunity opening.* This would be easier than she'd anticipated.

Alana slipped back into the house, went to her room, and came out a moment later wearing a backpack. She'd prepared it earlier that evening, packing everything she thought she might need. Still no sign of her guardian. She silently gave thanks for her good luck and hoped it would hold out.

The Range Rover was parked beside the house. It was unlocked and the key was in the ignition. It was left like that as a matter of routine; the vehicle had to be kept ready to move, and a misplaced or fumbled key could be the difference between life and death. Starting it required a passcode.

Alana, heart racing, opened the door, shoved her backpack inside, slid into the driver's seat, and turned the key. The dashboard and touchscreen lit up, asking for the passcode. She'd seen her bodyguards input it at least a dozen times: 7308. The engine thrummed to life and the headlights came on. Dirt churned as she reversed out, put it in drive and roared along the street. At the edge of the settlement, she turned on to Highway 33, heading west.

For the first few miles, Alana couldn't shake the feeling that she was being tailed. But there was nothing but blackness in the rearview mirror. After a while the feeling subsided, replaced by a mounting exhilaration. She'd done it! She felt a little bad about tricking her bodyguards – not to mention Noah – but she needed to do this, and her guardians had begun to feel like her jailers.

The highway passed through a few scattered villages she remembered from the journey the previous day. After a while the houses of Qaradagli appeared in the pool of the headlights. Just past the last house on the left was the turn signposted for Mammadbagirli and the archaeological excavations. She drove past it, killing the lights and slowing to a crawl.

The road went on dead straight for a quarter of a mile, easy enough to follow by moonlight. There was no actual border post, and Alana had no idea how far she could safely drive before reaching the security belt. Trusting her instinct, she drove until her spine began prickling, then pulled over into a field entrance and switched off the engine.

Her heart in her mouth, Alana stepped out of the vehicle into the deep, intimate quiet of a rural night. Shouldering her backpack, she walked toward the border.

In less than a minute, she had vanished into the darkness. The Range Rover's engine ticked softly as it cooled in the night air. Another minute passed by, and another. Then there was a faint rumbling sound, and a car, its lights off, came slowly along the highway. It turned in at the field entrance and pulled up behind the Range Rover. The driver's door swung open, and a man stepped out. He examined the Range Rover, finding it empty. Reaching back into his car, he took out a pistol. Tucking it in his belt, he set off on foot, heading the way Alana had gone.

Emine was woken from a dream in which she was a child again, milking her father's goats on their farm in the hills. The sound of a car roaring violently away in the street outside jolted her awake with her head jangling.

Her husband, Yusif, went on snoring. Knowing she wouldn't get back to sleep, Emine climbed out of bed and went through to the living room. She listened at the young lady Alana's bedroom door, but there were no sounds. Emine went through the kitchen and opened the back door to let in some fresh air. She could still hear the car in the far distance, dwindling away and leaving behind the quiet of an Elamxanli night. It would be dawn in a few hours, time to get up.

Ermine was about to go back inside when she realized that the quiet wasn't entirely normal. The chickens seemed more agitated than they should be at this time of night. Was there a fox about?

Taking a flashlight, Emine went down the steps and crossed the yard to the coop. The birds were clucking and unsettled. Emine shone her light through the fence, sweeping the enclosure; it found nothing but straw, a couple of chickens, a pail … and a large dark shape. She gasped and let out a choked scream.

There was a man lying in there. Emine could see his face, and knew him as the young blond agent, Rustam. His skin was white in the torchlight and streaked with blood, and Emine, who had seen such things before, knew at once that he was dead.

Alana picked her way carefully along the road. It was the same Highway 33 she'd driven along from Elamxanli, but from here on it hadn't been used in decades. The banks on either side had subsided, and weeds grew from cracks in the asphalt. She really needed a flashlight, but it was out of the question.

She'd gone a quarter of a mile when she came to an enormous mound of earth and rubble blocking the way. There was a sign board next to it, but she couldn't read it in the darkness. She guessed this was the demarcation: the beginning of the occupied zone. There was no fence, no barbed wire. Would there be landmines? That hadn't occurred to her until now, and the thought froze her to the spot.

There was no going back now. So long as she stuck to the road, she figured it should be safe enough. She climbed up the steep mound and slithered carefully down the other side, landing back on the asphalt. Alana had penetrated the edge of the security belt and was in Armenian-occupied territory.

It occurred to her that this was the very same road that passed through Khojali; she believed she could remember crossing it that night, heading for the hills. The memory of it made her shiver. It was as well for her that she had lost track of dates since leaving

England, and was wholly unaware that tonight was the twenty-sixth of February – the anniversary of the massacre. Every year from that night to this was now just a slab on a bridge over a featureless void, a causeway bringing her back to this place.

Peering ahead into the silvery moonlit gloom, Alana could neither see nor hear any sign of military guards. Stunted, spidery trees cast shadows across the dusty, cracked road ahead; some had put roots through the asphalt. All was silent and empty.

She began walking. The trees were like petrified sentries, and as she passed each one her skin crawled, as if expecting the gnarled bark to come to life. It truly felt like a road traveled only by ghosts, and as she walked, a fancy grew in her mind, that it was leading her not to her past, but into some kind of deathly netherworld.

Distance was difficult to judge, but she guessed she'd walked a few hundred yards when the way ahead was obstructed by a deep trench cut across the road, flanked by a dozen or more spindly trees. Alana hesitated, scared to approach this eerie copse. She forced herself forward, step by step. The trench was long, zigzagging away on either side. It was lined with sandbags, but had partially caved in, and rusted wire, empty food cans, scraps of plastic sheeting, and other detritus lay among the soil. Clearly, it had been disused for quite a while.

Alana braced herself against her own fears, climbed across, and hurried through the sinister trees.

The road resumed, ever more narrowed by the encroaching banks, obliterated in places by dirt and weeds. Far away to her left the lights of a vehicle appeared. She heard the deep rumble of a truck and shrank back into the shadows beneath a thorn bush. The truck seemed to be heading straight toward her across the open landscape; suddenly it veered, crossing the road about twenty yards ahead and continuing on northward. Gradually the noise and lights faded.

When it was gone, Alana moved on, more warily than ever. Soon she came to the spot where the ghost highway was crossed by a newer road, surfaced in grit, a pale ribbon laid across the landscape.

This was part of the Armenian front line. The occupying army had abandoned most of their fixed trench lines in favor of mobile defense, using purpose-built roads linking strongpoints made up of gun emplacements and entrenchments. Hard standings had been constructed at intervals along the new road; there was one near the point where it crossed the ghost road, and she could see the dim outlines of military vehicles and soldiers moving about.

As stealthily as she could, Alana scurried across the road, her flesh shrinking with fear until she was reclaimed by the shadowy obscurity on the other side.

The ghost road led straight through the black, silent nocturnal landscape. Alana had a sense of barriers closing behind her; there would be no going back. Another two hundred yards, another disused trench line, and another new road. The ghost road was increasingly blocked by dirt slippage, bushes and trees, the broken asphalt becoming patchy and disappearing altogether for long stretches.

Did this awful road have no end? She looked at her watch, tilting it to catch the moon's rays. Nearly half past three. A wave of fatigue was numbing her body, and she fought against it. She took a step and stumbled, kicking a loose stone; it skittered noisily across the road.

Instantly, a male voice came from somewhere up ahead.

Alana dropped to a crouch. The voice was close and distinct. Peering into the darkness, she thought she could make out the shapes of soldiers about fifteen or twenty yards ahead. Her tiredness was swept away by a surge of adrenaline, and her body tensed, ready to run. Away to the left, she made out the jagged outlines of derelict buildings: an abandoned farm, she guessed. The rational part of her mind urged her to head for cover there, but the irrational part regarded the ruined buildings with an animal dread.

Two flashlights turned on, lighting up the ground ahead. The beams flicked about, left and right, scanning the road. The nearest one began tracking right toward her. Alana was gripped by a paralysis, caught between the fear of discovery and the nameless dread of the ruins. Her terror was threatening to turn into panic when another sense whispered that there was some other, unidentified, threat behind her. She had walked into a trap.

The light had almost reached her when the rational mind won; she rose to her feet and moved softly to the edge of the road, up the shallow bank and across a patch of open ground, dropping down behind a half-collapsed wall.

Crouching among the tumbled concrete blocks, Alana heard the voice again, now slightly farther away; the flashlight beams left the road and began scanning the far side. She could see the soldiers silhouetted now, searching. After a while the lights blinked off, and silent stillness resumed. The sensation of a second threat behind her had gone.

Alana was shaking. She focused on regaining control, calming down, breathing steadily. She began taking stock of her situation. The wall was part of an outbuilding; nearby was a derelict house. If she could …

A twig snapped, right behind her.

Alana twisted round in time to see a dark figure rushing toward her. She scrabbled at the ground, instinctively searching for a weapon, and her hand fell on a half-brick. She gripped it and rose, lunging with all her strength at the figure. The brick glanced off the side of his head, and they went down in a struggling, tangled heap. Alana fought with the fury of panic, kneeing and clawing at the man; she tried to raise the brick for another blow, but the man gripped her wrist with a terrifying strength.

"*Stop,*" he hissed. "*Stop!*"

She twisted her wrist out of his grasp, and lost hold of the brick in the process; the man pushed against her, but she had her knee in his stomach, and managed to get both hands on his throat.

"Alana, stop! Stop, it's me, I—" Her thumb pressed into his larynx, choking off his voice. Seized by an animal instinct she didn't even know she possessed, she pushed down, closing off his resistance, all thought blotted out by the need to eliminate this threat. Her eyes, dazzled by the flashlights, failed to see the familiarity of his features.

A shred of cloud that had obscured the bright moon passed, and Alana recognized the face among the deep shadows, eyes bulging, mouth working. "Noah?" She let go of his throat as if she'd been electrocuted. "Oh my God, oh dear God …"

He raised himself on one elbow, clawing at his throat, struggling to recover his breath.

"Oh God, Noah, I'm so sorry." He gestured frantically for her to be quiet. She reached out to him, but he backed away. "I thought you were one of them," she said. "I thought you were gonna … oh my God I'm so, so sorry."

Noah shook his head and tried to speak, but all he could manage was a hoarse croak. "It's okay. I understand. I'll live."

"You followed me?" she said.

"Yes."

"You can't make me go back. I have to go through with this."

Noah sat up, breathing laboriously. He pointed to his throat. "You have water?"

Alana opened her backpack and gave him a bottle. "Do you hear me? I'm not going back with you." Now that the first moment of horror had passed, she was furious with him. "You can't stop me!"

It was too dark to make out Noah's expression. He took another sip, then handed back the bottle. "Does your grandfather know you're doing this?"

"Of course not."

"Then why do it?"

"I just have to, Noah. I need to know, I need to go home."

"Yes, you need to go home – to Elamxanli, to Baku."

"My home is *that* way," she said, pointing toward the ghost road.

"No Azeri has a home that way anymore, Alana. It is gone."

"For me it's still there, Noah. I have to find it. I can't let you stop me."

Alana went to stand up, but Noah gripped her arm. "Are you insane? We are in the security zone. There are enemy soldiers right there."

"I'll go around them. One way or another, I'm going on."

Noah sighed. "They named you Chichak rightly. What do I have to say to make you see reason?"

"There's nothing you can say."

"Very well." He stood up, took the pistol from his waistband, checked it and replaced it. "In that case I am going with you."

"Are you kidding me? You have responsibilities back there; you can't come."

"I cannot stop you, and Alana, you cannot stop me."

They waited in the shelter of the wall a while for Noah to get his breath back. There was no more argument; for better or worse, they were in this together.

"How did you know to follow me?" she asked.

"I was sitting up late with some case notes. I heard the car driving away."

As he spoke, Alana was shouldering her backpack and checking that the coast was clear. Noah was thankful that she was too preoccupied to spot the transparent lie and didn't think to ask how he'd know she was driving the car, or why he'd thought it was important to follow.

"I think they're gone," she said. "Time to go."

Rather than return to the road, they stayed in the cover of the ruined buildings, which were more extensive than they had seemed. "I guess this is the edge of Saricali," said Noah. "It was an Azeri village the Armenians destroyed. One of many like it in Aghdam district. They drove the Azeris out and burned their homes, their farms, their businesses."

Alana could almost feel the presence of the specters of the annihilated community, and was glad they only had to walk through the edge of the ruined village, not through it. For a short while, she and Noah stuck to the fields, but the moon was sinking, and it was getting hard to find a way in the deepening dark. There was also a risk of minefields.

"We should get back on the road," said Noah, leading the way over the bank.

His feet had barely touched the asphalt when there was a loud crack and a bullet kicked up the dirt in the bank next to Alana. She threw herself to the ground with her hands over her head. Noah did the same. A burst of automatic fire sent bullets thrumming over their heads.

The firing stopped as suddenly as it had started; there was a lull in which they could hear voices and running feet, then two blindingly bright lights came on, flooding the road, exposing Alana and Noah as clearly as daylight.

A voice – from a source invisible beyond the glare of the lights – called out a challenge in Armenian. Noah got to his knees with his hands raised and gestured for Alana to do the same. The voice suddenly blared out through a loudhailer, repeating the same challenge. Noah, visibly quaking, replied in Armenian. Pointing to Alana, he said, "*Amerikats'i.*".

Silence.

Noah whispered: "I told them you're American."

An urgent debate broke out beyond the lights, several men arguing with one another. It came to an abrupt halt, and the silence resumed. Suddenly the lights flicked off.

Alana was absolutely blind, colored shapes dancing in her eyes. She heard Noah calling out in Armenian, but there was no reply. She peered toward the sound of his voice.

"What's happening?" she said.

"I don't know."

Noah called out again, but the soldiers still didn't say anything or make any move to take them prisoner. Neither he nor Alana dared to move. Gradually the colored blobs faded, and Alana began to be able to see faintly. Cautiously Noah got to his feet and took a few steps forward. Nothing happened, and Alana followed him.

"They're gone," she said, and took a few more steps. Her boot hit something small and light, which skittered away with a tinkling sound. She squatted and felt around; there were several small metal cylinders. Cartridge cases. This was where at least one of the soldiers had stood to fire at them. "They're gone," she repeated. "I don't understand. Why would they just disappear?"

"I don't know," said Noah. "It happened after I said you're American."

"They let Americans through?"

"No, they do not let Americans through," said Noah. "I told them that in the hope they would simply arrest us instead of shooting us right here."

"So why didn't they?"

Noah shook his head. "I have no idea."

"I guess it's my lucky night. Let's get out of here before they change their minds and come back."

"You're not going on?"

She stared at him. "Well, obviously. Are you coming?"

Without waiting for him to reply, Alana walked on into the darkness of the ghost road.

29

Aghdam

The moon sank below the western hills, leaving nothing but faint starlight, partly obscured by clouds. Alana and Noah, picking their way step by step, were now deep within the security belt; this stretch of the ghost road was in use by army traffic heading up to the front line, and they had to hide several times when military vehicles came roaring along.

Eventually dawn began to lighten the sky, revealing a landscape flatter and blanker than Alana had imagined. The trees, which moonlight had sculpted into threatening, living shapes, became dull gray hawthorns and beeches; on either side was a brown wasteland of rank grass, broken here and there by ruined houses and streets that had been reclaimed by the land, leaving only impressions, like veins under the skin. They walked past a walled enclosure surrounding a complex that looked like a school or a small hospital, all in ruins and overgrown.

"We must be near the city," said Noah.

They walked on. The road, having run straight for miles, bent hard right and passed over a rise. As the sun came up and the light grew, they turned the bend on the brow of the hill, and the city of Aghdam came into view.

Alana gasped and stopped in her tracks.

Vast and flat it stretched, block after block fanning out, street after street, avenues, parks – all desolate and abandoned. Alana had seen pictures of German cities bombed in World War Two, the rubble, the hollow shells of buildings. Aghdam was like that, but with the devastation overlaid by the patina of a quarter century's abandonment. Within Alana's own lifetime this had been a thriving, bustling city of fifty thousand souls. Immediately below where they stood was a grid of suburban streets more than a mile from side to side; the main avenues and cross-streets were still there, but the cul-de-sacs and lanes had faded into the earth, and most of the houses were little more than stumps of walls. A few stood to first story height, their windows empty holes, brambles climbing up their crumbling brickwork. In the distance were the skeletons of office and apartment blocks, and the shells of public buildings, stretching away to the hills. The ghost road had brought them to a city of the dead.

Alana's skin crawled at the sight of it, and her heart quailed at the thought of passing through it. She had spent half her life among ancient ruins, and there was a part of her that was enthralled by one so vast and vitally preserved, but there was a horror here that she had never felt among the ruins of long-vanished civilizations. Only when centuries had washed away the memories, and the memories of memories, would the horror recede.

"I can't go through there," she said. The urge to turn back from this cadaver of a place was almost overpowering.

Noah pointed toward the green mountains of Nagorno-Karabakh rising close and clear beyond the city. "This is the only way," he said.

Alana's heart recoiled. She tried to imagine having the opportunity to walk through the ruins of Mycenae or Troy or Lepenski Vir or Çatalhöyük this soon after their abandonment. What excitement she would have felt at getting this close to the human horizon of those settlements. *Treat it as archaeology*, she told herself.

"All right," she said, taking a deep breath. "Let's walk."

The main road curved away north to join the city's main boulevard. Armenian military traffic used that route, so instead they struck out ahead along an avenue that ran straight as a die through the suburbs and the center of the city. Its asphalt was pitted, vegetation growing in the gutters and deep cracks.

For Alana, it was easy to picture the life that had once existed here before the apocalypse. They walked past broken and destroyed buildings, intersections where signs scabbed with rust pointed the way to indecipherable places. Some structures had been leveled to their foundations, but many stood as high as two stories. Close to the center they walked past office blocks sagging and broken, and older buildings with rows of arched windows now open to the sky. The commercial districts were so ruined and decayed it was impossible to tell if one was looking at a clothing store or a restaurant or a community center. And yet there were men and women in Elamxanli who had lived and worked here, or who had played in these streets as children.

Passing a row of stone store-fronts that still had parts of their roofs, Alana, acting on an impulse, went to look inside. All she found was a mess of thistles and brambles and chunks of fallen brick wall. The interior walls and floors were all gone. On the upper story, which must have been the store owner's apartment, there was a mural, preserved from erosion by the remains of the roof: a beach scene with a blue-green sea and palm fronds. The room beside it still had the faded remnants of cartoon wallpaper. Alana thought of the wall paintings at Çatalhöyük and the graves of children. There were too many ghosts here. She went back outside.

"Aghdam was the one of the last Azeri towns left in Karabakh after the fall of Khojali and Shusha," said Noah, looking at the derelict façade of a small mansion opposite. The ruins were as much of a shock to him as to Alana; he knew Aghdam's story, and had passed through it as a child en route to Baku, but like nearly all of his countrymen he had not set foot here since the genocide. "The Armenian forces came in the summer of 1993. By then our army was beaten; the population fled east toward Qaradagli and Aghjabedi, and most of the army fled with them. The Azerbaijani forces came back later and fought hard, but by then it was too late. The city was lost."

Alana sat down on the curb and took a drink of water, offering the bottle to Noah.

"The few people who remained here were driven out," he said. His voice was hoarse with emotion. "Then the Armenians began to destroy the city. They stripped everything they could and hauled it away to Khankendi – which they renamed Stepanakert – to repair the war damage there. Doors, windows, timbers, bricks. What was left they blew up or burned, although they used old Azeri tomb stones as stairs for public toilets and this public humiliation bolstered their ego."

"Fifty thousand lives," said Alana. "Did you ever—"

"Hush!" Noah held up a hand and stood listening intently. "Somebody is coming."

"Oh shit – let's go!" Even as Alana snatched up her backpack, a jeep accompanied by half a dozen soldiers on foot emerged from a side street at the end of the block ahead. "We have to double back," she said.

Noah grabbed her arm. "No time. This way!"

He ran into the derelict store, pulling Alana with him. She heard a shout from the soldiers, and the jeep revving. Noah clambered over the mountain of rubble with Alana at his heels, fighting through the clinging brambles. The rear of the building had half collapsed and was obstructed by vines and ivy. Noah hurled himself at it; fortunately it was thinner than it looked, and he went flying through, trailing greenery and landing in a heap on the ground. Alana scrambled after him and was helping him to his feet as the soldiers reached the front of the building.

Noah grabbed Alana's hand. "This way, quickly."

Behind the buildings was a stretch of open waste ground ridged with the stumps of destroyed buildings and littered with rusting scrap metal, rotten timbers, and broken glass. On the far side was a half-demolished brick wall; they climbed over and found themselves in a shallow gully that had once been a backstreet. They sprinted across another stretch of waste ground and dodged into an alley between two half-collapsed apartment buildings.

Alana glanced back. "I think we lost them."

They stopped to catch their breath. Across the street from the apartment buildings was a mosque. It stood tall and elegant, the only intact building amongst the devastation. Its stone walls were the color of bleached bone, stained with weather and neglect, the sky-blue paint that had once decorated it mostly flaked away, but the twin minarets still had their intricate tilework and onion-domed roofs. A herd of cattle grazing in the open ground had wandered in under the arched entrance; Alana and Noah pushed through them and slipped inside.

The vaulted interior was flooded with light from the windows, many of which still had glass; the floor was bare dirt. A few cows stood among the carved pillars, regarding the newcomers impassively.

"So this was the only building that survived the destruction," said Alana. "Miraculous, I guess."

"The Armenians might have acted without humanity, but they should know better than to desecrate a holy place," said Noah. "No doubt they feared the international outcry if they completely destroyed a mosque."

"Seriously?" Alana was almost lost for words. "Just look at this place! It's a pig barn! A Muslim holy place is filled with pigs! How sick are these people? They savagely massacred innocent women and children, burned cities, turned a million people into refugees, but they were afraid of the outcry if they wrecked *one building*?"

"A cultural symbol. The mosque of Aghdam is quite famous. I have read that the Armenian government even made some repairs to the roof, but clearly that is another lie fed to the media."

Alana shook her head in disbelief and sat down on a window ledge, taking a few photos to document this vandalism. "Think we're safe in here?"

Noah glanced out. "I think they lost us. We should go up the minaret and take a look; we can plan our route and see any dangers."

He looked tired, but the warm, reassuring smile was still there, and still comforted her. "Noah, you shouldn't have come. This is my mission; you didn't need to risk yourself."

"It is my duty to protect you and help you." He hesitated. "Besides, I lied to you earlier."

"What do you mean?"

"I didn't follow you just because I heard you driving away. Emine woke me. Alana, your bodyguard, the blond one ..."

"Rustam?"

"He is dead. Emine found him."

"*Dead*?"

"He was murdered. His carotid artery had been severed by a single stab wound to the neck. Whoever did it was an expert killer. Right

310

away I thought of that man who came for you in Switzerland. I couldn't find Uzeyir, but I fear he may have been murdered also, or abducted." Noah's eyes were wide. "Alana, I thought the same had happened to you. I couldn't find you."

Alana covered her mouth. "Oh my God, oh my God," she muttered.

"At first, I thought the car driving off must have been the killer, so I collected my gun and followed. I guessed it might head for the Armenian zone. I don't know what I thought I could achieve, but I had to find out who it was and what they had done to you."

Alana struggled to speak. "Was anybody else hurt?"

"I don't know. I only saw Rustam, poor man."

Alana remembered her last conversation with him, his dream of living in New York. "This was a professional murder," said Noah. "To sever that artery so cleanly and precisely is the work of a person trained to kill."

All Alana could think about was poor Rustam and his family. *Family.* She yanked open her backpack and pulled out the satellite phone. It had been switched off since the previous day to prevent it ringing while she was on her mission. Now it showed ten missed calls, all from Togrul. She called him.

"Ayna!" His throaty old voice gave her a surge of relief.

"Are you all right?"

"I am. But Ayna, I have been trying to telephone you since yesterday. I could not get through. What is happening?"

"Oh, you know …" She gestured helplessly, trying to think of a way of describing the situation that wouldn't cause alarm. "I'm with Noah."

"Thank God for that. Listen, my child, you must come home right away. Tell Noah to bring you. Let me speak with him."

"Grandfather, what's wrong?"

"The bodyguard, Salim Zardabi, the Iranian, is missing. His superior does not know where he has gone; he did not report in. But they tracked his telephone before he switched it off; he was heading west, toward Karabakh. Ayna, I believe he is a traitor. He may mean to harm you."

The balcony atop the minaret gave a panoramic view over the whole city. The mosque stood at the very center, surrounded by the remains of Aghdam's public buildings and clusters of apartment blocks. Alana and Noah stood in the small open space under the dome, trying not to lean on the flimsy-looking railing, which was all that stood between them and a sixty-foot fall.

Noah hoped the view would reveal a safe route out of the city. Alana gazed out along the avenues, across choked streets and crumbling ruins that stretched for miles in every direction. Nature was reclaiming Aghdam. Alana knew the processes by which it happened; the robbing of materials and the grind of wind and rain breaking down the structures, worms casting up tiny quantities of dirt, slowly blurring the ground, fallen leaves mingling with the dust to make new earth over the paving; moss and vines enveloping brick and stone. Given another century, the city would be nothing but grass and trees and mulberry bushes and a few scattered remains of walls, like ancient sites all over the world. Given still more time its story would become obscure and ultimately forgotten outside of remote legends, until someone like her came along to peel back the overgrowth and uncover the remains, trying to piece together the lives that had once existed here and figure out what had caused its abandonment.

Noah pointed. "I think if we go diagonally that way, we can reach the western suburbs. It would be a long route, but probably less likely to meet soldiers."

"Uh-huh. Good point."

He looked doubtful; none of the ways out seemed good to him. "Alana, I wish you would change your mind. We could wait here until dark and then go back."

"I'm not having this conversation. If you want to go back, you'll have to go without me." She looked at him. "I like having you with me; it means a lot. But I have to go on."

"I lied to your grandfather just now. I have never done that before. Telling him you were safe with me, and letting him believe are still at Elamxanli … What if Salim finds us out here?"

"Better than finding us at Elamxanli."

"He is your grandfather, Alana, but to me he is my savior, my second father. I owe him everything. It cuts me like a knife to deceive him."

Alana took his hands in hers. "Noah, I'm sorry. But I can't just turn back now. I've come too far. I have to see Khojali for myself; it's like there's something in me that will never be complete until I see it again." She squeezed his hands. "But I won't force you to do anything. If you *really* want us to go back, then we will."

Noah's blue eyes were fixed on hers, and she could see the conflict in them. He took a long time to answer. "Because of what I owe your grandfather, I would do anything for you," he said. "But for your sake, I would not do anything against your will. If you must go on, then we go on together."

Alana hugged him. "Thank you. You're the best."

Noah, startled, tentatively returned her hug. "I am not."

Suddenly she froze. "Did you hear that?" She peered down at the stairwell. "There's someone coming up."

Noah knelt by the opening. He could hear the echoes of footsteps on the spiral stairs. They were trapped. He glanced over the edge of the railing. "Do you have rope?" Alana shook her head. "Then there is no way out."

313

He drew his pistol and leveled it at the head of the stairs. Alana looked around and snatched up a piece of broken railing. "All right," she muttered, and braced herself.

The footsteps were getting closer. Suddenly they stopped and a man's voice called out: "Anyone up there?" Then more quietly: "I think there might be somebody up there already."

Incredibly, the voice spoke English; even more incredibly, the accent was Scottish. A few moments later a head appeared in the opening: a young man with thick, unruly hair and sandy-colored stubble, his pale skin blotched pink from the exertion of climbing. Noah instantly concealed the gun. The newcomer looked up and grinned.

"Oh, hi," he said, and called down, "Come on up, Jem, we've got company." He stepped up into the balcony, followed by a young woman in a striped woolen hat and green leather jacket who smiled shyly. "I'm Leo," said the man. "This is Jemma."

Alana managed to find her voice. "Alana," she said. "This is Noah."

"Did you come down from Stepanakert?"

"What? No. No, we didn't."

Leo looked out at the view. "Oh, this is bloody *awesome*," he said, taking out a camera and starting to take pictures. "Cost us 12,000 drams a head for the taxi, but by God it's worth it."

Alana and Noah exchanged a look. "Wait," said Alana. "You're *tourists*?"

Leo stopped taking photos long enough to give her a pained look. "Travelers," he said.

Jemma regarded Alana and Noah curiously. "You're not travelers yourselves?"

"No—" Noah began, but Alana cut him off: "Well, yes, kind of. We're here for research. We walked here."

"Walked?" Leo looked at her with admiration. "That's commitment right enough. We were in Yerevan; bumped into an Aussie lad at Garni Temple who told us about this place. You know what happened here, right?"

Alana gave a tight-lipped nod. The man's enthusiasm and his treatment of this place of atrocity as a tourist spectacle grated on her. "Yes, I do. There are people living – young people – whose lives were torn apart by it."

Leo nodded, but seemed oblivious to her point. Jemma noticed Alana's tone and nudged her partner. "Maybe show a bit of respect, Leo," she muttered.

"Eh? Oh, right enough. Aye, respect for the dead and that."

Noah broke the awkward silence. "So you have a taxi here?"

"Oh aye. Waiting a wee way down the street, out of sight." Leo lowered his camera. "You have to be careful here, right? I mean, technically it's a war zone; the army doesn't take kindly to visitors."

Alana raised her eyebrows. "You don't say."

Eventually, having taken their fill of the view, Leo and Jemma said their goodbyes and went back down the stairs. Alana was about to follow when Noah held her back. "I think we have found our way out of here," he whispered.

The taxi, a dusty and battered old Volvo, was waiting in a nearby side street, as Leo had said. Noah and Alana watched it covertly from a nearby ruin. After the mosque, the two travelers had set off to tour the city on foot while their driver sat waiting, smoking drowsily with his car radio burbling out Russian folk music.

"We should take it," said Alana.

"What do you mean?" said Noah.

"I mean pay the guy to take us to Khojali."

"And leave Leo and Jemma stranded?" said Noah.

"I thought that's what you were thinking? I mean, the guy likes it here so much." The callousness Leo had shown still rankled with Alana. "Let him suck up the awesome. Besides, we only want to get to Khojali; maybe the guy could come back for them."

"You would do that? Really?"

Alana sighed. "Oh, I guess not. So, what – you think we should share their ride?"

"I do."

They had to wait nearly three hours before Leo and Jemma returned. The travelers were delighted to find their new friends again, and were enthusiastic at Noah's suggestion that they share the cost of the return journey. However, they wouldn't be going all the way.

Rather than heading back to Armenia, Leo and Jemma were heading north to the ancient ruins at Tigranakert. Alana had heard of this place from her grandfather; it was a relic of the Armenian dominion in the period before the Romans. It was a powerful symbol of Armenian culture in Karabakh, and the occupying power was now pouring resources into studying it. The proximity of the two ruined cities – one of them Armenian and two thousand years old, the other Azeri and destroyed within living memory – created such a sick dissonance in Alana's mind that she could hardly think about it without wanting to bang her head on something. For the first time in her life she almost regretted the preservation of an archaeological site.

The taxi driver, a middle-aged Armenian with a grizzled beard and drowsy eyes, regarded his new passengers with little interest and demanded an extra 500 drams. Alana offered him a ten-dollar bill, which vanished into his shirt pocket in an instant.

Leo sat in the front while Alana and Noah squeezed into the back seat with Jemma. The Volvo coughed itself to life and set out along the central boulevard. This road was the main route along which scavenged building materials had been transported west and was broad and clear. Unfortunately, it was also used by military convoys going to the security belt and was occasionally patrolled. The taxi had only gone a few blocks when two soldiers peeled away from their vehicle and ordered it to pull over.

"Oh, that's not good," said Leo.

Alana's heart thudded as the squad corporal, a long-faced gorgon with furious eyes, stared in through the driver's window and barked at him in Armenian. Alana's hand shook; she pressed it against the seat to still it and felt Noah's hand cover it. He gave her his reassuring smile, but there was anxiety in his eyes.

"We're British," said Leo, leaning across. "Our pals back there are Americans."

The corporal gestured with the muzzle of his AK-47 and gave an order. Alana felt Noah flinch beside her. The driver translated: "He say you get out."

"Oooh shit," muttered Leo.

The soldiers covered them with their weapons as they got out of the car. The corporal snapped another order. Noah murmured in Alana's ear, "He wants our identification."

Alana's heart froze; her passport was in her backpack, but Noah had nothing. The moment they spoke to him, they would identify him as Azerbaijani.

Leo and Jemma dug in their packs, and Alana did likewise. The corporal glanced at their passports. Fortunately he didn't look closely enough to notice that Alana's had an Azerbaijan stamp. He glared at Noah and gestured at him to hand his over. Noah made a show of searching his pockets. "I … I don't have it," he said in English, trying to Americanize his accent. The corporal stared at him coldly and gestured again. Noah's mouth worked in confusion; there was nothing he could do. The corporal beckoned to men, who stepped forward, rifles at the ready.

On an impulse, Alana stepped in front of Noah. "I do apologize, sir," she said to the corporal. "My husband has left his passport at the hotel. *Again*." She gave Noah a withering look. "Honey, you are *so* careless. I swear this man would forget his own head if he didn't have me to watch it for him."

She beamed at the corporal while the taxi driver translated the gist to him. The response came back: "Which hotel?"

"Oh, er, in Yerevan, the hotel …" Alana began to flounder. Jemma mouthed a word at her. "Kantar?" said Alana, and Jemma smiled. "Yes, the Kantar Hotel, Yerevan."

The corporal stared suspiciously at her, then grunted something that sounded like a mortal threat.

"We go now," said the taxi driver, sweating. "Is okay. We go."

As they were getting back in, the corporal stopped Leo and seized his camera; he turned it over, extracted the memory card and pocketed it, then handed the camera back. "Hey! That's my pictures!"

"Back in car!" the driver urged. "We go now."

Leo got in reluctantly. As the taxi drove on, Noah murmured to Alana, "Thank you. That was good acting. You saved me."

"So did Jemma," said Alana. "Thank you."

Jemma smiled sweetly. "That was a scary one, wasn't it? What's up with you two?"

"Oh, just wandering somewhere we shouldn't," said Alana. "Leo, you lost your photos. I'm so sorry; it's all our fault."

Leo chuckled. "If I've learned one thing from the wild ways of the world, it's never to keep your memory card in your camera when you're not using it." He fished a second card out of his pocket. "Here's my photos. Corporal Clott back there is now in possession of, if I remember rightly, a fifteen-minute video of the escalators at Heathrow airport and a dozen shots of my auntie's back garden in East Kilbride."

The last devastated blocks of Aghdam city went by, and after about a mile the outskirts gave way to scrub and farmland. The fields, no longer cultivated or irrigated, were brown and bare, their only crops thistle and bramble. The farms were ruins in the distance. A little way farther on, the road converged with the Gargar river and Alana began to see farms that were intact and still working.

They were coming to the end of the militarized zone. The mountain foothills reared up, a massive arm flung out onto the plain of the Karabakh Steppe. The river hugged close to the base of the hills, and the road followed it. Exhilaration began to take hold of Alana. Ahead, a second mountainous ridge marched across the plain toward the first, forming a gap through which the river flowed; that was the gateway to Nagorno-Karabakh. Just beyond was Khojali. Alana was trembling.

Near the tip of the southern range, the road divided, and with it the travelers. Alana and Noah's way lay straight on, but Leo and Jemma were going north to Tigranakert. They all got out to say their goodbyes. Although they had known one another for only a couple of hours, for a brief spell they had become friends. Noah shook hands with them both, while Alana hugged Jemma and pecked Leo on his stubbled cheek.

"Enjoy Tigranakert," said Alana. "And give my regards to East Kilbride."

"Aye, right enough," said Leo. "Mind and find that passport, Noah. Travel well and stay whole, the both of you."

The doors slammed, the engine roared, and the Volvo drove away up the dusty road.

"So," said Noah as it dwindled to a speck and silence settled. "Now we walk to Karabakh."

319

30

Karabakh

There was a copse of bare birch and hawthorn, through which the Gargar flowed, splitting in two around a dart-shaped islet of pebbles and mud. On a mossy log on the bank sat Noah, looking up at the hills, which were turning gold in the early afternoon sun. A little way up the bank, Alana lay dozing under the trees, wrapped in a blanket, head pillowed on her rucksack.

Noah was lost in thought, his fingers working the beads of his *misbaha* – thirty-three ovals of red carnelian and pale onyx. There were no prayers on Noah's lips; he was scarcely religious at all, but the *misbaha* had belonged to his father, and before him his grandfather, and he found that working it aided contemplation.

To say it was strange being in Karabakh again would be an understatement. Noah's feelings went in every direction, like the meandering river. Elation, dread, longing; all those sensations were shot through with guilt that he had helped Alana come here. She had set out of her own volition, but he had brought her to Azerbaijan in circumstances that were bound to set her course toward Karabakh. Noah understood the draw of this place; it was his birthland too, and he yearned for it. But his memories were clear, and he had never forgotten the terror that was here. If he'd been more open with her, perhaps he could have persuaded her to turn back last night.

"You haven't slept …"

Noah turned. Alana was sitting up, blinking at him. Her eyes were pink with sleep and fatigue. "I had a little sleep," he said. This was a lie; he'd closed his eyes for a while, but no sleep had come.

"Aren't you frozen?" she said.

"I am used to it. Besides, this jacket is a good one, made for mountain climbing." He watched Alana roll up her blanket. "Emine will miss that," he said, and smiled.

"I know. Your community storage will miss this as well." She took out a bulky brown plastic sachet, which he recognized as one of the council's emergency ration packs. Alana shrugged guiltily. "I snuck in the storeroom yesterday and took a few. Don't worry – I'll replace them." She tore the top off the sachet. "I just hope I brought enough. I didn't know I'd have company." She peered at the label. "Let's see, we have mac and chili with sides of cheese crackers, baloney, cookies … and I'll be darned, there's even coffee and powdered creamer. And what's this?"

"It's the heating device," said Noah. "Give it to me, I'll set it up."

"No, I got it. You go get another one from my pack. You're hungry, right?"

While they waited for their meals to warm, they sat on the log and talked over Alana's plan. It was simple enough – to go to Khojali.

"You intend to just walk into the town?" said Noah.

Alana shook her head. "No, I need to go to the last place I remember. That's my grandfather's house in the hills."

"You know where it is?"

321

"Not exactly. But I researched it; I figure it's somewhere off the road near a place called Aggadik."

"That is correct."

"D'you think it's still there? Can we find it?"

"The first question, I do not know. The second: if it's there I believe I can remember how to find it."

Alana touched her ration pack. The chemical heater had done its job, and the bag was piping hot. She passed the second one to Noah. As she did, she noticed him peering intently at the trees on the opposite bank. "You keep looking like you're watching for something," she said, spooning mac and chili into her mouth.

"I'm uncomfortable. Something is not right. Don't you feel it?" Alana shook her head. "Last night," said Noah. "Those Armenian soldiers in the security belt. You don't think that was strange?"

"I … guess so." At the time Alana had been alternately too frightened and too relieved to think clearly about it.

"They *let* us pass."

"Yeah, that was pretty odd. What about it?"

"It's not just that they let us pass; they *vanished*." Noah struggled to articulate his feeling that it was as if the soldiers had been embarrassed and skulked away, as if they were not supposed to be there in the first place. "It's crazy, but I believe they let us pass because they had orders to do so. I believe they were not intended to be there at all."

"Noah, my brain's kind of fuzzy right now. I don't quite see what you're getting at."

"Remember what you said about what you saw from the archaeological site? What the professor said about the defenses?"

"Bobbie? She said they looked less active than usual. She thought maybe the Armenians were cutting back their defenses. That's what gave me the idea … Oh."

"Exactly! Alana, we know they have a spy; they knew you were coming. I believe the troops in the security belt had instructions to clear a path for you to pass through."

Alana stared at him. "That's ridiculous."

"Those soldiers should not have been there. They realized their error when I said you were American – and they vanished." Noah shrugged and gestured with his spoon. "You say it is ridiculous. But there it is. How else to explain it?"

In a quiet forest glade where the trees thinned out and the land gave way to a sheer-cut precipice, a small herd of fallow deer stood grazing the scrubby grass. A young buck's ears twitched at the touch of falling snow; he walked aside from the group and began scraping his short antlers on the bark of a silver birch, working down the side of his neck; he shivered, shaking his whole body, and stood absolutely still, listening, smelling the air.

The birdsong in the forest was muted, the air slow-moving and empty save for the falling flakes.

In an instant, the silence was cut by an unearthly loud squawking, high-pitched and harsh. The buck started back, and in the same moment there was an ear-splitting bang and something tiny slammed hard into the tree trunk where the buck's body had been a moment before, kicking off a chunk of bark.

Birds fluttered up from the branches. The buck bolted; the other deer scrambled to their feet and ran, vanishing through the trees like water through a drain. The high-pitched squawking went on.

Vahe Grigoryan lowered his rifle, cursing under his breath, and unhooked the sat phone from his belt. Nearly an hour he'd spent stalking deer and getting nowhere, and just when he'd had the perfect shot lined up …

"Yes?"

A familiar voice: "Go. Destination Khojali. Coordinates to follow." There was a click, and the line went dead.

Vahe slung his rifle and ran back through the forest. He'd strayed farther than he'd meant to, and it was over a quarter of a mile to the road. But he knew the place well, and ran direct, bursting from the trees at the exact point he'd left the pickup truck. His men – four of them – were dozing or smoking and looked up in surprise.

"Go!" he shouted. "Get in! We're going to Khojali!"

Vahe jumped into the front seat as his driver started the engine, the others grabbing their weapons and scrambling over the sides into the truck's bed. With a roar and churning of grit, the truck pulled away.

Ever since leaving the taxi, Alana and Noah had followed the river into the valley, keeping their distance from the road and the small settlements that clung to it. Although they had left the security belt, they were reluctant to come into contact with local people.

Less than a mile on from their rest stop, they approached a sizeable village. The land straddling the river was densely packed with little fields of olive trees and kiwi fruit vines. Deviating south, Alana and Noah trekked up the hillside to skirt around the village and its surrounding farms. Soon they had a panoramic view of the valley bottom, with its spread of houses and patchwork fields beside the winding, tree-lined ribbon of the river.

"This must be Asgaran," said Noah. "See there, the castle."

At the far end of the village, perched on a high mound above a bend in the river, dominating everything around it, stood the ruins of a stone fortress. Square and stolid, with a round tower at each corner, it looked exactly like a European medieval castle, with a fortified bailey stretching down from the mound to the river edge.

Togrul had told Alana about the fortress of Asgaran. It had been built by his ancestor, Panah Ali Khan, the founder and first ruler of the khanate of Karabakh. The khans had kept a strong garrison in the fortress, using it as their principal military base and main point of defense against invasion from the east. After the Russian empire took the overlordship and the threat declined, Togrul's grandfather – Alana's great-great grandfather – had focused his dwindling resources on maintaining his palace-fortress at Shusha, and Asgaran castle had fallen into decay. Alana shivered. She had never known what it was like to look on an ancient monument and know that she belonged to it, that its stones were part of her lineage and her very self.

"We should keep going," said Noah softly.

A slate-gray overcast had been rolling down from the north, and as Alana turned her back on Asgaran the first flakes of snow began to fall. A rough track led upwards, winding through the goat pastures, climbing ever more steeply until it mounted a long ridge, from which the whole vale of the Gargar could be seen. They had walked about half a mile when Alana realized that Noah was no longer beside her. She turned and found him standing looking southwest along the valley. Thin flecks of snow swirled around him on the wind. He beckoned to Alana and pointed.

Alana stood by him and looked out over the valley. "What is it?" she said.

"See, there. You don't see it? Those lines?"

It was hard to see through the haze of falling snow, but Alana could make out the meandering line of the river and the road running straight then forking about a half a mile away. Beyond was a blur in which she could make out the faint blobs of buildings.

"You don't know what that is?" Noah said.

Alana shook her head, although she felt a stir of dread in the pit of her stomach.

"That is Khojali," he said, and looked at her. "You have found what you sought."

Fine snow grains were beginning to touch the birches and the bare hawthorn branches, dry flakes like ash tumbling off and falling onto the chattering surface of the river. A broad-set figure in a black hiking jacket brushed aside the twigs and walked down to the strand of pebbles by the water's edge. He turned his large, square-set head this way and that, his small eyes scanning the ground, then knelt beside a moss-covered log. The moss had been flattened in places, as if a person had sat on it.

Salim Zardabi touched the green with his thick, blunt fingers. Something caught his eye, and he reached down between the pebbles beneath the log, drawing out a torn triangle of plastic wrapper. On it, printed in English, were the words *Beverage Base Powder, Orange, 34 gr—*

Searching farther up the bank, Salim found a faint impression in the rough grass where a person had lain. And in a patch of soft mud at the far end of the strand, he discovered two sets of footprints, one immediately following the other, heading southwest.

Salim grunted to himself in satisfaction. He was on the right track. She had come this way, and she was not alone.

He'd nearly caught her in the darkness last night on the road near Mammadbagirli. He'd picked up her trail and found the DMX Range Rover abandoned at the roadside, but just as he was setting out to pursue her on foot, another car had arrived. Acting on instinct, Salim had hidden and watched a man get out – a man who was visibly armed. Despite the darkness, Salim had recognized him as the young doctor friend of Karabakhsky's. Failing to notice Salim's car parked in the field entrance, the man had set off on foot.

326

Hanging back to watch what they did, Salim had tracked them both through the security belt, but lost them in Aghdam when they ran from the Armenian patrol. After that it had taken him hours to pick up their trail again and follow it to the riverbank below Asgaran.

Squatting, Salim examined the footprints. They were fresh; no more than an hour or so old, which meant he was gaining on her. If he couldn't catch up with her before the daylight failed, he wasn't the tracker his father had trained him to be.

Alana's thigh muscles were burning with fatigue, almost at the point where they would begin to turn numb and fail under her. She had dozed for maybe an hour during their halt by the river, and her head was starting to swim. But she kept going.

After that brief, heart-stopping glimpse of Khojali, the dirt road had turned sharply southeast, closing off the view of the valley. It followed the line of a deep vale through which a tributary of the Gargar flowed. The track rose and fell, winding left and right, following the contours of the hills, climbing constantly toward a forested mountain ridge in the distance. Light snow dusted the grass on either side. It was just as it had been twenty-five years ago, when her feet last trod the hills above Khojali.

The physical pain and weakness in her muscles scarcely impinged on Alana's consciousness; the exhilaration eclipsed everything, the hunger for what lay ahead. In her imagination it took the form of a glowing heavenly light shining down on her grandfather's house, illuminating the truth, the answer to her existence.

Breasting a last steep rise, they came to a place where the dirt road leveled off, turned a bend by a jagged outcrop of rock, and there it was. The old hunting lodge of the khans.

It wasn't like her imagination, or even her fragments of memory. A weed-grown, rutted track led off the road, crossing a slope of rank grass dotted with blackthorn bushes. On a broad flat area at the head of the slope, below the forest edge, stood a building. It was hardly a house. To Alana's eyes it looked more like a tumbledown barn of adobe, stone, and lumber. There was no divine light. But she knew it all the same.

"This is it," she said softly.

Noah stopped beside her. "Yes. It has changed, but yes, this is it." He glanced at her. "We are back." he said. "And on just such a day …"

Alana looked at him. His eyes were distant, remembering.

"It was you, wasn't it?" she said.

Somehow, on some unconscious level, she had always known it; now she saw it as clear as day. "The boy. I can't remember the name …"

"Neymar," he said. "I was called Neymar in those days."

"Neymar," she repeated. "Yes, that was it."

"My mother called me that, even though my given name was Noah."

Alana reached out to him. "You were there, you saved me and brought me here."

Noah took her hand. "It was the goatherd who saved us. He found us in the hills, freezing. I led you out of Khojali, but without him we both would have died."

Alana thought she was about to laugh for joy, but what came out was a choked sob. Her chest heaved, and she began to cry uncontrollably. She threw her arms around Noah, and he enfolded her, swaying her gently while she shuddered and sobbed.

It felt to Alana as if she would never stem the flood; years' worth of emotion, dammed up so firmly she'd had no idea it was even there, was bursting out of her. Eventually the torrent slowed and abated. Embarrassed, she pushed herself away from Noah, wiping her eyes.

"I'm sorry…"

"You should not be sorry. If I—"

Alana squeezed his hand. "Shall we go take a look?" She walked up the weed-grown track toward the house, and he followed.

It was very different from the hazy image in her memory. In its heyday, the Karabakhskys' lodge had been a fine, albeit modest building. A two-story central block in pale brick with a veranda was flanked on one side by a low stone wing containing the kitchen and dairy, and on the other by the old stables. Nobody lived there now. The veranda had lost its paint and the railings were falling apart; the discolored adobe of the stables was cracked and broken, and the kitchen wing was little more than a shell.

Alana looked in through the kitchen door. It had been burned out and was nothing but a mess of charred lumber and tiles overgrown with weeds.

"I remember eating here," said Noah, looking in beside her. "The cook – I have forgotten her name, but she came from Aggadik and had a pretty daughter – made the best *plovs* I ever tasted, only she used goat instead of chicken."

"It's stopped snowing," said Alana, glancing up at the sky. "Think we could spend the night here?"

"Possibly. The main part of the house might be habitable … What's the matter?"

Alana was gazing at him intently. "Noah, why didn't you tell me it was you, that you were Neymar?"

Noah shrugged. "Because then we – you and me – would have become all about the past. I want us to be all about the present." Her heart fizzed at his words, and the warmth in his eyes as he said them, but then he laughed. "So much for that hope. We have been living in the past since we first touched Azerbaijani soil."

Alana studied his face, his lips speaking, his beautiful green-blue eyes with their reassuring smile. He had been there through it all; he understood her better than any person living, knew the forces that had made her. He met her gaze. Everything else seemed still and silent, as if the world had been muted. Their faces drew towards each other, and their lips, as if drawn by magnets, came closer. Alana's eyes closed.

Noah drew back suddenly, as if he'd been stung, and turned away. "I remember sitting there," he said. Alana opened her eyes, startled, to find him pointing at the middle of the kitchen, where a jumble of charred lumber lay overgrown with weeds. He stepped across the room. Alana watched, bemused. Had she imagined the moment that had just come and passed? No; the buzz of it had been palpable, still tingling on her skin.

"At the table, eating," he said. "I saw out of that window – yes, that one – my father arriving! I ran – yes, I ran through that door! I went to find you! I see it all now ..."

Alana followed him through the broken doorway into the main part of the house. The fire must have been confined to the kitchen, because the larder and the hallway, although derelict and dank, were untouched by it. Noah turned left, as if following a sound or smell undetectable to her.

"It was in here ... your room was through this doorway."

Noah had to lift aside the door and frame, which had fallen away from the brickwork. Alana followed him into the room beyond.

And there it was: the little bedroom with its small stained-glass window – still miraculously intact though crusted with grime – and little hearth choked with rubble. The walls still retained most of their plaster, which was still a dirty white. She remembered it instantly. Above the space where her bed had been, a moldering horse cloth hung from a nail, its gold embroidered serpents and silver flowers still visible.

330

She spoke softly, almost in a whisper: "I remember …" She reached out and touched the cloth.

Noah watched her closely. Was she remembering it as he did? Could she see her grandfather, Neymar's father, Neymar himself, the way he could? Could she smell the beechwood smoke of the hearth, the aromas of hot meat and spices from the kitchen? To him it was as vivid as reality itself.

"Alana?" he said. No response. "Alana?"

Her eyes were distant, almost opaque, her mind no longer here, no longer now.

"*Ayna*?" he said.

31

"Ayna?" She looked up at the sound of her father's voice. "Don't go to sleep."

How silly, she thought – as if she could! The forked tree root dug into her back, but she was scarcely aware of it. Her senses were alert to the cold, to the muttering of frightened voices around her: a husband and wife talking urgently; an old man looking for his son; the low murmur of a mother trying to comfort her child …

These few dozen people – mostly families with children – had dropped aside from the exodus to get their bearings and ask after those who had got lost or been left behind. Ayna's mother was talking to a man called Abdullayev. His son was missing, and the man was in tears; Ayna's father tried to encourage him, while her mother went from group to group with the missing boy's mother, asking after him.

Ayna could feel her brother Hakan shivering beside her. He and Leyli had been in the house when the attack began, and there hadn't been time to dress them warmly; Hakan's shoes had been thrust on his bare feet and left untied.

"Here," she said, and took off her precious pink woolen scarf, offering it to him.

"No," said Hakan. He could hardly speak, his teeth chattered so much. "Leyli needs it more."

Leyli was beside their father, his arm around her; her lips were growing dark and bluish, her eyes glazing. Ayna twined the scarf around her sister's neck, tucking it under her chin, and kissed her cheek.

Their mother returned. Her face was taut. "Is there any word?" said Mr. Abdullayev eagerly, but Nurbanu shook her head. The distraught father squatted on the ground and clasped his head in his hands, rocking back and forth on his heels. Ayna watched, fascinated and terrified. She was dimly aware that this man was the father of the refugee boy, Neymar, who had admired her dog, Rolan.

The dog. Ayna's heart stopped. She hadn't seen Rolan since he'd yanked the leash from her hand. She jumped to her feet and snatched at her mother's sleeve. "Mom! Where's Rolan? Rolan isn't here! Have you seen him?"

"What? No, my cherub. Listen, are you ready to start walking again? I—"

Ayna didn't hear the rest; her mind was overwhelmed by a vision in which see saw her sweet dog lost, lonely, and frightened. Her grief for him was like a punch in the chest, all the worse for the piercing shame of not having thought of him until now. Before her mother could stop her, Ayna took off, running as fast as she could back the way they had come, back towards Khojali, stumbling on the beaten snow, calling out "Rolan! Rolan! I'm coming!" Her mother's cries didn't reach her. Her mind was full of the horrifying image of her beloved, lost and alone.

How long she ran she didn't know; it was only as the river water lapped over the tops of her rubber boots and trickled down to her feet that Ayna came back to her senses. For the first time she took in her surroundings and realized that she was utterly alone. She paused and looked back, confused. Where was she? How had this happened?

She heard a dog barking in the distance; it could be any dog, but somehow, she knew it was him. "Rolan!" she squealed, and ran on, scrambling up the bank, heart racing, oblivious to all danger, heading for the familiar streets of Khojali.

Tengiz had secured the scarf around Leyli's neck and checked her pulse and breathing, and was about to suggest that they all get moving again when Nurbanu began to scream: "Ayna! Stop! *Ayna*!"

Before Tengiz could react, Nurbanu took off after her daughter.

"Allah have mercy," he muttered desperately. Turning to Mrs. Abdullayev, he thrust Leyli into her arms. "Please, look after her. And my little boy there. I'll be back. If I am not …" He hesitated. "Just go on. Get these people moving. If they don't get to shelter soon, hypothermia will get them. I will find you. Now go!"

Tengiz ran after his wife. For a woman in her condition she had got surprisingly far. He found her among the trees near the river, leaning against a trunk, doubled over in agony.

"Nurbanu! What is it?"

She fended him off. "It's nothing, just a pain."

"What kind of pain? Nurbanu—"

"I can go on, Tengiz. I have to find Ayna."

"*Nurbanu—*"

"I have to!"

Gasping for breath, she set off again, plunging into the river, which came up to her knees. Tengiz waded in after her, guiding her to the shallow ford, where the water was only ankle deep. It was painfully cold. He could hear the sporadic chatter of gunfire, but it was far away now, echoing among the hills. They climbed the bank and found themselves on the road. An Armenian military vehicle stood at the street corner, so they cut across a construction site to the main Khojali road. They could only hope that Ayna was heading for home, and hadn't gotten lost, taking off in some entirely random direction.

It was a long and dreadful walk through the silent streets. Death was everywhere; corpses lay in the gutters and gardens, and the freezing, still air was tainted with the odor of their blood and the stench of gun smoke. Nurbanu felt like her abdomen was being squeezed by steel bands, but she ignored the pain and staggered on, holding on to Tengiz's hand. At every corner they halted, looking out for soldiers. Twice they had to hide while a patrol passed by.

They were in their own home street when suddenly Nurbanu gripped her husband's arm and hissed: "There she is!" The tiny shape of a child stood beneath an overhanging bush, silhouetted against a white wall behind. Nurbanu knew that shape instantly and hurried across the road. Ayna burst into tears the instant her mother's arms enfolded her, and the familiar, comforting voice murmured her name over and over.

"I couldn't find him," Ayna sobbed. "I heard him bark but I couldn't find him!"

"Hush, my darling, hush. Look, your feet are soaking wet!" Nurbanu looked at her husband. "Perhaps we can get home and find some dry clothes for her?"

Tengiz was looking anxiously up and down the street. "It's not safe. Come, we need to go." Ayna was lifted into her father's arms.

"But it's right here, we can—oh!" Nurbanu clutched at her belly. Leaning against the wall, she doubled over, her hand over her mouth to muffle a guttural scream.

Before Tengiz could act, there was a shout in Armenian, then a babble of voices. Ayna's head was obscuring his view, and she saw the soldiers before he did. She saw their guns raised, heard the shots.

Her father realized the threat too late to escape it; he instinctively twisted to put his body between the gunfire and his child. Ayna felt him stiffen convulsively, giving a strange hacking cough, and then they were falling.

The next thing Ayna knew, she was on the hard ground, her knees grazed, the weight of her father pinning her down so that she could scarcely breathe. She pushed at him with her free elbow, but he didn't move. Ayna couldn't understand it; she shoved and prodded, but her father lay still as stone.

"*Tengiz!*" Her mother flung herself down at her husband's side, shaking him and wailing his name, but he wouldn't move for her either. Two soldiers seized her by the arms and pulled her away, screaming and kicking her heels and crying curses on the soldiers. They slapped her, spitting abuse at her, and half-dragged, half-carried her along the street and through a gateway.

Ayna's little spirit was galvanized by the sight. With a rush of strength out of all proportion with her size, she wrenched herself from under her father's body. He still showed no sign of moving, and Ayna realized that he had become like the other people she'd seen lying in the street. She was too stunned to feel the full horror of it, and backing away, she turned and ran after the soldiers.

Reaching the gateway, even in her confused state she recognized the entrance to her own home – the back yard, the path to her father's medical office, and the steps up to the terrace and the house. The terrace doors were wide open, the living room curtains flapping out in the damp breeze. Ayna climbed the steps, lifted aside the billowing cloth and looked inside.

Through everything that followed, what she saw would never entirely leave her; it was etched in her brain as immovably as the elaborate engravings on the great silver samovar on the side dresser.

This magnificent vessel had belonged to her maternal grandmother, and her mother loved the ritual she enacted in the brewing and serving of tea for guests in the accompanying set of crystal *armudi* glasses.

The room was illuminated by a kaleidoscope of flashlights in the hands of soldiers whose numbers Ayna could not guess – it seemed as if the room was filled with them. Two held her struggling mother, pinned by the arms with her back against the samovar. The moving flashlights made it look like a grotesque, violent dance. Ayna stood on the threshold, unable to move, unable to speak.

Then the man came. The man whose face would be more deeply grooved into her unconscious memory than any other part of the nightmare. The soldiers' jeering and abuse stilled, and they stood back.

The man was dressed like the others in combat fatigues, and he had an ammunition belt slung over his shoulder. His face was lean, olive-skinned, and hawkish with a long nose and a black beard that gleamed as if oiled. His eyes were as dark and shining as the beard. They scanned the room like a predator, and fell on Ayna, standing in the doorway.

He gestured, and Ayna realized that he had a savage-looking knife in his hand. "Take that one," he said.

Every pair of eyes in the room turned to her. Her mother saw her and screamed in anguish. "Run, Ayna, run!" Ayna couldn't move. The man with the devil's face stepped toward her mother. "Run, baby, please," she begged. "*Please*, baby, run my sweet—" The man gripped her shoulder in one hand, and with the other drove the knife into her belly. Ayna could hear the strange grunting noise he made as he slit her mother from navel to breast.

As the nearest soldier reached out for her, Ayna found her legs and ran.

32

The white walls retreated from her until they became a distant blur. Alana's skin prickled and went numb; her joints and bones ached as if the toxins that had lain frozen in her brain for twenty-five years were melting into her bloodstream. Her head was dizzy, but she didn't feel she would faint because she hardly felt she was present at all. She swayed, and firm hands gripped her elbows, steadying her.

"Alana? Are you okay?" She mumbled something, but Noah couldn't make it out.

She had found what she had come looking for. Alana's instinct had been right: life and memory were intertwined with place. She had believed that if she came here, to where it had happened, the memory would be found. She had scraped away the lowest layer of dirt and uncovered a pit of vipers. Her mind recoiled from it.

"No," she muttered. "That can't be right."

"What can't be right?" said Noah. "Alana, what's the matter?"

She turned to him, grabbing his wrists. "It's false, a false memory, it can't be true. It *can't* be!"

Her eyes were wide, the lashes trembling, her breathing labored; she was on the verge of panic. Her fingers dug into Noah's forearm,

338

pressing on the bullet wound. He suppressed the pain and spoke calmly.

"Whatever it is, we will resolve it," he said. "Tell me."

"I can't." She felt that if she said it out loud, that would somehow make it true. "I can't."

Her nails squeezed harder, and Noah couldn't help wincing in pain. Alana's fingers jumped away. "Oh my god, Noah – your wound! I'm so sorry." She looked at him, and her eyes lost their glaze, as if his pain had jolted her out of her stupor. "Oh god, Noah, what have I done to you? Dragged you all this way ..."

"You didn't drag me; I came willingly."

"Everything I do causes misery and danger and death to the people around me. I should never have come here. If I'd had any idea what ... Oh god, what have I *done* ..."

Alana sank down on the floor, her head in her hands, and sobbed. Noah tried to comfort her, but she pulled away; she couldn't bear to be touched; it felt as if she would infect him with whatever wicked, baneful thing was in her.

Noah knelt on the floor near her, but not so near as to trigger this inexplicable reaction. Outwardly it looked like madness, but Noah realized that she had remembered something. He had feared this, guessing that anything her mind had taken such care to bury so thoroughly could not be disinterred without terrible pain. And he could imagine the kinds of images that were now flooding her brain. He saw them too. For most of his life they had haunted his nights, wrecking his sleep, unsettling his mind. From time to time they still came; he could sometimes sense when the demon would visit, and would stay awake through the night, obliterating the evil with work.

"It was me." Alana's voice was quiet, cracked. "It was me. It was all my fault."

"What was your fault?"

Haltingly, piece by piece, she told him the story of that night, of her parents, of how it was that he, Neymar, had found her alone in the street. Noah's flesh crawled as she spoke; not only at the nightmare memories it stirred in him, but at the deathly way she took the guilt on herself.

He took her hand, and this time she didn't recoil.

Vahe signaled his driver, and the pickup truck pulled off the road onto a sidetrack opposite the turn for Khojali. They followed the winding track, climbing steeply, for about half a mile. "Stop here," said Vahe. The truck drew to a halt under a stand of trees beside an isolated farmhouse. Vahe opened the door. "From here we go on foot."

Taking his AK-47 from the footwell, he climbed out and gave a nod to his men, who picked up their weapons and jumped down from the truck bed.

"The girl is two klicks in that direction," he said, pointing to a shallow ravine climbing up between two hills. "Our contact has eyes on her. She's with a companion, a young Azeri male. The man may be armed, so keep your heads on straight – but no shooting unless you have to. As for the girl, capture her but *do not kill her* under any circumstances. If she comes to harm, Vartan will have your families' skins for curtains."

"What about her companion?" said one of the men, checking his rifle's magazine.

Vahe shrugged. "Him you can carve into dog's meat, but the girl stays intact. Mark you – intact."

"No games?" said another man, a tall, lean individual with a jarhead haircut and a badly broken nose. The others laughed.

For answer, Vahe swung the butt of his rifle into the man's stomach, doubling him over, then gripped his throat and pulled him upright. "Alive and unharmed," he growled. "Now move out."

The men fanned out on either side of the track, weapons ready; at Vahe's nod, they began trekking up the ravine toward Aggadik.

When Alana came fully to her senses, her head was resting on Noah's shoulder, her face pressed comfortably against the rolled fabric of his coat and sweater in the crook of his neck. His arm was around her.

She felt safe in the compass of his strength and goodness. She had never felt anything like this with any man before. Noah was absolutely selfless, unfailingly courageous. Twice in her life he had saved her, and both times for the same reason: her own reckless, headlong searching for something that was beyond her.

"It wasn't your fault," he said. "How could it be?"

"If I hadn't gone crazy, if I hadn't gone back for my dog …"

"Alana, you were four years old and traumatized. I was there, remember. You were *four years old*. You are not to blame."

"Then who—?"

"The Armenian soldiers. The Soviet military who helped them. The people who began the war. *They* are responsible. Your family and mine were murdered by the men with the guns, not by you, not by me. I have had guilt all my life because I survived when other children did not, but we did not cause the killing."

She looked up at his face. "Noah, how did you get to be such a good guy?"

He laughed. "Oh, just lucky I guess."

"My needle's been in the red for so long now, I feel like I've got nothing left inside of me."

"You are hungry?"

"No, I mean … forget it. Now you mention it, I guess we ought to eat something."

Noah opened her backpack. There were four meal packs left, but her bottles were all empty. "We have no water," he said. "I believe there's a stream a little way down the hill. It should be good for drinking." Alana went to stand up. "No, you stay and rest. I'll go." He gathered up the empty bottles and went out.

There was a steep wooded slope behind the house, leading up to a rocky bluff. Noah guessed there would be water flowing from up there somewhere. He walked a little way along the lower tree-line until he came to a cleft in the hillside. Following it down the slope, he found a spot where the ground broke and a spring emerged. He knelt and scooped up water in his hand, sipping it. It was ice-cold and crystal clear.

He had filled two bottles and was unscrewing the cap on the third when he began to get a creeping feeling that he was not alone. It started as a vague sense of unease and grew to a kind of burning in his skin.

Without moving or turning, he slowly laid down the bottle on the grass, and reached under his coat for the pistol tucked in the waistband of his jeans.

A voice spoke behind him, as deep and harsh as a mountain gorge: "Touch that weapon and I'll go through you like a brick through a window."

Noah's hand froze a few inches from the pistol's grip.

"Put your hands behind your head and stand up … Now turn around."

Noah knew the voice instantly, even though he'd only heard it a handful of times and was prepared for the face. Togrul Karabakhsky had been right about the identity of the traitor. Salim Zardabi unarmed

342

was unsettling; on the other end of a handgun the cliff-like features and gimlet eyes were horrifying.

Salim snatched the pistol from Noah's waistband and stood back. "The *xanim*, where is she?" he demanded. "Is she alive?" Noah didn't know what to say – would it be safest to lie and tell Salim that Alana was dead and gone? Salim answered the question for him: "If she has come to harm, I'll kill you myself."

Noah swallowed the surge of horror at the mistake he had nearly made. "No, she is alive and well."

"Are you sure? She hasn't been taken yet? Then where is she?"

"What do you mean, *taken*?" The gun muzzle twitched impatiently. "No, she hasn't."

"So where is she? Why are you alone?"

Noah gestured at the spring. "I came to get water."

"And left her unguarded? Allah give me patience! You fool! If any harm befalls her, you will answer for it to Karabakhsky."

Noah's mind, racing, looking for a way to deflect Salim, tripped and fell headlong. "If … if … *what*?"

Salim's jutting brow rose a fraction, and there was a hint of irony in his eyes. "I know the khan suspects me. His doubts have been useful to me; I've kept my gaze sharp, and my own suspicions to myself. Last night in Baku I discovered the truth; I set out immediately, afraid I might already be too late. I picked up the *xanim*'s trail at Elamxanli and tracked you both to here."

"But if you didn't kill Rustam and Uzeyir – who did?"

"Who says they are both killed?"

Noah opened and closed his mouth, dumbfounded. It had been fixed in his mind that both the bodyguards were dead, and that he was the only protection Alana had left. But he'd only seen Rustam's body; that Uzeyir was dead too was his own assumption. An assumption based solely on the idea that Salim was the traitor. Like falling blocks, each realization slotted into the last: if Uzeyir was alive, he must have killed Rustam; and if that was so … he could be here.

After Noah had gone out, Alana sat for a while on the floor, hugging her knees and trying to calm her mind.

It was no use. She stood up and went through to the hallway. She wandered up the stairs, looking into abandoned bedrooms littered with the detritus of the lives that had been lived there – oddments of furniture, fragments of decoration clinging to the damp walls, pieces of broken crockery. It had been a fine house, and Alana couldn't understand why nobody from Aggadik had taken it over. She wasn't to know that while its lands had been appropriated, few locals had dared enter the house in the past quarter-century, believing it to be haunted by the ghost of the old khan, bent on taking vengeance for his slain family.

Other than that little bedroom on the ground floor, none of the rooms felt familiar to Alana. Her whole time here – weeks, months – had been spent it in the near-catatonic state her grandfather had described to her.

She went to the main door, which gaped open to the snowy weed patch that had once been the front garden and stable yard. There was a memory shard here, in which she ran through this doorway, chasing the heels of Neymar, filled with hope that some member of her family had been saved. Her brother? She couldn't recall. Alana clutched at the memory, but it ended in darkness, and she knew that this was where the utterly blank period began; her mind, in excruciating pain, had at that moment shut the door to memory, locked it, and buried the key. The key was now in her hands, but as in this house, the rooms it unlocked had decayed or been emptied, and in some cases burned out. From that moment to her earliest memories as Alana May Fulton, growing up in Malibu and Beverly Hills, was a gap that no amount of stimulation could fill.

It had stopped snowing, and the clouds were beginning to break up, revealing patches of a grayish-blue sky. It would start getting dark soon, and she and Noah would have to make a decision about sheltering here for the night. Alana walked out across the yard; it was strangely less cold in the fresh air than in the damp indoors. Where had Noah got to? A pang of anxiety touched Alana's heart. She'd lost track of how long he'd been gone. Surely he should be back with the water by now?

As if in answer, she heard a footstep from beyond the ruined kitchen wing, and turned expecting to see the familiar, reassuring face, and her heart warmed in anticipation. But nobody appeared. The sound halted the moment she turned. Had she imagined it? "Hello?" she called warily. "Noah, is that you?"

There was no response, no sound, but some instinct told her that whoever or whatever it had been was still there among the blackthorn bushes.

"Noah, if this is your idea of a joke, I'm not laughing."

A man emerged from behind the end of the kitchen wing, and she nearly jumped out of her skin. In place of Noah, it was the compact, dark-haired bodyguard. Alana's breath choked in her throat, and her initial terror turned into astonishment and then relief. "Uzeyir! Thank God! What in the world are you doing here?"

He smiled broadly. At this distance, Alana didn't notice the wariness in his eyes as he walked toward her, or how his face relaxed at her greeting. All she saw was the familiar slanted grin. "Is my mission to keep you safe," he said. "I am sorry deeply for losing you in Elamxanli. I got – what do you call it – distracted, like a decoy. When I learn what has happened, I come chasing. You are okay?"

"I'm okay, yes." She was embarrassed. "Listen, I'm sorry I lit out without saying anything."

"But all okay?"

"Yes, all okay."

He was silent a moment. "Is good."

Alana wasn't sure if this was a comment or a question; there was an odd tone to his voice that could imply either. His smile had that curious twist in it, and now the feeling that it conveyed some secret, sneering amusement was more unsettling than ever. She had a feeling that he was appraising her, weighing her up. She wished Noah would come back.

Uzeyir took a step forward. Instinctively Alana stepped back. "Do not be afraid," he said. "We are here to keep you safe. Is all that matters."

"We?"

He nodded toward something behind her. Alana caught a sudden odor of tobacco smoke; she turned to find a man standing there. He was middle height and thick-set, dressed like a hunter in combat fatigues, and armed with an assault rifle. A cigarette was cocked nonchalantly between his lips. That he had come so close without her noticing terrified her. The man smiled.

"That is Vahe," said Uzeyir. "He will help keep you safe."

Her unease about Uzeyir turned to certainty. Without a second's pause, she turned and ran.

Ignoring the instinct that wanted to make a run for the house – where she'd be trapped like a mouse in a bottle – Alana headed for the trees. The direction Noah had gone was barred by Uzeyir, so she veered left. From the corner of her eye she saw him reach for his thigh, where there was a holstered handgun. Expecting at any moment to hear a gunshot, she pressed on harder, running for her life.

The trees were less than twenty yards ahead … fifteen … ten … She sprinted past a blackthorn, and in that split second a shape loomed up to her right from behind the bush, a rifle swinging low; it contacted her knees with brutal force, and she fell headlong on the damp turf, rolling over and over. Before she'd even stopped tumbling, there were hands on her arms, biting into her like pincers.

"I've had doubts about Uzeyir Khalilzade for a while," said Salim. "Yesterday I heard from a contact in the Ministry of Internal Affairs who was looking into him for me. Uzeyir's story is that he and his parents were Azeri refugees from Khankendi who came to Baku in 1994. Well, my contact traced the records of the Khalilzade family in Khankendi back to the 1980s. They were recorded as being killed – husband and wife, along with all their children, three boys and a girl – when the city fell to Armenian forces in 1991."

"So how could they be refugees in 1994?" Noah asked.

"They couldn't. The parents of the man we know as Uzeyir used the dead family's identities when they crossed into Azerbaijan. The real Uzeyir Khalilzade was murdered in Khankendi when he was six years old. The state protection service agent calling himself by that name is not him."

"What does that mean?"

"Who can tell? If you want my opinion, it means Uzeyir's parents were Armenian sleepers, and their son was groomed to be a deep-cover agent." Salim was about to say more, but was interrupted by a sharp bang somewhere in the distance. It echoed back and forth among the rocky hilltops. "That was a gunshot. Where is she?"

Noah pointed. "Her grandfather's house, that way."

"Take me to her!"

Salim had holstered his weapon while he talked; now he drew it again. They sprinted through the trees and across the hillside. Noah's mind was filled with the face of the gunman from the country road in Switzerland; he imagined blood, Alana lying wounded or dead. He cursed himself for taking so long, and Salim for distracting him.

Noah had come farther down the mountain than he'd thought in his search for water, and it took several exhausting, anguish-filled minutes to run back up. As the house and its outbuildings came into view, they slowed and took cover.

"It might have been a hunter," Noah whispered. "Or a farmer shooting crows?"

"On a goat farm? That was a handgun, my friend." Salim grunted and drew out the pistol he'd taken off Noah, offering it back. "You know how to use this?"

Noah nodded and took it back. He checked the chamber, the bodyguard's narrow eyes watching him closely.

"Follow my lead," said Salim. Raising his weapon and keeping low, he emerged from cover.

From a distance the house looked empty and peaceful. There was no sign of life or movement. With Noah following, Salim approached the door of the ruined kitchen. There was nobody inside, and he moved on cautiously to the hallway. The little bedroom was clear, and to Noah's dismay, Alana's backpack was gone.

Sticking close to the wall, Salim crossed the hallway to the doors opposite; one was ajar, the other hanging on by a single rusted hinge. The detritus littering the threshold of the broken doorway was undisturbed, but there were distinct scuff-marks in the dust in front of the other, half-closed door. Silently Salim drew Noah's attention to it and crept slowly along the wall toward it. He was two short paces away when they both heard sounds of movement inside: a soft scrape and then a creak.

Adjusting his grip on his pistol, Salim took another step, and another, reaching for the doorknob with his left hand. Then, with a single, quick movement he thrust the door wide, simultaneously swinging his body into the opening and leveling his gun.

All Noah could see was Salim's back. He braced himself for gunfire, half-expecting to see Salim shot down at his feet. There was a pause, then Salim's shoulders sagged as he lowered his weapon. He turned away with a sigh. Peering past him into the room – which had been a study, with a once-ornate desk now rotting under piles of junk – he saw a goat munching at some vines that hung into the room through the broken window. It glanced briefly at the intruders, then went on eating.

Noah opened his mouth to speak, but Salim hushed him, indicating that there were still rooms unchecked.

None of them proved to contain Alana or any clue to explain her absence. Noah and Salim were crossing the hallway to the front door when Salim suddenly halted and bent down. He picked up a flattened cigarette butt, obviously freshly extinguished.

"The *xanim* does not smoke, no?"

Noah shook his head. He'd been clinging to the hope that Alana had merely gone for a walk – he knew all too well how impulsive she could be – and that despite what Salim said the gunshot had been some farmer potting at wildlife.

Outside, Salim searched the ground for further clues. "There was a struggle here," he said, pointing to the rank grass and dirt in front of the doorway. Even Noah could see that the grass had been damaged in a couple of places, and there were scrapes on the frozen dirt. The thin dusting of snow had been trampled by several pairs of feet.

Although the dusk was deepening rapidly, Salim picked out a clear trail leading down the slope toward the road. There the snow on the beaten surface showed the prints heading downhill, crossing other sets of tracks going uphill.

"Six, maybe seven, came up here and went back down," said Salim. He studied the confused prints but couldn't tell whether any might be Alana's.

Under the thick cloud, the feeble light was fading by the minute. There was scarcely enough to make out the point a hundred yards down the slope where the prints cut away from the road, leading toward the head of a ravine. Noah and Salim inched downward, following it. Near the drop, where a stream fed out of a culvert and flowed into the ravine, they found a body. Here was the explanation for the gunshot they had heard. Salim knelt beside the corpse and switched on a pocket flashlight: a young man in camouflage gear; he was lean, with an angular face and broken nose. The top half of his face had been blown away by the bullet that had ended his life.

"You think Alana could have done this?" said Noah.

Salim shook his head. "See there, the tracks go on. This was some dispute between them."

"About what?"

"Who can tell with such people?" Salim gazed down the ravine; it wound away, deepening, dotted here and there with trees and rocky outcrops. "There should be a road at the foot. They will have a vehicle." He shook his head and said with grim finality: "She is long gone." He switched off the flashlight.

Noah's heart sank. His fears for Alana and his own feelings of remorse and guilt were matched only by the question of how he could possibly bring this dreadful news to Togrul Karabakhsky. It would destroy him, heart and soul. His beloved grandchild was gone, and with her all his hopes for Karabakh.

33

Shusha

As the slope grew steeper, Hayk ran harder, powering along as if he were on springs, his breath clouding in the freezing dawn air. The route between the lower town and the high palace was usually his favorite part of the daily run; it was the closest sensation he had to a homecoming. The palace signified Vartan, and Vartan had always meant love and honor. But no more.

The asphalt road divided, giving way to an uneven cobblestone roadway inside the old town walls. Although long disused, Shusha's medieval defenses still stood to their full height on the north side, a massive rampart pierced with arrow-slits and round towers at intervals.

Normally Hayk would have been aware of every nuance of his surroundings: the walls, the trees, the ruins of the old town, the road beneath his feet, the very air; but today he scarcely noticed any of it. He had lived his life on the edges of his own self; from as early as he could remember, he had been trained not to reflect, not to look inward, but to keep his consciousness always on the surface, in his eyes and ears, at the tips of his fingers, alert to every scent, every vibration, every shift of the breeze. In a single moment, that had all changed. Ever since reporting his failure to Vartan, Hayk had been struggling not to collapse inwards, focused solely on his own wretchedness.

As he ran the last few yards, Hayk was passed by a pickup truck filled with men. The gates of the palace-fortress swung open, and it drove in. Hayk followed.

The vehicle swung to a halt in front of the main entrance. Vahe got out, and his men dismounted from the truck bed, hauling with them a slight figure dressed in jeans and hiking jacket. The figure was female, and although she was hooded, Hayk knew right away who she was. He knew every detail of her person and her history, and his loathing was so strong that he wouldn't pronounce her name even inside his own head; to him, she was just "the woman."

Hayk's skin prickled with cold, and nausea rose in his gorge. The process that had begun a week earlier – his mind retreating within itself, backing away from the enormity of his own failure – progressed still further. Hayk had never felt sorry for his own pain before; the self-pity eased his nausea, producing something almost like euphoria.

The woman was tied wrist and ankle, but she struggled like an eel, gagged screams coming from beneath the hood. Vahe's men carried her up the short flight of steps to the palace entrance. Hayk hesitated, then followed at a distance.

Archimandrite Gevorg Harutyunyan was in the palace's guest day-room, reading a theological life of Saint Mesrop, when he heard a commotion below the window. Putting an ivory place marker between the pages, he set down the book and, wheezing, lifted his bulk from the chair. By the time he reached the window, the noise had moved indoors.

He left the room. A gallery ran all around the upper story of the palace's inner courtyard. Harutyunyan was in time to see a group of

Vartan's thugs carrying a tied, struggling woman across the court, her screams echoing around the stone walls.

The priest was astonished. Vartan, it appeared, really had succeeded at last. That morning, Harutyunyan had been in Yerevan at a meeting of the conclave of the Holy Apostolic Crusade for Artsakh when he received Vartan's message inviting – no, *demanding* – his presence at Shusha, where he would witness the culmination of his plans. The girl was as good as secured, Vartan had claimed, and soon they would fully possess Shusha and its territories – a hinge screwed to the door that would open on a new era for the Republic of Artsakh. After centuries, Karabakh would be recognized legally as part of Armenia.

Harutyunyan had the gravest reservations about every aspect of Vartan's plan, founded on a distrust of the man himself, of his motives, and the plan's legal pretensions. Harutyunyan remained convinced that, if Armenia were to benefit, the woman must die.

As he watched the disorderly procession pass under the opposite arch into the central block of the palace, the priest noticed a man dressed in dark gray sweats following at a distance. He stopped before the arch, hesitating. Harutyunyan recognized him as Vartan's quiet young assassin, Hayk. Harutyunyan knew of the youth's failure to secure the woman in England and Switzerland, and could guess at the shame he must be feeling. Harutyunyan studied his face; even at this distance the boy was beautiful, the disfigurement of the jaw making him, in the priest's eyes, all the more desirable. Harutyunyan stroked his long beard, fingering the golden cross that hung there, fighting down his feelings.

The boy was visibly engaged in a similar struggle, his face working. Harutyunyan felt pity for him. His failure was hardly surprising – he was a killer, not a marshal or a jailer. A trained, honed, experienced killer. The priest's skin tingled. He knew what he had to do.

* * *

Noah hauled himself up the steep slope, gripping tussocks of grass. His fingers hurt, and he felt like he could collapse from fatigue. Ahead, Salim powered up the ravine like a robot, his strong limbs working tirelessly. Noah paused to give his burning muscles a moment to relax.

The night had felt like it would never end. After finding the corpse, Salim had continued following the trail. Traversing such a dangerous terrain in almost total darkness was slow, arduous going. Salim would only use his flashlight intermittently and briefly, to double-check that he was still on the trail; the risk of enemies seeing the light was too great to use it more. Hour after hour they picked their way downward, across the side of the mountain.

It was near dawn when they reached the dirt road. In the emerging light, Salim found the tracks of a vehicle in the mud. It had been parked for a while before turning around and heading away southwest, back the way it had come.

Salim and Noah followed its tracks until the dirt road joined the highway. There, to Noah's horror, Salim had flagged down the first vehicle to come along – an early morning delivery truck. At gunpoint, he forced the driver from his cab, and leaving him by the side of the road, the two Azeris drove off along the Khankendi highway.

The road passed by Khankendi itself, skirting the foot of the high plateau on which it stood, following the valley bottom and then winding up into the mountains again in a series of hairpin bends. Salim seemed to know exactly where he was going. Halfway up they reached a turn signposted ՇՈՒՇԻ. Noah knew just enough of the Armenian alphabet to recognize the name of Shusha. They took the turn, climbing ever higher into the green mountains.

Abandoning the truck in a side road near the outskirts of Shusha, they had struck out southeast across country. It was as arduous as

354

the night's trek; they had the benefit of daylight, but the drawback of extreme fatigue. Noah was nearly at the end of his strength. There was also the increased risk of being seen by the enemy.

Reaching a ledge near the lip of the second forest ravine they had crossed since leaving the road, Noah sank down to get his breath. Salim paused to wait for him. Noah could sense the bodyguard's impatience.

"What makes you think they brought her here?" said Noah.

Salim drummed his fingers on his thigh. "There are reasons. Got your breath back? Come, let's go."

"What reasons?"

"Look, HACA is a terrorist organization; they have links to the Armenian government, but no base in their regional capital. So she won't have been taken to Khankendi. But the local warlord, Vartan Sarkissian, is a HACA leader. His headquarters is in the old palace of Shusha."

"You mean Togrul Karabakhsky's palace?"

Salim nodded. "The same. Now come, we're nearly there. Just a little way now." He held out a hand.

Noah allowed himself to be hauled to his feet. The thought of Alana in the hands of people who had so casually put a bullet through the head of one of their own men – not to mention hunting him and Alana at Gstaad – filled him with dread and lent him new energy.

"Lead the way."

Alana worked to control her breath. The hood smelled foul, and the crude gag cut into her mouth, but she counted each breath in and out, slowing and steadying the rate, preventing herself hyperventilating, and above all trying not to cry. If she started crying, she knew it wouldn't stop. She would fall apart like a cracked pot.

She guessed she was in some kind of cell. It was cold, the floor was damp and hard under her backside, and the wall pressing into her back felt like bare brick. Leaning forward, she could raise her tied hands just enough to touch it.

The past several hours were a blur made up of one hideous image after another, all conjured up in her blinded state from the terrifying sounds around her. Her body hurt all over; her knees and shoulder ached from the first fall when she'd tried to run, and since then she'd been buffeted and bumped and shoved for miles. At one point – she wasn't sure how long after her capture – one of the men had tried to assault her. Her captors had stopped for some reason; all was quiet, and then this man's hands were on her, groping, his voice muttering hungrily. Suddenly a voice yelled furiously, and a gun went off, shatteringly close to Alana's head, making her skull ring and her ears whistle. Then she was lifted and carried again. Downhill, always downhill. The trek went on and on, until Alana believed her torment would never end. Then there was a truck and a jolting, painful journey by road. Meanwhile, the darkness beneath her hood had begun slowly to give way to the dim light of morning.

And now she was here, wherever this was. A big building of some kind, from the length of time it had taken them to carry her through it – up steps, around corners, down a staircase, and into this dank, freezing cold room. Nobody had spoken to her; this silent treatment, as if she were a parcel being delivered, terrified her more than anything so far.

Alana was exhausted, aching, but her body trembled with adrenaline. She had to clear her head, because if she let terror take charge, she would lose her mind. She tried to think of something good and comforting. Her thoughts went immediately to her father – not to the man who had given her life, but to John Fulton.

Alana heard his voice, a fragment of a conversation from years ago. She was twelve, and it was summer vacation; they were in a boat on

Lake Isabella, below his cabin in Sequoia, fishing. Alana remembered hooking something big, and the pull of it nearly yanking her out of the little boat. *Never panic*, her father told her afterward, *never despair. When you're in a bad situation, focus your mind on how to change it. Don't think about how to get out of it; that's too big, think about that and you'll panic. Just look for any little thing that will shift the balance.*

Her mind was still out on that lake, looking into her father's eyes squinting against the sunlight glittering off the water, when there was a rush of footsteps outside the door; she heard it squeal open. A male voice barked a command in Armenian, hands grabbed her and lifted her off the ground.

"Get your hands off me!" Alana yelled. "Let me go!" All that came through the gag was a wordless shriek of terrified rage. A man – huge, immensely strong, and stinking of sweat – swung her over his shoulder, knocking the breath out of her.

He walked faster than the men who had carried her before; he swung round a corner and went up a flight of stairs almost at a run. As far as Alana could tell, the route was different; she recalled an echoing space like a big hall, but now it was just corridor after narrow corridor. Then more stairs, twisting upward in a spiral, and at last she sensed open air blowing cold and fresh.

The man stopped; his powerful hands swung Alana down and planted her on her feet. The hood was whipped from her head, a flood of brilliant sunlight seared her eyes and sweet-smelling air rushed into her nostrils. In the midst of the glare was a blurred face, and a male voice said:

"Welcome."

"Stay low," said Salim quietly.

They had emerged from the trees lining the side of the last ravine. Before them was a steep slope falling away to their left; to the right

357

it rose up to an almost sheer rocky bluff, at the top of which stood a high wall of white stone topped by battlements and bracketed by stubby round towers.

The palace-fortress of the khans of Karabakh. The trees obscured most of it from view, but even from this glimpse it was a formidable place. Noah knew of the reputation it had acquired since the Armenian invasion. Part of it was used as a prison where inmates were kept in dreadful conditions; some were Azeris captured while trying to revisit their old homes in Karabakh.

Noah regarded it with dread. "If Alana is in there, how can we possibly get to her?"

Salim, studying the walls and the bluff through binoculars, grunted. "This is no good. We need to get closer and get a better view."

He started to move, but Noah gripped his arm. "We can't go out there in daylight! We'll be seen!"

"There's nobody on the walls, and only one security camera that I can see, and it's pointing along the wall, not outward. Come on."

Keeping low, they left the cover of the trees. Within a few yards they were at the foot of the bluff, which shielded them from sight of anyone on the walls above. Salim began to climb, with Noah following. The bluff was less precipitous than they had looked from below, and they had little trouble until the last stage, where the rock reared up in a sheer face. The two men skirted it, finding a way diagonally up the right-hand edge of the bluff.

They looked cautiously over the lip of the final ledge. In front of them, a steep grassy slope ran up to the foot of the walls, about a hundred feet away. The whole northern face of the fortress was now in view; on the right, the curtain wall they had seen from below abutted a massive hexagonal tower, four stories high from buttresses to battlements, jutting out to the edge of the ravine.

Salim took out his binoculars again. "That camera is dead," he muttered. "The cable is broken. They have no eyes outside the walls." He pointed toward the angle of the curtain wall and the great tower. "That's a blind spot, not overlooked by any point in the fortress. That's where we go in."

He climbed up over the ledge, and with Noah following began to traverse the slope. They hadn't gone more than four paces when a man stepped out from the trees to their right. "Halt."

Noah's heart stuttered and almost stopped. The man was dressed for mountain hiking and was armed with an assault rifle; to Salim it was instantly recognizable as an AK-47 variant used by the Armenian military, but to Noah it just looked like a fearsome weapon. At least two heartbeats thudded in Noah's chest before he recognized the man as Uzeyir.

"It's good to see you again, Salim," he said with his familiar twisted grin. "You've wandered far from home. Abandoned your post, have you?"

Salim's basilisk eyes glared at him, his heavy jaw set firm. "Traitor," he said.

"No, Salim, I am no traitor; I am utterly loyal to my motherland. Loyal to the death."

Quick as a snake, Salim went for the pistol at his belt, simultaneously lunging sideways. He wasn't fast enough; Uzeyir's rifle banged once; the bullet caught Salim full in the chest and he doubled over, dropping the pistol. Noah watched in paralyzed horror as Salim's body tumbled down the slope and fell over the edge of the sheer drop.

Anger seized Noah, and he moved toward Uzeyir, heedless of the rifle muzzle now aiming at him. Something slammed into his skull. The light flickered and went out. He had the sensation of falling, but never felt himself hit the ground.

* * *

Out of the dazzling blur, the voice spoke again: "Welcome to the home of your forefathers." The voice was male: smooth and deep and soft, and heavily accented. Alana's eyes struggled to adjust to the light, tearing up in the icy wind. The blur resolved, and she saw a man standing before her. He was only middling height, but held himself erect, proud and domineering in an immaculate slate-gray overcoat and red silk scarf. His hawk-nosed face was lined but handsome, framed by dark hair turning gray and a neatly trimmed beard.

"I know you," Alana whispered. "I …"

The hideous, horrific image remained clear in her mind, having been excavated from the deepest levels of her unconscious memory less than a day ago. She could see the silver samovar, her mother's blood, heard the screams and saw the face of the young soldier wielding the knife. That soldier had aged in a quarter-century, but had changed little. Alana stared at him in horror, her insides turning to ice.

He regarded her with fascination, like a connoisseur beholding a rare treasure – almost in ecstasy. He bowed.

Alana couldn't speak; she felt she'd be sick if she tried to utter a word.

"Come," said Vartan. "Look at the view."

He beckoned, and for the first time Alana took notice of her surroundings. They were standing in an open space atop a castle tower. It was a hexagon about fifty feet across, the walls topped with round-tipped Islamic-style crenellations. At two opposing corners were small square turrets.

Vartan gestured at Alana's ankles. "Let her be free to move." The giant guard who had carried her up produced a knife, stooped, and cut the zip-tie. The one securing her wrists behind her was left in place. She tried to take a step, but her legs were numb, and she stumbled. Vartan caught her by the arm and steadied her.

Alana recoiled from his touch. "You killed my mother," she said.

"I did?" He sounded mildly surprised, like a man being told he'd taken someone else's drink from the bar.

"You murdered her. She was pregnant and helpless and innocent, and you murdered her."

Vartan sighed. "Oh. I see. Well, that does sound like the kind of deed I might have done. When did this occur?"

"It was at Khojali."

"Ah. Khojali. Well, in that case it was strictly in the line of duty. I was a soldier then."

"I saw you. It was cold-blooded murder."

"Wait – was she the lady of the silver samovar?"

Alana's jaw worked up and down, and she clenched her fists; if she'd had them free, she would have launched herself at this lizard of a man. What was the universe doing to her? It was as if the life she had known – California, New York, England – had been a momentary dream, and she had been dumped back into her former existence, to find the same people still there: her grandfather, Noah, and now the murderer of her mother, a man she had thought of as a figment of her nightmares.

"Well," said Vartan. "That explains why the lady possessed such a fine vessel. It was Karabakhsky's! How fitting. I wish I had known. Would you like to see it?" Alana lunged at him but was instantly snatched back by the guard. "Perhaps later. For now, come and see the view."

The giant shoved Alana gently but firmly, and she moved reluctantly to the north battlement, where Vartan stood gazing out.

"Behold what might have been yours," he said.

Alana looked, and was awestruck. The weather had cleared, and the sun shone out of a wintry blue sky. Before and below her, the folded, rippling hills of Karabakh filled her sight, green and glorious, toothed with jagged rock, clothed in forest and field, rising in places to mountainous heights, dusted here and there with snow. Away to the east, the deep Hunot Gorge cut through the hills like a knife-stroke, sheer walls of rock through which ran the Gargar river on its winding way to Khojali, Asgaran, and Aghdam, a river steeped with history and blood. The south battlements overlooked the palace, with its round tower and the slender minaret of the old mosque. Beyond was the town of Shusha, spread across the surface of a sheer-sided plateau like a model on a table. The whole city was a fortress within a fortress; no wonder the khans had chosen it for their stronghold.

As she turned to the east, toward Baku, Alana remembered the afternoon, little more than a week ago, when she and Noah had stood on the summit of the Maiden Tower, looking this way. She had wondered then what lay beyond the horizon, and whether the answers to her questions could be found in Karabakh.

"It is magnificent, is it not?" said Vartan. "Almost all that you can see from here was once ruled by your ancestors. Until Armenia came to liberate it, Togrul Karabakhsky personally owned a great portion of these lands."

Alana found her voice. "Liberate it? You *stole* the land. Before you came, Armenians and Azeris lived together in peace in Karabakh. You came and destroyed all of that. A million Azeris were murdered or driven out. There's a word for what you people did here: genocide."

Vartan's genial countenance slipped. He looked at her with such hate, Alana thought for a moment he would kill her right there and then. With a visible effort, he regained control of himself. "Armenia owned these lands long before there was any such thing as Azerbaijan. They are Armenian by right of history."

362

"History? I know this region's history. I lived through the worst of it, thanks to you, you son of a bitch. I know the deep past well, and let me tell you, there is no national immemorial right to land in this part of the world. There's only the living bond of birth and life. *A million people.* It was genocide."

"Words," he said. "What are words? A web of traps and deceits. I care only for what *is*: the Armenian mission for Artsakh – and what shall come to pass: the successful conclusion of that quest."

As he spoke this last phrase Vartan looked at Alana in a way that told her that whatever that quest was, its conclusion somehow involved her.

"So, are you going to tell me why you've abducted me?"

Vartan smiled. "I will do more than that; I will show you."

34

The explanation had been prepared for her, like an exhibition.

Below the summit of the great tower was a library. It had long fallen out of use and was a picture of disorder and decay. Tinted light streamed in through two large stained-glass windows, illuminating walls lined with bookcases. With a jolt Alana recognized it as a near-duplicate of her grandfather's library in Baku, but on a much larger scale. There was even a slanted scribe's desk under the window and a great table piled with books and papers, disarrayed and thick with dust. Volumes had been dragged from bookcases and lay tumbled on the floor. Detritus and broken furniture littered the room.

A space on the table had been cleared and dusted, and on this three items had been neatly laid out: a map, an old parchment, and what appeared to be a shapeless lump of silvery metal.

"The key to Artsakh," said Vartan, "which you call Karabakh, lies here."

Alana was pushed toward the table. Her hands were still tied behind her, increasingly numb from the loss of circulation. She looked at the articles laid out. The map showed Karabakh, with parts of the mountainous territory between Shusha and Khojali shaded blue. The parchment looked to Alana like some kind of legal document; it was very old and bore a heavy wax seal below a series of illegible signatures. The text was written in Russian Cyrillic script.

"You know what this is?" Vartan asked, holding up the chunk of metal so that it gleamed in the light from the windows.

Alana shrugged. "Silver?"

"No," said Vartan. "But nearly as precious as silver and becoming ever more valuable. This is pure, refined cobalt." He turned the piece in his fingers, and reflections moved across his face. "Azerbaijan has its oil wealth. Karabakh too is rich in mineral deposits. Lately it has been discovered to be plentiful in cobalt." He nodded toward the map. "Very plentiful."

Alana gazed steadily at him. "So much for historic entitlement. This is all about money, isn't it?"

"Everything is ultimately all about money, Miss Karabakhsky." Vartan stroked the piece of cobalt. "You know what they use this for? There are many uses, but above all for lithium-ion batteries. Every cellphone, every laptop computer, every tablet, every electric car, every rechargeable device – all the things that are the life-blood of modern civilization – they all require cobalt, and the demand increases constantly. The lithium battery industry is worth over thirty billion dollars annually, rising exponentially every year."

Alana said nothing; instead she focused on keeping her face impassive, controlling her breathing. She knew all too well that this man was a sadist who relished inflicting hurt and sorrow. It was in the way he studied her face as he talked, looking for a reaction. Whatever he wanted from her, the more pain he could cause in extracting it, the more he would enjoy it. Alana was determined to deny him that pleasure.

"You see where this is leading, yes?" said Vartan. "Hundreds of millions of dollars in cobalt lies beneath Karabakh. *You*, Ayna Chichak Karabakhsky, can play a part in releasing this treasure from the earth."

Vartan set down the piece of cobalt and snapped his fingers. Seemingly out of nowhere, a servant appeared with a tray on which were two glasses and a tall crystal decanter sheathed in chased silver; Vartan poured a measure of amber fluid into each glass. "This is Ararat," he said. "Armenian brandy, thirty years old and quite superb." He held out a glass to Alana, oblivious to the fact that with her hands bound she couldn't take it even if she'd wanted to. The rich, blooming aroma of it touched her nostrils. "No? You are missing a treat. When Winston Churchill was served Ararat by Stalin, he liked it so well he ordered cases of it delivered to England."

Turning back to the table, Vartan ran his fingers across the map.

"Hundreds of millions in cobalt under these hills – this so-called Black Garden. But we have an insurmountable problem. Cobalt is costly to mine, and the Republic of Artsakh does not have the capital to begin. We have approached mining corporations in the United States and in Europe, but they – at least, the reputable ones who can be relied on not to rob us – will not invest here. They are afraid, because despite all our work, all the blood we have spilt, and the effort we have expended, Nagorno-Karabakh is still recognized internationally as belonging to Azerbaijan."

He drained his glass in one, and slammed it brim-down on the map, right over Shusha.

"*Twenty-five years!*" he yelled, making Alana flinch. "A quarter of a century of possession, and those foreigners dare to refuse us our rights!" He turned to face her, his features contorted by rage. Alana saw in her mind's eye the knife, her mother's blood, the face of the young soldier. She took a step back and collided with the huge guard. "You can help us," said Vartan, his voice suddenly soft, almost pleading. "Help us. Help me."

Disorientated and terrified, Alana heard herself say, "How?"

It was an expression of curiosity, not willingness, but Vartan's eyes lit up. He snatched the antique legal document from the table. "This is a deed of rights to Karabakh," he said. "An instrument of the Treaty of Gulistan, signed in October of 1813, which established Russian overlordship of the Caucasus. Under the treaty, various khanates were recognized, including this one. This deed grants the right of owner-ship and fief of Karabakh to Meghdigulu Khan Javanshir, who was at that time Prince of Karabakh."

Vartan regarded the document as if it were toxic. "It has never been revoked. It was endorsed by the Republic of Azerbaijan in 1919 and again in 1990. Foolishly, Togrul Karabakhsky neglected to take it with him when he fled from Shusha. Yet, so long as it remains in existence, no foreign company will invest in any conspicuous ventures here."

"Then why not just destroy it?" said Alana.

"You think I would not, if it would do any good? Your grandfather made a notarized copy many years ago, which has been laid before the International Court of Justice. He seeks United Nations recognition of his claims, and hopes it will provoke the UN into taking action against Armenia's possession of Nagorno-Karabakh." Vartan looked at Alana keenly. "You are Karabakhsky's heir, the final remnant of the khanate, the last princess of Karabakh."

"I'm no such thing. I'm Alana Fulton, I don't have any official legal connection to Togrul Karabakhsky."

"You are incorrect. When your grandfather sent you into hiding, your adoptive parents signed a paper confirming the arrangement. Karabakhsky kept it, and a week ago it too was laid before the court as part of his legal case. You are officially his granddaughter and heir."

Alana's mind reeled. Heir to these mountainous green hills, this palace, the castle of Asgaran, and above all to the heritage of the khanate! Even though it was only an heirship in principle, it was enough to make her giddy.

Vartan's eyes shone with excitement. "If you were to sign an affidavit abdicating all title to these lands, the Karabakhsky claim would be destroyed. You would be compensated, of course. I am sure I can persuade my friends to grant you ten percent of profits from any mineral extraction operations."

Alana stared at him, stunned. "Not a chance in hell."

"Do not say so right away; at least think about it."

"I will never help you to rob my family. You'd have to be insane to even think that!"

Vartan gazed at her regretfully. "Then have I brought you all this way for nothing? You have made me very sad." He came close and stroked her cheek. Her skin shrank at his touch, and she would have recoiled from him if the giant hadn't been gripping her by the shoulders. "Very sad indeed. Because if you will not help me willingly, you will unfortunately have to be forced."

"I don't care what you do to me, I'll never sign anything. What use would it be, anyway? The courts would never accept an affidavit signed under duress."

"They will accept an affidavit signed and notarized in proper form, before independent international witnesses. There will be no visible duress."

Alana stopped herself from saying *I don't understand*; she felt a creeping certainty that she didn't want to.

"Having delivered you to me, Uzeyir Khalilzade is at this moment traveling back through the security belt to Azerbaijan. By this evening he will be in Baku. There he will report to your grandfather that you are safe and recovering in the refugee settlement where you were staying until a few days ago. You were the target of an assassination attempt by the Iranian Azeri bodyguard Salim Zardabi. The third bodyguard was killed, and you were injured. You are not well enough to travel yet but will be soon. Your friend Noah Abdullayev will speak by telephone with your grandfather to confirm this story."

"*What?*"

"Abdullayev will be only too eager to comply, because he will know that if he does not succeed in convincing your grandfather, you will be killed." Vartan looked at his watch. "It is now one o'clock. The telephone call will occur this evening at seven, once I have received confirmation that Uzeyir has reported in Baku."

Alana felt sick at the knowledge that Noah had been captured and started shaking with horror. "I won't sign your document. I don't care what you do to me."

"To you? Who said I would do anything to you? You have twelve hours to agree to sign. If you do not agree, Noah Abdullayev will be killed. You will witness his death; it will not be quick. Then you will have a further twelve hours to reconsider. If you still do not agree to sign, Uzeyir will be instructed to terminate Togrul Karabakhsky. Only then, in the knowledge that you have ended the lives of two men dear to you, will you be put to death, and the Karabakhsky line will be extinct."

Moving with as much haste as his bulk and ecclesiastical dignity would allow, Archimandrite Harutyunyan strode through the palace's great hall, stopping here and there to peer in among the arches of the side galleries. He had searched half the palace without success. The door at the end of the hall opened onto a colonnaded cloister surrounding the fountain courtyard. There he found what he was looking for. Among the columns, seated in the shadows under a palm, was the young man with the deformed jaw: Vartan's assassin.

His back was turned, and Harutyunyan approached warily. "You needn't try sneaking, reverend father," Hayk said quietly. "I heard you coming from the other end of the hall."

The priest forced a laugh. "You know me by my tread? That's quite a trick." He took another step. "Hayk is your name, is it not?"

There was no answer. Hayk kept his back turned, gazing across the courtyard at the pattering fountain. Vartan had antifreeze added to the water so it could keep running throughout even the harshest winter; this was kept a secret, because it amused him that unsuspecting guests might be tempted to drink from it.

Harutyunyan edged closer, until he stood by the young man's shoulder. "I sense your pain," he said. "It is natural in God's eyes."

Slowly, like a snake uncoiling, Hayk rose from his seat, turning to look at the archimandrite, taking in the portly belly, the black cassock, the long graying beard with the ornate cross hanging within it, and finally the watery eyes draped with layers of bags. Harutyunyan quailed under the boy's aggressive gaze – his eyes were as hard and black as a serpent's.

"You sense nothing," said Hayk.

Harutyunyan's instinct for self-preservation warned him against pressing further, but he did so anyway. He had a purpose in mind of the greatest importance, worth risking his own life for. "I know you are hurt," he said. "When we serve to our utmost ability, yet fate robs us of our goal, it is bitterly hard. And in drinking the cup of disappointment, it is doubly bitter when there is betrayal mixed in the dregs."

The effect on Hayk was subtle but visible; the eyes remained hard as glass, but his lower lip wavered, and he shifted his weight forward. "What betrayal?"

Harutyunyan had prepared his next words carefully. "The betrayal of a son's love for his parent. You love Vartan, do you not, as a father? Your entire life has been dedicated to his service, yet now he makes you feel as if you have failed him, when it was not in the least your fault."

Hayk's eyes glittered; Harutyunyan knew he was a hair's breadth from provoking a violent reaction, but he pressed on, trusting his own intuition. All men, no matter how dangerous, were malleable; it was a matter of finding the soft places. "Had it been up to me," the priest went on, "I would have had you kill her in England."

Hayk nodded. "You tried to kill her. My father was angry. It nearly ruined everything."

"On the contrary, I nearly *saved* everything. I would have had you kill her because to stalk and kill is your talent, your calling. You are no kidnapper of girls. Alive, Ayna Karabakhsky is a danger to us all." Harutyunyan paused. "Especially to you."

"How to me?"

"Vartan believes that he can force her to sign away her inheritance. He believes that this will make the world accept Armenian sovereignty in Karabakh and recognize our republic. Alas, it will do nothing of the sort. It will merely draw the world's attention all the more closely to the fact that the Karabakhskys still have legal title here. They are not fools; they will suspect that the girl has signed under duress. They will call her to testify in person."

"And then what?" said Hayk.

"And then we will be undone. At best, international recognition of our possession will be still farther away; at worst, it will be beyond our reach forever."

"But the woman's family won't own the land anymore. And she won't be able to testify in person."

Harutyunyan peered thoughtfully at the young man. "I see. She will be put to death?"

"Yes."

"And you will be the one to do it, no doubt?"

Hayk's reptilian eyes gleamed. He nodded.

Harutyunyan sighed. "It is, as I thought, a betrayal. My son, you are being deceived. Have you never heard the fable of the Wedding Band and the Knife? Truly? I thought all Armenian children heard it in their cradles. Come, sit beside me and I will tell it to you."

The archimandrite sat on the stone bench. "You will not sit? Well, you are younger, fitter, and considerably lighter on your feet than I. So … it seems that in a distant province of Armenia long ago there was a merchant who accumulated a great deal of wealth and built up a large and grand family. He acquired a fleet of ships and a good deal of land.

"There lived at the same time in the same province a lord – a fine warrior nobleman who had great success in battle and had retired to his estate. Now, it happened that through a long and complicated series of misunderstandings and happenstance, which would serve to fill a dull winter evening by the fire but with which I will not try your patience, the merchant and the warlord came to dispute the ownership of a large tract of valuable land. Each believed he held title to it.

"The merchant and the warlord battled for the land. The warlord sent his men to terrorize the merchant's tenants and burn their barns, and the merchant raised the prices of the goods he sold to the warlord to a degree that threatened the warlord with bankruptcy.

"So at last the dispute was brought before the king, who was renowned for his wisdom in judgment. He summoned the warlord

372

and the merchant to his hall. He heard their arguments and looked at their scrolls, and could see nothing to tip the balance. So he set before them two salvers, on each of which was laid out a knife and a golden wedding ring. 'You will now choose between blade or band,' said the king. 'Make your choice according to how you would see this dispute settled, and I shall decree who has the better claim.'

"Each man was offered a salver, and each made his choice. The warlord chose the knife. 'How will this settle your claim?' the king asked.

"I will kill my enemy," the warlord replied.

"Why, then his son will inherit his claim," the king said.

"Then I will kill his son, and his son's wife, and his brothers and daughters. I will slay his whole family, and the land shall be mine."

The king shook his head. "It shall not, for under the law the claim will escheat to the king. Would you kill the king, then?" Of course, the warlord would not. So the king turned to the merchant, who had chosen the wedding ring. 'Explain your choice,' he commanded.

So the merchant bowed and said, "I would resolve this dispute by marrying my son to my enemy's daughter. I know he has one unwed." The warlord laughed at the idea that he would let his precious daughter marry the merchant's pampered son. But the merchant insisted that he should; for in the fulness of time, the wedded couple would have a son: "And that son would be both my heir and yours; he would inherit all our lands and wealth. Thus are great dynasties built."

The king heard this and said, "You have chosen well. Therefore I decree that the disputed land belongs to the merchant, and the warlord's claim is void."

Harutyunyan looked up at Hayk. The young man was gazing across the courtyard at the fountain. The wintry sun had risen above the palace roof and was glittering on the dancing water. "And what of it?" Hayk said.

"Vartan has the heart of a warlord," said Harutyunyan. "You may think it likely that he will let you kill his enemy's family once he has his signature, and so press his claim. Yet he has the mind of a merchant, and that will determine his course."

Hayk looked down at the priest, his eyes blazing. Harutyunyan knew he was almost there. Just one more push. "You think he would marry his son to her?" said Hayk incredulously. "He has none, save me."

"Not his son," said Harutyunyan. "He will force her into marriage to himself. The child of Vartan Sarkissian and Ayna Karabakhsky will inherit this land for Armenia."

"He wouldn't do that," said Hayk.

"He would. Search your heart; you know this is true." Harutyunyan watched the emotions ripple across the young man's face and calculated his next words with finesse. "The woman you hate most in all the world will supplant you." He lowered his voice to a hoarse murmur: "I know your story. I know your heart. Only you can stop this."

In the angle between the great round tower and the main palace wing was a suite of two small rooms. Here Hayk had lived for almost as long as he could remember, during the periods when he wasn't away training or on missions. A living room and a tiny bedroom, both spartanly furnished. There were no personal traces in either: no pictures, no mementos – no books except for training and weapons manuals, an atlas, and a Bible, and no ornamentation but an ivory crucifix, before which he prayed morning and night.

Hayk stood at the narrow window looking across at the former family wing, which now housed the district offices, stores, and the administration section of the prison. In its cellars, where few people ever ventured, were the secret holding cells, reserved for prisoners who did not officially exist. Hayk had learned from Vartan's secretary that the woman was being held there.

She will supplant you. The archimandrite's words had gotten into Hayk's bloodstream like an intoxicant. And they were true, he could feel it. *Only you can stop this.*

Abruptly, Hayk left the window and opened a drawer. From the selection laid out inside he chose his favorite combat knife: a neat, double-edged blade with a black rubberized grip. It was time to bring all this to an end. Sheathing the knife, he tucked it into his waistband and left the room.

35

The waters of Lake Isabella were deepest blue, a thick inkiness almost as dark as indigo. Above rose the crinkled green peaks of the Alta Sierra. The two fishing lines were limp on the water, the floats rising and falling with the water lapping against the boat's hull. Reflected Californian sunlight rippled on Alana's face beneath the brim of her beige Loro Piana fedora.

John Fulton watched his daughter's face; her earnest concentration was something to see in a kid her age. Being here with her was a dream he'd once thought could never come true. In his imagination it had always been a son, but the reality of Alana was better than any dream. Seven years had passed since she'd come into their lives. He wondered if she ever thought of her past, but then pushed the question away, as he always did.

All Alana's thoughts were bent on her fishing line, and the length of it hanging invisible below the surface, in another world. She was fascinated by all things buried or submerged. Her float bobbed suddenly, then vanished. The pull was so strong it almost yanked the rod from her hands; with a shriek of panic she jumped to her feet and would have fallen over the side if her father hadn't grabbed her and pulled her back. Taking the strain on the rod, John helped her reel in a fourteen-pound brown trout.

"You should never panic," he said as he disgorged the hook, and they watched the wriggling fish swim away. Alana always insisted on letting them go. "When you're in a bad situation, don't think about how to get out of it. That's too big – it'll swamp you like a wave, and you'll panic. Like just now. Instead, focus on how to *change* it. Look for any little thing that will shift the balance."

"I didn't have time to think."

"There's always time. The human brain works fast. Doesn't matter if it's a business deal going bad or a big trout; look for the loophole in the contract, get your foot against the gunwale, just do something that changes a desperate situation in your favor."

When Alana closed her eyes, she could remember that wonderful day on the lake as if it were yesterday, hear her father's voice, see his gentle eyes glittering. Even here, in this dungeon beneath a fortress in a dangerous land that was worlds away from Lake Isabella, she could feel the warmth of the California sun.

Reluctantly opening her eyes, she looked around the room. The walls were of brick and stone, with remnants of damp plaster. There was a small window near the ceiling. Her ankles had been tied again, but at least she no longer had the hood.

Vartan's words kept going round and round in Alana's head, like the refrain of some hateful song. Was the remote possibility of her family regaining Karabakh worth dying for? But would signing Vartan's affidavit really save her grandfather's life? What was to stop HACA killing him anyway? Or her, for that matter. As long as she was alive, she would be able to rescind her signature.

The realization hit her so forcibly, she gasped aloud. Of course Vartan would have her and her grandfather killed, no matter what;

surely it was the only way to ensure his hold on Karabakh? But if she didn't comply, Togrul Karabakhsky would definitely be killed.

Alana's mind was so preoccupied she was barely conscious of the pain in her shoulders, burning with the strain of being twisted, or the zip-tie biting into her wrists. How could she get out of this? Struggling to her feet, she could just make out that the window was at ground level, but it was too dirty to see anything more. It was barred, but the metal was badly rusted, and the window might be big enough to climb through if she could get it open. With her hands and feet tied? The impossibility of the idea wrung her heart, and she began to despair.

Her father's voice murmured in her memory. *Don't think about how to get out of it. Focus on how you can change it. Shift the balance.*

In what little way could she change the situation? Think small. Alana scanned the room, noticing for the first time that there were chains set into the wall right above where she had been sitting. They had manacles attached, like relics of the Inquisition. She almost retched at the sight of them, imagining herself clamped and rotting in this dungeon forever. Dying here. Being zip-tied was awful enough, but that …

A door opened in Alana's mind, admitting a chink of light into the darkness.

Sitting down again, she doubled over, wedging her tied wrists under her butt, wriggling her body backward into the loop made by her arms. Her arms were long and her body lithe, and with an effort that tore at her shoulder joints, she managed to squeeze through.

Her hands were now in front of her. That was one little change for the better. Now for the next. With more contortions, Alana delved into the tiny coin pocket in her jeans. "Please god let it be still there," she whispered. "Please, please … ah!" A sharp stab in her fingertip told her she'd found what she was hoping for: the scalpel blade she'd borrowed at the dig site two days earlier.

It only took a few seconds to slice through the plastic strip around her ankles. But no matter how she twisted her hands, she couldn't bring the blade into contact with the zip-tie around her wrists.

Wedging her back against the wall, she placed her feet together, pigeon-toed, and carefully inserted the blunt end of the blade between the edges of her boot soles, so that a half-inch of razor-sharp steel protruded. She'd just got it poised when there was a sound of heavy footsteps in the corridor, coming closer. Alana froze, holding her breath. The footsteps passed by and receded. Pausing to steady herself, she brought the zip-tie slowly, carefully down on the blade. The moment they touched, the blade dislodged and fell on the floor.

She swore, fumbling around on the wet, gritty stones.

Just as her fingers touched the blade, she heard sounds again outside her cell. Voices. Two men. One sounded like he was challenging the other. Trembling, Alana reset the blade between her soles, gripping it more tightly this time. It wobbled and nearly fell. The voices stopped, then came the jangle of keys.

They were coming for her.

Alana lowered the zip-tie onto the blade again. They touched, and the blade held firm. She applied pressure and the steel began to bite into the plastic. A key rasped in the lock and the door swung inwards with a groan. Alana flinched, and the scalpel fell to the floor. She quickly moved her feet to hide it, and rested her arms, still bound, on her knees. Keeping her feet together, she hoped it wouldn't be noticed that her ankle tie had been cut.

To her surprise, the man who entered was neither Vartan nor the huge jailer. He was medium height, and slim, dressed in dark gray sweats and a tight black blouson. His head was lowered, as if he were catching his breath or fighting some inner pain, his face indistinct in the dim light. He closed the door and took a step toward her. His face came into the light. Instantly Alana recognized the gunman who had hounded her from Cambridge to Gstaad. The same chillingly beautiful eyes and the sculpted face marred by the deformed jaw.

He stood, staring intently, studying her, searching her face. He seemed wary of her – afraid even. He squatted down and studied her even more closely. Alana shrank back against the wall in horror. His eyes flicked back and forth across her features, as if he were reading his fortune there.

"Who are you?" she said. He didn't seem to hear her; his gaze continued wandering across her face; then, as if by chance, his eyes met hers, and on an impulse, she asked: "What's your name?"

There was no glimmer of a response. She guessed he didn't understand English. He held her gaze. Alana had to struggle not to look away. Despite her terror, something in her refused to be cowed. He reached behind him, and his hand came back bearing a knife. Its blade was double-edged, about five inches long, and extremely sharp; he touched his thumb on the edge, and even this light pressure drew a thread of blood.

Alana suppressed her mounting panic. Was this part of Vartan's plan to terrorize her into complying? "I could reward you," she said. "Help me get out of here." She studied his face, trying to discern any reaction. "My family is rich. Very rich. Do you understand? Do you—"

"I understand English very good." For the first time there was a flicker of life in his eyes.

"My family will reward you if you help me."

"Your family?"

"Yes, my family. They're very, very rich."

"*Your* family?" His gaze hardened into a stare filled with outright hostility. The point of the knife turned toward her. "*Your* family?"

380

"Yes …"

"I had family once." His voice was quiet but crackled with emotion. "Good family."

There was a silence, and Alana felt compelled to ask, "What happened to them?"

"We lived in a village. We are happy there, mother, father, sisters, and me. Little boy. Then men came, killing everyone. I was afraid, my mother was afraid, all of us. So we run away. Us, other families, all run away to the hills. Although I am afraid, I have my family, I know I am safe with them. Father protects me, mother protects me, nothing bad happens because of *family*.

"So we walk at night through hills, always afraid bad men will find us and kill us." He paused and touched his chest. "But I know I am safe, because my family love me, they protect me and my sisters from all dangers. I love them, I trust them.

"We stop to rest. Other families also are there. Then something happens. I do not know what it is or why it is, but my sister is gone. And then my mother leaves me, and then my father leaves me, and it is just me and my other sister, all alone with strangers. I cry out for my mother and father, but they are gone. And then the bad men found us."

Alana's flesh was crawling, nausea rising in her gullet. This couldn't be real; what he was saying was just stark, staring impossible.

"A lady tried to save my sister, but the bad men shoot them both. I saw it. All the people around me are screaming, running, dying, blood on the snow … A man picks me off the ground and runs, but a bullet hits me here …" He touched his misshapen jaw. "My face is all blood, and I am unconscious, so the man thinks I am dead. He puts me on the ground and runs away. Now everyone has left me. All family gone, all friends gone. Abandoned."

Tears were streaming down his face, and he dashed them away angrily. Alana stared at him in horror and disbelief. From her buried, long-ago memories a name surfaced.

"Hakan?"

"Some bad men found me. They take me to their commander, captain named Vartan Sarkissian. This bad man, he take care of my wound, gives me food, and he is my friend."

Alana's mind whirled, a vortex of confusion. The killer who had dogged her, murdered people to get to her, was her *own brother*? "I don't believe you. It's impossible."

"My family abandoned me, left me to die. Because of *you*. They loved you, not me. Vartan saved me, protected me, became my true father."

"He murdered our mother!"

Instantly the knife blade was against Alana's throat. Hayk's eyes blazed. "The woman who left me? That mother?"

Tears bloomed in Alana's eyes. "You can't be Hakan. It's not possible; Hakan died; Hakan would never side with the man who butchered our mother; Hakan loved m—"

The knife pressed, scoring her skin. "Say that name again and it is the last thing you ever say." His free hand clenched and unclenched slowly. "I am not that name. It is dead. My family abandoned me. You abandoned me. Vartan is real family to me. He protected me, loved me, taught me to fight."

Alana tried desperately not to move; the slightest pressure against the knife would cut open her throat. The fire in Hayk's eyes subsided. "And he taught me my great purpose. I will destroy the family who betrayed me." Hayk lifted the blade and pointed it at Alana. "You first."

He let those words sink in.

Alana made one last effort. "You don't have to do it. I remember you, this isn't you. None of us meant to leave you. It was my fault, not our parents'. I was just a little girl, I panicked, I didn't know what I was doing. I would never have left you. *I loved you.*"

Hayk's eyes welled up. His mouth worked, struggling to form words. Alana felt him weakening, changing his mind; her memory of her brother, the love they had shared as children, convinced her that he wouldn't hurt her.

He shook his head and thumped his temple with his fist. "Is too late," he said, and jabbed the knife toward her face. "Too late for you, for me." He raged and sobbed: "All family betray me, even Vartan. He will not let me complete my destiny, I feel it."

"What do you mean, your destiny?"

"I will not be let to kill you. Harutyunyan says he will make you marry him."

"*What?*"

"Now I see you, I believe it is true. I am betrayed again!" Hayk yelled, flecking her face with spittle. "I will be abandoned again! Lost again!"

"No! I won't abandon you. Not again. Come with me, leave Vartan. We'll be together again, brother and sister."

Hayk was too wrapped up in himself to hear her – except for the last three words. "I have no sister!"

In a blaze of fury he lashed out with the knife.

If he hadn't been so shaken by emotion, Alana would have died in that instant. The crosswise slash, designed to lay open her left carotid artery – a stroke that Hayk had delivered many times – went wide. Alana recoiled, and the edge brushed the side of her face, a gentle stroke leaving a searing pain in its wake.

Hayk, squatting on the balls of his feet, lost his balance. Before he could recover, Alana lunged, her wrists still bound, snatching blindly, and found herself gripping the wrist of his weapon hand. Screaming in terrified rage, she held on determinedly as he tried to shake her free. With all her strength, Alana launched herself upwards; her weight bore him over, and they went crashing to the floor in a struggling heap, his wrist still clamped in her grip.

Hayk was a veteran of close combat; she'd caught him off balance once, but it wouldn't happen again. His free hand snaked up her body and found her throat; the fingers and thumb closed in on her windpipe and squeezed.

Alana tried to pull her head up, but his hold was too strong. Her lungs labored, but no breath came; her vision began to blur and dim, and her grip on his wrist started to fail. Consciousness began to slip away, and her fighting spirit subsided into resignation. *So this is it*, she thought. *This is how I die ...*

As her vision went black, she heard muffled sounds, as if from underwater – a door opening and a shout. The grip on her throat suddenly slackened and she was lifted in the air – an almost pleasant floating sensation that lasted for less than a second before she fell violently to the floor. She rolled over, coughing, gasping for breath. Voices were yelling. Her sight cleared to reveal Hayk locked in a furious struggle with the huge jailer.

They were right above her. The guard had Hayk in a choke-hold and seemed to be trying to reason with him – all Alana could make out in the guttural stream of Armenian was the name "Vartan" – but the young man was oblivious. Nobody would give anything for Hayk's chances, clamped by the neck in the giant's huge arms. But Hayk moved like a snake; with one hand he snatched at the guard's groin, twisting, and with the other he jabbed backwards, catching him full in the eyes.

The guard screamed and released his hold, pawing at his eyes. As he staggered blindly and Alana watched in horror, Hayk went at him like a mechanical demon, punching and kicking him in the face, the body, the limbs, moving faster than Alana could follow. The half-blinded giant staggered, trying to hit back, but he was too slow. All he could do was lumber, blocking as many blows as he could, and lunge futilely as Hayk drove him into the corner. The knife had fallen to the floor in the first clash – now Hayk scooped it up by the point, spun it in his fingers, and drove it toward the guard's chest.

The giant was just quick enough – he seized Hayk's wrist and twisted. Hayk gasped in pain and the knife flew across the cell, clattering to the floor. The giant lifted him bodily and hurled him against the far wall. Hayk tumbled to the ground and lay motionless. The giant, his face a bloody mask, stared down warily at him, suspicious that this might be some trick.

Alana saw her chance. The door was wide open, the guard distracted, and the knife lay just a couple of feet from her; if she grabbed it, she could finish cutting the tie on her wrists and make a run for it before he noticed she was gone.

Surreptitiously she crawled to the knife. Her hands closed on the grip, but in turning it awkwardly in her bound hands the blade scraped audibly on the stone floor. The guard turned and saw what she was doing.

"*Hey! Mi dipch'ek' danaky!*"*

He strode toward her. In panic, Alana lurched to her feet, trying to balance. The giant's massive hands seized her: one by the arm, the other by the neck. Struggling with all her might, she fell back against the wall, and the tie she'd half-cut with the scalpel came apart. The knife was still in her hand, and as the giant closed on her, bearing down, she felt a sharp pressure in her chest and heard the slick, rasping sound of the blade driving to the hilt into flesh and bone.

And then she knew truly what it was to die.

*   Hey! Don't touch that knife!

The giant's hideous, battered face was inches from hers, looming over her, eyes bulging from their sockets. His weight bore down on her, and she buckled under it, sliding down the wall. As she reached the ground, the giant fell away from her, landing across her legs with a crash like a sack of cement, bloody saliva oozing from his lips, the knife handle protruding from his midriff. The wet warmth on Alana's right hand, which she had taken for her own blood, was his. The pain in her chest that she had thought was the knife blade had been its steel pommel.

Gibbering in horror, Alana fought to free her legs from beneath the dead giant's weight and scrambled to her feet.

Before she could even think what to do now, the giant gave an unearthly groan and levered himself upright. Dribbling blood, he looked down at the knife in bewilderment, then at Alana. Disbelief turned to rage, and with the hilt still sticking out of his body he rose agonizingly to his feet and staggered toward her.

Alana backed up against the wall. The giant's colossal hand took her by the throat and lifted her off the ground, swinging her like a doll, preparing to hurl her against the stones as he had done to Hayk. In desperation, she snatched at the knife handle and wrenched it with all her strength.

The giant bellowed and released his grip. Alana fell to the floor, and before she could struggle to her feet he was on her again, grabbing at her hair and her arms. Something brushed against her face, and she realized it was the manacle chains that had so disturbed her earlier. Without thinking, she snatched up one of the manacles and, squirming in the giant's grip, whipped the chain over his head. With a strength and agility she never would have guessed she had, she clawed her way onto his back, drawing the chain around his neck, and hauled on it, leaning back with clenched teeth.

He bucked under her like a bull, roaring, writhing with such strength that the iron eye anchoring the chain to the wall began to move, but he couldn't rise to his feet to exert his full might. Alana held on, straining, and slowly the giant's resistance weakened. He subsided and collapsed, Alana holding on until every last trace of movement had dissipated.

Her breathing was labored, and her hands were shaking violently. With an effort she uncoiled her fingers from around the chain, and only then did she realize the enormity of what she had done. She had killed a man. Rolling off the corpse, she recoiled from it, appalled at her own ferocity.

Less than a minute had passed since the guard had entered the cell, and now two men lay dead, one of whom she had killed, the other her own brother.

The small part of her brain that could still think clearly told her not to stay and ponder this incredible shock. Crossing to the door, she peeked into the corridor. It was empty and silent, bleakly forbidding in the dim light of a single bulb. Recalling the route she'd been brought along an hour or so earlier, she turned right and started walking.

36

Making her way cautiously along the dim, silent corridor, Alana thought she could hear muffled thumping and shouting somewhere and paused to listen. The echoes in the passage made it impossible to tell where the sound was coming from. It seemed nearby.

The noise stopped, and Alana resumed walking. She reached a corner where a side passage branched off to the left; it was dark, with a stairwell at the end in a pool of light. Ahead the corridor ran straight, ending in a right turn. If Alana remembered correctly, the stairs led up to the main palace levels. She headed toward them.

She'd only gone a few steps when the noise started up again. It was now much closer: fists hammering on wood and a voice shouting in Armenian. Several doors led off the passage; the noise came from a heavily barred door halfway along. Someone was locked inside and desperate to get out. The voice, although it spoke Armenian, was familiar.

Alana leaned close to the wood. "Noah?"

The banging stopped. "Alana?"

There was a grille in the door, and she slid it aside. With a flood of mingled delight, relief, and distress, she saw Noah's eyes looking back at her from the darkness within.

"How did you get out?" he said. "Are you all right?"

"I'm okay. Your face! What did they do to you?" Noah's cheek was bruised and swollen, his nose and mouth bloody.

He touched his face, and she saw that his wrists were tied. "Just a friendly Armenian greeting. I thought I heard screaming just now. What happened?"

Alana was examining the door. There was a heavy iron ring, and below it a large keyhole. "I can't open it. I need a key. Wait …"

Leaving Noah, Alana retraced her steps to the turn. The corridor was still deserted. She made her way back to the door of her cell, and hesitated. Nothing on earth could have repelled Alana with the same force as the prospect of going back in there. She took some deep breaths and, with a supreme effort of will, went inside.

The guard was slumped against the wall with the chain around his throat and the knife protruding from his body. His face was a deathly blue-gray, the tongue sticking out between bared teeth, and the dead eyes staring at the ceiling. Hayk lay crumpled, face-down, the side of his head matted with blood. Hesitantly, Alana stepped toward him. Protruding from the pocket of his blouson was the heavy bunch of keys he must have obtained from the guard. Alana drew them out. As they came loose, they jangled, and the body gave a guttural sigh.

Alana lurched back in shock, almost falling over. *Hayk was still alive.* She stared like a rabbit watching a wolf, but he didn't move. He was out cold. His face was partly visible, and she tried to discern any recognizable trace of her lost brother. But the image of the little boy in her memory was too indistinct and remote. She didn't for a second doubt what he had said, it fitted too closely to her own recollection of that awful night – a recollection that until now Alana had believed was unique to her, the only survivor. Should she do something to help him?

389

The thought – born entirely of instinctive compassion – jolted her back to the present. Whoever this man had once been, there was nothing of Hakan in him now.

Closing her fist around the keys, she stepped away. Her eyes fell on the knife handle, and she wondered if she should retrieve it. A weapon would be useful. She touched the hilt, but the thought of drawing it out of the corpse revolted her. What was she thinking? What was she turning into? Instead, she felt around on the floor and found the scalpel blade. This would have to do.

With Hayk still alive it would be safest to lock the cell door. Alana pulled it closed and examined the keys; there were at least half a dozen that might fit. She was about to try the first when she heard footsteps coming from the direction of the main prison section of the complex.

Cursing under her breath, Alana hurried back to the dark side passage. Glancing back around the corner, she saw a man in guard uniform coming along the corridor. She backed silently along to Noah's cell. His face was pressed anxiously to the grille. He was about to speak, but Alana hushed him. The ring held three keys that might fit this lock. The guard's footsteps were almost at the corner. In desperation, Alana pressed herself back into the doorway and held her breath.

The heavy footsteps reached the corner and paused a second. Alana's eyes were shut tight, hoping the darkness would be sufficient to conceal her. After a second's hesitation, the footsteps continued, receding along the main corridor.

"Quickly," Noah hissed.

Alana began trying the keys, her fingers trembling and fumbling. The second one turned with a heavy clunk, and the door squealed open.

"Allah be praised!" said Noah, but before he could say anything else, Alana's arms were around him squeezing him tightly.

"Thank God," she said. "Thank God. You poor thing, what did

390

they do to you?" She kissed his face, her tears running off her lips on to his bruises.

"It's nothing," he said. "Tell me how you got out."

"No time for that. Hold out your hands." She fished out the scalpel blade and cut the zip-tie from his wrists. "Now we have to find a way out."

Consciousness came slowly to Hayk, hanging back like a nervous animal, reluctant to return. Finally he surfaced into a wave of skull-crushing pain. He raised his head off the floor, wondering where he was. A cold, dank room, with a tiny window near the ceiling admitting a fading light. In the gloom he saw a huge bulk beside him: the body of a huge man. Now he remembered where he was.

Dragging himself up, Hayk crouched over the corpse, inspecting it curiously but dispassionately, his gaze moving from the protruding knife to the chain wrapped around the throat.

Who could have done this? The woman? That was impossible; she could hardly weigh more than a hundred pounds soaking wet. And yet she was gone. Her friend, maybe? Equally impossible – he was locked up tight. Then perhaps the spy, Uzeyir. A string of suspects ran through Hayk's mind, each more unlikely than the last. Patting his pockets, he realized that the keys were gone.

Hayk knew he was to blame again, but his guilt was buried beneath a towering black cloud of wrath. He recalled his training – *When you have to kill, just kill. Do not talk, do not torment your target, do not enjoy it. Just end the life and move on*. In his passion Hayk had forgotten this most basic rule. That would not happen again.

He stood up and was overwhelmed by a vortex of dizziness and nausea. The side of his head was sticky with blood, and he had trouble focusing. Hayk waited until the spell calmed, then, drawing the knife from the guard's body, he wiped the blade and stepped out into the corridor.

Alana led Noah up the stairs; two flights up they came to a broad passage lined with tall windows. It had once been a fine gallery connecting the main palace to the family wing. Now only function-aries used it, and it was shabby and neglected, the windows coated with grime. Alana hesitated. She had no idea how to get out of the palace. She wasn't sure she wanted to leave yet; the thought of that historic deed in Vartan's possession nagged her.

"I know a way out," said Noah. "Your grandfather told me all about the palace; he loved to show me plans and reminisce about it for hours. There is a door over there ..."

He led Alana to the far end of the gallery, where there was a small side door. The handle was stiff with disuse, but it opened, grating on rusty hinges. Alana was surprised to find herself in a well-kept ornamental garden. The light was dying to dusk.

Noah closed the door quietly. "If we go to the end of the garden," he whispered, "there is a small mosque and school. The Armenians do not use it, obviously, but they have a fear of desecrating holy places – remember the mosque in Aghdam. It's right under the fortress wall; it will be the safest place to try to climb over."

Keeping close to the palace wall, and covered by the deepening darkness, they crept through the garden. Halfway along, the wall gave way to an arched colonnade: a cloister around a courtyard planted with vines, shrubs, and agaves; in the center a fountain pattered, all illuminated by soft lights under the arches.

They moved on, painfully conscious that the light and the lack of cover made them dangerously conspicuous. The cloister ran to the corner of the building, enclosing the courtyard on both its outer sides;

just beyond, the great round tower rose. Here the gardens ended; ahead, the domed roof and slender minaret of the disused mosque stood silhouetted against a lilac sky.

Noah crouched by the corner, looking and listening. The only sounds were the muted noises from the prison and a dog barking somewhere in the town. Nudging Alana, he began creeping across the space between the palace and the mosque. He'd gone several steps when he realized Alana wasn't following him.

"Come!" he hissed.

Alana was rooted to the spot. "I have to go back to the library," she said.

"What?"

"There's a document belonging to my grandfather, to my family. Look, there's no time to explain, I just have to go back." The deed was drawing her back like a magnet; neither she nor her grandfather would ever be safe so long as it was in Armenian hands.

She began heading back the way they had come. Noah followed her, bewildered and frustrated. As he caught up with her, they both heard a sound, clear in the evening stillness: the groan of the gallery side door opening and closing.

They both slipped behind the cloister's corner pillar. "We have to get out *now*," Noah whispered urgently.

"No." Alana stepped into the shadows of the cloister and crept along it, keeping to the shadows, pausing now and then to listen. They were nearly at the point where the courtyard joined the palace when Alana heard soft footsteps. She ducked down between a pillar and huge urn overshadowed by palm fronds, pulling Noah down with her.

The footsteps were barely discernible above the tinkling of the fountain, betrayed only by an occasional scrape of grit on stone. They crossed the courtyard and stopped nearby. Not daring to move or breathe, Alana peeked through the gap between the fronds. Nothing. Her heart pounded so heavily she was afraid it must be audible. There was another soft scrape, less than a yard away, and she almost gasped aloud. Noah's body tensed beside her. A second soft crunch of grit and the footsteps receded.

Alana rose gingerly to her knees and glanced over the urn. The courtyard was deserted. Nearby, a grand double door stood wide open. Nudging Noah, she stood and approached it warily.

It was dark within, but Alana could make out a vast space. "The Great Hall," said Noah. Faint light leaking in from a side corridor revealed a hall two stories high, with two levels of colonnaded galleries on three sides. At the far end were tall arched windows, beneath which the hall bent away to the left. The shadowy shapes of furniture loomed threateningly.

The corridor from which the light came was on the right; Alana guessed that the way to the library must be in that direction. Followed closely by Noah (who was wishing she would see sense so they could get out now), Alana flitted through the shadows to the corridor. It was broad, lined with paintings and statuary, with doors at intervals and lit by sconces. It was deserted and silent, except for extremely faint noises in the distance. As Alana and Noah moved along the corridor, the sounds resolved into the clattering and chinking of a kitchen at work. They passed a side passage leading to a door from which all the noise was coming, and then the corridor angled to the right, widening, with several more passages leading off.

Alana glanced at Noah, who shrugged. Despite the tales he'd heard of old Shusha, he had no idea where they were. Trusting to intuition, Alana kept following the corridor; it was heading generally northeast, toward the end of the palace where the hexagon tower stood.

Approaching each alcove and doorway with caution, Alana marveled at their luck at not meeting anyone. As if in response to the thought, a door opened right beside her; there was a gasp, and Alana found herself looking into the astonished face of a man. He was no taller than her, and his face, framed by a thick, graying goatee and a perfectly bald head, dissolved in horror at the sight of her. He opened his mouth to cry out.

Noah moved instantly; before the man could utter a sound, Noah had seized him by the collar, clapped a hand over his mouth, and pushed him backwards into the room. Alana followed them in, closing the door behind her.

They were in a snug, comfortable room furnished as an office and lounge. A cozy blaze burned in the stone fireplace. Noah spoke quickly and fiercely in Armenian. The terrified man shook his head, seeming not to understand. "I asked him where we are and how to get to the library," said Noah. He repeated the questions, tightening his grip. The man glanced at Alana; something in his eyes told her he knew exactly who she was. He shook his head again.

Alana glanced around; on the desk was a letter-opener, a thin steel blade as sharp as a kitchen knife. Picking it up, she rummaged through the drawers, finding a flashlight, which she pocketed, and in the bottom drawer a small, snub-nosed semi-automatic pistol, old and worn.

"Here, take this," she said, handing the pistol to Noah. Then she pressed the point of the letter knife against the man's throat. "Talk," she said.

She was disheveled, dirty, wild-eyed, her face smeared with blood, her voice seething with fear and anger. The instant the blade touched his skin the man broke down and began babbling piteously.

Noah translated, leaving out the pleas for mercy. "He is lord Vartan's secretary. He doesn't know who we are or what's going on."

"He's lying. Tell us how we get to the library in the tower."

The secretary talked rapidly, gesticulating. "He says if we spare him, he will show us the way."

Alana was suspicious and didn't withdraw the blade. "Okay, but if he puts a foot wrong, I will end him. Tell him that."

Somewhere inside Alana, the woman she had been until today listened with amazement to the words coming out of her mouth; she could never have imagined herself talking like that to anyone. She was no longer that woman, and never could be again, not entirely. She had killed a man tonight in self-defense and felt she could do it again in anger. Something had been awakened in her. Had her grandfather been there to witness it, he might have called it the spirit of her warring ancestors, the spirit of Banuchichak, the legendary warrior maiden for whom she had been named.

With the secretary leading the way, they crept along the palace corridors. Alana was half convinced that the Armenian would lead them into a trap. It was only when they passed a branch corridor where there stood a marble statue of a nymph and a griffon that she knew they were in the right direction; she remembered passing it earlier that day. The branch corridor led to the prison, and ahead lay the way to the fortress keep containing the library.

A little way along, the secretary led them into a room – an unfurnished, echoing chamber, off which three doors led. The secretary made for the door opposite, beckoning them to follow. Alana's suspicious hackles rose again.

"That's not the way," she said.

Noah glanced from her to the secretary, who smiled nervously and beckoned. "The tower is straight ahead," said Noah.

"He's trying to trick us." Alana remembered passing through this room on the way back to her cell and strove to remember which door she'd entered by. "It's this one." She pointed to the door on the right.

"Are you sure?"

Alana looked from one door to another. Behind one of them led the correct route; the other might lead to a trap. "I … I remember …"

Noah turned to the secretary. "Which is it?"

There was no reply. They were alone in the empty room; the secretary had vanished without a sound.

The air was a confusion of odors; in Hayk's nostrils they mingled bewilderingly, refusing to yield up information. He had learned the woman's scent in England, a blend of perfumes of rose, jasmine, of laundry detergent, of products laced with coconut, mint, and berries, and underlying it an individual musk. He could have tracked her anywhere by it, but he could no longer detect it; most of its ingredients had been left behind on her journey, and Hayk's senses had been badly marred by the head injury.

In the fountain courtyard he thought he detected a trace of her, and again in the great hall, but it eluded him. Where would he go if he were in her situation, having just killed a guard? The answer to that was simple enough: he would want vengeance. Hayk left the hall and climbed the stairs leading to the central palace apartments.

At the head of the staircase he met Vartan coming out of his study. Hayk halted in surprise.

Vartan's momentary smile disintegrated. "My son, what happened to you? My God, your head is bleeding!" Reading the look in Hayk's eyes and noticing the knife still streaked with blood in his hand, Vartan's expression hardened. "What did you do?"

Hayk's mind was almost as confused as his senses. He had half expected to find Vartan murdered, and after what Harutyunyan had told him he wasn't sure that that would be such a terrible thing. "You betrayed me."

"I beg your pardon?"

"I have served and trusted you all my life, and you are betraying me."

Vartan's voice was soft, wary. "I do not understand. Explain yourself, my son."

Hayk brandished the knife. "Now you have her, you will discard me. She will give you Karabakh and herself, and I will be left behind – as I was then. As I will always be!"

"Have you been dreaming?"

"No! The reverend father opened my eyes, but I see for myself what you will do. You will marry the woman and deny me my right to kill her, and you will have a new son."

Vartan began to see what had happened; if Archimandrite Harutyunyan had been within arm's reach at that moment, his blood would have been on the floor and his head on a pike. "You see nothing. That bastard son of a pig that calls himself a priest is a liar. To think that I would favor this bitch over you? That I would betray my own son? The idea is preposterous." Disregarding the wavering blade, Vartan stepped close to Hayk and cupped his face in his hands. "You know how it shall be. When I have what I need from her, she will die at your hand, and in that moment you will tell her who you are, that she dies by her own brother's hand."

Hayk's mouth opened and closed. "I ... I ..."

"You already told her, didn't you?"

"Forgive me, father, I ..."

Vartan's eyes narrowed, and his hands bit into Hayk's shoulders. "Did you kill her? Is that her blood on your knife?"

"I ... I tried to."

"Did she do this?" Vartan indicated Hayk's injured head.

"No, she—"

"*Help! Lord Vartan, sir!*" Along the corridor Vartan's secretary,

Kamo, came running; he staggered to a halt, struggling for breath. "The woman," he said. "She's out … loose … man too, with her …" Vartan shot a glance at Hayk. "I know … know where they're going."

37

There had been no sound of a door opening or closing, and yet they were alone in the room. There wasn't so much as a stick of furniture to conceal a man: just the two heavy doors ahead and one to the right, any of which would make a very noticeable noise.

Noah touched the wall, which was built of smooth cut stone. "Togrul mentioned there are concealed passages in the palace. There must be an entrance in this wall."

Alana grabbed his arm; if there was ever a time for pondering architectural history, this was not it. "Come on. We're gonna have the whole fortress on our backs any minute now." She opened the right-hand door. It led to a dark passageway running in the direction of the tower. "I recognize this. I was right – he *was* trying to lead us the wrong way."

Using the flashlight she'd taken from the secretary's desk, she led them through a series of heavy oak doors. They came to a large chamber, filled with crates, old furniture, and junk, looming eerily in the beam of the flashlight. There was a window deeply recessed in the thick outer wall of the tower. It was bitterly cold.

"I remember this," said Alana. "We're directly below the library."

In the corner was a door leading to a spiral staircase. Now that her goal was near, Alana's fears, which had been suppressed by the exhilaration of the escape and the search, were growing. The secretary must have raised the alarm by now, and escape would be virtually impossible. Vartan's men might even be waiting for them in the library above.

The staircase wound up and up, and eventually they came to an iron-bound door. It opened with a groan. like a soul in torment. Alana cringed and cast her flashlight beam about, picking out the tables and desk, the disordered bookcases, chairs like the skeletons of beasts, animated by the moving light, discolored tapestries hanging from the opposite wall. There was no one there; just the hush of abandonment and neglect.

"Lock the door," Alana whispered, and crossed to the central table.

Noah secured the bolt. Then he went to the large double door, which he guessed led to the palace's main living apartments. There was a big iron key in the lock; it was stiff, but turned with a dismal grating and clunked home.

"Do you have the document?" he hissed, hurrying to Alana's side.

She was rummaging among the dusty papers and books scattered in teetering heaps all over the surface of the vast table. "It's not here!" she said. "It was right there, with these things!" The map was still laid out, and the silvery lump of cobalt, but there was no trace of the deed. Alana's legs almost gave way as the enormity of her mistake hit her, the sheer folly of assuming that such a priceless document would have been left right here where Vartan had shown it to her. "How could I be so stupid?" she cried out.

"Sssh! They might—"

At that moment, the handle of the main door turned slowly, with a hollow, agonizing squeal. The door shook.

Alana and Noah stared at it in horror. A heartbeat passed, and then a heavy pounding began, reverberating through the room. There were voices raised. They were trying to break the door open.

"Out, now! The stairs!" Noah ran for the door leading to the spiral staircase.

Alana was rooted to the spot, staring at the table. *Where Vartan had shown it to her – right here*. Why had he shown it to her here, on this table, in her ancestors' library? From all he had said, she suspected that he had this much in common with Togrul Karabakhsky: in his own twisted way, Vartan liked things to be in their proper historical place.

"It's here," she muttered. "It must be …" She looked over the mountains of papers and manuscripts, the stacks of books and boxes on the floor, the chests of drawers, the cupboards, the cases, thousands of old volumes on the shelves. It would take days to search it all.

Noah was at the stairway door; his hand was on the bolt, ready to release it, when he heard heavy footsteps on the stairs.

He backed away. "They're coming that way too," he said, and looked around frantically. "There's no other way out." The pounding on the main door was joined by hammering at the stair door. Noah ran to the windows. The tall stained-glass panes contained only one small panel that opened for ventilation; Noah looked out into the night. He had stood at the foot of this tower and knew that the drop must be at least thirty feet onto a rock-strewn slope. They had no rope – in desperation he wondered if they could fashion something from the wall hangings. He touched one; it was damp and rotten from a leak in the roof above and fell apart in his grip.

Alana was still staring into space, seemingly oblivious to the cacophony and the horror of the situation. She was trying desperately to think. *Their proper historical place* … Where in this room would her ancestors have stored such a document? Alana gripped her temples, trying to stave off the panic threatening to suffocate thought. Into her mind came a memory of the library in her grandfather's house in Baku. She saw him taking out an ancient parchment: the illustration of the siege; it came from a chest with lots of long, shallow drawers. *In here I keep my most precious documents ...* Togrul's own grandfather had created that library as a replica in miniature of this one.

Leaving the table, Alana paced about the room, but there didn't seem to be anything like it. Meanwhile, the pounding on the door had changed to battering, as if they were beating it with rifle butts. The flashlight beam caught the corner of a chest draped with a sheet. She tore back the sheet ... and there it was. An identical chest of drawers.

"Alana, what are you doing?" said Noah. "We have to find a way out of here!"

"Wait! I think I've got it."

She pulled out the top drawer: empty. The second was filled with papers and maps. As she rummaged through them, the beating on the main door stopped abruptly. There was a pause, and then a burst of automatic gunfire. The wood around the lock splintered, but the door held firm.

"They're coming in!" Noah readied the pistol and aimed at the door.

Alana opened a third drawer, then a fourth. Lying on top of a heap of maps and pictures was a centuries-old parchment written in dense Cyrillic script, bearing a wax seal and myriad signatures. "I've got it!"

Her words were drowned by another long burst of gunfire. Splinters flew from the door and the lock ruptured. The doors swung inward, the light of two powerful flashlights leaping into the room.

Noah had a glimpse of Vartan armed with an AK-47 and another man beside him with a handgun; Noah squeezed off two rapid shots, grabbing Alana by the arm just as she snatched up the deed. He pushed her down behind the table, fired once more and dived down beside her, pursued by a torrent of gunfire that threw up a storm of paper and dust.

"I got it," said Alana, frantically rolling up the unwieldy document.

"Good for you."

Noah heard the clicking of a rifle magazine being changed; he swung up and fired two more shots; dazzled by the lights, he aimed for the source of the beams. An answering shot came out of the darkness, hitting the table next to his head, and as he ducked back into cover there was a fresh burst of automatic fire.

Still the pounding on the stairway door went on, and a laugh came from the darkness. "Cease, Vahe!" said Vartan's voice, speaking English. "We have them trapped like little Azeri mice."

Noah checked the pistol; it was an old Russian-made Makarov with only an eight-round capacity. He tried to remember how many shots he'd fired already. Four or five? Sensing someone moving stealthily to flank them, he leaned out and fired a warning shot.

"No need to take them that way, my son," said Vartan from the darkness. "Let these grapes wither on the vine."

An unaccustomed anger boiled up in Noah; he stood up and fired toward where he sensed the second man was. Two shots, and then a click. The weapon was empty. He'd hit something – there was a gasp of pain from the darkness, followed by a wild burst of gunfire. Noah leapt back into cover as a snowstorm of shredded paper filled the air.

"I'm out," said Noah, covering his head. "No more bullets."

Alana stared at him, clutching the rolled-up deed. "I'm sorry, Noah … Noah, WAIT! NO!"

Before she could stop him, Noah rose to his feet, tossing away the pistol and putting his hands up. Squinting against the glare of a flashlight, he said in Armenian. "I surrender."

The flashlight was lowered, and he saw Vartan staring at him intently. "It seems you have no choice, friend." He gestured with the AK-47 and said in English: "Let Miss Karabakhsky show herself."

"Just take me. Let her go."

Vartan laughed. "You think you can bargain?" He broke off in irritation and yelled, "Vahe! Stop that racket!" The hammering from the stairway door ceased. Covering Noah with his rifle, Vartan crossed to the door and unbolted it.

Alana peeked over the top of the table, surveying the room. Hayk was half-lying in the middle of the floor, gripping his right arm where Noah's shot had clipped him. From the stairway door, three men spilled into the room. Alana recognized the leader as the man who had abducted her at Aggadik.

"I tell you again, I don't care what you do with me," said Noah. "Just let Alana go free."

"I will do as I please with you," said Vartan. "But she is staying here. Also, I am sick of your mewling." He raised his AK-47 to his shoulder, aimed at Noah, and squeezed the trigger.

A gunshot cracked. Noah flinched, his body stiffening in anticipation of the bullet. It never came. The AK-47 fell from Vartan's hands, clattering on the floor, and he crumpled up and dropped. There was a second gunshot, and Vahe fell with a hole in his forehead.

A figure stood at the far side of the library, looming in the torchlight. He had entered the room unheard, apparently through the solid tapestry wall. He was heavily built, with a face like a rock formation and small eyes like black stones.

"Salim," Alana whispered.

His face was bloody and bruised, but Salim Zardabi was alive. Behind him was an open door – one of the old khan's concealed entrances, disguised as part of the wood paneling and half-covered by a tapestry.

405

"Come!" he barked. "Quick!"

Noah ran, grabbing the paralyzed Alana by the elbow and hauling her to her feet. Vahe's remaining men recovered from their astonishment, diving for cover as Salim's firing pursued them with lethal accuracy. Hayk scrambled for his dropped pistol, grabbing it with his left hand and firing back.

Passing Vartan's body, Alana snatched up his AK-47 and, turning in the doorway, vented her anger and indignation with a long burst of fire. The rifle's powerful recoil wrenched her shoulder, and the bullets sprayed wildly around the room. Hayk kept shooting, his rounds slapping into the woodwork.

Noah stumbled and almost fell, gasping, but Alana grabbed him and pulled him through the door. Salim slammed it behind them and barricaded it with a table.

"Follow," he said.

"We thought you were dead," said Alana as they followed him across the room to a second door. Salim paused as he opened it and drew back his mountaineering jacket, revealing a Kevlar vest with a scar where Uzeyir's bullet had struck. His lips drew back wolfishly from his teeth and his tiny eyes sparkled.

"Not so easy to kill."

The door led to another spiral staircase. Salim led them upwards. Halfway to the top of the tower a door stood open, and through it came a cold night breeze. Salim urged them through, and they found themselves on the rampart walkway of the fortress's northeast wall, the tower looming above them. Salim crossed to the battlements and reached into an embrasure; a climbing rope hung there from a grapple.

"This I climb in. I hear shooting and come. Lucky for you." He quickly secured the rope more firmly, tying it around one of the stone uprights.

Alana looked out at the drop; the moon was bright, and she could see a grassy slope twenty feet below, strewn with rocky outcrops.

"You first," said Salim. "You most important."

Alana didn't waste time arguing. Salim looped the end of the rope around her waist, and within seconds she was being lowered down the wall. In the moonlight, it crossed her mind that she was playing a part in some ancient Azeri fable of princesses and castles. Intoxicated by fatigue, relief, and adrenaline, she almost laughed aloud.

Noah came down second; as he touched the ground he staggered and leaned against the wall for support. He seemed exhausted. Alana put a hand out to steady him, but he pushed it away. "Noah, what's wrong?"

"Nothing, I'll be fine." His voice was hoarse, his breath coming in gasps.

"Noah, let me …" Alana touched his side and felt dampness. She pulled back his jacket. The side of his shirt was soaked in blood from armpit to waist. "Oh dear God, Noah …" She remembered him stumbling as they were escaping through the door. Hayk's bullet had hit him in the side just below the ribs and must still be inside him.

Salim reached the ground. He sensed immediately that something was wrong and took in the situation at a glance. He grunted and walked a little way along the wall, coming back with a pack he'd left hidden in the angle of the tower's foot. From it he took a dressing pad and handed it to Noah, who pressed it to the wound.

There wasn't a moment to waste; the fortress garrison would be mobilized within minutes – if they weren't already – and a full-scale hunt would get under way. With Alana supporting Noah and Salim leading the way, they picked their way down the slope. Noah was weakening rapidly, and by the time they'd negotiated their way to the foot of the rocky bluffs his breathing was like a broken bellows. Alana strained to support his growing weight as his strength failed.

Below the bluffs the sloped eased off and the going was less arduous. But Salim drove them on without pause or pity.

After two hundred yards the ground began to rise again, and as they breasted a ridge, they heard the roar of an engine in the distance. A rough farm track crossed the vale from the Shusha road, and bounding toward them along it was a heavy vehicle festooned with floodlights. A shout of triumph rang out above the roar of the engine; they had been spotted. A spatter of gunfire broke out, but the shots went far over their heads.

Salim cursed and, seizing both Alana and Noah, he physically hauled them over the rise. Then, setting his neck under Noah's armpit, he hoisted him up over his shoulder and began to run.

Alana glanced back. The vehicle was less than a hundred yards behind them, bouncing wildly on the stony track, its floodlights splashing their glare across the slopes.

As he ran, holding Noah firmly with one hand, Salim reached inside his jacket and drew out something that looked like a toy pistol. He passed it to Alana. "Go! Make light!"

The pistol was an orange plastic flare gun. With another glance back – the truck was down to fifty yards and closing fast – she halted, steadied herself, aimed skyward, and pulled the trigger. The pistol cracked, and a red flare shot up, trailing a long arc of smoke.

Alana ran on, straining to catch up with Salim, whose strength and stamina seemed limitless. The slope suddenly reared up at forty-five degrees, and Salim went up it like a hill pony, with Alana struggling behind, bent almost on all fours.

The farm track petered out, and from behind they heard the Armenians dismounting from their truck. The floodlights illuminated the slope, and they opened fire. A bullet thwacked into the turf next to Alana's hand; she yelped and threw herself headlong up the hill, hauling herself up with hands and feet. The soldiers came on after them. Alana fought for breath, feeling that this nightmare climb would never end, that this hill had no summit.

It had, and as they reached it, ahead Alana saw a moonlit landscape rising gently, a vast open hillside with a forest at the crest. There was no hiding place, no cover – it was a killing ground.

The soldiers saw the same thing; as they came over the lip Alana and Salim where twenty yards out on the hillside: sitting ducks. Without breaking step, Salim twisted, firing back at them wildly, trying to keep their heads down, but it was no use.

Alana glanced over her shoulder; she had one brief glimpse of them – half a dozen men standing or kneeling or just coming into view, raising their rifles to their shoulders, silhouetted against the white dawn-like glare of the floodlights. The image lasted about half a second, then there was an ear-splitting whooshing noise and the lip of the ridge erupted in an orange fireball, consuming the soldiers. The shockwave threw Alana off her feet.

She lay there, stunned, ears ringing. The next thing she knew, Salim – with Noah still draped over his shoulder – was helping her to her feet.

"What happened?" Her own voice sounded strangely muffled in her head.

Salim pointed. Farther along the hillside, a single spotlight shone down from the sky. It came rushing toward them. A black shape, with lights winking on its body, resolved into a helicopter. Alana could scarcely hear its noise above the ringing in her ears, but she felt the wind from its rotors. The spotlight beamed flicked back and forth across the hillside, searching for them. Salim waved, and the helicopter descended.

Alana, her senses battered and confused, was vaguely aware of heavily armed soldiers in full combat gear leaping out and taking up defensive positions, of hands reaching out to help her aboard, of Noah being laid gently on the floor of the aircraft, and of Salim talking to an officer, shouting above the noise. And then they were ascending. Floating, it seemed to Alana, floating heavenward.

Noah opened his eyes to see her gazing down at him, her face bathed in the red glow of the aircraft's interior light. He believed that he had never seen anything so beautiful – a fitting sight to behold before closing his eyes forever.

"Noah, I'm so sorry." Alana touched his cheek; tears were streaming down her face. "This is my fault, all my fault."

He tried to open his mouth to deny it, but no sound would come. He shook his head weakly and smiled. She stooped and kissed his forehead.

Alana was pushed gently but firmly to one side. A medic opened up Noah's jacket and deftly cut away his shirt. As he began cleaning and pressing a pad on the wound and preparing a syringe, Alana felt her hand gripped. She looked down to see Noah's blood-covered fingers curling around her own, and she squeezed back. His teeth were chattering, but he tried to smile.

"Noah, I love you," she said. "I've been falling in love with you since I first saw you. I can't lose you now that I've found you."

The medic's needle slid into Noah's arm, and morphine flowed into his blood. The grip on Alana's hand slackened, and his eyes began to close. She wanted to scream, to grab hold of his soul, force it to stay in his body. She thought of the two of them long ago on the hillside above Khojali, surrounded by death and huddled together for warmth, and her flesh ached for every lost moment from that day to this. She subsided in despair and wept.

38

Spring was coming to Baku. The perennial wind called Khazri, which carried the chill of Russia across the Caspian Sea, had eased, and although its summer rival Gilgavar had not begun bringing warmth from the south, the air was balmy. Standing on the balcony of her room, Alana breathed in the atmosphere of the Old City; the usual smells – the coal smoke from the neighbors' samovars and the faint undertone of traffic fumes from the modern city beyond the walls – were joined this morning by the rich aromas of food cooking for the spring festival of *Novruz*: the sweet *shekerbura* pastries with honey and saffron, the cloves and cardamom of the *pakhlava* desserts, and *shashlik* kebabs grilling on coal fires. Alana savored it all as she watched the early pedestrian traffic pattering through the narrow street below.

The *Novruz* holiday began today, and would last for five days, during which the Old City would be filled with festivities, ritual games, feasts, parades, and the lighting of bonfires – a nod to the old Zoroastrian beliefs. In the Karabakhsky household the first day of *Novruz* was especially notable this year because it was Alana's grandfather's birthday. Togrul Karabakhsky was ninety years old. The house was being prepared for a special lunch, to which close friends and family were invited, and this evening there would be a big party at the famous Mugham Club restaurant, which was an ancient caravanserai near the Maiden Tower. Alana could hear the noises from the kitchen below, and the tread of servants – specially hired for the occasion – on the stairs and landing. It was rare in these twilight days of the Karabakhsky dynasty for the household to be so full and so busy.

It would soon be busier still – John and Catherine Fulton were flying in today to join the celebrations. Alana hadn't seen her parents since disappearing from Gstaad more than a month ago. She had mixed feelings about it all; she was happy for her grandfather, but the prospect of both her families meeting made her nervous. It was difficult enough having the two strands of her life co-existing in her own mind; bringing them together in the same room might be like joining matter and antimatter.

"What are you thinking about?"

The touch of his hands on her shoulders, his deep voice; she tilted back her head to let him kiss her cheek and reached up to stroke his face. "How are you this morning?"

He touched his side, where the bullet had entered. "It pinches a little, but you know what – I think I may go for a gentle run today."

She turned to him, settling into his embrace and looking up at him. "You can't run – you're only a few days out of the hospital."

Noah laughed "Who's the doctor, me or you?"

His eyes sparkled with the same warm, reassuring smile that had first drawn her to him in the lobby bar of the Gstaad Palace Hotel. The words she'd said to him on the helicopter – when she was sure he was dying – had never been repeated. It wasn't that she hadn't meant it in the moment; rather, it hadn't felt seemly somehow once they were back in the real world. Everything had moved so fast. But

412

now, looking into his eyes a sudden spark of pure joy made her say it again: "I love you, Noah."

His smile grew like a single note resolving into a full tonic chord, and he touched her face. "I love you too."

Alana laughed. "Isn't it strange? I mean, we've known each other – what, four weeks?"

"Twenty-nine days, eighteen hours, and forty-five minutes," he said. "Give or take a little. And no, it is not strange. It is the most natural thing in all creation."

And there on the balcony, in the balm of a Baku morning, he kissed her.

The security guards manning the Old City gateway had raised the barriers to ease the flow of revelers arriving for the first evening of *Novruz*. Elsewhere around the ancient citadel people were trickling in from the sea-front promenade, but it was at the Qosa Qala Qapisi – the medieval double gate – that the greatest crowds came in.

Neither the security guards nor any member of the public took any notice of a solitary dark-clad figure who sidled in stealthily through the gate and passed among the shadows by the booths opposite the tourist information office. He moved softly and was adept at not being noticed.

He had also evaded notice twenty-four hours earlier, when he had emerged in the dusk from the security belt near Qaradagli, unnoticed by any of the diggers on the archaeological site there.

The only person who had noticed or interacted with the strange figure was the truck driver who had picked him up near Aghjabedi and given him a lift as far as the outskirts of Baku. That truck driver would never bear witness, because he was now lying in his cab on a patch of waste ground dotted with oil derricks in the Sabayil district, with his throat cut.

413

Near the Museum of Archaeology and Ethnography – where Alana had spent many hours whenever she wasn't at Noah's hospital bedside – the street forked. The man followed the left way, keeping to the shadowy side of the street, following the winding way down toward the Maiden Tower.

Alana threaded her arm through Noah's as they walked along the street. She had never seen Baku quite so throbbing with life. They wove through a flock of teenagers in fantastic colorful costumes in the traditional Azeri style – the girls in long dresses with beaded gauze veils, the boys in gold-braided tunics. They were followed by a group of men dressed as medieval soldiers in spiked silver helmets, decorated shields, and carrying spears.

"This is wild," said Alana. "This happens every year?"

"Every single one," said Noah.

Alana glanced back, realizing that they'd got ahead of the rest of the group. Togrul Karabakhsky, with his steward on one side and Catherine Fulton on the other, was keeping up a good pace for a man of his age, but he was still slow. Alana had tried to persuade him to take a cab, but he'd insisted on walking – he wanted to "feel his city" and besides, a cab would take even longer to get through the crowds. For the evening he had transformed from his domestic outfit and – honoring his American guests above *Novruz* tradition – put on a finely tailored double-breasted suit in dove gray with a sky-blue tie. Catherine took the old gentleman's arm, and John Fulton walked beside her.

The meeting of the families had gone better than Alana could have hoped. Her mother was in a state of high nervous excitement, but had managed to rein herself in, and her father was his usual relaxed, charming self. Over lunch, Togrul had wanted to know everything they could tell about Alana's life with them, and the Fultons had supplied that wish in plenty.

"*Amore*, please slow down – don't leave your *Maman* behind." Catherine smiled at Noah. "I understand you guys being wrapped up in one another, but darling, we old folks don't have your zest."

Alana paused to let them catch up. "*Maman*, please don't ..."

"Don't what? Share my daughter's joy?" Catherine simpered at Noah, who smiled and gave a little bow.

"The youth – they are our future," said Togrul. "I could not be more happy for them."

Alana hadn't blushed this much since high school. "Come on," she said. "We'd better move, or we'll be late."

Baku was lit up like jewels against the black velvet night. The Maiden Tower was bathed in white floodlight, standing above the rooftops like a torch, and the modern city's triple Flame Towers were lit up in green, red, and blue, the national colors of Azerbaijan. The illuminated spires and the lights of the tree-lined promenade shimmered on the waters of the bay. Alana glanced up at the Maiden Tower as they turned into the street leading to the *mugham* restaurant; the trauma of all she had been through, combined with the exhilaration of being still alive and being here with Noah and her family, made her feel as fragile inside as an eggshell. At any moment she might laugh for joy or burst into tears.

She didn't notice, in passing the tower, that she was watched from the shadows beyond the floodlights. The little shiver she felt she attributed to the evening air and the sleeveless dress she wore under her light jacket.

In the restaurant's entrance passage they found Salim standing guard. Alana met his eye and smiled. The ugly, stony face glimmered momentarily with warmth before resuming its implacable, impenetrable gaze.

The octagonal interior of the old caravanserai had been laid out with three long tables arranged in a U and set for ninety guests – one for each year of the host's age. They glittered with silver and glass on vivid scarlet cloths. The space between was spread with Turkish carpets, and the open stone cistern in the center – where pack animals had once been watered – was laid out with silver urns and artefacts from the ancient days of the camel caravans. Most of the guests had already arrived and were being served drinks while a *mugham* band played softly in one of the arched recesses. Togrul's entrance was met with a round of applause and murmurs of delight.

While the old gentleman began a long round of greeting the guests – many of whom were old friends from Karabakh – Alana and Noah went looking for their places at table.

"I believe we're at the head, *amore*," said Catherine. "Quite naturally, of course."

"This place is fantastic," said John.

Catherine rolled her eyes in ecstasy. "Oh, it's so exquisite I can't stand it – look at these fabrics. And the food!"

The dining and serving tables had been laid out with an array of Azerbaijani dishes – there were pilafs and shashliks, breads, and a rainbow of fresh fruits and salads. Alana identified each dish to her mother.

"Well, it all looks delicious, *amore*. I say, isn't your grandfather a darling! Such a gentleman. I can see where you get it from. I mean, I always thought it was *my* influence – but it's in the breeding, of course. Didn't I say so, John, on the flight, our little Alana is … Why, *amore*, whatever is the matter?"

Their seats were near the middle of the central table. As Alana pulled out her chair, she realized that it was in exactly the same spot where she and Noah had sat on their previous visit. The music was the same, and the aromas of food and the susurrus of people, and for a dizzying moment she was back there, with Uzeyir's sharp eyes on her, and his knowing smirk.

She recovered. "Nothing, *Maman*, I'm okay. I just got a little headrush."

John took her arm to steady her. "But sweetheart, you didn't stand up – how can you get a headrush?"

"I don't know, daddy, but I'm fine. Noah, could you pour me a glass of water?"

The other guests, talking animatedly among themselves, were beginning to take their seats. Togrul finished his round of greetings and sat down with Alana and Noah on his right, and John and Catherine on his left. Alana was introduced to various old friends of her grandfather – including at least two who were high up in the government of Azerbaijan – but she was too distracted to take in their names. She sipped her water and tried to shake off the bewildering sensation that had taken hold of her.

She came out of it with a startling suddenness, like a swimmer surfacing, into a chorus of clinking china and loud conversations. Noah was talking with a naval officer sitting opposite them; the man, who was bald, with a long face and thin black mustache, was clearly high-ranking. Alana knew enough Azerbaijani to gather that Noah was thanking him warmly, while the officer smiled and made little disclaiming gestures with his half-eaten *shashlik*.

"This is Captain Krivotsyuk," said Noah to Alana. "He is a distant cousin of your grandfather's. I owe him my life."

"You do?"

"Those soldiers who rescued us from Shusha were from his regiment." Noah lowered his voice to a whisper: "Unit 641, the Azerbaijan navy's special forces."

The captain nodded politely to Alana. She smiled and thanked him as best she could in his own language.

As the food and drink were consumed, the party grew looser and noisier. The *mugham* band played loud and lively music, and there was dancing. Togrul caused much laughter by persuading a blushing Catherine to join him in a traditional Azeri folk dance. Spinning around with Noah, the heady music saturating her, Alana forgot all her unease and gave herself up to the joy of the moment.

There was a moving interlude when, at Togrul's request, the band's singer – a young woman dressed in embroidered silks with a beaded headdress – sang *Sari Gelin*, the beautiful folk lament. Togrul took Alana's hand as the plaintive, exquisite voice filled the stone building. "Your grandmother's favorite song," he whispered to her. "She would have been happy tonight to see you. Happy indeed."

Shortly after the song finished, Togrul vanished. Alana was wondering – with a qualm of anxiety – where he had gone, when Noah drew her attention to the upper story gallery. Her grandfather appeared there, hands resting on the balustrade, looking out over his party. His steward, Rashad, who had helped him up the stairs, stood just behind him with Mary, his housekeeper. A bell rang, the octagon fell silent, and the guests looked up.

"Dear friends, family, and guests from other lands," Togrul began, his deep but fragile voice filling the stone space. "Welcome to Baku. Please accept my most sincere thanks and blessings for being present at this, my ninetieth birthday celebration."

He spoke in Azerbaijani. Alana had learned enough to follow some of what he said, and Noah translated quietly for the Fultons' benefit.

"My life has been long, and I have tried to live it so as to bring honor and joy to those who are dear to me. As all of you know, *Novruz* is a time of renewal. But it is also a time when we honor our ancestors and our departed loved ones by visiting their graves. For me, that is not possible; my son, my beloved wife, my parents, and my forefathers all lie in Karabakh, our homeland, where none of us now may tread. None, that is, but the bravest.

"For this reason, it gives me joy and pride beyond measure, beyond my greatest hopes, that among you sits my granddaughter, Ayna Chichak Fulton Karabakhsky." Alana felt every pair of eyes in the place turn to her, and she blushed again. "Light in my darkness, sunshine in my days, my Ayna, you survived the atrocity at Khojali, and have come back beyond all hope from America, and out of the prison fortress that our Shusha home has become. You are the last of my line, and I hope the foundation of its continuance. I call on all here present to raise their cups to my own Banuchichak, Khanim Ayna, princess of Karabakh."

Every voice gathered there joined in the toast while Alana looked up at her grandfather; he appeared to be weeping for joy, but it was hard to tell because her own eyes were blurry with tears.

As the acclaim subsided, Togrul wiped his eyes and began to talk of history and ancestry. The deed that Alana had brought back from Shusha had been displayed on an easel, and Togrul – with allusions to the folk history of Karabakh – described its importance.

While he spoke, Alana found herself staring at her glass, her mind filling with unwelcome images: the cell, the guard's weight on her, the gunfire, Noah's bleeding body in her arms, Vartan's eager, evil eyes daring her to join in his plan to gain Karabakh's wealth, Uzeyir's jeering grin, the snow-swept hillside above Gstaad, where the gunman lurked somewhere in the trees ... She heard *mugham* music, and saw the dark shadow of an armed man prowling into the *caravanserai* restaurant, seeking her, and Uzeyir gliding in to intercept him ...

With a sick jolt, Alana realized that although the music was only an echo in her head, this last image was not just a memory of that other time; it was occurring right now. The black-clad figure was there, moving stealthily through the shadows under the entrance arch. Alana shook her head and blinked. Her grandfather's voice came back into focus, and the figure under the arch was no longer there. Had she imagined it? She turned to speak to Noah, but he was gone.

Her father saw her bewilderment. "He went to speak with your grandfather about something." Alana got up. Her legs were weak and her hands trembling. "Are you all right, honey?"

"I'm fine, daddy. I won't be a minute."

There was a door right by the entrance, which led to the kitchens and a service stairway to the upper floor. Alana opened the door quietly so as not to interrupt her grandfather's speech and closed it behind her. A short passage, brightly lit, led to the staircase. There, with his head resting on the lower stone steps, lay a waiter in a pool of his own blood. His throat had been slit, hanging open like a second mouth.

Hayk was here. Her grandfather was in lethal danger. For an instant, Alana was paralyzed with horror; then she recovered herself and raced past the body, bounding up the stairs. Just beyond the first turn, near the top, she found Salim.

He was sitting with his back to the wall, apparently asleep. Coming closer, Alana saw the blood on the front of his white shirt, at the level of his heart. Even as she stooped over him the circular crimson patch spread rapidly. Salim's eyes opened, and he beckoned weakly. Alana crouched at his side, taking his blood-soaked hand. He tried to speak but had no voice.

"Salim, oh God, what can I do? Wait, I'll call an ambulance …"

She went to get up, but he gripped her hand with sudden ferocity, shaking his head. He forced a whisper: "*Acnabi … Armani.*" Foreigner: Armenian. "Take," he said, and pointed toward his pistol, which lay on the steps a yard away.

Alana's brain snapped into focus, and anger filled her heart – a burgeoning fury that her enemies, not content with Karabakh, should steal in here, violating, killing, destroying. Taking up the gun, she stooped and kissed Salim on the forehead. "Thank you," she said.

At the top of the stairs was a corridor left and right. Getting her bearings, Alana went left. The corridor was lined with doors leading onto the upper story balconies. She had passed several, looking for the right one, before she remembered that there was one continuous gallery running around the whole upper story. Whichever door she chose, she would get to her grandfather.

Alana skidded to a halt. As her fingers touched the door handle a gunshot rang out on the other side. She heard screams and commotion. She turned the handle, but it was locked.

She was too late.

With a scream of animal rage, Alana fired into the door lock, squeezing the trigger again and again, the pistol jolting violently in her palm. On the fifth shot, the lock gave way and the door swung open.

The scene on the balcony hit her eyes as a frozen tableau caught in a split second. Togrul lay on the floor, pale as a ghost, a gunshot wound in his left arm, cradled by Mary and Rashad. Noah was locked in a desperate struggle with the intruder; his hand was clamped around the gunman's wrist, the pistol pointing at the ceiling, and the gunman's other hand was at Noah's throat. As Alana entered, the two men twisted round, and she saw that it was not Hayk, but Vartan himself, teeth bared in a furious snarl as he fought to free his gun hand from Noah's grip.

Noah was between Alana and Vartan, and she couldn't get a clear aim. Suddenly, Vartan let go of Noah's throat and drove his fist into the wound on his side. Noah doubled over in pain. Vartan shoved him aside and leveled the gun.

Every detail stood out to Alana's heightened senses, precise and vivid: Noah falling back, an expression of horror on his face; Vartan's features contorted, his jaw working, mouthing some curse in his own language; the glint of lights on the pistol as he raised it; the black hairs on the back of the hand gripping it. All sound seemed to withdraw, and Alana's senses zeroed down to just vision and reflex in that slice of a single second as the gun's muzzle swung upward. It swayed toward Togrul, but wavered and turned back to Alana, as if Vartan couldn't decide which of them he hated more. Then it swung to Togrul, and the knuckle of Vartan's index finger paled as it began to squeeze the trigger.

Alana fired. The bullet caught Vartan full in the chest. She fired again and again. He staggered back against the balustrade, his hand still gripping the pistol. There was a high-pitched wail of fury as Mary launched herself at him, seizing a full bottle from the table, and in one swift motion slamming it into Vartan's head.

The warlord teetered back over the balustrade, hung for a second, then fell, to a chorus of screams from the guests below. Alana rushed to the balustrade and looked down. Vartan's body lay spread-eagled on the carpets, his head on the flagstones, a pool of blood spreading around him.

It was over; the threat that had stalked her from her college rooms at Cambridge to the dungeon at Shusha was ended.

"Banuchichak," said Togrul. There were tears in his eyes, but he was smiling. "My Banuchichak." He glanced up at Rashad, then down at his arm. "Well, this was not the finale I had in mind for my birthday. Now, would somebody mind getting me a doctor?"

Appendix

A Short History of Karabakh

Nagorno-Karabakh, which lies within the Karabakh region, is among the most ancient and culturally important areas of Azerbaijan, but its recent history has been marked by conflict. In the eighteenth century, Armenians living in Azerbaijan tried to claim Azerbaijani land. In 1923, the Soviet government established the Nagorno-Karabakh Autonomous Oblast (NKAO), which comprised 4,400 km2 of Karabakh.

In the 1980s, Armenian claims to land were revived and prompted an attempt by Armenia to annex the NKAO. This led to the deaths of 216 Azerbaijanis, the wounding of 1,154 more and the expulsion of 250,000 from their historical lands.

In late 1991 (by which point the Soviet Union had collapsed) the conflict escalated, and Armenian forces began to operate in Nagorno-Karabakh. The Khojali Genocide of February 1992 ended with thousands of Azerbaijanis dead or captured, and the town destroyed.

The town of Shusha and the district of Lachin, between Armenia and Nagorno-Karabakh, were occupied in May 1992 and in the following year Armenian armed forces captured six more Azerbaijani districts around Nagorno-Karabakh – Kalbajar, Aghdam, Fuzuli,

Jabrayil, Gubadli and Zangilan.

The United Nations (UN) has repeatedly tried to intervene:

On 30 April 1993, the UN Security Council adopted Resolution 822, which required occupying forces to leave the Kalbajar district and other parts of Azerbaijan.

On 29 July 1993, the UN Security Council adopted Resolution 853, which called for the immediate, unconditional withdrawal of occupying forces from the district of Aghdam and all other occupied areas of the Republic of Azerbaijan.

On 14 October 1993, the UN Security Council adopted Resolution 874. This required the immediate implementation of the reciprocal and urgent steps provided for in the Conference on Security and Co-operation in Europe (CSCE) Minsk Group's "adjusted timetable", including the withdrawal of forces.

On 11 November 1993, the UN Security Council adopted Resolution 884, which condemned recent ceasefire violations and the resumption of hostilities. The Resolution specifically denounced the occupation of Zangilan and Horadiz, attacks on civilians and bombardments of Azerbaijani territory. It demanded the unilateral withdrawal of occupying forces from Zangilan, Horadiz and elsewhere in the Republic of Azerbaijan.

Armenian armed forces remain within Azerbaijan's territory and during the conflict, over 1,000,000 Azerbaijanis have become IDPs, 20,000 people have been killed and 50,000 have been wounded.

Sources

https://barassociation.az/news/609
http://unscr.com/en/resolutions/853
http://unscr.com/en/resolutions/884
http://unscr.com/en/resolutions/822
http://unscr.com/en/resolutions/874

Map

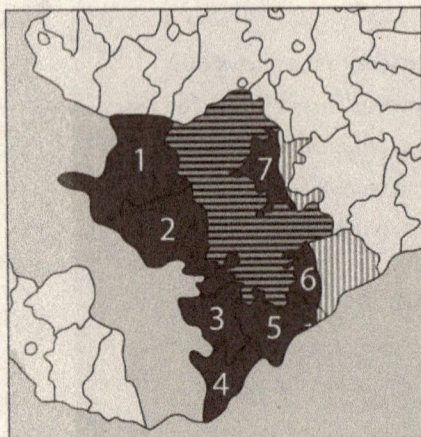

Map of occupied districts before the 2020 war. The former Nagorno-Karabakh Autonomous Oblast is shown in horizontal stripes and pre-2020 Azerbaijan-held territory in vertical stripes. 1. Kalbajar, 2. Lachin, 3. Quhadli, 4. Zangilan, 5. Jabrayil, 6. Fuzil, 7. Agdam.